THE
PROFILER

Helen Fields is the author of the twelve novels that have sold more than a million copies internationally. Her books have been translated into more than twenty languages. Her Scottish set crime series featuring DI Luc Callanach has captivated audiences globally. Her books have been long listed for the McIlvanney Prize and the Ian Fleming steel dagger award. Helen is a former criminal and family law barrister. She splits her time between West Sussex and Edinburgh.

For more information visit Helen's website www.helenfields.com or find her on X (formerly twitter) @Helen_Fields.

T0315286

PRAISE FOR HELEN FIELDS

'A super-tense, in-your-face thriller that will keep you up all
night reading!'
The Sun

'Fields at her compelling best as a mistress of suspense and tension.'
Daily Mail

'What a read! This has potential for a TV series.'
Prima

'I was on the edge of my seat.'
Yours

'This twisty, claustrophobic thriller is ideal for fans of
The Sanitorium.'
Candis

'Fields has written yet another haunting and absorbing thriller.'
My Weekly

'With a fiendishly clever premise and a kick-ass heroine to root for,
The Profiler is pure page-turning perfection'
Susi Holliday

'A new novel by Helen Fields is always an excitement and this may
well be her best and most gripping thriller yet. Absorbing, powerful
and surprising, *The Profiler* is an unforgettable experience.'
B P Walter

'Fields, a master of psychological suspense, is in top form as she
spins a harrowing, nonstop story populated with complex, fully
formed characters.'
Jeffery Deaver

'A wonderful, compulsively gripping rollercoaster of a read.'
Liz Nugent

'Absolutely AMAZING. Tense, engrossing and gripping with a truly
unique main character in profiler, Connie Woolwine.'
Angela Marsons

HELEN FIELDS

THE
PROFILER

avon.

Published by AVON
A division of HarperCollins*Publishers* Ltd
1 London Bridge Street
London SE1 9GF

www.harpercollins.co.uk

HarperCollins*Publishers*
Macken House, 39/40 Mayor Street Upper,
Dublin 1 D01 C9W8, Ireland

This Paperback Edition 2025
24 25 26 27 28 LBC 5 4 3 2 1
First published in Great Britain by HarperCollins*Publishers* 2024

A catalogue copy of this book is available from the British Library.

UK ISBN: 978-0-00-853356-4
US ISBN: 978-0-00-871319-5

This novel is entirely a work of fiction. The names, characters and incidents portrayed in it are the work of the author's imagination. Any resemblance to actual persons, living or dead, events or localities is entirely coincidental.

Typeset in Sabon LT Std by Palimpsest Book Production Limited,
Falkirk, Stirlingshire
Printed and bound in the United States

For Diccon

Who helped me start this wonderful, tempestuous journey

Chapter 1

There is a moment for women – no more cacophonous than a petal falling from a dying flower – when good intentions have cost them their life, and they know it. That moment, so brief it would barely register on any clock, stretches long into the coming void.

Chloe Martin, stuck in her moment of eternal regret, stared at the foot separating her door from its frame as time stood still. You never knew when it was your turn, she thought. How could her day, her boring, run-of-the-mill day, have come to this? Where were the signs from the universe? Where was the sense of impending doom? It didn't matter, now, that she always carried a rape alarm in her handbag, and it didn't matter that she never walked home alone in the dark. It didn't matter that she always put a lid over her drinks to prevent spiking, or that she never engaged in online dating. Because now she was in the thick of it, facing a shadowy figure at her door who had knocked and cried out for help, and she had rushed there so fast, so worried for the safety of a stranger, that she had failed to engage the chain.

'Are you okay?' she'd called out. 'What's happened? Do you need an ambulance?'

The foot, encased in a brown leather boot, was in her door before she'd seen the face beneath the hood. The darkness had shielded her assailant between a line of trees and her flat, the road beyond so near and yet so far. Too late, she realised that her exterior light wasn't working. She didn't need to look up to know that it had been smashed. Now that her adrenaline was flowing, she was able to put two and two together and come up with precisely four, no trouble at all. This was no random attack. Whoever the owner of the boot was, they surely knew that she lived alone. And they'd known to wait until after dark.

Perhaps they even knew that she had been brought up to provide assistance when asked. To reply when someone spoke to her. To smile politely and walk away demurely when men cat-called her on the street. Not to reduce herself to the level of men who were crude in social situations. Not to slap the hands that touched her on the crowded tube, only to remove herself from the area.

The burden was on her, as it always had been on women. Not to wear provocative clothes. Not to make bad choices. Not to encourage or put herself in danger. And she hadn't. She hadn't. She just fucking well hadn't. And yet danger, mortal danger she suspected, had come looking for her just the same. Now she was opening her mouth to scream because it was only 9 p.m. and there should still be plenty of people awake to hear her, but there was a fist heading for her face and she couldn't let the door go and run because then the owner of the fist would have free rein to enter and she wouldn't stand a chance, and she couldn't slam the door shut because they were already pushing on it and—

The fist smashed into Chloe's mouth and seemed to stay there as her uninvited guest walked forwards into her apartment, pulling away only when he kicked the door shut. Chloe's hand went to her mouth and came away grainy with spiky shards of teeth, and the pain from that hadn't even begun to register when her attacker grabbed her arm and pulled her forward so she landed on her knees, and, Jesus, she was seeing flashing lights and hearing blood pulsing through her head, and—

Chloe vomited. The fight erupted out of her and washed the formerly immaculate hardwood floor with stinking, blood-streaked bile, splashing up the side of still-rolled birthday paper that she'd bought earlier that day. It was – had been, anyway – white with tiny gold stars and little pink hearts on it. The gift destined to be lovingly wrapped therein sat next to it, still in the bag. She had time to hope as the boots approached, that if the worst happened, her sister would find that bag and know that the giggling squirrel soft toy was destined for Chloe's soon to be three-year-old-niece, Vivienne. Ridiculously, she was relieved that she had already bought the batteries for it, currently in the same bag, because it felt mean to give a gift to a child without ensuring the batteries were included. Her niece loved squirrels. Chloe tried to take her to the nearby park every weekend. They would run around, squirrel (her niece pronounced it 'squirl') hunting, until it was too dusky or gloomy or rainy to see into the trees any more, and time for hot chocolate and teacakes.

The man who had violated her home, and her face, grabbed her by the hair. Chloe reached out to the plastic bag, as if touching it once more, holding onto it, could break her out of this nightmare realm and into the reality in which she was

3

supposed to exist, where she got to meet the man of her dreams and play in the park day after day with her own giggling girl, showering her with plush squirrels and soft maternal kisses. As she was being dragged along her hallway to the back of the apartment, the bag slipped from her reach. The tears Chloe cried were for what she believed was about to happen, not just to her, but to the people who loved her.

He said no words as Chloe's legs free-wheeled in the air trying to gain traction on the terracotta tiles, slapping and scratching the hand that gripped her messy bun, ripping tufts of hair from her head as they went. Much as she wanted to scream, breathing was her priority. The pain in her bile-coated mouth and sheer bloody panic combined to make the world's most toxic gobstopper.

He kicked her bedroom door fully open, and Chloe wished, desperately, that he would say something – anything – and it occurred to her that she had never before in her stupid life wanted to hear the words, 'If you do what I tell you, if you let me do what I want, I promise I won't kill you.' Two minutes ago, she'd have thought the idea of being grateful for such a threat was insanity. Now, nothing else mattered.

'Pl—' Her lips managed to form the right shape to emit the single syllable before the monster grabbed her by the throat and hauled her up onto the bed. 'Pl . . . nu . . . nu . . .'

From the lounge, Chloe's landline began to ring. It was a life raft, just tantalisingly beyond her grasp, and she was never going to be able to reach it, no matter how hard she swam. Her attacker stopped moving and listened as her answerphone message kicked in.

'Hi, this is Chloe Martin. I'm not available right now, but leave your name and number and I'll call you back as soon as I can.' Her voice sounded impossibly cheery. Death had not

4

even occurred to her as an option as she'd recorded the brief message. It was a mirage. Something in the distance she didn't really believe in.

'Don't hurt me,' she sobbed, the words finally forming, delivered with an accompanying bloody froth and broken teeth. Her attacker, no more than a huge presence, mask concealing his lower face, simply grunted and pulled cable ties from a coat pocket.

'Hey, Chlo-Bo.' Her sister's sing-song tones echoed her message as they beamed through the phone line into the living room. Chloe cried louder. Big braying sobs of terror and loss. 'Whatcha doin'? My baby girl is waiting for her auntie to come over tomorrow night for cake and candles! We're counting down the hours so I said I'd phone you to make sure you don't forget that it's someone's birthday tomorrow.' Giggling in the distance. 'Whose birthday could that be?'

'Please . . .' Chloe begged. She held out a desperate hand only to find it grabbed, gripped and tied to a pole of her metal headboard.

'Is it Daddy's birthday?' her sister asked.

'No!' her niece shouted.

Chloe turned her head and stared at the cable tie. Why wasn't she fighting? If all she had were minutes to live, why wouldn't she give as good as she got?

He reached for her left hand. Chloe tensed her stomach muscles, shot her legs up, and smashed a knee into his face. As he staggered back, Chloe scrambled up the bed, pulling desperately on the one cable tie connecting her to the headboard.

'Is it Mummy's birthday?' her sister teased.

The cable tie wasn't budging. She got up on her knees ready to fight some more, grabbing the lamp from the bedside table and ripping it from its socket, brandishing it in front of her.

'No, it's not. It's not your birthday, Mummy!' Her niece could barely get the words out through her laughter.

Chloe took the deepest intake of breath she could manage. 'Help!' she screamed, hoping against hope that the people in the apartment above hers were home from work, or that the elderly lady next door had her hearing aid switched on, or that someone was walking in the alleyway behind her building.

Her attacker put his head down and charged across the bed, arm up, ready to take whatever blow Chloe could muster with the lamp. Head butted head. She smashed the lamp into his side, falling off the edge of the bed as she swung, and above the rasping breath and groans of exertion, the popping sound of her arm leaving its socket trumped all.

'Then whose birthday can it be?' her sister shrieked joyously as Chloe screamed and begged.

'Mine!' her niece replied. 'Mummy, it's my birthday tomorrow. You know it is! Silly Mummy.' And they laughed and laughed and laughed.

Her attacker hauled Chloe back up onto the bed as she screamed. He tied her previously free arm to the headboard as she thrashed her legs. He fitted a gag over her mouth as the pain and panic left her flitting in and out of consciousness.

'Auntie Chloe?' her niece called from the lounge down the line. 'Are you okay? Mummy, is Auntie Chloe okay? Why isn't she coming to the phone?'

'I don't know baby, but we'll see her tomorrow, I promise,' her sister said.

You won't, Chloe thought. God help us, you won't see me tomorrow. And I won't see Vivienne grow up. I won't take her to New York for her eighteenth birthday. I won't become her legal guardian if anything happens to you, and you'll never know that the moment you asked me was the proudest of my life. I won't get to buy her wedding veil. You won't come to me in tears when teenage Vivienne is mean to her mum. And she won't know how much I loved her. A year from now, she'll barely remember me at all.

'Okay. I love you, Auntie Chloe. See you tomorrow. Don't forget my present!'

I didn't forget, Chloe thought. I hope you love the squirrel. I don't want to die. I don't want you to have to find out that someone killed me. I don't want to be scared like this.

'Sorry we missed you, Chlo-Bo. Love you, girl. See you tomorrow.' Kisses into the phone. More giggles. A dead line.

Chloe lay still. The pain in her mouth, her head, her shoulder were at fever pitch, and yet they couldn't touch the overwhelming tsunami of sadness that was dragging her under.

Rape me then. Hurt me if you have to. But let me live. Let me live. Let me live.

She could see the words of her thoughts hanging in the air between them, written in clouds of tiny black, buzzing insects.

He drew scissors from a voluminous pocket and cut her clothes open down the middle, then down each sleeve and leg, pulling the sections of cloth away slowly and letting them drift to the floor.

For a moment or a minute or an eternity, Chloe passed out.

She was at a party but she couldn't remember who it was for. It felt strange because she was sure they should have been celebrating, but there was her sister in a corner being comforted by her brother-in-law, and as Chloe walked past another room, door locked, she was certain she could hear her father sobbing, and something had to be very wrong for that to be real because she had never, ever seen her father cry. Even at her mother's funeral, her father had held it in, dignified (or was it repressed?) to the last.

7

And then Vivienne ran past, something fluffy in her arms. Delighted, Chloe ran after her, chasing happily through the house as they had done so many times, calling to one another as they slowed down and sped up, nearly catching, nearly being caught. What was in her arms? Chloe couldn't quite see. Its face looked like any other sweet, stuffed toy but its tail end was painting a ragged dash of red on the wall as Vivienne ran, and now Chloe felt the early rumblings of nausea. The low boil of something not quite right. She was catching up to Vivienne now, close enough to see into her arms, close enough to see her niece's face, but she wasn't laughing; she was crying. And she was holding a squirrel which was strange because Chloe was sure she'd only just bought Viv a squirrel and hadn't given it to her yet. In fact, she really had to get on and wrap it, because it was dark and she had a whole day of work ahead of her before her niece's birthday party tomorrow. And if that was tomorrow then where was she now, and why was everyone – absolutely everyone – crying?

Chloe woke up, choking, trying to scream, only to waste the noise as it filtered through a soggy, stinking rag around her mouth, and the pain. The pain. The fucking pain. The enormity of the terrible, mind-twisting, devastating, fucking pain.

She wanted to die.

And now she knew why everyone was crying in her dream.

Chloe lay still for she had no choice, and cried with them until the end – her end – came far too slowly and painted red.

Chapter 2

Necto Corporation's office in the United Kingdom doubled as a botanical garden. Prime London real estate had been dismantled, brick by brick, steel girder by steel girder, and replaced with lush greenery, flowers, insect colonies and curved glass. The staff spent their days in beautiful bubbles, looking out at the inner-city haven, within structures that rose up from the earth between the exquisite trees and stunning blooms. The cafeteria was built into a vast dome that featured a stream and fruit trees, rows of vegetables between rows of tables, while butterflies and bees kept the air alive. Necto was the future – biotech specialising in the human brain. Their American headquarters situated just outside San Diego were the envy of companies across the world, both for the stunning landscaping and the futuristic office space. The UK office was a little less prestigious and a fraction of the size, but the staff were working on the same projects for the same types of clients.

Midnight Jones was late for work and it was only Tuesday. It didn't matter that she'd stayed an hour late the previous night, nor did it matter that she'd worked fifty hours the previous week. Late was late, and it showed a poor respect for self and a disregard for the commitment of others – or so said her line manager, more regularly than anyone on Midnight's team felt was really necessary.

She dodged a double-decker bus, stepped over a cold pile of fish and chips that someone had dropped on the pavement the previous evening, and entered the haven that was Necto's gardens. Midnight breathed deeply, knowing that for the next nine hours she would be taking in machine-conditioned air. In the beginning, she'd fallen for the scent of cut grass and petals, believing the hype that the air in her office was pumped in fresh from the gardens to keep her brain stimulated and her senses relaxed. That had lasted until a shame-filled, late-night cigarette outside a Battersea pub, five years earlier, when she'd bumped into a member of building support staff and learned that the true origin of those fragrances was carefully procured perfumes pumped into the air-con system. A few seconds after his miniature whistle-blow, he'd thrown up into a nearby skip and staggered off, presumably with no memory of his indiscretion the next morning. That was another thing. You didn't share company information with anyone. Not ever. There wasn't even access to the internet inside Necto, at least not at Midnight's pay grade. The internet, they'd been told in training, was a distraction that could only lead to wasted time. More than that, it was a route in for hackers and a route out for valuable company secrets.

Today Midnight was late because her twin sister's carer had been delayed. It was the only reason Midnight was ever late. It still wouldn't matter to her boss. She swiped her card at the first security point, left her mobile phone in a locker, had her bag checked at the second, and entered her thumb print at the third. At the lifts, her security pass automatically dictated which floor she went to. The lift headed down.

Only the top two floors were gifted with natural light, comprising breakout rooms and a large auditorium, a cafeteria and client consultation suites. The lift went past level −1 which was production. Necto's products ranged from virtual reality training headsets to electroconvulsive therapy units, and from polygraph machines to psychogalvanometers that measured physical responses to emotional stimuli. The development team was on −2. Those guys were the kings of the hill. She'd heard but never been able to confirm rumours of a masseuse, a sauna and hot tub, a gym, and a personal chef for lunches and snacks. From blue-sky thinkers to designers and coders, they ruled the company roost. When Midnight's team were sent for training sessions, they might make it as far as the Eden cafeteria at ground level. The development team had been sent to Singapore and Bora Bora in recent history. The difference was replaceability.

Midnight was bright in the grand scheme of things. She had a first-class degree in social sciences, and a master's degree in psychology and neuroscience. But the developers were a breed apart. One-of-a-kind doctorate-wielding geniuses who could command pay at a level Midnight could only dream of. They, unlike her, could not be replaced by a throng of other suitable candidates desperate to join the Necto family. Midnight thought about that every single day. She was blessed in many ways, and she knew she had to stay grateful both for the vastly better than industry-standard pay packet that gave her the means to care for her sister, but also for the opportunity to work in a globally revered technology company. She loved her job, and she was more than fortunate. But still. Replaceable.

The doors opened at level −3. Applications made up the largest team in Necto's offices, and they were still understaffed and overworked. Their job description was simple: they took the data that Necto's equipment gathered and translated it into something their clients could use. Different teams could be found beavering away on a variety of projects. Medical were in the middle of a highly profitable bout of testing new drug efficacy. Psychiatric were doing great work assisting in-community mental health patients, and working with pharmaceutical companies to suggest new prescriptions and organise drug trials.

Then there was Midnight's team, who spent all day, every day, profiling.

'Miss Jones, you decided to join us!' her line manager called across the network of pods, each of which contained a desk, chair and computer with virtual reality glasses and had the ability to close off your pod for privacy, a little like an electric soft-top on a car. 'Shall we talk?' As if saying no was an option. Her manager ushered her into his pod and shut the privacy hood.

Midnight fought the urge to fold her arms, which would also earn her a hostile body language chat.

'So, you know what I'm going to say,' Richard Baxter began, adjusting his already-perfect tie, and smoothing steel grey hair that wasn't out of place.

'I can only apologise,' Midnight said, injecting more emotion into her speech than she really felt. It was thirty minutes. Necto owed her a hell of a lot more than that for all the hours she put in. 'My sister's carer was late and I can't leave the house until they've arrived. The health network I use to provide the care has been unreliable lately and—'

'Let me stop you there, Midnight. What's one of our founding principles that you're failing to apply right now?' Richard asked, a little smile on his lips that Midnight fancied slapping lightly, as if it were a fly that could be shooed away.

Instead, she took a deep breath before answering, keeping her voice low and sickeningly compliant. 'Ownership.'

'Right first time. Ownership. That means taking responsibility for our performance. If we want to claim the victories, we also have to own the deficiencies. Are you with me?'

'I am,' Midnight said. 'And I know this is my responsibility, but my role as a carer comes with some issues . . .'

'Yes, sure. Talk to me about that. What exactly is it that's making you late again?'

'My twin sister, Dawn, has severe special needs. She can't be left alone. If I leave our flat before the carers have arrived, it can be dangerous, and I have no family I can call on to help.'

'Yes, I think you've mentioned your twin before.' Midnight most certainly had. At least a dozen times. 'But you see, it's still your responsibility to engage a good carer who will be there on time. It's no good passing the chaos on to Necto. You know we can't pick up the slack. A good team needs all its players to be on the ball. Am I right?'

Midnight gave her brightest grin. If Richard could see the scorn in it, he kept it to himself.

'You're right. My fault. I'll stay late to make up the time and take a shorter lunch break.'

Richard turned his head slightly to one side, eyebrows raised. 'And . . .'

'And I'll apologise to the team,' Midnight said. 'They shouldn't have to pick up the slack. Thanks for being so understanding, Richard. You're a great manager.'

'Oh my goodness. You're a keeper. I mean, not if you're late again, obviously. That'd be too many strikes. But otherwise you're a keeper. Now get going, Miss Jones. Time and Necto wait for no man.'

13

Midnight wanted to scorch his ridiculous sayings onto his face.

'You bet,' she said, grinding her teeth as she waited once more for the pod to transition out of privacy mode, turning away before he could offer her a sweaty-palmed modern manager's high five. Walking slowly through the maze of pods, she issued a few, 'Sorry I'm late!' calls, receiving a variety of sniggers from her co-workers in response.

Her desk was in the far corner, amid a horseshoe of three that made up Midnight's mini-team. She threw her bag onto the floor next to her chair and tried not to look at her closest friend, Amber, certain Richard was still watching for any un-Necto-like behaviour. Behind Amber was an empty seat recently vacated courtesy of a transfer, resignation or firing. They hadn't been told which.

'Did you get the taking-up-the-slack lecture?' Amber whispered without taking her eyes off her screen.

'Yup. And a quick reminder that I have to own my deficiencies. He hasn't used that one for a while. How's the system running today?'

'There's been a software update so it'll be a couple of minutes before you can download any data. You want a coffee? You look like you need one. I'm due my screen break.'

Necto either allowed or enforced screen breaks – Midnight wasn't sure which – during which time employees had to move away from the screen to protect their eyes and reduce headaches, a fact they widely advertised when seeking plaudits as a good employer. What they didn't say publicly was that their own testing had proved employees actually increased their output after breaks.

'Coffee would be great. Dawn's carer was late again, so I didn't get any breakfast or a shower this morning, and I'm

14

going to have to work late tonight to make up for not getting here on time.' Midnight knew moaning was a bad way to start the day, but the lack of flexibility in her life was draining. She was so reliant on agency carers, some of whom might stay late if asked, but it was never guaranteed at short notice, and it wasn't as if she had a network of personal contacts to plug the gap. She turned her attention to Amber to get her mind off it. 'Anyway, how was your night?'

Amber responded with a grin and a wink that, combined with her dyed-crimson pixie cut and false eyelashes, made her look more like a naughty schoolgirl than the employee of a powerful corporation. She was trying out a new dating app and regularly regaled Midnight with tales of disastrous dates and hilarious hook-ups. 'Oh God, tell me once I've had caffeine. It's too early for any detailed descriptions of debauchery,' Midnight groaned.

'Fair enough. The debauchery debrief can wait, but I guarantee you're going to want to hear it. The man was a built like a viking!'

As her friend disappeared towards the kitchenette, Midnight logged in, went through the security measures, and got down to it. Her assignment was profiling applicants to ensure each was suitable for their chosen higher education course, both academically and in terms of their interests and personality.

Amber delivered steaming coffee in a reusable bamboo cup before sliding into her own seat and getting back to work, whispering, 'Lunchtime!' to schedule a retelling of her previous night's exploits. Midnight imported her first project of the day.

It was from Thames Environmental Sciences University, whose campus was only a short walk from her flat, evidenced by the number of drunk students passing her door on Friday and Saturday nights. The degrees they offered were all very theme-specific – the sciences, geography, social history, environmental law, politics, global economics and so on. That meant selecting students who showed both good strategic skills and high social conscience scores. She downloaded the first application – geography degree – fairly straightforward.

Her screen displayed an applicant number and a series of coded data scores. Midnight began to assess the profile. Somebody somewhere had just been sent an email or a text message that told them their application profile was '. . . now being assessed by Midnight J at Necto. You're a step closer to your future.' It was a nice touch, if slightly dramatic. It was all designed to integrate Necto into daily life. They didn't want to be that big scary tech company who developed programs that could read your mind – cue the conspiracy theorists. Instead, Necto branded themselves as the good guys, making the world better, finding a solution for every problem, even the ones you didn't know you had.

Midnight studied the profile. The applicant's interest levels were high for geography-related content. Concentration scores were average for what was expected intellectually at degree level. Socialisation and confidence was a little down but still within the client's parameters. The applicant got more excited about sport than anything else – notably football and cricket. No interest registered for illegal stimulants, maximum score there. Low-level interest in alcohol. Various other markers, but all within the university's acceptable range. Midnight confirmed it as a profile A, meaning that the application hit an average score for all the university's requirements. She filled in the digital form, then sent it off for the university to process. Some happy person would be getting a course offer by the end of the week.

Her coffee was cold. Midnight considered sneaking away from her desk to fetch another, but she wasn't due a break for forty minutes, and Richard had a sixth sense for when a rule was being broken, so she cracked on. The next application was for a male – the only identification factor revealed as it affected some of the biological scores – course unspecified, which was unusual but not impossible. TESU allowed testing before students had decided on a specific pathway. Overall, the university required a high level of analytical thinking, with moderate empathy. Cognitive and creative scores both had to be at the top end of the spectrum. Competition for places was tough. TESU was internationally renowned and always oversubscribed.

She entered the data file and began looking at the various test scores. 'Damn it,' she muttered. 'Must be a system error.' Midnight removed her headset and scooted her chair across to Amber's. 'You getting any corrupt data through? I just got a set of results that have to be a glitch.'

'Nope, all normal here. You tried unplugging it and plugging it in again?'

Midnight rolled her eyes. 'You're funny. Bugger, must just be my system.' She rolled back to her own workstation, deleted the file she was working on, downloaded the data for a second time and took another look.

Same results again. All the levels were at the extreme edge of the readings. Midnight sighed. A problem like that meant going back to the original, raw files to figure out where the process had gone wrong and that was going to slow her output down. She had no hope of hitting her daily work target if she didn't get moving. Had to be done though. Necto was obsessive about tracing the root of system errors. She put up her pod's privacy hood and prepared to figure out where the software might have hit a fault.

Chapter 3

The equipment Midnight wore was exactly what any applicant would wear during testing: a headset featuring a band with sensors to register brain activity, a visor that both showed images on a screen and had a camera that recorded eye movement and pupil dilation, and a glove that monitored heartbeat, blood pressure, finger movement, oxygen levels and perspiration. None of it was painful or uncomfortable, and for the most part the applicants were never aware of just how much of their functioning was being monitored, yet the data it fed back was powerful at levels Necto was still investigating.

At a basic level, the software could figure out if you preferred tea to coffee, men to women, sailing to skiing. But it was so much more than that. Show an image, and it would know where your eyes settled, how they followed, if you were aroused or repulsed, interested or bored. And a million, million other tiny things. But the really clever part was that the test adapted to each applicant's levels. If you exhibited signs of excitement at one image, the computer would show you similar images until your excitement maxed out or you got bored, then it would move on to something new. Nothing was sacred. Nothing could be hidden. And what your future employer or organisation didn't know about you by the end of it, to be honest, wasn't worth knowing. It was psychometric testing imbued with artificial intelligence that was learning at a faster rate than Necto could harness, and Midnight was in awe of it. Amber said it made the CIA's lie detector system look like something from the Neanderthal age. That, in fact, was still an understatement. When the software was first released, there had been complaints about invasion of privacy, but like most things, people got used to it. The reality was that almost no one understood just how powerful it really was.

All Midnight had to do was replay the precise series of images the applicant had seen and establish where the software had gone wrong. Necto's profiling system did fail, occasionally. Not even Necto was infallible. Midnight donned the headset, sat back, and programmed the computer to replay the test sequence.

It began, as every test did, with a bird's eye view drifting slowly over a serene lake at sunset, hazy mountains on the horizon, with low-level inoffensive music in the background. The narrator told Midnight to relax and breathe normally, to imagine she was simply watching TV at home. Nothing to worry about.

And so it began. From images of courtrooms, to university lecture halls, environmental footage that ranged from polluted rivers to diseases, and dying cattle. And then the glitch hit.

The applicant had no empathetic reaction to the dying cattle. None at all. The average score at that point, Midnight could see, was in the mid-range. So the computer stepped it up a gear. Midnight watched animals being slaughtered in abattoirs.

Still nothing registered in terms of a reaction that would make the university think the applicant would be a good match for one of their courses. The computer, trying harder to register a reaction, showed images of baby animals being tortured. Midnight squeezed her eyes shut until the clip finished playing, then checked whether it was Necto's equipment that had malfunctioned as opposed to the software, but the applicant's pulse readings were stable, his oxygen levels were normal and eye movement was still being recorded. The equipment had been operating perfectly.

She assumed it would stop. The screaming, the horror. But on it went. More footage followed, each clip more terrible and graphic than the last. Finally, the applicant's pulse rate went up and his pupils began to dilate, but by then the computer had reached the limits of what it could offer and turned instead to images of drugs and alcohol. Bottles of wine and beer were shown, people laughing in pubs, couples smoking huge hand-rolled cigarettes, men staggering down the street almost too inebriated to walk. No response. The applicant's pulse rate was so slow he might have been asleep. Needles and bongs, drug users staring glassy-eyed into the abyss. Nothing. Then a woman snorting cocaine and staggering gleefully towards a window, shouting happily to the people down below, before stepping out onto the windowsill. Kicking off her stilettos. Midnight was gripping her armrests. The woman took another step forward, spread her arms wide, then stepped forward one more time.

'Don't!' Midnight pleaded.

But the woman did. Whoever was holding the phone camera lurched too late into action, succeeding only in showing the last two seconds of her journey to the ground, and the crumpled mass of designer clothes around a corpse that had imploded into a single lump on the pavement.

The applicant's pulse rate exploded into the equivalent of a hundred-metre sprint. Midnight checked the data. His palms were sweating at that point, his breathing rapid, pupils fully dilated. He made no attempt to close his eyes to shut out the images. The applicant's brain activity showed arousal without empathy. Midnight grimaced. But the computer still hadn't reached the upper limit of the data scores yet, so on it went.

'Holy crap,' Midnight muttered as the footage rolled.

She couldn't watch. The sounds alone were enough to have her grinding her teeth. Focusing instead on the data feed, Midnight watched the applicant's vital signs for distress and found none. The movies continued, the software trying in vain to find the applicant's outer limit of emotion. The noises were beyond the reaches of anything Midnight had ever imagined. She felt sick. Her hand flew to her mouth and her eyes opened, looking for an exit. Right in front of her a person was being flayed with some sort of wire whip. Midnight froze.

'Oh fuck. This isn't okay.' She tried to look away but the horror of it kept her gaze glued to the image. Her hands and jaw were aching.

The data told her that the applicant was breathing faster. His heart rate was up to ninety beats per minute, and that still seemed wrong because Midnight was aware that her own pulse was going at a good hundred and twenty, probably more. But unlike her vital signs, full of panic and desperation, trapped in a visor which she could not fight and from which she should not flee, the applicant had been having a completely different experience.

His pupils were dilated. His eyes had not closed once, his hands were relaxed. His brain activity showed engagement and excitement. High-level stimulation. But still not – *still fucking not* – at the maximum.

21

A new video began to stream of a woman tied to a bed and Midnight closed her eyes once more, humming a song to herself, one her mother used to sing to calm her sister down, back in the days when either of her parents were still interested in the concept of parenting.

Two more minutes passed of the computer trying to figure out where the applicant's boundaries were. One hundred and twenty seconds of hell. Weeping, sobbing, pleading. Midnight sang louder and louder, forcing her mouth to form the words of the song to keep her brain busy enough that she didn't have to listen.

'Will you make me a cambric shirt?' She began the song again. 'Parsley, sage, rosemary and thyme.'

Finally the noise stopped. Midnight didn't trust it. She sat there a little longer with her eyes firmly shut, until the sounds of Christmas carols began to play, children giggling, the crackle of a wood fire in the background.

Taking a deep breath, she allowed herself to look once more. The scene was beautiful and postcard-familiar. Family and gifts. Giving and sharing. Food and drink. Safety, she thought. Comfort. She took a look at the applicant's data. His pulse, finally racing at the end of the last set of images, had dived back down to sixty beats per minute. He hadn't even carried the adrenaline with him into the new section of the test. His brain was showing no activity other than the basic minimum required to keep him alive.

'Who the fuck are you?' Midnight whispered.

The footage shifted again. Men, women, children. Different races. Different economic backgrounds. Workers in different jobs were shown. Various places of religious worship. Styles of home. Shops, restaurants, transport. The computer went through it all like clockwork, not a glitch in sight.

Midnight sat there, numb and heartsick, wondering how she was ever going to get those images and that audio out of her head. The thought of going home that night to her innocent, lovely sister, having witnessed those things, made her want to throw the visor across the room.

'Do your job,' she told herself. 'It was probably computer-generated. That couldn't have been real.'

The remainder of the footage, blissfully mundane, took thirty minutes to play, during which all Midnight could think of was getting out of that room, taking the lift back up to the ground floor, and walking in the clean air, then finding somewhere to drink the strongest alcoholic beverage money could buy. She took off the visor then lowered her privacy hood.

'Shit, woman, what the hell were you doing? You look like you just ran with the bulls and lost.'

'Yeah, weird thing, not sure I know. I mean, I thought it was corrupt data, but everything was working fine and now I don't know.' Midnight wasn't making any sense, and she knew it.

'You due a break? You look like you could use one,' Amber said.

'In a minute. There's one last thing I can check. I'll break after that.' Midnight gave an impression of a smile that felt more like a grimace.

She extrapolated the data, double-checking the results as she went through every category. There was no question about her recommendation to the university. As far as Midnight was concerned, the applicant wasn't fit to study any subject, at any educational establishment in the world. What she needed to do was complete her report and finalise the profile, and she fully intended to include a special message to TESU to make absolutely sure the applicant didn't slip through the rejection net and apply at a later date.

She raced through the work, keeping her focus on going straight to the bathroom afterwards to splash water over her face and use the hand sanitiser to kill whatever germs might have been spread through a process of psychological osmosis that felt all too real.

Midnight waited. Her computer was operating unnaturally slowly. The submitted data had to be chewing up the inside of her machine. It was doing the same to her brain.

'Come on, come on, come on,' she willed it.

Her computer responded with a profile code and a blinking cursor.

'What the fuck is this now?' Midnight asked her screen, rubbing her eyes and checking the phrase she'd never encountered before – hadn't even known was a possibility – in spite of the thousands of data profiles she'd processed.

The computer didn't care. It wasn't changing its mind. Midnight downloaded the raw data onto a separate drive in case an update corrupted it, doubled up with transferring it onto a pen drive to show her manager, and logged off to get advice on how to proceed.

The applicant was a Profile K.

Chapter 4

The Applicant

He finished a sudoku and stood to stare out of the window. People scurried to and fro on the street below, completely unaware of him. Even if they noticed him looking, so what? He was just a man, cigarette in one hand, mug in the other, watching the world go by.

That week he would start a new job, and in preparation, he intended to tidy his flat. He needed to do a quick food shop too, and that was annoying because he hated lugging carrier bags back from the supermarket. The only thing he disliked about living in London was that car ownership was impractical. He'd enjoyed driving in his late teens and early twenties, but he didn't have a garage, and the idea of trawling the streets at the end of the day looking for parking was intolerable. He'd recently come into possession of a motorbike, which was something, but still not as practical as a car.

He took one last drag and stubbed out his cigarette. Ten a day, as evenly spaced as possible time-wise, was what he allowed himself. He had rent to pay, and a future to save for.

His list of chores for the day remained incomplete. It was washing day, and he had extra to do from – he struggled to find the right words to describe it in his own mind – the things he had done. It had been more than a day now and he still hadn't seen anything reported on the news, which was both good and disappointing. Good, because it meant there hadn't been any witnesses or nosy neighbours calling the police at the time. Disappointing for obvious reasons. There was something fascinating about the idea that a squad of detectives would be trying to figure out who'd done it, to unpuzzle the mess he'd left behind.

He liked puzzles, preferably mathematical ones, but he was also good at general knowledge, memory, word searches and sequencing. He'd always liked technology and had been good at science at school. The act of testing himself was fun, which was why he'd chosen to try the new profiling software. He'd been fascinated with Necto's psychometrics ever since he'd first read an article about it, so when he'd received a letter three months earlier with a free voucher, he'd signed up just days later. The letter had said Necto would keep his results on file for any future employer, which was amazing given that he'd been considering a career change at the time. More importantly, it had talked about the test as if it were a game of chess (he'd always loved chess), as if it would be him versus the machine. He'd once written a story about exactly that at school, for which he'd won an award. How could he have resisted?

It wasn't the first time he'd undergone psychological assessments – he'd done plenty of those at Moorview College – but what Necto did had been mind-blowing. It was difficult to put his finger on the exact moment during the test that everything had changed for him, but he'd felt it like a lightning bolt.

Now he was struggling with his discipline. Leaving chores undone so late in the day wasn't like him. He was distracted. He'd caught himself several times recently, halfway through a task and unable to remember what he was supposed to be doing.

The thing with the woman was that he should have taken photos. That was annoying him. He'd watched so many series in preparation, listened to so many podcasts, that he'd lost count. Even so, he'd been overwhelmed by the sudden rush of excitement. His planning had been amateurish. If he had photos to look back on now, it would all feel so much more real. Surely the police had to find her soon, then he could read about it in the newspapers. Help remind himself of the details.

His only hope was that his parents wouldn't see the coverage and decide to pick it all apart while he was with them over the weekend. They did love a good in-depth discussion of news events, especially when it came to crime. It wasn't so much that he cared what they thought of him – not that they would ever find out that he was the perpetrator – just that they were going to ruin it for him. They were both so incredibly analytical. His father had been an actuary and his mother was once an editor for a scientific magazine. They loved to read, were careful with their investments and came from conservative backgrounds. His father had attended a private school while his mother went to a grammar. They'd have been a sure match for one another had online dating been a thing when they were in their early twenties. Now in their late sixties, they still lived in his childhood home in the country. When he'd moved out, they'd given him the deposit and first six months' rent money for his flat, but not provided enough to buy somewhere, because apparently he needed to be taught to be fiscally responsible. He sighed. The price he was paying for their generosity was high enough anyway. Lunch every Sunday, lending a hand with the washing-up (the dishwasher wasn't a good use of water or electricity) and a game of Scrabble or cribbage while they discussed the week's events. The coming visit would be full of questions about his new job.

'Fuck it!' He grabbed the packet of cigarettes and pulled another roughly out, jamming it between his lips and taking a silver teardrop-shaped lighter from his pocket. He loved the lighter, and he wasn't given to loving material things, but this felt good in his hand. Smooth, cold, heavy. He flipped open the tip of the droplet and flicked his thumb downwards to light a spark, then kept the flame burning to stare at it as he took his first drag. God, it was beautiful. The extra cigarette was another step down a pathway into addiction, but he was fit and healthy. Strong, too. He'd rarely had to test that in his lifetime, but the girl had fought and kicked, and there had been other tests of his strength recently too. He'd prevailed. That had felt good, the sense of physical dominance. He'd thought it was all going to be about the blood, but pushing his body to its limits had been incredibly liberating.

Someone buzzed at the outer door. He skipped down the central stairwell to find that a parcel had been left outside. Ripping open the packaging, he considered what he was going to do next. Not next as in later that day. Next as in . . . bigger things. Viewing Necto's footage three weeks ago had been an awakening and, holy crap, it had been really, really good. He didn't have the words for it. There was no metaphor that would ever do it justice. Only now there was nothing to look forward to.

The delivery would help, chef's knives so sharp they might have been destined for an operating theatre rather than a kitchen. He drew one from its metal block. The sound it made was pleasingly reminiscent of a sword being pulled from its scabbard in a black and white movie, that long *tsssssss* followed by the tiniest spark as its tip hit the air. From the fridge he took out an onion, aimed the knife above it and added just enough pressure to keep the cut clean. Straight through, effortlessly, with the satisfying crunch. Again. The blade was flawless. And again. He took a moment to shed the skin, then began dicing. Smaller and smaller, the pieces went. The juice ran from the flesh until the board was a sticky wet mess. He cut until those cubes were as small as he could make them, then rinsed the knife, added salt and pepper to the vegetable mound, and took eggs from the fridge. He might as well have omelette for dinner. Cooking was good for him. It was one of the activities he'd learned at college that kept him focused and purposeful – the weighing and measuring, the precision, the ability to start and finish a process. And he was hungry again now. Ravenous, in fact. He needed to do something. Mostly, he needed to keep his mind off Jessica.

His phone pinged with a text message. He sighed, put down the knife carefully, and took a look at the screen, feeling a momentary sense of combined exhilaration and panic.

Congratulations, it read. Your profile is now being assessed by Midnight J at Necto. You're a step closer to your future.

Midnight. That was quite the name. He wondered what the J stood for – and which was the surname, and which the first name? It had to be a woman, surely. He spent some time imagining her at her desk, drawing up his profile. Was her hair light or dark? What was her skin tone? How tall was she?

'Midnight J,' he said, as he cracked eggs into a jug and began to whisk. What would his profile reveal? The man who lived within the rules he'd been taught, or the new version of him, authentic and liberated? It hardly seemed fair that she was getting to know him so intimately, while he had only half her name.

Maybe he would change that. How hard could it be? He was good at puzzles, after all.

Chapter 5

Midnight took the sort of breath usually reserved for free-divers and walked up to Richard Baxter's desk.

He checked his watch as she entered his pod area.

'Screen break?' he asked.

She couldn't help but glance for the thousandth time at his wedding ring. What the hell type of person had married him? That was what Necto should really use psychometric testing for – checking out your intended. They'd make even more gazillions than they already did.

'I need to report an issue.'

'That's what the technical teams are for. Follow the Necto code!' He almost sang the words.

Midnight closed her eyes for a millisecond against the corporate bullshit.

'Yeah, there's nothing wrong with my system. I did all the checks. I mean, I followed the Necto code. It's just that—'

'Did you go back through your training manual? Almost

every question you have can be resolved by tracing the information tree.' He was still typing as he spoke.

Midnight wanted to talk to him about manners. About human resources. About shoving the Necto tree where it would be extremely difficult for him to retrieve it.

'It's a profiling anomaly and the training manual is clear that we're supposed to report any profile-related issues to our line manager, so that would be—'

'Are you struggling because you're overtired? I know I was hard on you about the lateness but it's for your own good.' Richard gave her a synthetic smile. 'And honestly, I have to say that wasting more time with this conversation when you've already turned up late is—'

'What's a Profile K?' she blurted. 'Because we weren't trained on that. I looked it up and it's not mentioned anywhere.'

'There's no such thing as a Profile K,' Richard said, the saccharin in his voice now fully dissolved. 'You've either made a mistake or someone's messing with you.'

'Messing with me how? Why would anyone think a Profile K is funny?' she demanded.

Baxter held up a finger towards her face, shushing her. Midnight stared, incredulous.

'Miss Jones, it's a joke. A poor joke, in fairness. When the profiling codes were put together, it was necessary to find a code for someone who failed on all counts – no empathy, past all boundaries on whatever depravity scale the software could throw at them, inappropriate responses that went beyond sociopathy and into the extremes of psychopathy. A code had to exist, so they gave it a K for killer, which I personally do not find amusing. But no one can hit those scores, and as far as I'm aware, even within military and special operations applicants, no applicant has ever returned a Profile K. Whatever you're concerned about, I'm certain you don't actually have one now.'

'As reassuring as your management skills are, I do, in fact, have one. So what are we going to do about it?' Midnight asked.

'You might consider softening the tone,' Baxter said.

'You might want to rethink dismissing this out of hand. The term "Profile K" might have been some idiot's idea of a joke, but I just checked the raw data. I viewed the footage and photos this applicant saw and I studied his responses at the same time. I've never seen anything – I mean *anything* – like it.'

'Okay, let's unpack that,' he said. Midnight figured she was thirty seconds at best from punching him in the face. 'I believe it's important to recognise that women can be extremely sensitive, so some of the content you viewed, while upsetting to you, is probably only a little over the line for most men.'

'Richard,' Midnight said.

'Yes?'

'You need to shut the fuck up. I'm taking this to Sara Vickson.'

Midnight turned on her heel and headed for the exit. She walked past the lifts and into the door across the hallway where the senior staff had their offices. The corridors were wider, and the lighting was kinder. Plants lined the hallway, and here and there an item of designer furniture could be found, not that anyone was ever going to get caught sitting around instead of working. Around a corner, a smiling personal assistant was ready to greet her. Midnight didn't bother smiling back. She knew that look. It said, gosh, it's lovely that you're here, and let me see if I can't make you an appointment for a month or so hence.

'My name's Midnight Jones and I have an appointment with the Director of Operations,' Midnight said. 'Apologies, I'm a couple of minutes late, so I need to go straight in. I'd hate to keep Ms Vickson waiting.'

The fake smile morphed into a frown.

'The director doesn't have an appointment in her calendar,' the assistant said. 'You must be mistaken. I've never missed anything like this before.'

'Then it's you who shouldn't keep her waiting. I don't want to open my meeting with a complaint. Not a good look.'

'I'll need to check with her first. She's very busy today, and if I let you in . . .'

'By all means,' Midnight said. 'Feel free to check. Just do it fast.' She could hear footsteps at the far end of the hallway and there was zero chance it was anyone other than Richard fucking Baxter. She had to make it to Sara Vickson before he did.

The assistant walked out from behind her desk and selected one of the six doors leading to much larger offices. Midnight should have stayed where she was. Instead, crossing her fingers as if she were still five years old, she walked as quietly as she could directly behind the assistant, waited until Sara Vickson's door was open, and pushed through.

The assistant gasped. 'Ms Vickson, I'm sorry but Miss Jones said she had an appointment—'

'Not now. I'm too busy for whatever this is.' Vickson didn't even look up from her laptop.

'No!' Richard shouted from the end of the corridor. Now he was running.

The assistant was trying to push Midnight back out.

'This is important,' Midnight said. 'It can't wait. I know I'm not following procedure but I wasn't getting anywhere with my line manager.'

'Not true,' Richard burst in behind her. 'I was handling this. I have it under control. I'll be making a referral to HR. Miss

Jones failed to follow instructions. She obviously hasn't processed a file properly.'

Sara Vickson glared at them all, her bronze-varnished nails hovering in mid-air above her keyboard as she ran a delicate tongue over perfectly glazed lips. Her assistant shrank into the background.

'It'd better be good,' she said, 'or you're all fired. Every single one of you.' Vickson shook her ash blonde, loosely curled ponytail, as if flicking away flies.

There was a moment of stunned silence. Midnight recovered first.

'I have a Profile K,' she said. 'And for the record, it's definitely not a mistake.'

Vickson closed her laptop softly. 'You,' she told her assistant. 'Hold my calls.' The assistant scurried out.

'Sorry,' Midnight murmured to her as she went.

'And you, go and file your report with HR. That's not my problem.' Richard took a small step backwards and blushed.

'He'd better not,' Midnight said. 'He was extremely misogynistic and suggested to me that I made a profiling error because I'm female and therefore oversensitive.'

Richard paused too long to make any denial credible.

'It seems you two are quits then,' Vickson said. 'You, be more respectful to your line manager. Chain of command within Necto is very clear. And Mr Baxter, if you want to have a discussion about how oversensitive women are, you should schedule that chat with me instead.' He opened and closed his mouth twice, then gave up. 'Good, you can go.'

Richard exited, shutting the door as he went. Midnight waited to be invited to sit. It didn't happen.

'Tell me about it,' Vickson said. 'You caused enough of a scene getting in here, so this had better make compelling listening.'

Midnight kept it short and factual. When she finished, Vickson stared at her, tapping her Mont Blanc pen on the desk as she chewed her bottom lip.

'Just so I understand, what is it you think we should do with this information, Miss Jones?'

Midnight frowned and shook her head. 'I . . . I suppose I thought you'd have the answer to that question.'

'No, you have the answer to it. You see, this is not me asking you what will happen. I'm asking for your thoughts. Really, I'd like to know what you expected when you brought this to me.'

Midnight took a moment to think about it. 'Well, I guess we should notify TESU of the details, not just give them a yes or no to the applicant. They need to know what they're dealing with here. I think we should also consider notifying the authorities. I mean, the coders may have been messing around when they called it a Profile K, but this man has no limits. He could be – probably is – abusive in relationships. There's no doubt in my mind that he's very dangerous. The university might want to release the applicant's details to the police so they can check him out.'

Vickson was nodding. Midnight felt better already, just getting it out there.

'Wow. That's a lot,' Vickson said. 'You went right from igniting the engine, to warp speed in just a couple of breaths. So let's break this down. Our contract is – in this case – with TESU. Only TESU has the legal right to discuss applications with the police, and that would be a matter for them. It's simply not within our purview to make recommendations or suggestions to clients about these things.'

Midnight felt herself shrinking. 'But . . . we have to. I mean, we should. Richard said there has never been an actual Profile

K before. If that's true, then this person is . . .' The words wouldn't come and she finished her sentence with a weak shrug.

'This person is what? A data set. That's all they are to us, and that's not to dismiss your concerns, but you're talking about what scientists would say is no more than potential energy. A mindset that we happened to pick up, that might never come to anything. Miss Jones, it's not a crime to be a sociopath or even a psychopath. Not all of these people act on their impulses. You know, some of our clients are actively looking for people like your Profile K applicant. If I were to talk with anyone about it, I'd be giving our military clients a ring.' She gave a brief bray of laughter that Midnight did not return. 'So listen, I understand why you're concerned, and I think it's admirable that you're taking your job and our corporate responsibility so seriously, but the bottom line is you cannot report someone's psychology to the police.'

Midnight rubbed her eyes. Vickson was right, of course, and she felt more than a little stupid. 'Could we at least warn the university?'

Vickson got up from her desk and walked to where Midnight was standing. 'Miss Jones, what's the first thing applicants see when they put their digital signature to their application? I mean, before they've got the headset on, or the glove. Right at the start.'

'You mean the terms and conditions of testing?' Midnight asked, sinking further into her humiliation.

'Bingo! Terms and conditions,' Vickson confirmed. 'Those state that we undertake not to use test results for anything other than to provide our client with a suitability assessment for employment or education.'

'Got it,' Midnight confirmed quietly.

'Perfect. So you don't need to worry about a thing. This is

what the process is for. The system works. And yes, there might be some bad apples out there.' Midnight felt about an inch tall. 'But you're not a police officer, and Necto isn't some Orwellian Big Brother set-up.'

Midnight sighed. 'Sorry to have wasted your time, and for the whole, you know, bursting in thing.'

'That's all right. It was a welcome break from statistics. Not that I'm encouraging you to do it again, and you shouldn't undermine your line manager like that.'

'I'll apologise,' Midnight muttered, heading for the exit.

'Miss Jones, before you go. You didn't download any of the data on this applicant, did you?'

'I put it onto a separate drive on my computer in case you wanted to see it,' she said. 'I hope that wasn't wrong.'

'Not at all. It was a sensible precaution. Email it to me and I'll take a quick look, if that makes you feel better, then delete the file your end. We have strict rules about how data can be stored, as you're aware. Talk to no one, not even your fellow team members about this. Loose lips lose lawsuits.' Another of Necto's favourite bastardised sayings.

The conversation was over.

The assistant didn't turn to look at Midnight as she plodded past and made her way back down the hallway, heading for the toilets. Her relationship with Richard Baxter would never recover, and, for the first time, Midnight thought that perhaps he had some justification for not liking her. Amber was going to think she'd lost her mind. Even she was looking back on the decisions she'd made that morning, wondering what the hell she'd been thinking.

The mirror was not her friend. It told a story of a young woman who worked too many hours and who worried too much. Pale skin that hadn't seen enough sunshine was the main problem, but there were other factors, like when had she last had sex? When had someone last hugged her, who wasn't her sister or a close girlfriend?

'Maybe it's self-pity vibes driving all the men away,' she murmured.

Back at her desk, she emailed the care agency pleading an emergency at work and asking for late cover. She'd have to pay them double time, of course, but she needed to let off some steam. The one thing that wasn't difficult was persuading Amber to go drinking with her after work.

Midnight emailed Sara Vickson the file of raw data then deleted the copy from her desktop, tossed her pen drive into the back of her desk drawer, and downloaded a new set of data to profile. Her desk phone rang five minutes later.

'This is Sara Vickson. I've identified the problem. We recently started allowing interested parties to use certain locations, such as TESU, to undertake testing for their own purposes. He wasn't applying to take a course at the university at all. His profile should never have ended up on your desk. In the circumstances, I decided to mark the file as corrupt and have taken him off our system completely. Well done for flagging it. I'm impressed. Bear in mind that Necto does like to recognise and reward its keenest staff. And the legal team has asked me to remind you of the non-disclosure agreement contained within your contract. You should take a look just to familiarise yourself with its terms.'

'Legal team?' Midnight's stomach plummeted.

'Of course. You seemed sufficiently concerned about matters that I consulted them. Any breach of confidentiality in this matter would result in the immediate termination of your employment with Necto, without an ongoing reference.' Vickson paused momentarily. 'And in fact, a breach of confidential information would also mean that Necto would be able to sue you for damages. Between us, biotech companies really can be awfully litigious. I've never known our legal team to lose a case.'

'Um . . . okay,' Midnight mumbled.

'But the main takeaway here, is well done, as I've said,' Vickson added brightly. 'It's good to know you're on your toes. I'm sure you'll make good choices.' The line went dead.

So that's that, Midnight thought. It was the juicy carrot and barbed stick approach. Vickson had handled it. The Profile K had been deleted from the system. Midnight had been given a pat on the head for her vigilance, and at the same time threatened with dismissal if she mentioned the Profile K to anyone else. And what the hell did being sued for damages mean? Could they take her flat and what few savings she had? Could they force her to put Dawn in a home? She was guessing Necto could do pretty much whatever they wanted. The message had been clear. Her hands were shaking and her head was thumping. She knew her only option was to keep quiet.

If only forgetting what she'd seen were as easy as deleting computer files.

Chapter 6

Bake Me A Cake had doubled its profits from the previous year. The cash profits, in reality, weren't all that much to shout about, but the trajectory was heading in the right direction and that was what Jessica Finch cared about. Her company – her baby – had been born only two years ago, and now she was paying her rent, making her bills, and this year she might also manage a holiday as well.

She put the finishing touches to the batch of cupcakes and traybakes she would take around several businesses in the Clapham and Battersea areas the next day and began washing up. Other people might begin to resent the mess, the grind, and the floury fingermarks on everything, but Jessica loved it. She'd loved it when her mother had first begun teaching her to bake at the age of four. At twelve, she'd won a baking competition, and the prize had been a cake decorating course in the summer holidays. When it had finally dawned on her that it could actually be her career, she'd never looked back. Jessica, at thirty-one years old, was literally living the dream.

It wasn't rocket science. There were recipes to follow, techniques taught by other people, and quality ingredients. All those things mattered. But Bake Me A Cake wasn't just about how light her sponges were or how evenly distributed the fruit was in her tea loaf. Her business was thriving because she'd persisted in reaching out to local businesses and making friends with them. She didn't just turn up with her cake delivery each day, take the money and run. Every drop-off involved careful scheduling so she could spend plenty of time chatting with the people who bought her cakes. She knew the names of the security staff on each door. She always had a few extra treats up her sleeve to offer to the right people. And Jessica Finch was never, ever caught without a smile on her face. Her mother had taught her that, too. It wasn't fake and it wasn't forced. Jessica meant every smile that lit up her face. But my goodness, didn't it make doing business easier?

Some time, there would be the space in her life for other things, too. She'd like a girlfriend one day. Someone to curl up with in the evenings and watch a movie. A special person of her own to walk along a beach with, holding hands. Right now she didn't have time to meet anyone. Pubs and clubs were exhausting and time-consuming, and online dating wasn't for her. She would just have to wait and meet someone organically, maybe at one of those beautiful offices she visited every day, with all those glamorous women in their designer suits.

A timer went off. She removed a batch of shortbread from one of the two huge ovens in her kitchen that had necessitated a loan, and which she'd finally paid off just one month earlier. Now they were hers. Everything in the flat was hers, and that was good because back in the days before she'd admitted to herself that she was more attracted to women than to men, she'd lived with someone who'd been unkind. That was her catchall phrase for what she'd endured. The split had been painfully disruptive, although not emotionally painful at all, she'd been so ready for it. There had been boring arguments over who'd bought what, and for the most part Jessica was willing to let go of material possessions. She drew the line at kitchenware.

He'd been less reasonable. There had been arguments so severe that some of her beloved plates, scales and moulds had been thrown across the room, and she hadn't liked that at all. But it was all replaceable, save for those pieces from her mother that she'd inherited and treasured. Those pieces, she'd moved first, so her then boyfriend, Billy, couldn't destroy them.

Men, Jessica had realised in the final throes of a row that had started with an accusation that she was frigid and ended with him throwing eggs at her, were not for her. Her clothes and hair streaked with yolk, shell crunching underfoot, egg white rendering the floor a slippery minefield, she'd cleaned up the mess she'd made of her life with a smile on her face. It was all good. You broke a few eggs in life. If that was the price she had to pay for a brighter future, then she was willing to pay it. In truth, her relationship with Billy had never been that great. She just didn't like to think about the really bad times. He had a temper, and he preferred women who did what they were told. But it was water under the bridge for the most part. She hadn't seen Billy in person since, although he'd contacted her. Persistently. Not always nicely. Some of it had been disconcerting. Those times, she'd made new plans, picked herself up again, changed her mobile number, moved out of the area, and just kept on carrying on.

She sprinkled a light dusting of caster sugar on the shortbread and grated some orange zest over the top.

'Living the dream,' she said.

It was 10.59 p.m. and she was dead on her feet. Time for a quick shower, a few pages of a book, and she'd be asleep before she could finish the chapter. Jessica reached up to run her fingertips over the edge of a glass jelly mould in the shape of a crown. 'Goodnight, Mum,' she whispered. 'Love you.'

Chapter 7

The pub on Battersea Park Road was full of beautiful, tired people. Some were tired because they weren't working enough, the remainder because they were working too much, but the overwhelming sense was of eye-rolling ennui.

Amber had been drinking red wine all evening and her lips were stained purple. Midnight had stuck to bottled beer which was less likely to give her an acid stomach and a hangover, but it was fair to say they'd both drunk more than was advisable for a school night.

'You okay?' Amber slurred slightly. 'You've been a bit weird all evening. And why was Richard giving you the evils all afternoon?'

'It's nothing. Well, it's something, but they're hitting me with the confidentiality stick so I can't talk about it. Suffice it to say, if there were an Oscar for having the shittest day at work ever, I'd be writing my acceptance speech right now. Richard hates me more than ever, which I wouldn't have thought possible at seven o'clock this morning, but apparently, I still had new depths to plumb.'

Amber knew better than to ask. Confidentiality breaches at Necto were not tolerated, and no one wanted to be part of one. Instead, she held her glass in the air, red wine sloshing dangerously from side to side.

'I salute you, most troublesome of the Education Team. Long may you piss Richard off!'

'Cheers to that.' Midnight clinked her glass against Amber's.

'Hey, listen, my brother just split up with his girlfriend. I know relationships are tough for you, but I honestly think you guys—'

'No way,' Midnight said. 'I'd hate it if anything got in the way of our friendship. And you're right, relationships are pretty much impossible for me. I've got to face facts. My parents aren't coming back, not until they're too old to travel or run out of money, by which time they'll be expecting me to support them too. No one wants the sort of commitments I've got, Amber. I rarely go out more than once a month, and when I do, I can't go far in case I get called back to Dawn. Plus, having people to mine is really difficult.'

'I know. But at some point, you'll have to live a little. More than just three hours at a bar with me, or a takeaway and movie night. I mean, when did you last have sex?'

'You mean with an actual human rather than just in my imagination?' Midnight laughed. Amber didn't.

'Sex is important, not optional. It reminds us that we're alive. I've got a great idea! Next time you can get a carer for a Saturday we'll go to Battersea Power Station. The shopping centre in there is amazing.' She raised her eyebrows dramatically high. 'Even better, we'll go to the JOIA bar in the evening, put on some heels, layer up the bright red lipstick. The men who

46

drink there are both gorgeous *and* rich. I guarantee you'll get phone numbers.'

'To do what with? It's not like I can take anyone home with me and I can't stay out all night.'

'Sex doesn't take all night,' Amber grinned.

'It doesn't, but I'm not a Clapham-Common-quickie-against-a-tree kind of girl, thank you very much.'

The barman turned off the lights behind the optics. 'Shit, it's that late already?' Midnight checked her watch. 'I've got to go. You coming?'

'No, I'll linger with the last-to-leave crowd but I'll text you when I get home. Don't worry about me. Go get a taxi.'

Midnight grabbed Amber and kissed her temple noisily. 'Thanks for coming out. I needed this!'

'Go!' Amber ordered. 'And don't be late tomorrow. Richard will crap himself with excitement if he gets to have a chat with you in his pod two days in a row.'

'Gross!' Midnight shouted as she dashed for the door, bumping straight into a man who was already looking past her towards Amber. 'Sorry.'

He stepped back out of the door without a word and let her pass. Midnight crossed the road to look for a taxi and headed for a nearby junction with no luck, then tried a different street, aware of the fact that Dawn's carer would be getting increasingly cross.

Twenty minutes later, an empty taxi finally raced past. Waving madly, she stepped out into the road behind it. The driver slowed to a stop. Midnight raced up, shouting her address as she climbed in and hoping the smell of booze on her breath wasn't overpowering. She relaxed and drifted, glad she'd stopped drinking before spinning-ceiling syndrome set in, but having had enough that she'd be asleep the second her head hit the pillow.

The taxi driver slammed on his brakes and Midnight slid off her seat, hitting the floor hard.

'Fuck, what's this now?' he muttered.

Midnight picked herself up to see a horizon of flashing blue lights.

'Terrorist attack?' Midnight asked.

'We should get out of here,' the driver responded. 'Get your belt on.'

He pulled across the road to start a three-point turn as an unmarked car with police lights inside approached from behind, beeping madly.

'I've got to get home. My sister needs me,' Midnight said. 'Oh God, we're still more than a mile away.'

'You can't get out here. I'll find a different route.' He completed his turn, headed back the way they'd come and turned off to avoid the junction.

'What the fuck?'

'What is it?' Midnight asked.

'No way through. We'll have to wait it out. I've got cars behind me now.'

Midnight lowered her window and listened. Sirens – lots of them – but no gunfire, no shouting or screaming. There was no one running panicked down the street, just people opening their curtains.

'I can't wait,' Midnight said. She grabbed £20 from her wallet. 'Here. Keep the change. I'll walk.'

He released her door and Midnight hopped onto the kerb, trying to figure out the fastest way home. She had no choice but to head towards the police lights. Going back the other way would take her in the wrong direction, and she wasn't about to start wandering down unlit side streets late at night when she'd been drinking. Crossing the road as officers were hastily sectioning off a road with crime scene tape, she couldn't help but stare.

Uniformed officers were positioned a few metres apart along the road. Police vans and some unmarked white vehicles were centred around a line of trees further down, behind which floodlights were being hastily erected facing a white gazebo. A stream of white-suited personnel, hoods up, shoe-covers on, were moving between vehicles, the tent, and one of the houses.

Midnight knew she had to leave, but the scene was captivating in the worst possible way.

'Excuse me,' another passer-by called to the nearest police officer. 'Can you tell me what's happened? I live on this road and I need to get to my house.'

'Not possible right now, sir, I'm afraid,' the officer said. 'Is there somewhere else you can go temporarily?'

'No. That's my house, I've been working late, and I need to get to bed. Could you please explain what's going on?'

The police officer kept it friendly and polite. 'A serious crime has been reported, sir. A unit will be over to speak with you to ask if you witnessed anything.'

'Is someone dead?' he asked.

No sugar-coating with this guy, Midnight thought.

The police officer sighed. 'That would be correct, although I can't share any further details.'

'What house number?' the man insisted. 'It might be someone I know.'

'Sir, you'll be made aware of the facts as soon as we can release them. It's important that we proceed in a way that's respectful to the family of the deceased and that best supports our investigation. I'm sure you understand.'

Midnight could see flashes going off in the dark down the street. They were taking photos. The gazebo had to be protecting the exterior scene. Sooner or later they'd be bringing out the body. It was macabre, standing there waiting to catch a glimpse of it all. She wasn't alone, either. Other people were walking up, straining to look. Shame flushed her cheeks with blood.

'Dawn,' she gasped. 'God, I'm so bloody late.'

Tearing herself away, she began a slow jog home.

Twelve minutes later, she found Dawn's carer fast asleep on the sofa. Midnight rushed through to check on her twin sister – her own mirror image – but Dawn was peacefully dreaming, the sides on her bed up to prevent her from falling out. Her curtains were closed, her night-light was on, and she was wearing the fresh pyjamas Midnight had left out. All was well with the world.

Back in the lounge, she gently shook the carer's shoulder to wake her up.

'Hey, sorry I'm so late. A lot of roads are blocked. There's been an incident.' It was only a white lie, but she still felt ashamed at the time she'd spent gawping.

'Not a problem. I'll fill in the timesheet tomorrow. Dawn was okay. She asked for you a couple of times and didn't eat much, but she had a glass of warm milk before sleep. I had to read her favourite book three times before she'd settle.'

'She finds it harder to get to sleep if I'm not here,' she explained.

The carer exited as Midnight filled the kettle. Sleep wasn't going to come as easily as she'd hoped. The point of going out for drinks was to banish the horrific images from earlier in the day. Now that footage felt closer than ever.

The images had to have been computer-generated, she told herself. Artificial intelligence was more than capable of that. There was no way Necto would have sourced and used that footage.

'Looked fucking real,' she argued with herself.

That was ridiculous. It had to be illegal. Probably just possessing it was enough to break a few laws. But the noises, the screams . . . who wanted to artificially generate stuff like that?

Taking her drink to bed, Midnight tried not to think about anything; not Necto, not the crime scene, not her lie to the agency so she could go drinking. What sort of a person was she becoming?

Perhaps a little more like her mother and father. A framed photo of them sat on the windowsill in Dawn's bedroom. It had seemed important to remind her sister that she did have a mum and dad, that they had once been a complete family. Dawn wasn't communicative enough to express it in words, but Midnight knew she missed them. When you grew up with so few people around, unable to attend mainstream schools or birthday parties, family was everything. For the first two years after their parents had left, Dawn had been tearful from time to time, and more confused than normal. Midnight had religiously read her sister the postcards and showed her their parents' location on a globe, until she couldn't stand it any more. Why pretend they were coming back? Why keep them alive in Dawn's mind just so her sister could carry on missing them? Midnight had filled the space their parents had left, and become Dawn's everything.

It seemed to her now that her parents had always planned to leave. They'd trained Midnight well, slowly increasing her caring responsibilities through her teenage years, going away for weekends once the girls turned sixteen. Midnight had even gone home on alternate weekends while at university, partly to give her parents a break, but more for Dawn than for them. A twin was a twin, whether or not they inhabited the same intellectual world you did. Her parents had waited until Midnight had graduated from her master's degree, then announced their intention to start travelling. At first, Midnight had assumed they meant they were going on a cruise and would be gone two, maybe three, weeks. But then they'd put their house on the market so they had a pot of money to draw from as they went. They started discussing destinations like Australia, South America, China and India. Still, Midnight hadn't really got it. They weren't going on holiday. They weren't taking Dawn with them. And they weren't coming back. Six months later they were gone, leaving only a monthly allowance to help with rent and care for Dawn. Midnight had to cover all the utilities and food bills, and she was coping all right until her parents' payments petered out after two years.

The contact was regular at first, and there was always a letter on birthdays. One Christmas they even swung through the UK on their way to Turkey from Canada. They were full of praise for Midnight's care of Dawn. It had taken her four days, a whole bottle of wine, and a slow-boiling rage to ask them to start contributing again to the cost of Dawn's care. The pittance the government paid didn't even cover the basics.

The excuses flowed thick and fast. Her parents claimed their money was going down faster than they'd anticipated. Their pensions were worth virtually nothing. They couldn't risk touching capital, given the fact that interest rates were dropping. She had a good job, things were working out for her, weren't they? And if Midnight felt she couldn't cope, she could always talk to the doctors. Dawn would qualify for a place in a home. Midnight could visit at weekends. She shouldn't feel guilty about wanting to get on with her own life. They clearly didn't.

Midnight had left the hotel where they were all having lunch, wrapped Dawn up in her coat, hat and scarf, and got her out of there. She hadn't seen her parents for the remainder of their trip home, and they hadn't tried to call.

Perhaps they were just tired of it, and the terrible, horrible, worst thing of all, was that part of Midnight could understand how they felt. Admitting that to herself was like setting off an internal bomb. Understanding that she wasn't good enough or big enough to never have felt that, had made her physically sick.

So yes, there was something of her parents in her. Because it was hard putting someone else before yourself every single day. It was exhausting, worrying and being scared, making plans then changing plans, keeping medical appointments and ticking the endless boxes that needed ticking to keep her sister alive, fed, stimulated and healthy. And oh God, *yes*, Midnight had days when she didn't want to do it any more. Days when the lure of a travel agent and an airport were so hard to resist it left a knot in her stomach. She hated her parents so much for getting up and leaving and living their own lives. And she hated herself for wanting the same.

The difference was that she couldn't do it. Would never do it. Because when she walked into Dawn's room at the end of each working day, her sister's face would light up. The love they had for one another made her sister's physical and intellectual limitations irrelevant. She was half of Midnight.

Midnight and Dawn. Their stupid, hippy parents' idea of amazing twin names. They were the same height, the same build, had the same hair and the same face. The only real difference was that Midnight had been born without any complications at all, but Dawn's brain had been starved of oxygen, the umbilical cord wrapped perilously tightly around her neck, leaving her brain-damaged before she'd taken her first proper breath. She could walk short distances but got tired and wobbly. She could feed herself finger food, but cutlery was too hard for her. She could say odd words but not fit them together into sentences. She could feel love and experience pain, but would never be able to form adult relationships or make decisions. Their grandparents were all gone, and there were no aunts, uncles or cousins to bolster the family tree either. The two of them were the sum total of the family left in the UK.

So Midnight had to get her head together. Her job at Necto could not be put at risk. Tomorrow morning she would go in not just on time, but early. She would switch back into super-efficiency mode. If she could stomach it, she would even apologise to fucking Richard.

And she would keep Dawn safe. That was all that mattered. Not her day. Not her evening. Not tomorrow's hangover. Just Dawn. Midnight finished her tea and tried to sleep.

Chapter 8

Almost every night, Midnight's sleeping brain took her into the past. Her first day at school was a recurring dream, and Midnight never fought it.

She'd long since realised that her sister, who was so like her physically that they could fool their parents when they were asleep, was not the same as her on the inside – that was how her mother had explained it to her.

They'd been inseparable since birth, in spite of their parents trying to persuade Midnight to make other friends with girls at the park or who lived nearby. But Midnight didn't want anyone else, because how could that be fair when the only person Dawn had was Midnight?

School made the gulf between them real. Midnight had put on her white shirt and blue jumper, grey trousers and black shoes. She'd packed a lunch with help from her mother, and put a pencil, a handkerchief and a miniature doll in her bag, just in case she got scared. Not that she would, she'd told Dawn. She was a big girl now.

Their parents had walked her to the playground. Her father had carried Dawn all the way, and she'd been howling with laughter as he'd horsey-galloped along the pavement. Their mother had taken a photo of Midnight at the school door, head up, smiling and looking confident. Dawn had smiled too. There were people everywhere, children running and playing, and the late summer's cut-grass scent rolling off the school field in warm waves. Then it had been time to go in. Her parents and Dawn had waved. Midnight had waved back, and that was that.

In the corridor she was given a peg to hang up her coat, and looked around for Dawn to take her coat and hang it up too. There was a table for lunchboxes, and Midnight looked back to show Dawn what to do. A seat had been allocated for her, and Midnight sat dutifully. Her name, which she already knew how to spell and write, was on a laminated piece of paper in front of her, but Dawn's was missing. All day long, every few minutes, she reached for her sister's hand, only to find nothing but air. Once, she reached out and took the hand of some boy by mistake who wrinkled his nose and shouted 'Yuck' so loudly the whole class heard. The day dragged.

By the time she was told to put on her coat, Midnight was in tears. She raced out, the teacher calling her back in line, to stay with the class until her parents appeared. Midnight ignored her. Because there was Dawn, red-eyed, twisting her hands, arms outstretched. And there was her mother, because their father was at work, looking exhausted and frantic. But then Dawn was in her arms and nothing else mattered. Midnight didn't care that her sister couldn't speak like her, or spell or write. They were half of each other.

'Thank goodness,' her mother said. 'Dawn's missed you so much.'

No, 'How was your first day?' No, 'Was everything all right?' Not even a, 'Did you make any friends?' Just the realisation, as far as a five-year-old could process anything so adult, that her mother had spent a whole day alone with Dawn without Midnight to entertain her, for the first time ever. As far as Midnight could tell, their mother didn't seem to have enjoyed it much at all.

They walked home, Dawn in the pushchair she'd grown out of a year earlier, and went straight to their room. Midnight took off her new uniform and put on the clothes that matched Dawn's own outfit. Then she pulled the sheets and blankets off their beds, pushed the frames together, and made a magical tent. Inside, she put all the pillows and cushions she could find, drew the curtains and took the torch from the utility room. She found Dawn's favourite picture books, they cuddled up together in their special world, and she made up wonderful stories about unicorns and princesses, and tigers and knights.

When Dawn fell asleep, Midnight went downstairs to get some tea. Her mother, white-faced and tight-lipped, was on the phone to a friend, talking about exhaustion and stress. There was no dinner cooking so Midnight got herself a croissant and some fruit. Her mother's hand shook as she lit a cigarette. In the corner was a pile of washing yet to be done, with several of Dawn's bibs on the top. Dawn didn't like eating without Midnight by her side. A nappy was wafting from the bin so Midnight tied up the top of the sack. Dawn was being potty trained, but she was taking her time to learn.

Her mother put down the phone. 'Is Dawn okay?' she asked.

'She's asleep. Did you have a bad day, Mummy? You look upset.'

'Not a bad day exactly,' her mother said. 'Just a long day. But that's okay. I'll get into a routine.' She walked to the fridge and took out a half-full bottle of white wine. 'I'm glad you're home.'

Midnight awoke at the same point in the dream she always did, trying to figure out how much she remembered accurately and how much of it was her brain filling in the blanks. She rolled over, knowing sleep would take its time coming again. Her parents had been good with Dawn in the early years before Midnight had started school. Not just good, but loving, patient and kind. The sad truth was that from that point on, it had all been pretty much downhill. It might have been exhaustion, perhaps the repetitiveness or restrictiveness of each day. There was so much they couldn't do, that they stopped trying to do anything at all. And it was hard work, there was no denying it. Her parents stopped socialising with friends who had children the same age as her and Dawn, because they had to sit and watch those friends get their lives back, finding their freedom again as their kids spread their wings. While their old friends started going out to the theatre or the pub, on romantic weekends or pursuing new hobbies, Dawn and Midnight's parents grew tired and bored, distant and disillusioned. They just weren't cut out for the hand fate had dealt them, not long term. Both she and Dawn had paid the price.

Chapter 9

'Whatever else happens on this case, there's no way I'm exposing a member of this woman's close family to identifying the body,' Detective Inspector Jock Ruskin announced to the team standing in a circle around the bed. They included a home office pathologist, a photographer, a blood spatter analyst – talk about a waste of time there, he thought – two other detectives from his team, and the head of the crime scene processing squad who'd been called to the worst atrocity any of them had ever witnessed. In any other place, at any other time, they'd have looked like some deranged cult.

'Right, everyone, let's get on. I want to get the body moved as soon as possible to start checking for trace evidence,' the pathologist said. 'Jock, I'll begin the postmortem as soon as we get her back to the mortuary. Preliminary findings at noon tomorrow.'

'That's all right. I think I figured out the cause of death,' Ruskin muttered, his gruff Scot's accent all the more pronounced for the fury and devastation he was trying to control. He was a heavy-set man who nevertheless carried himself lightly, with thinning hair that he was only amazed he hadn't lost years earlier courtesy of the job. The job took everything after a while.

This one was going to leave a stain in his memory, and he knew it. The second he was off-duty, he'd be in his garage punching the heavy bag swinging from the beams, until his fists hurt so badly the pain was all he could think about. It was really just self-harming, but when you could hide abuse in the guise of exercise, no one seemed to care. Better than the alternatives that some of his colleagues used to dull their pain: drink, drugs, or taking it out on their partner. The latter happened more often than Ruskin cared to think about.

One by one, the team disappeared to get on with various tasks, until only Ruskin and the photographer remained.

'Would you mind standing back by the wardrobe please?' she asked. 'I need to get some wide shots first.'

Ruskin shuffled away, careful to make sure he was treading only on the mats protecting the carpet, avoiding leaning against furniture so he didn't smudge any fingerprints. There had to be a forensic trail, he told himself. The fucker who'd killed the woman must have been there for hours. Literally hours. Often, when talking about crime scenes, his squad talked in hyperbole, but the current murder defied even the most extreme adjectives.

The photographer was rearranging her lights to get close-up shots of various areas of the victim's body, but all the photos would show exactly the same thing.

'Bring back the death penalty,' the photographer muttered as she snapped. Ruskin didn't think she'd even registered that she was speaking aloud.

He didn't agree with the death penalty, personally, and he'd seen a lot of dead bodies. But this? The death penalty would be far too kind an ending for this bastard.

The pathologist re-entered the room as the photographer exited.

'How're you doing, Jock?' he asked. 'You picked up a bad one today.'

'They're all bad ones if I've been called in,' Ruskin replied. It wasn't untrue, but it was disingenuous, and Ruskin knew it. On his personal scale of tragic to absolutely fucking monstrous, this was at the fuck-this-job-I'm-getting-a-plane-to-anywhere end of the scale.

'I have some preliminary questions,' Ruskin said. 'I know you don't like this before you've had a chance to—'

'That's fine,' the pathologist interrupted. 'I'll make an exception. You want to know when this happened, and if she was alive when the wounds were inflicted. Given the extent of the bleeding, you know as well as I do that she was alive. So, to the thing that's really bothering you, was she actually conscious during the . . .' He made tiny noises in his throat as he sought a suitably professional word.

'Torture,' Ruskin gave him. 'Let's call it what it was.'

The pathologist didn't bother repeating the phrase. 'She died, I believe, two days ago but I'll confirm that later. I'd say she was conscious, for a substantial amount of the event. My assessment of that might change if I find drugs or alcohol in her system during the toxicology screening, but I doubt it.'

'Because that was the point. Why go to such lengths if she wasn't going to suffer, right?'

'I'm not a psychologist, but I concur. That would seem to be the logical conclusion. Anything else?'

'How long did it take her attacker to do this much damage?' Ruskin asked. 'I need to establish a timeline, and the more accurate the better when we're screening for witnesses and checking CCTV.'

61

'Hard to say. It's detailed work. I'll have to do a reconstruction of sorts.' He paused and neither could look the other in the face. A reconstruction – whatever material was used to practise on – was hard to imagine. 'Not less than an hour, four at most. Somewhere in between.'

Ruskin stared at the flesh and bone that used to contain what seemed a sort of magic. A personality, a conscience, a sense of humour, ambitions, phobias, desires – all had once inhabited the corpse on the bed. And all of it, every nuance and memory, had been soaked into the bed sheets as she'd slowly died. Was it still there, somewhere? If he wrung it out into a bucket, would the magic be dissolved in her blood? He never got over it, no matter many bodies he saw.

'How many cuts on her body in total?' Ruskin growled the question.

'Difficult to say right now. I counted eighty between the back of her wrist and her elbow. Given that both sides look the same, multiply that over the body, allow extra for the trunk. And the face. At least two thousand. That's a conservative estimate. I'll have my assistant get you an accurate count, but it'll take time.' Ruskin nodded. The pathologist gave him a look that only those concerned in the day-to-day management of violent deaths understood. 'I'll give you a minute.' He left Ruskin alone with the body.

It was a hard thing to look at, and a harder thing to look away from. The devastation wrought upon the flesh was absolute and yet – Ruskin hated himself for allowing the thought to be born into a coherent sentence – and yet it was hypnotic, if not sickeningly beautiful.

The pattern carved slice by slice into her flesh was mesmerising. It had to have been made by a scalpel, the individual cuts little more than a millimetre apart, and not deep. Just enough to show the flash of red between the strips of pale tan. Alone, any one cut would barely have bothered her. Not enough to warrant a trip to the doctor, or the pharmacy even. A plaster maybe, over the worst of them.

Ruskin spread a sheet of protective plastic over the windowsill and allowed himself a moment to recover from the uncharacteristic dizziness that was rocking his world.

Her killer was sick, but he'd dealt with sick men and women before. It was perhaps the only given in his job. Some people were sick because they were born that way. Others were sick because their parents or their abusers, sometimes their husbands or wives even, had made them that way. That wasn't what bothered him.

Dangerous? Tick that box. Ruskin ground his upper teeth hard over his lower set. The scene was no lovers' quarrel gone wrong. It wasn't even long-term abuse. This wasn't coercive control or domestic violence. It was obsession, maybe stalking. Perhaps, he thought, the start of something really, really bad. Something the British newspapers would shout about so loudly that pretty soon they'd have reporters calling from all over the globe. Even the possibility of more of the same wasn't what was making him light-headed.

What bothered Ruskin, he realised, boiled down to a single word.

Patience.

'Sir, would you speak with the relative who called it in? She's refusing to be escorted home until she talks with you,' a constable asked, calling the request through a one-inch gap between the door and the frame.

'Of course,' Ruskin said. 'Keep her outside. I'm on my way.'

*

Lily Aguter wasn't crying when Ruskin reached out and shook her hand. She didn't cry when he escorted her to a police van and held the door open for her to climb inside so they could speak privately. She was keeping it together, he thought. More people did than the public realised. British stiff upper lip was real, particularly combined with shock and the most destructive thing of all – hope. That was the killer. The metaphorical killer, he corrected himself in his head.

'I take it you didn't go into the bedroom?' Ruskin began. No point beating around the bush. He had some hope to destroy and it was best done fast.

'No, I couldn't get into the flat at all. I have a key and it turned in the lock but there was something blocking the door. That's when I called the police. I could see a couple of inches into the hallway, and there was a mess and what I thought was maybe, you know, um . . . blood?'

Ruskin tried not to be too kind. He'd learned that early on in his career. There was something about the kindness of strangers that made human beings crumble.

'It was blood,' he said. He wasn't rough or harsh, but facts needed to be spoken plainly. 'Your sister owns the apartment?'

'Yes, but she had friends visit sometimes, occasionally they'd stay over. Maybe she wasn't alone, you know? It's possible that she's somewhere else and—'

There it was. Fucking hope, dancing excitedly in your peripheral vision, making everything worse again. 'Ms Aguter,' Ruskin interrupted her. 'There's no doubt in my mind that the deceased person inside is your sister. I saw a photograph on her bedside table of a young woman holding a toddler in a yellow coat. Is that your sister?'

Lily's chin was wobbling now and her breathing was fast and shallow. 'Um, yes, that's her with my daughter Vivienne.

Are you sure it's her, because you don't know her and some of her friends have similar colouring.'

'The deceased was wearing an emerald ring, quite distinctive, on the middle finger of her left hand. Is that familiar?'

She sobbed, which was all the confirmation Ruskin needed. It went two ways with reactions. A heavy breath out was relief. The sob was always a positive identification. Ruskin waited as long as Lily needed until she could speak again.

'What . . . what . . .'

'What happened?' Ruskin helped. Lily nodded. 'We'll know more after the postmortem which will begin as soon as the body can be transported to the mortuary. The pathologist is with your sister now. There's no doubt that her death was an act of criminal violence. We should talk about the details when you're at home and have some support.'

Lily kept both hands pressed against her mouth, eyes wide and circling as if looking to escape.

'For now,' Ruskin continued, 'if I can press you to help us very briefly. I have a few questions and they're important. Was your sister . . .'

'Chloe,' she whispered.

'Chloe,' Ruskin said unwillingly. He hated the moment he had to begin using the name of the deceased. That was when he got sucked into their life. Every fact he learned from that point on would be a body blow. He felt it all so deeply that really he had no business being in the police game. 'Was Chloe in a relationship? Is there anyone we should be looking for?'

She shook her head.

'No ex-boyfriend or ex-husband who might have done this?'

Another headshake.

'And had Chloe mentioned anything to you about being worried, scared, stalked, uncomfortable?'

Lily managed a small, 'No.'

'Did she have a passport, and do you know where she kept it? It's a fast way for us to pull all her official details from any databases.'

'I want to see her,' was Lily's non-sequitur.

'That can't happen here, I'm afraid, and it's best that you don't see her. People often think they need or want that as some sort of closure, but . . .' He closed his eyes momentarily and the image of Chloe's formerly beautiful face marred by hundreds of tiny slashes flashed up. 'It would be upsetting, and it would ruin the last memory you have of your sister. Perhaps you could think of someone else who—'

'Was she . . .' Lily leaned forward clutching her stomach. 'Was she raped?' She clapped both hands back over her mouth the second she managed to eject the words.

'We don't know yet,' Ruskin said. 'We'll be able to tell you in the next few days.'

Lily nodded and turned her face to stare into the blue-ribboned darkness, crying quietly. Ruskin watched her falling tears reflected in the passenger window. She dashed them away.

'Her passport's in her bedside table. She was twenty-eight years old and five foot five tall. Her driver's licence will be in her wallet. Her handbag's usually on the back of one of the dining chairs. There was no boyfriend. She was lonely but she wouldn't use the internet to date. It scared her.' Lily laughed and it turned into a half-scream as she reached for Ruskin's hand.

He gripped hers in response and let her dig her nails into his flesh. She was on the brink of a chasm he himself had seen. In that second, he was the only thing keeping her from falling in. He didn't move. She had to step back from the ledge all by herself.

'She missed my daughter's birthday party yesterday afternoon,' Lily said eventually. Ruskin thought of the wrapping paper he'd seen in the hallway, still rolled up with an elastic band. 'Vivienne was so upset. I knew straight away that something was wrong. Maybe if I'd left the party that minute, if I'd driven over immediately. Could I have saved her, do you think? Was there time? Afterwards, I just cleared up. Why didn't I get in the car and check on her?'

'We don't have a time of death yet,' Ruskin said. 'But I've been doing this a lot of years. We suspect Chloe died more than a day ago. You might have found her body sooner but I don't believe you'd have been able to change anything. I'd like to check her mobile phone and her emails. If you know her passwords, that would help.'

'I can help with that,' Lily said. 'Just tell me one thing. Did she suffer? I mean, she's dead so I know . . . I realise . . . that it would have been awful. But was it terrible? Would she have known much about it?'

Ruskin wrapped his free hand over the one of Lily's that was still holding his. 'She's not suffering any more. That's what you need to keep remembering. Chloe's okay now.'

Chapter 10

Slightly worse for wear, Midnight arrived at work early in accordance with her decision from the night before. Dawn's carer had been mercifully prompt which allowed Midnight to dash into a chemist for paracetamol, followed rapidly by a cafe pit stop for a double espresso and a cherry Danish. The three things combined had reduced the hangover by a good fifty per cent by the time she took the lift down to her department.

'I've just never heard of anything like that happening around here,' one woman was whispering. 'I mean, we all know to be careful on Clapham Common after dark but this was in her own home.'

'My husband has already said I'm not to walk anywhere alone until they've caught whoever did it.'

Midnight exited and walked along the corridor to her department. Richard Baxter was nowhere to be seen, and Amber wasn't at her pod – no surprise there – so Midnight busied herself downloading enough data batches to get her through to lunchtime. It was only when Amber hadn't arrived by 9.15 a.m.

that Midnight checked her voicemail. The only message was from Amber.

'Midnight, please pick up,' Amber sobbed. 'I need you. Call me, please, as soon as you can. I don't know what—' The call ended abruptly. Midnight listened to the call details. Amber's message had come in the previous evening.

She dialled Amber's number. 'Come on, pick up.'

Straight to voicemail. Midnight ended the call and immediately tried again, only to get the same result.

Richard Baxter walked past her desk and Midnight waved to stop him.

'Morning, Richard. Sorry to start the day like this but I'm concerned about Amber. Has she called in sick or anything?'

'I can't discuss another employee with you. That would be a breach of confidence, and after yesterday I think it would be best if you confined yourself to worrying about your own work.' His lips were pinched almost white.

Midnight mentally shelved the apology she'd been planning, but softened her tone.

'Of course, it's just that she left a voicemail on my phone last night. I only just picked it up and she sounded . . .' What could she say? The last thing she wanted to admit was that she and Amber had been out midweek drinking. Not that there was anything wrong with that, but Richard would find a way to make it feel disappointing. 'She sounded unwell. Like, maybe, very unwell indeed.' He shrugged. 'Perhaps, as her manager, and I know you're conscientious about your team – we're all grateful – you could ask HR if she called in sick. You don't have to tell me anything. But you could, you know, check it out. On your own.'

Richard sighed. 'I will ensure that I've undertaken all my managerial duties. You know, when I tried to stop you going to Sara Vickson about the Profile K, I was actually trying to help you.'

'By threatening to report me to HR?'

'You rather forced my hand on that score. Just so you know, I opted against that course of action. I believe you've learned your lesson. As it happens, I need your assistance. I've been informed that we have a new team member joining your group today and he'll need help getting used to the procedures. I'm assigning you as his probationary mentor. Here he is now.'

'Is this Necto's way of punishing me for yesterday?'

'Necto is a global corporation working to the highest professional standards. It doesn't punish its employees,' Richard chastised quietly. 'Perhaps you should just be grateful that you've still got a job.'

Midnight tried not to roll her eyes as the man approached, smiling warmly at her.

'Eli Sand, this is Midnight Jones,' Richard said. 'She'll be looking after you. Questions should be directed to her in the first instance. Midnight will show you around the office, and explain lunch breaks, screen breaks, et cetera. You'll be her shadow for the next month.'

'Hi,' Midnight said. 'Welcome.'

Richard nodded his satisfaction and walked away. Midnight struggled to keep her face neutral. It wasn't unknown for Necto to announce new team members without warning, and she had always suspected they liked keeping their employees on their toes, but the timing was more than a little suspicious. Best-case scenario, Sara Vickson was trying to keep her extra busy to stop her thinking about the Profile K. Worst-case scenario, Eli Sand had been strategically placed to keep an eye on her. He looked far too confident and relaxed for her liking, and good-looking if you liked men with shaped eyebrows and designer stubble, which Amber most definitely did. Midnight wished her friend was next to her, making her usual inappropriate comments.

'I hope you don't mind mentoring me. You must be so busy. I was told you're one of the best here so it's a privilege to—' he began.

'Listen, Eli, I'm sorry, but I need to put my pod hood up for a while. A colleague hasn't come in and I got this weird call, so I need to locate her. This is your station.' She pointed at the empty desk behind her.

'Go ahead. I hope she's okay. You must be scared after the murder last night. It was kind of close by, right? Have they released the victim's identity yet?' He sat in his chair and began adjusting the seat position.

Midnight stared at him, feeling increasingly sick. She hadn't factored Amber's absence into the previous night's police operation, but now that it had occurred to her, her insides were a fountain of panic.

'Some people were just talking about it in the lift. I hadn't realised it would get this much publicity,' she said.

'It's everywhere. News, radio, papers, internet. What planet do you live on?' he asked, wide-eyed.

Planet Dawn, she wanted to say, too busy dialling Amber's number again to explain. Midnight lived in a world that demanded every second of her time, all her energy, and a military routine just to get out of the door in the morning. So no, she hadn't put the TV on, picked up a paper, or looked at her phone since getting out of her front door. And now, fuck-fuck-fuck, her best friend who was fairly drunk when she'd left her last night wasn't answering her phone.

'Calm down,' Midnight told herself. 'Amber's fine. There's no way it could have been her in that house. She couldn't have got ahead of me.' Still no response from Amber's mobile.

71

'Could you show me how to calibrate my headset? They went over it pretty fast in training,' Eli said.

'Not now,' Midnight snapped. 'I mean, I'll help you later. Sorry. Bad timing.' She tried Amber – straight to voicemail again. 'I'm off to the media centre. If you get stuck, just look busy until I get back. If Richard asks, tell him I'm in the women's toilets. That always shuts him up.'

Midnight disappeared before Eli could ask her any more questions and headed for the lift. One more floor down was a media centre where certain websites and media outlets could be accessed. Every now and then employees needed information about the outside world available only on social media or through news channels, usually for client research, less often for personal reasons. It was supervised, and the only feed was incoming, so no one could export company secrets.

She waved her ID tag at the door, knowing HR would immediately be alerted to her visit, and rushed in.

'Good morning,' an overly perky media assistant greeted her. 'What is it you'd like to access today?'

'News feed, any channel, relating to a murder in south London last night. Whatever has the most details.'

'Gosh, that's a gruesome start to the day! Are you sure?'

'Yep,' Midnight said, crossing her arms.

'If you insist. Here you go. This is the feed from London Watch.' She turned a screen in Midnight's direction and stepped away to allow Midnight to scroll through the available information.

She skim-read. The deceased was believed to be in her twenties, Caucasian, found alone in a one-bedroom apartment. She hadn't yet been named as police were still talking to witnesses and were in the process of having the body formally identified. Her killer had not been apprehended and a major investigation and manhunt had kicked off around the city. Anyone with information should contact the Metropolitan police, etc., etc.

'Goddamn it,' Midnight muttered. 'Where the hell are you, Amber?'

'Sorry?' the assistant called from her desk.

'Talking to myself. Is there nothing more detailed than this?'

The media assistant wrinkled her nose. 'Why would you want more detail than that?'

Midnight realised she could have put it better. 'I meant in terms of the investigation. Not as in the death or the body. It's close to where I live. I have a sister who lives with me.'

The truth of that statement hit home as she was saying it. Her flat wasn't far enough from the murder scene for her to take anything for granted, but Amber lived even closer, maybe a quarter of a mile to the west. Even so, Amber shouldn't have been anywhere near there. Unless, Midnight's brain insisted, Amber staggered out of the bar just after you and was bundled into a car, and then—

'I shouldn't worry, ninety per cent of women in the UK are killed by someone they know, and most stranger attacks are terrorism related.' The assistant whispered it, as if imparting some dirty secret. 'Approximately seventy-five per cent of murdered females are killed in their own home, so statistically it's very likely the victim was killed in a domestic incident, probably by a partner or ex-partner.' She gave a broad grin that Midnight couldn't force her face to return. 'I'm a bit of a true crime nut.'

'Sure,' Midnight muttered. 'Makes sense. I just, er, walked past the scene last night and I think it freaked me out a bit.'

'Oh my gosh.' The assistant leaned in, breathy with excitement. 'Did you see anything? Were they carrying out the body?'

'All I could see was a tent, lots of lights and people going back and forth from vans, in and out of the house.'

'That'll be a scenes of crime unit,' she said. Midnight couldn't help but think that smugness while discussing a recent murder was about as tasteful as flirting during a funeral.

'I should be getting back to my desk. Are you able to notify me of updates?'

'Absolutely. I scan the news regularly while I'm on duty. Write your company email address here.' She pushed forward a pad of paper.

Midnight left her details and returned to the lift, grateful to be away from Little Miss True Crime Sunshine. As she re-entered her department, she could see Amber stripping off her coat and talking animatedly to the new recruit. Midnight forced herself not to run the length of the office.

'I did my first degree at King's and my master's at LSE,' Eli was saying. 'I couldn't believe it when I landed the job here. It was so competitive. They say Necto only accepts two per cent of all job applicants. Is that true?'

'No idea,' Amber replied. 'The only statistic I care about right now is how many people they fire.' She gave a burst of laughter. 'Hey, Midnight—'

'Where the hell have you been? I've been calling you. Was your phone off?'

'I didn't exactly come from my house. It was a late night and I didn't have a charger with me.' She shrugged and had the decency to look sheepish.

Midnight flopped down into her chair and motioned for Amber to come closer to her. 'Are you okay?'

'Better than okay,' Amber said. 'As long as Richard doesn't give me one of his lectures. I've avoided him so far.'

'You left me a message.' Amber looked blank. 'You were crying, asking me to call you. I was terrified.'

'Ah,' Amber scrunched up her face. 'Yeah, sorry about that. A former hook-up of mine came into the bar as you were leaving and he started giving me a load of shit. Said he was going to get his own back, threatened to follow me home. It was pretty nasty.'

Midnight sighed. 'Please don't tell me you made up with him and it all ended in hearts and roses.'

Amber smiled sweetly. 'I love that you care about me, but no, I'm not a total idiot. As I was phoning you, he tried to grab my mobile which was why I got cut off. One of the barmen waded in at that point – you know the really tall one with the man bun and the tattoo of a grapevine down his left arm? – he got my phone back and kicked the guy out. The barman let me stay a while to make sure I was safe, we got chatting and sort of decided it might be wiser for me to stay at his for the night. In the circumstances, you know?'

Midnight nodded. 'Yeah. I get it.'

'So, do you want to hear about it, or are you just going to be all quiet and judgey?'

'I love it here already,' Eli said, giving them both a sly wink. 'Is it like this all the time?'

'I wish!' Amber said, giggling. 'Oops, here comes Richard. Look busy, people.' She sank into her chair and began furiously tapping keys.

Midnight scooted her chair across to Eli's. 'Let me show you how to calibrate your headset.' She held out her hand and he passed it over.

Richard took a seat at another desk and began an earnest conversation about appropriate workwear with some poor soul on the team next to theirs.

'Hey,' Amber hissed. 'I really am sorry. I didn't mean to freak you out.'

'No, I overreacted,' Midnight said, slipping the headset on. 'Go to settings, Eli. There was a murder last night, that's all, so when I got your message then couldn't get hold of you . . .'

'That's awful.' Eli joined in. 'Did you actually think she was dead?'

'Oh crap, Midnight, is that it? I'm so sorry!'

'No, not really. Logically, I knew it couldn't be you. I got freaked out at work yesterday and was a bit hyped up. Probably shouldn't have gone drinking.' She shook her head and managed a smile. 'You know, I actually went to the media suite and looked up the details of the murder to check it wasn't you!'

Amber frowned but only held it for a few seconds before beginning to laugh. 'That's actually really nice of you. I mean, I was off having the best sex of my life with grapevine guy, but it's the thought that counts. I'm pleased I'm not dead, but at least I know you've got my back.'

Midnight took off the headset and handed it back to Eli.

'I'm pleased you're not dead, too. Just don't leave me any more messages like that.'

'Can I go drinking with you guys tonight?' Eli asked. 'It sounds amazing!'

'Yes!' Amber mock punched the air. 'We have a new recruit.'

'Sorry, I won't get another late carer for ages. You'll have to wait.'

'She has obligations,' Amber told Eli. 'Stick with me. I'm the fun one.'

Richard began patrolling the office again, and they all returned their focus to work.

Midnight reorientated herself. She'd overreacted about Amber, and as much as she'd tried to hide it, she'd been furious when she'd found out the truth. Was there an element of jealousy to her reaction? Yup, absolutely. Midnight had been there plenty of times before. At least she could admit it to herself. It was hard, never being able to disappear off to someone else's place on a whim and indulge in a night of wanton, careless sex. Whenever Midnight met anyone she liked, she spent hours agonising over their personality, their commitments, when to tell them about Dawn, how they might react. It was a slow poison. If she didn't tell people and they got into something with her, they seemed annoyed when she finally admitted what her life actually looked like. If she told them straight away, they got scared and disappeared.

It wasn't Dawn's fault. Midnight had never resented her sister for it. But her parents? That was different. They'd left without considering what it would mean for Midnight's own personal prospects. Only she didn't think that was true. More likely, they knew exactly what they were doing and couldn't have cared less.

Midnight shook herself. Self-pity was quicksand, and she couldn't let herself get stuck in it again. She completed thirty-nine more profiles before her internal phone began flashing.

Chapter 11

Jessica wheeled her Bake Me A Cake cart into the reception area of the office space in Clapham that was one of ten stops she had scheduled for that day. The 11 o'clock stop was often her most lucrative. Most people hadn't eaten since breakfast, and all it took was for one person to appear with a slice of blood orange meringue pie or a chocolate mousse doughnut and everyone would come running.

In that particular office, the same man was always waiting ahead of her arrival. She looked around, hoping he was ill rather than just late. Usually, she was grateful for every penny her customers spent. His, she could do without. Much as it went against her nature to be so mean, he gave her the creeps – he had from the first day he'd asked for two of her cream buns. He hadn't even looked at them, just kept on staring at her until she'd handed him his change and called the next customer forward. After that, he'd barely missed a trip to her trolley, ordering the same thing every time, staring at her just a little too long and far too intensely. Two cream buns. He'd never asked her out, never said anything inappropriate, but just thinking about him standing so close she could feel the warmth of his breath on her lips . . . who did that?

A queue was forming. It was always a pleasure to see how excited people got about the treats she made. The fact that the man she thought of as the Cream Bun Creep wasn't there was just the icing on the cake. She mentally excused her own pun and began serving.

Thirty minutes later, she was in her van and preparing for the next stop when two young women walked past. One reached out to the other and brushed a stray lock of hair from her shoulders. Just like that, Jessica couldn't breathe. Her heart hurt. To have someone who felt able to reach out and touch her so gently. No stress. No anger and resentment. Just sweet, reciprocated love.

'No more waiting,' she told her reflection in the rearview mirror.

Life balance had to be achievable. There were hours enough in the week for both baking and dating. Waiting was wasteful. You never knew how long you had. Her mum had been taken far too young and Jessica wasn't prepared to delay finding happiness one day longer. She was going to be proactive. The positivity made her smile.

The rest of the day flew by in a haze of greetings and brief exchanges, of dashing from one office to the next. By mid-afternoon she'd sold out and taken orders from two office canteens for cake deliveries later in the week. Making money without standing around hand-selling items was where her business needed to go. The only downside was that she needed to head out of town to stock up on ingredients. She took a deep breath. Sorting out her love life was going to have to wait a few more hours.

By 4.30 p.m. she was paying for ingredients. Having loaded it all into the car, Jessica took one look at the traffic trying to exit the car park and decided to treat herself to a coffee and toasted sandwich at a nearby cafe. It was 5.20 p.m. before she turned up the radio and headed for home, and nearly 6 p.m. by the time she turned into her road to park.

She noticed a space, which during rush hour was cause enough for a celebratory glass of wine later, and began heading for it a little faster than she would normally have driven on the residential street, but there were no pedestrians that she could see.

Joining in with a song at the top of her lungs as she got into position for a parallel parking manoeuvre, Jessica felt different. Making decisions was good. It was time for her to move on. The world was her—

The motorcycle hit the side of her car, smashing down hard onto the concrete as the driver thudded against her window then dropped to the floor.

'Oh my God!' Jessica screamed. 'Oh, no, no, no! Please let him be okay.'

She ripped the handbrake upwards and opened her door carefully so as not to slam it into his head. He was lying in the road, one hand trying to get his visor up, otherwise not moving.

'I'm so sorry,' Jessica said, kneeling by his head. 'I don't know how it happened. Are you in pain? Are you bleeding?'

The visor finally came up. 'I'm okay,' he said. 'I don't think anything's broken.' He struggled to sit up.

'I really don't think you should move until you're sure you're okay,' Jessica said. Two other cars were approaching now, slowing to see what was going on.

'Why don't we see if I can get up off the road, then figure out what needs doing. We don't want to cause a tailback at the junction.'

He planted a hand behind him and pushed until he was sitting up, flexing his shoulders, and twisting his head right and left.

'But you might have a head injury or a problem with your spine.' Her imagination was in overdrive. 'The cars will just have to wait.'

Right on cue, a vehicle at the end of the road began beeping.

'Help me up?' He extended his hand. 'My legs feel okay, and the bike's out of the way so they should be able to get by.'

'If you're sure.' Jessica pulled him to a standing position and supported him to the pavement. The traffic began creeping past.

'Bloody rubberneckers,' he said. 'Could you help lift my bike so I can see what the damage is?'

Jessica's heart began beating a little less crazily. If he was thinking about his bike, then he really was okay. No serious injury probably also meant no police. Not that she'd have hesitated to call them, but dealing with the insurance company was going to be bad enough without worrying about the potential for a court appearance and a driving conviction. There was no way she could afford to pay a lawyer, and if she lost her driving licence she'd lose her business and her income too. She wasn't even sure how the collision had happened.

'Sure,' she said. 'After that, my flat is just a few doors down. Why don't you come in and I'll get you a drink. You can check for injuries, make any calls you need, and we can exchange details.'

'Sounds good,' he said. 'Thanks.'

Together they picked up the bike which, she noticed, horrified, looked fairly new. He walked it to a safe spot and set it on its stand, circling to assess the damage.

'I'll need to call a garage to pick it up, but it could have been much worse. Thankfully I was only going about ten miles per hour, so the damage looks minimal.'

Jessica felt the relief wash over her. 'Okay, let me finish parking my van, more carefully this time, and we'll go in.' She took a deep breath and got back in the driver's seat, noticing the dent in her driver's door and the smashed mirror, a tiny voice inside already telling her that's what happens when you start thinking things are on the up.

As she opened the boot to take out her handbag and the items from the shop, she looked over at the motorbike driver. He was vaguely familiar even with his helmet still on and his leather jacket done up to the neck, but she couldn't quite—

'Is that heavy?' he called.

It was his voice that did it. Up to that point it had been softer, more muffled, as if it hurt him to speak. But now she was sure, and while it changed nothing at all, it changed everything.

The Cream Bun Creep was walking over, hands outstretched, to take her shopping from her. Jessica stood still, bags hanging at her sides, staring at his eyes in the slit of his helmet.

'Um . . . do we . . . know each other?' she asked softly.

'I don't think so,' he said. 'Here, let me take those.'

'It's fine,' she said. 'But I think you do know me. I sell cakes to some of the companies around here. You're a regular customer, right?'

'Oh my God,' he said. 'That's you? Sorry, it's difficult recognising people out of their normal routine. Plus, I just tried to knock some sense into the road with my head, so I'm not on my A-game here.' He grinned.

Jessica didn't feel quite as relieved as she had earlier.

'Yeah, you usually order the cream buns,' she replied, the thought making her feel a little queasy.

He opened his mouth as if to reply but staggered to the side instead, clutching his head.

'Wow, headache! Do you mind if I take you up on that offer of recovering in your flat? I'm really hoping we don't need to call that ambulance.'

Fuck, Jessica thought. Truly fucking fuck!

'Sure, follow me. I'll make us both a cup of tea.'

She didn't want him to have her address, let alone actually set foot in her flat, but she also didn't want him calling an ambulance if it wasn't strictly necessary. The potential claim was just a long list of numbers building up in her brain, from the repairs to his vehicle, replacement leathers and helmet, to compensation for his injury, then the inevitable hike on her own insurance premium and repairing the damage to her van. It could cost her thousands. If he was hurt, genuinely injured, then so be it, but she couldn't help feeling that there was something off. Something too convenient about it all.

He followed her up, pulling off his helmet as he walked, and plucking the keys from her fingers without asking as she went to open the door. That was presumptuous, she thought. Domineering, in fact. A sort of micro-violation.

Jessica chided herself. She was being a bitch. She had just knocked the man to the ground. She should be grateful he wasn't badly hurt.

'Got anything stronger than tea?' he asked as they entered, the flat door opening directly into her lounge. 'That was a bit of a shock. I could do with something to steady my nerves, and it's not like I'll be driving home.'

Jessica plastered a polite smile on her face.

'Sure, I've got red wine, vodka or single malt whisky. Does any of that work?'

'Glass of wine would be great. We can always move on to

the hard stuff later.' He winked as he said it and Jessica's heart sank. She headed left into the kitchen area. The length of marble-topped counter separated the living space enough that she felt better having an obstacle between them, even if he could still see her.

As for moving on to the 'hard stuff' later, he surely had to be leaving in fifteen minutes, thirty tops. She needed an excuse.

'Actually, I have a lot of baking to do for tomorrow, so I probably shouldn't drink. I can call you a taxi, or is there someone who can come and get you? A girlfriend, maybe?'

'Sadly, not. I'm single. What about you, as we're getting to know each other?'

'Boyfriend,' she said, pouring the smallest glass of red she could without looking inhospitable.

'But you recently split up with him, right?' he added smoothly. 'One of the girls at work you chat to mentioned it. Messy break-up, she told me. You okay? That stuff can be rough.'

A loud click sounded in Jessica's brain as if she'd just found the right combination to a safe. Because what were the chances of the Cream Bun Creep driving past her at that specific moment? What was he doing in the area in the first place? She put the stopper back in the wine bottle and returned it to the shelf rather than leaving it out as on ongoing invitation.

'I'm fine. I'm not the kind of girl who allows toxic men in their life, so I ditched him. I'm not making that mistake again,' she said, hackles up. Enough was enough. If she had to cope with an increased insurance premium next year because of a claim, that was starting to feel like a small price to pay compared to spending time with the Creep. 'Listen, let's just exchange insurance details and let the professionals deal with it. I really should get on with baking.'

'Great, I'd love to see where the magic happens,' he said, taking a sip of wine. 'Don't let me stop you. I can watch you work while I assess my injuries.'

'I don't actually feel comfortable working with anyone else here. I guess I'm a bit of a . . . private baker.' The words sounded ridiculous, but it was the best she could do.

'Of course. I'll go, then. We should notify the police, too. That's the right thing to do, I think, with an accident where someone suffers an injury.'

Bastard. Jessica drove a knife into the top of a bag of flour. She didn't want the police involved. Police meant an investigation and the threat of charges, resulting in exponential stress and risk to her livelihood.

'Whatever you think,' she said, smiling.

'I think as long as I can take my time recovering here, then I don't need to do anything rash. Tell you what, I'll settle myself on the sofa, maybe close my eyes for a while. Perhaps I could call and order some food? If I start feeling better, we won't need any formal investigation. Not even the insurance companies. I'm sure we can settle this ourselves.'

She gripped the knife hard enough for her knuckles to ache.

'There are some delivery menus on the coffee table,' she replied sweetly. 'My treat. And of course, stay until you feel well enough to go home.'

He deposited his leather jacket on the back of a chair, grabbed the menus and laid on the sofa.

Jessica busied herself measuring out water. The thing was, now that she was over the shock of it, she wasn't sure she'd even been in the wrong about the accident. She'd been at an angle in the road, certainly, as she was reversing, but over the line enough for the motorbike to have collided with her? That didn't feel right at all.

'I forgot to ask,' she called to him. 'What were you doing in my road? Passing through, or visiting someone?'

'Just cruising around, getting to know the area,' he said lightly.

Jessica stopped what she was doing and tried to look only casually interested.

'Any particular reason?' she asked.

'You know what it's like, when you're in your twenties you want to live in the middle of everything. You don't care about noisy bars or people out on the street day and night.'

'Uh-huh,' Jessica said.

'But now I'm more interested in other stuff. Nights in, more privacy and intimacy, somewhere a bit quieter.'

Don't say it, Jessica thought. Please don't say it.

'So I've been looking for somewhere new to live, and this road seems particularly nice. You wouldn't happen to know of any flats that are up for rent?'

'You . . . want to live on this road? I wouldn't recommend it,' Jessica said. She wanted to scream. 'There are much nicer places around here, nearer the park, for instance. And this road is on a bus route, so the noise starts at six a.m.'

He stood up and walked to the kitchen counter, leaning across and staring into her eyes.

'I think it'll suit me just fine,' he said. 'Especially given what happened today. It just feels like fate.'

Chapter 12

Midnight picked up her desk phone.

'Midnight Jones,' she said.

'Media update for you, on that murder?'

'Yeah, actually it doesn't matter now—'

Whoever was on the end of the line – not the same young woman she'd seen that morning – wasn't listening.

'The police have named the deceased as Chloe Martin. If this is personal to you then the rules are that I must notify human resources at this stage, and they will provide you with support.'

'It's not, and it really doesn't—'

'Okay, good. So, Chloe Martin, twenty-eight years of age, was murdered approximately thirty-six hours before police found her body.' The media assistant sounded bored. Midnight was tempted to tell her how disrespectful she was being, but that would have lengthened the call and it was after 6 p.m. already. 'She was unmarried, lived alone, looks like she answered the door to an intruder who was thought to be in her flat for several hours, before leaving in the morning. Your basic nightmare really.'

'Thanks for the update,' Midnight muttered.

'Yup, and . . . I see. You're on the education team. So that's the connection.'

'I'm sorry, what are you talking about?'

'Chloe Martin worked for Thames Environmental Sciences University. Did you hear from the client about it today?'

The room began to spin.

'Um, yeah, that's it,' she managed. 'Did the police say what department Chloe was in?'

'Just a moment.' A few clicks followed. 'She was an admissions officer. Oh, she wasn't our TESU contact, was she? Because senior management would need to be notified.'

'No, she wasn't our contact. Are any other details available?'

'The usual. Her family has requested privacy. There'll be a memorial service at an appropriate time. All contact to be made through the police. There's a phone number in case anyone has information.'

Midnight took a few deep breaths before trying to speak again.

'And how did she . . . what happened?'

'Doesn't say. Adjectives are "violent and brutal", so not good,' she understated skilfully.

Midnight hung up and turned to Amber who was in the midst of working furiously to make up for the time she'd missed that morning.

Amber raised her eyebrows. 'You okay?'

'Need water. Come with,' Midnight stood, giving it a second before trying to walk, then lurched towards the kitchenette. Amber followed. Eli, mouth hanging open, watched them go.

*

'What's going on?' Amber asked, following her in.

'Shhh!' Midnight whispered, putting the kettle on before shutting the door and grabbing a couple of mugs from the cupboard, then motioning for Amber to join her on the floor.

They sat together, backs against the wall. Midnight raised the mugs in the air and clinked them together a few times.

'Have you joined some invisible orchestra?' Amber asked, wide-eyed.

'You want to tell me you're completely sure they're not listening to us?'

'You mean . . . Necto? In the kitchen? I think that would be both weird and illegal,' Amber replied slowly. 'What's up with you?'

Midnight clanked the cups a few more times, leaning close to whisper in Amber's ear.

'That thing I told you about last night – or couldn't tell you about – is the reason I was so worried about you this morning. A woman got killed. I think, or I feel like maybe I know, who the killer is.' She stared at Amber wide-eyed, chewing her bottom lip.

'The murder that was on the radio this morning?'

Midnight nodded. 'I went past the scene last night.'

'The one you were worried might have been me?'

'Exactly.'

'How can you possibly know who the murderer is? And why do we need to whisper?' Amber asked. 'I've got to stand up. The floor's too cold and I want a peppermint tea.'

Midnight followed her up but stayed close. 'I found something yesterday, a profile from an applicant who tested at TESU. Have you ever heard of a Profile K?'

Amber stared at Midnight, turning her head slightly sideways and frowning. 'Are you serious?'

'Shit, yes,' Midnight said.

Amber put one hand to her mouth but she couldn't hold it in, bursting into laughter.

'That's not a real thing, babe. Profile K is a joke they tell in training meetings. It doesn't really exist. It's just code for the point at which you break the software's boundaries. Oh my God, is that what you're freaked out about?' Midnight frowned. 'Hey, I'm sorry, I'm not laughing at you – well, I sort of am – but not really. I love that you take all the crap we do so seriously, but Profile K isn't a thing. That murderer was just another bastard who got told no. It'll be the usual story. Your Profile K, on the other hand, is just some weirdo who fell asleep with his eyes open during Necto's boring tests.' She took one of the mugs from Midnight's hand and dropped a teabag in it before pouring hot water.

'The boss didn't think it was a joke,' Midnight said, still quiet but more than a whisper.

'Richard? He takes everything too seriously. Ignore him.'

'Not him. I went to see Sara Vickson.'

Amber dropped the teaspoon she'd been stirring with.

'Shut up! You did not. How the hell did you get an appointment with Vickson?'

Midnight's face reddened. 'I lied and said I had an appointment, then I barged in. That doesn't matter. But Vickson made me promise to delete the files, fed me Necto's "Loose lips lose lawsuits" bullshit, and basically threatened me with dismissal if I told anyone. She told me Necto's files on the applicant had been wiped.'

'Jesus, why are you telling me this? Just this conversation could get us both fired. What the fuck?' It was Amber's turn to whisper. 'And why exactly do you think the dead woman has something to do with your Profile K applicant?'

'She worked at TESU, in the admissions sector no less. They run all the on-site testing, sign everyone in, explain the procedure. That means it's possible that she met the Profile K applicant in person. She might have booked him in for his test, shown him to his booth, or even just bumped into him in a corridor. I mean, what are the odds?'

Amber stared into her steaming mug. 'It's not a direct link.'

'It feels pretty fucking direct to me.'

'I'll accept a disconcerting coincidence. Even so, you still wouldn't know who the murderer is because we aren't given names, just an applicant number.'

'It doesn't feel like a coincidence. There's a geographical proximity, a timing proximity and the fact that he took our test which was within the victim's work remit. That's three links, Amber.'

'Loads of people around here work for TESU, it's a big university. And millions of people a year take our tests. Combine that with the statistics in London – so many people, so many psychos – that I think you're blowing it out of proportion. Leave this alone. It won't end well.'

Midnight rubbed her temples. 'Yeah, that's what Vickson said.'

Amber crossed the kitchen to hug her. 'I know you're freaked out. It must be hard having Dawn at home and worrying constantly about caring for her, but this isn't your problem. The police are investigating. That freak – your Profile K – is just a random anomaly.'

'Random anomaly or not, this particular freak has my first name, the initial of my surname, and he knows where I work. As soon as I accessed his profile, he'd have been sent the standard message.'

'Okay, but Necto employs thousands of people. He doesn't have your full surname or your home address. Switchboard won't give out your details if he doesn't have your surname. More importantly, he has no idea how much information a profile really gives us. I'm pretty sure you're safe.'

'Really? How many Midnights do you know?'

Amber shrugged. 'Just one, but she does virtually no social media, is very sensible and careful in her private life, and isn't normally quite so paranoid, so I think she'll be just fine.' She smiled. 'Midnight, you've got enough on your plate. Now let's see if we can't persuade our new teammate – cute dimples, good hair – to come for a post-work drink so we can find out all about him.'

'Sorry, I can't. You go. Give me all the gossip tomorrow.' She forced a smile onto her face. 'Just don't sleep with him. Not this week. I can do without the HR nightmare when he ends up heartbroken.'

Amber pouted for a few seconds before grinning. 'You're no fun. Probably right, though. He looks a bit too clean-cut to be my type. And I think the barman might have a few miles left in him yet. Now *that* is the gossip you really need to hear.'

'Save it,' Midnight said. 'Even if Necto aren't listening to our conversations, those details require alcohol.'

Amber gave her a thumbs up and opened the door. Richard Baxter stepped back sharply, dusting down his suit jacket as if he'd suddenly found himself dirty, which probably wasn't so far from the truth.

'Everything okay?' Amber asked sweetly.

'I could ask you the same. You've been in there longer than it takes to make a hot beverage. The kitchenette is not a common room.'

'Put it down to pre-menstrual tension,' Amber said loudly. 'It's a sisterhood thing.'

Richard's cheeks glowed to match his tie. 'That's enough, I think. Back to your desks.'

'It's actually after hours, so we're heading home. See you!' Amber finished, giving a bright smile and walking off jauntily to her desk.

'Miss Jones, a word,' Richard said quietly. Midnight swallowed a sigh. 'I'd have thought, after yesterday, you'd have been more careful about keeping your nose clean.'

'Sorry, do I have something on my face?' She made a show of brushing it left and right.

'That's not what I meant,' he snapped.

'Really? Because otherwise I'd have to assume that you were standing outside the door listening to a private conversation. Aren't you usually gone by this time?' Her voice sounded snippy and terse, but she couldn't seem to adjust it to normal levels of office obsequiousness.

'Apparently my leadership skills were needed for longer than usual today. Did you fill your profile quota?'

Midnight flexed her shoulders. 'I just need a few more minutes,' she said.

'Then I'll hang around until you're finished. Any problems, let me know.'

Midnight waited until he was back at his desk before returning to hers. She was going to be late for Dawn – again – but she really couldn't leave until her work was done and the day's distractions had left her behind.

'You sure you won't come for a drink with us?' Eli asked breezily as he put on his coat.

'Can't. I've got to finish up here then get back to my sister. Have a great time,' she said. 'Hope you had a good first day, Eli. Sorry we didn't get to chat. What department did you say you'd transferred from again?'

'I'm new to Necto,' he said.

'Wow, and you got straight into profiling without going through any other departments first? They usually have new people do a few months with other teams before putting them in here.'

'Guess I got lucky,' he said. 'See you tomorrow, Midnight. Thanks for your help today.'

Amber stepped forward, smoothing her hair with one hand as she checked her watch.

'Come on, you're buying the first round. Newbie's duty,' Amber told Eli, motioning towards the door.

Midnight watched them go then flicked onto a new profile, but her brain wasn't on it.

Dawn wasn't the only reason she'd opted not to go for a drink with Amber and Eli. The timing of having a new person in her team stank. Yesterday, she'd pissed Richard off and stormed into Sara Vickson's office, and today some new recruit turned up unannounced, straight in, without the usual lengthy introductions and processes.

Coincidences were for romance novels and insurance claims, not real life. Eli had been sent to spy on her. She really should have warned Amber not to let anything slip, but even Amber had been . . . what? Dismissive? Unbelieving? Midnight shook her head. That wasn't fair. Amber was her best friend. If anyone was behaving badly, it was her. She was uptight, irrational and losing perspective. Time to get back to work.

Midnight made it through to the end of the day's work quota, then headed home. Thirty minutes on a bus, stopping at every traffic light, every junction and every stop. It would have been quicker to have walked, but it was dark and she didn't feel like being on the street. By the time she unlocked the door, Dawn's carer had her coat on, bag on her shoulder, ready to go.

'I'm so sorry, it's been one of those days—'

The carer left. No goodbye. No chat. No acceptance of the apology. Midnight didn't blame her. She'd be paid a good sum of overtime, but that didn't make up for the lost hours with her own family. Time, she thought. Would there ever be enough of it?

'Dawn, sweetheart, I'm home!' She dropped her coat on the floor and kicked off her shoes as she made her way through to her sister's bedroom.

Dawn was propped up in bed in her favourite pyjamas, the pale pink ones with pandas on. On the stand in front of her, a Disney movie was playing on her iPad. She looked up as Midnight entered, extending her arms for a hug.

Midnight dropped the side of the bed and hopped up next to her sister, sliding an arm around the back of her shoulders and pulling her close, whispering sweetnesses to her: how much she missed her, how much she loved her, how pretty she looked. Dawn stroked Midnight's face and stared deep into her eyes.

Most of the time, Midnight thought it was Dawn who needed her, but on nights like this when the world seemed unbearably cruel, she knew the reality was that she needed Dawn more.

Fate was a bitch. Her sister should have been out in the world, partying, loving and succeeding. She should have been able to shine her beautiful light anywhere she chose. Instead, their small flat was her whole world. Every time Midnight considered sending her away for a few weeks' respite care, the idea that Dawn wouldn't understand what was happening destroyed her. They'd never been separated for long, and not at all in the past few years. So this was their life. Happy, in spite of the limits of their existence.

They fell asleep together, tangled in one another's arms, as a Disney prince kissed his princess and they walked forward into their happily ever after. Midnight slept peacefully for an hour, until in the darkness, in a shower of London's less-than-clean rain, a stranger began knocking on their door.

Chapter 13

Peering through the spy hole, Midnight could make out the figure of a large man; no one she recognised. She thought of Dawn in bed, vulnerable. Then she wondered where the rape alarm was that she'd been given during a protest a couple of years earlier. He knocked again while she was considering her options. Her heart was thumping.

'Hello?' he called. 'This is the police. Anyone in?'

'Police? Why?'

'Miss Jones, is it? My name's DI Ruskin. I wanted to discuss an incident with you.'

'Can you hold your ID up to the spy hole please?'

He did so. It looked in order, but really, how the hell would she know if it was fake?

'Give me a minute!' She went to the kitchen and grabbed a knife from a drawer, holding it behind her back as she opened the door a few inches, her foot strategically placed to stop it opening any wider.

'Thank you, Miss, and sorry to call late,' he said. 'I wanted to talk to you about Chloe Martin's murder.'

Midnight felt her jaw drop.

Thank God. Necto – either Sara Vickson or Richard Baxter – had obviously seen sense and decided to contact the authorities. She could admit to having kept a copy of the data on the USB stick, and it wouldn't be her responsibility any more.

'Of course, come in,' she said, stepping aside.

The policeman stared at the knife she was gripping.

'Is there a problem? Do you need help?'

'Oh, no, you're fine. I just wasn't sure who it was when you knocked and what with the murder and everything . . . My sister lives here, and I'm conscious that my security isn't what it should be.'

'I understand. You can call the station if you like. They can verify who I am, give you a description.'

'No, you're here now. I appreciate the offer, though. Come in. Sorry about the state of me. I fell asleep as soon as I got in from Necto, where I work. You know that already. Coffee or tea? I'm putting the kettle on anyway. It's such a relief that you're here. I can't tell you how many times I've thought about coming to you.'

'A cup of tea would be very welcome,' he said. 'Normally I'd have phoned ahead, but I couldn't trace a number for you.'

'I suppose work couldn't give it to you,' she said, clattering mugs. 'Data protection and all that.' She caught sight of the clock. 'It's only nine thirty! It felt like I'd been asleep for ages. So, do you want to start or shall I just tell you everything?'

'Let's sit first. I'd like to make notes, if that's okay. You've got a nice place here. I like all the bright colours and pictures. How old's your little sister?'

Midnight shrugged. It was a question she'd had before.

'Dawn's my twin actually. She has enhanced needs. But she's fine, in all the ways that count. We live a happy life. Milk? Sugar?'

'Neither,' he said, picking up his tea and letting Midnight lead the way to the bright orange sofas.

'Are you in charge of the investigation?' Midnight asked as she sat.

'Part of a large team. We need to figure out who did this, and fast.'

'And that's where I come in,' Midnight added.

'If you can help, we'd be very much obliged.' He took a notebook from his pocket. 'So, you're probably wondering how I found you.'

'Well—'

'Thankfully, much as some people aren't all that keen on the idea, we have a comprehensive system of CCTV on our main routes in this area. You were at the police cordon, the night we found Miss Martin's body, and we're hoping you can tell us about anyone else watching with you.'

Midnight tried to speak, couldn't, and sipped tea instead.

'That's it?' she murmured.

'Yes. Sorry if I put the wind up you. We traced your route home, nothing more high-tech than that. It's just that, without sounding too macabre, the perpetrators of these sorts of offences are often fascinated by the aftermath. They – I can say *he* with a fair degree of certainty – will have been waiting for us to discover the body. There were signs that this was a very unique offender, of a sort who might have been attracted back to the scene to watch.'

Midnight nodded, her disappointment making her tea taste sour. She'd been so relieved to think she'd been taken seriously. All she'd wanted was to pass on what she thought she knew to someone who could do something about it.

'You think he might have been there, with me,' she said. 'That's why you're here.'

'That's it,' he said. 'We could see your face clearly, but there were a few people there, hoods up, gloves and scarves on, who the CCTV doesn't show clearly. So, was there anyone who stood out to you? Acting, I don't know, a bit too intense, maybe secretive, or excited?'

'I'd have to think about it,' she said. 'Do you know anything at all about the man who did this?'

He shifted in his chair. 'You'll appreciate that I can't discuss the investigation at this stage. It's natural to be curious, though.'

'But you don't think it was anyone she knew? A boyfriend or a stalker, her landlord or something?'

'That doesn't appear to be the case. So do you have any recollection of anyone catching your attention?'

Midnight tried to cast her mind back, but she'd been drinking at the time. It was all just a rush of negative emotions.

'There were maybe two people near me. Both men. One quite elderly. He had a small dog with him, on a lead.'

'Yes, well remembered. It was a Jack Russell terrier. We've traced that gentleman. What about the other man?'

'I'm not sure. Can I ask, did you check at TESU where the victim works? She must've come into contact with lots of people there. Perhaps it was someone from the university. Some . . .'

Don't say applicant. You can't. You'll lose your job. Necto will sue you.

'You know, someone relevant to her specific department?' she finished.

'We're checking all angles, including TESU. But good thinking – you've obviously been following the case.'

'Only because I walked past. Not for any other reason.'

'Sure,' Ruskin said, setting his empty cup carefully on a

coaster. 'So nothing you can recall then, just the tiniest detail? Might not seem relevant at all to you.'

'Not really. Like you said, it was dark. The other guy, I'm sure it was a man, was taller than me, probably around six foot, bigger build than me but not like a body builder or anything. Black jacket.' She pulled the strands of the memory together in her head. 'Shiny, I think. Like, some of the police vehicle lights were reflecting off it. Not like a mirror, just not like cloth. Leather maybe?'

'That's good,' Ruskin said. 'Anything else?'

'I didn't get a look at his face, but I did see his hands. They were pale. I think that struck me because he was all wrapped up, scarf over his face, but no gloves. If I'm wearing a scarf, I've always got gloves on too.'

'So, Caucasian. No gloves. What about lower clothing? Shoes?'

'Can't help with that, sorry.'

Damn it, find a way to give him a clue. Come on.

'Will you be bringing in a profiler?' she blurted. 'Because that's part of my job. I mean, I'm not a profiler, I just translate data. Not that my employer can help you because that's not what they do either, so definitely don't try talking to them.'

Fuck, fuck, fuck!

'A profiler won't be able to help on a single murder. They work on patterns of behaviour, links between cases and so on. And we definitely don't want any extra deaths to investigate, this one's enough. So no, in spite of all the true crime documentaries, we're not in profiler territory.'

'Of course you're not. I don't know why I asked. It's just that whoever did this must be, you know, really screwed up. Are you able to tell me how he killed her? I'm not being . . .' she paused '. . . inappropriate. It's just that it was obviously violent, and I think it would be better if I knew what actually happened, rather than just imagining worst-case scenarios.'

Ruskin looked at her, a long stare, but gentle. 'I can only tell you what will soon be announced. Chloe's cause of death was failure of heart function caused by blood loss.'

Midnight's hand flew to her mouth. It was a few seconds before she could speak. 'He stabbed her to death?'

'Not exactly. There was a scalpel-type blade involved, multiple injuries, but it wasn't a . . . normal type of attack. This man is very dangerous. Uniquely dangerous, I think.'

'I see,' Midnight said. 'Got it.' A bead of sweat trickled down her forehead.

'Are you okay? I didn't mean to upset you.'

'It's just the thought of it,' she blurted. 'With my sister here, and unable to leave if anything happened. This was within walking distance. I'm not sure I'd be able to protect her.'

'Miss Jones, I can assure you, events like this are incredibly rare. If you're careful and take normal precautions, you're perfectly safe in this part of London. Like you said, it'll probably turn out to be someone Chloe came into contact with who took an interest in her. I'm going to leave you to get some rest. Here's my card.' He put it on the table. 'Call or email if you remember anything.'

'I will.'

He saw himself to the door. Midnight locked it behind him, shaking her head. How had she not managed to do more? She'd had a police officer in her flat, and still not talked about her suspicions.

'Midnight?' Dawn called, all the consonants mushed into the vowels. Her own special construction of the name.

'Hey, what are you doing awake? It's sleepy time, you.' Midnight walked into her sister's room.

'Is Daddy home? Mummy?'

Dawn didn't ask about them very often, but when she did it was a knife in Midnight's heart.

'No, honey. No Mummy or Daddy. We're still having our special time without them, remember? Just you and me, together forever.'

Her sister gave a huge grin and settled back down on her pillow.

'You not leave?' she asked.

Midnight's stomach hardened and she fought back tears. It was the first time Dawn had put it all together, or at least the first time she'd put it into words.

'Not ever. I'm going to be with you every single day. You never have to worry. But I'll be grumpy if I'm tired tomorrow, so we should get some sleep, okay?' She kissed her sister on the forehead and smoothed her hair.

'Love you,' Dawn murmured softly.

'I love you too, sis. Always.'

She closed Dawn's door, went back to the kitchen and poured herself a glass of single malt whisky from the bottle she'd hidden at the back of a cupboard the Christmas before.

Dawn had to come first. She needed to set her suspicions aside. Put her paranoia to bed. She knew nothing. What she couldn't do, under any circumstances, was risk her job. Necto were clear about their position, and confidentiality was key.

'Not my problem,' Midnight said aloud, tipping the contents of her glass down in one go. 'That's all there is to it.'

Sleep took its time letting her in.

Chapter 14

By the time Midnight turned eight years old, their parents had managed to enrol Dawn in a day centre. The difference in their mother had been remarkable.

She'd started wearing make-up again and styling her hair each morning. There were lunches with friends, and shopping trips. She appeared years younger, and her father's smile had returned as a result. Dawn was doing okay too, forming connections, and being kept interested in life. There were days out to petting zoos, and physical therapy made into games. Toys were provided that helped with dexterity, and play kitchens and bathrooms had been built to help students practise the basics. Their mother would pick Midnight up from school, then they would drive to Dawn's educational unit to collect her. At home, Midnight would find ever more imaginative ways to keep Dawn entertained while she got her homework done. And every evening, she tucked Dawn into bed in their shared room, even though she could have moved into one of her own, and she never missed reading her a bedtime story.

One Saturday shortly after their fifteenth birthday – marked by a sky so blue that Midnight had woken up and simply stared out of the window for a good thirty minutes – their parents had taken them to the beach. They hadn't tried that since they were four years old when Dawn had scooped up a handful of sand, eaten it, and thrown up for hours. But that day, they made it before the roads got clogged and the crowds arrived. A handful of dog walkers were already there, but otherwise they had the place to themselves. Dawn sat on a blanket and stared at the ocean. She didn't fiddle or get bored. She just watched the waves whooshing in then fizzing as they rolled back out across the pebbles. She followed the swooping gulls with her eyes and breathed the salty air. It was the calmest Midnight had ever seen her.

They spent three hours on the beach, and in that time not one passer-by could have noticed the difference between them. Midnight leaned over and rested her head on Dawn's shoulder, and for the briefest of moments her sister had looked down at her and smiled gently, not like the child who was inhabiting her brain, but like the sister she would have been, aged fifteen. All Midnight did for those minutes and hours was watch her, drinking it in, trying to cram the memory into her brain.

Then they'd climbed back into the car because her mother had an appointment at the salon later in the afternoon, and Midnight remembered that she'd been asked over to a friend's house. On any other day she wouldn't have even considered it, but Dawn had been so calm and happy that perhaps for once she could risk leaving her parents to look after her twin for the evening.

'Mum, Dad, Elodie is having a few people over tonight, and they've invited me. I can walk there if you don't mind picking me up. It should be finished by—'

'We're going out,' her mother said. 'We can't change our plans now. Why didn't you mention it earlier? Seriously, Midnight, you've got to get more organised. You can't just expect us to drop everything because you forgot to give us notice.'

Her father said nothing. That was his way. He chose neither one side nor the other, which meant, in fact, that he always sided with their mother.

'I never go out,' Midnight said. She kept her voice calm. No point giving her mother ammunition in the form of accusing her of rudeness. 'I haven't been out this school year. Not at all. I stay at home with Dawn every evening.'

'Don't say it like that's a chore! Your sister's right next to you.' Dawn was looking at the shells they'd picked up off the beach and was perfectly happy.

'Of course it's not a chore!' Midnight cried. 'But I spend every evening with Dawn, and all my time at weekends. I should be able to go out sometimes. You're out every single weekend, and it's not fair. I should be able to do other things too.'

'You're so ungrateful! You go off every day to your nice school, where you're doing very well in classes, with a bright future ahead of you, and your sister has nothing. Nothing! You should be thinking about her, not yourself.'

Midnight wanted to snap back. She wanted to tell them how much she did, compared to what they did. She wanted to remind her mother how much wine she used to drink before they found a day centre for Dawn. But she didn't. She didn't because she already knew it wouldn't change a thing. And because she already felt guilty, every single day, for the way her life had worked out compared to Dawn's.

Instead, she stared out of the window and watched the world go by, reaching out to hold Dawn's hand. She would make the world a better place, Midnight decided. She would take the gift of a healthy, fully functioning brain, and use it to build a better future. Dawn would be happy and safe. They would live in a community where the people around them were happy and safe too. She would make her parents see that she'd used every day of her education purposefully. And she would care for people, the way her parents seemed not to care about anyone but themselves. She would be a force for good in the world. Most importantly, she was going to make damned sure that she never, ever, turned out like her parents.

Chapter 15

The Applicant

He lay in bed trying desperately to sleep but he had an itch, and it was proving increasingly difficult not to scratch it. His new job was demanding but interesting, and he'd thought he would be ready to rest. But here he was, thinking about finding a woman. Deciding how he would choose her. Cross-referencing mentally with his diary and figuring out when he'd have time to fit in all the preparation.

The police were looking for him now, but there had been no knock at his door and there was no Photofit picture in the newspapers, no CCTV footage being played on the news cycle. Did they have his DNA? Probably. There were disconcerting blanks in his memory of the time he'd spent with Chloe, of which he had no recollection, and God only knew what he'd done. His gloves, new clothes and hat wouldn't have kept every stray skin cell off her body, but then there had been all that blood – a million tiny waterfalls by the end – and most of what would have been on her body would have been washed into her duvet or onto her carpet by the end. He knew forensic testing was impressive these days, but it didn't seem likely that they'd managed to check every drop of her spilled blood for someone else's DNA.

The problem was that replaying in his head what he'd done with Chloe just wasn't fulfilling. Unlike so many of the serial killers he'd read about, for him, remembering the kill was a flatline, less exciting every time he thought about it. With every hour that passed, the excitement faded until all that was left was a step-by-step guide to murder.

It was 3.47 a.m. and no amount of turning over his pillow was helping. He wondered who else was awake, and what they were thinking about. Chloe Martin's sister was, for sure, and he was pretty certain he knew what she was thinking about. He'd seen her on a news clip, accompanied by police officers, as they made an appeal for witnesses. She was good-looking, and he could see a resemblance to her sister, but she wasn't exactly what he wanted.

What about Midnight J? The person profiling him had been on his mind. It had been a risk, taking the test, but of course at that stage, he hadn't done anything wrong. Now all that had changed, and someone out there might just have the skills and insight to see him for what he was about to become. He pulled his mobile from its charging cable and looked up Midnight as a surname. It was most common, he found, in one area of Iran and what amounted to a handful of people in Canada. Midnight as a first name, though, was becoming increasingly popular for both boys and girls. He thought about the message from Necto, sent to give him a hint of a personal link without imparting any real information. Surely they wouldn't have revealed the surname of a staff member? Midnight J had to be the equivalent of Jenny B or Simon T. Meaningless in the grand scheme of things, but familiar enough to make a big company seem like a close friend.

He tried a couple of different social media sites, looking for anyone called Midnight living in London, with a surname that started with J. To begin with he found absolutely nothing, but several pages into his search he hit gold. King's College London had published a list of students graduating from their master's courses seven years earlier, among them, one Midnight Jones who had completed her MSc in Psychology and Neuroscience.

Perfect for Necto, he thought. Perfect for profiling. Worrying for him. Midnight Jones wasn't just some grunt pressing a few buttons. She understood the human brain. Perhaps she even understood his brain. His stomach dropped with anxiety as his pulse rose with excitement. Midnight Jones was a potential threat, but he wondered if she was also something more magical. Had she known what he was going to do before he even did it? Did she know what he was planning to do next? And wasn't that, if he told the whole, naked truth, why he'd taken the test in the first place – because after all the years of hiding and conforming, it felt liberating to have the possibility of being seen?

He found Necto's website, knowing he shouldn't, and pressed the 'Contact Us' icon. A box flashed up, into which he typed the new email address he'd registered and the subject line, 'Please help me find my old friend'. He was breathing more heavily as he typed and could hear his blood pulsing in his ears.

Hello, I do hope you can help me. I did a master's course at King's but lost contact with a friend who was studying psychology with me. Her name is Midnight Jones, and a mutual contact said he thought she was now working at Necto in the profiling department. Please could you pass this

*on to her? My email address is above if she wants to write
back.*

Many thanks for your kind assistance,
Gemini D St John.

Don't do it, he thought. This is not a game. It's an unnecessary
risk.

He clicked send.

Stupid, stupid boy, his mother said inside his head. Idiot.
Deviant.

He told her to shut up, something he'd never have the courage
to do in real life.

Now he couldn't sleep at all. Midnight Jones was not just
a potential irritation, she was a genuine threat. Every time he
thought about something else, there she was, hovering in the
periphery of his mind. An irritating fly.

Flies, of course, needed squashing. They were dirty nuisances
who kept coming at you until you dealt with them.

He stretched and clicked each knuckle individually. He didn't
want to think about Midnight Jones any more. Just her name
made him feel nervous. Better to find something to take his
mind off her.

He concentrated instead on a mental picture of the girl who
worked at a nearby supermarket. He'd thought about the things
he could do with her a few times before, and always dismissed
the notion. It was risky in a place he'd visited thirty, maybe
forty times. Preliminary research had returned a couple of
interesting statistics. The average British person would spend
eight and a half months of their life in a supermarket. On
average, an adult went to a supermarket three times a week.
At least he only went every five days, so he wouldn't be their
most regular customer.

He hadn't worn gloves when he'd started going there, so his DNA would be on some baskets and a few tins of food he'd touched then put back. They'd be able to compare it with the biological evidence he'd left at Chloe's. All of which was ridiculous. He lived in London. Where else in the UK would you find such busy supermarkets? If he stopped going now, there wouldn't be any recent CCTV of him in the shop. He didn't need to go inside to see her. She worked the tills, and the glass frontage provided an exquisite, brightly lit fishbowl for him to watch her. Across the road was a coffee shop where he could busy himself at his laptop to view her unnoticed. Not that he had any solid plans, but the first Saturday he'd noticed her, he'd found it hard to tear himself away.

Her name was Mae. She had black hair, dark, shining eyes, and flawless skin. She'd run his purchases through the till with a grace he'd found hypnotic. Mae was most often on till number 3, and at weekends, her shift ended at 10 p.m. when the supermarket closed. The coffee shop had been shut by then, but he'd passed the time between a bus shelter, a cemetery and the steps of the local library, drinking her in.

That had been before Chloe. Before the inspiration for Chloe, even.

Mae lived in one of Clapham's poorer areas. There weren't many of those left, but it worked for him. The rich were prone to calling the police at the drop of a hat, in a huff of how-dare-they and not-in-my-neighbourhood pomposity. Go outside and actually deal with a problem? Absolutely not. But a phone call from a suitably riled member of the upper crust was to be avoided. Mae's neighbours were more likely to assume a drug deal had gone wrong and come to scavenge from the remains.

Every muscle in his body was taut. Throwing back the bedclothes, he made his way to the shower. If he was lucky, there would still be a little hot water left in the tank.

It turned out the water was tepid which was better than freezing. His excitement had manifested itself bodily. He tried to work it out. Screwed his eyes shut trying to imagine the sounds Chloe had made, and the way her body had felt through his latex gloves. Nothing.

'Fuck it!' he screamed, punching a crack in a tile that left a line like a mocking smile in front of him. 'Fuck you!' He punched the tile again. That wiped the smirk off its face. Again and again and again. Crumbling shards fell onto his wet, cold feet, and blood dripped onto the whole sorry mess. He couldn't help but bend down to capture it on his fingertips before it disappeared into the waste pipe, concentrating on the silken texture of the liquid. It both soothed and invigorated him.

He dried off and stared in the mirror. Sunday night he would follow Mae home again. Not to do anything. He might never do anything. It was too much of a risk after Chloe, and if Jessica ever found out, there was no chance at all for their happy ending.

But he could go and see. Double-check Mae's route home. Finesse the logistics. He liked that. He had a very mathematical mind.

Perhaps that would be enough, the planning and double-checking. If he could only get Jessica to fall in love with him, he was sure he wouldn't hurt any woman, ever again.

His knuckles were throbbing. He would have to clean the wound out and bind it up. There would be the inevitable questions from his mother. He'd heard those questions before, of course, when there had been other events, other injuries. The police had been round to his parents' address, but they'd never been able to prove anything, and his father was highly regarded in the community, which had helped.

He'd denied everything when questioned by his mother and father, but they'd given him that look that only parents can give. That long, silent appraisal. He wondered if all parents were that knowing, or if it was only his.

Funny thing, they'd never asked him directly if he'd hurt anyone. It was almost as if they didn't want to know.

A girl had been pushed off her bike, leaving her badly grazed and cut on the asphalt. Her attacker had stared briefly as she'd sat up crying, then run away. He'd been in the area. His parents had asked where his bike had been that day, and what he was wearing. Could anyone confirm he'd been with them? But never, 'Did you do that thing to that girl?'

A young woman had her arm sliced by a razor blade as she'd been getting into her car after a party, late at night. On that occasion, local police didn't even bother saying that anyone had seen him there. They just started poking around. 'Is there anyone who can say they were with you?' his parents had asked that time. 'Was there something you were watching on TV that you can tell the police about?'

On it had gone. Little incidents, minimal harm done. The shifting sands of his parents' emotions became predictable. Angry with him and embarrassed by him. Frustrated by his lack of concern and worried for their own reputations. Keen to keep him busy in his room, at the same time desperate to get him out of the house. Until they sent him away to Moorview College. Then afterwards, when he'd moved to London, with their financial help. He suspected they considered it a small price to pay to have him gone.

He got back into bed, wondering if Mae was asleep or awake. Perhaps she had a boyfriend who stayed over. That wouldn't do. Men just complicated things.

'We'll see,' he said, flipping his pillow one more time.

Killing again was inevitable. He'd known that even before he'd forced his way into Chloe's flat that it couldn't possibly just be the once. In childhood, he hadn't given any thought to the sex of his victims. They'd simply been a means to an end. An experiment, in reality. With adulthood, it seemed his tastes had become more refined. It was women who called to him now. Women on park benches, women in playgrounds, women sitting in chairs at the hairdresser for anyone to stare at through the window. Women at work. His world had become one giant menu, and all he had to do was find the dish that was precisely to his taste. Did women even think about it, he wondered. Who was watching them, following them, who was making a note of the bus they caught and the car park they preferred. Routine was no woman's friend. It made tracking them all so incredibly easy.

Just like Mae. Beautiful Mae, with her perfect skin and graceful hands.

He wanted her. He wanted to undo her. To experience her.

Tomorrow should really only be about following her home, he knew that. But just thinking about it, anticipating it . . . he had to be realistic. He wouldn't be able to hold back. Mae was a feast laid out on a table in front of a starving man.

There was no point pretending. Mae would be his, just as soon as he had the right tool for the job.

Chapter 16

Chloe Martin's face was the first Midnight saw the next day, and she was beautiful. Hair, dark blonde but streaked with sun-bleached strands, with a tiny smile on rosebud lips and a crinkle at the top of her petite nose. It was hard to be sure of her eye colour from the image, maybe hazel, maybe grey, but her eyes were set wide across her face giving her an elfin look. Her skin had yet to be touched by the years. Midnight increased the size of the image on her mobile phone. Chloe looked like someone Midnight might have been friends with.

At Necto, there was a message flashing on every screen. 9 a.m. meeting in auditorium. Attendance mandatory. Empty pockets requirement.

Amber and Eli stumbled in together, laughing.

'Hey, you,' Amber said. 'Feeling better than yesterday?'

'Sure. You're just in time. Our presence is required in the auditorium.'

'Me too?' Eli asked. 'Are we in trouble?'

'Not yet, but I'm sure Amber will find a way to get us there,' Midnight murmured. 'Come on. Oh, and it's empty pockets.'

'Empty what now?' Eli asked.

'Pockets. Don't worry. It just means they want us all focused exclusively on them and taking no notes. Don't worry about it.'

'Ugh. That means I can't even take my coffee with me,' Amber groaned.

'Especially not coffee,' Midnight said. 'There should be no chance whatsoever of you experiencing any pleasure during a company announcement. Let's go.'

The auditorium was a vast round space with swirls of concrete benches. Up above, the atrium was surrounded by circular staircases lit in mood-enhancing colours. Every seat was full, and staff were standing on the stairs. It was a full company presentation, as far as Midnight could make out.

'They were trying for Guggenheim?' Eli asked.

'More like a sci-fi prison,' Midnight said. 'Nowhere to hide.'

'Come on, Midnight,' Amber said. 'It's not that bad here. You'll make Eli think he made a mistake. Necto could be worse. The cafe's great, the building's set in some of the most beautiful parkland in London, and the pay is the best in the UK at our grade.'

'Plus, a free juice bar, right?' Eli said enthusiastically. 'The last place I worked at only offered water for free. There was nothing like this. It's like being upgraded from economy to first class.'

'Where was that?' Midnight asked.

'A medical recruitment company, you won't have heard of them. I was filling in time until I could apply here, but I needed another position on my CV first.'

'Ugh, the dreaded CV,' Amber said. 'At least you'll never need to update it again if you like Necto. No one leaves here willingly.'

A young woman stood up and pushed to the front of the crowd, not quite daring to stand at the podium. She waved madly to quieten the crowd.

'Just quickly while we're all together,' she said breathlessly, 'given what happened two miles from here, if anyone wants to join our safe travel group, there's a route plan on the company digital notice board. You can walk in or home with an organised group or take public transport together.'

There was a rumble of concerned consensus as she walked away. Midnight gave Amber a brief glance but she was deep in conversation with someone from a different department.

Eli leaned forward and looked at Midnight intensely. 'Are you worried about it? I can't imagine how it must be for women, knowing there's a man out there who wants to do such violent things to them.'

'We live with it all the time,' Midnight said. 'It just gets very real when there's a body in the local mortuary.'

'Have you ever been attacked by a man?' he asked.

Midnight gave him a long look as she wondered why he'd asked and if she should answer, then Sara Vickson appeared from a lift, flanked by five people Midnight had never seen before.

'It's starting,' Eli said unnecessarily.

Vickson was shown to the podium, and the lights dimmed to leave her bathed in a soft golden glow.

'They've brought Vickson in, so it must be important. Normally these announcements are handled by someone lower down the food chain,' Midnight whispered. 'They must be about to hand out the Kool-Aid. Don't eat or drink anything they offer you.'

Amber managed to giggle and shush her simultaneously.

'Your time is precious,' Vickson dispensed with small talk niceties. It was a thing at Necto to never waste a second when they could be making money instead. 'So the headline is this – today we opened an office in our forty-third country.' She paused for the obligatory excited response. Amber, Eli and a fairly large percentage of the crowd clapped enthusiastically, as Midnight performed the action of her hands hitting without generating any audible applause.

'Congratulations to the biotech company with the most fingers in governmental pies. Every dictator and diplomat in the world must be in their pocket,' Midnight whispered to Amber.

'That's how they can afford to pay us the big bucks,' Amber grinned, rubbing her thumb against her fingers.

Once the cheering and clapping had subsided, Vickson continued.

'But Necto never rests on its laurels. In recognition of our continued expansion, we want to keep expanding your horizons too. We want a multi-skilled, three-hundred-and-sixty-educated staff. So this is a doubly exciting day.'

Eli whispered something to Amber that Midnight couldn't hear, and Amber nodded, briefly touching his arm with her hand. Midnight shifted across the bench a few inches to join in, but they'd stopped muttering by the time she was within hearing range.

'First, there'll be plenty of training, so no one need be concerned about being dropped in at the deep end,' Vickson continued. 'Second, this is going to be a lot of work for Necto, so bear with us, but it's being done for your benefit. We always have and always will put worker happiness at the core of what we do.'

There were a few low-level coughs at that, but no one was either stupid or brave enough to actually heckle.

'The best workforce is a flexible workforce, so we're making some departmental changes. We don't want anyone stagnating, and it's a good idea to have you all cross-trained so we can move you between departments to wherever we have the greatest need.'

'But yesterday was only my first day,' Eli said quietly.

'Don't worry, they won't move you,' Amber said. 'Not this soon.'

'For many of you, the move will only be to different stations within your current department. Some of you will be moving to a different department altogether. I myself will be transferring to become Director of Client Affairs, so please don't think these changes don't affect us all. I see this as an opportunity and a challenge. You should too. Your new assignments are up on the board at the front.'

'Ooh, old school,' Amber muttered.

Vickson coughed loudly to silence the background noise. 'You have thirty minutes to find your new posting. We've provided drinks while you chat about the changes. After that, you should return to your original desk where you'll have ten minutes to pack your personal possessions, then go directly to your new station. Your security passes will automatically update for access to a new floor. Any questions, just ask your new line manager.'

Vickson headed away, followed by her entourage. It was like watching the American President with his bodyguards, Midnight thought, only Vickson earned substantially more.

'Is that it?' Amber asked. 'No, "Good luck, see HR if you're unhappy, we're grateful for all you do." Jeez. Come on. Let's see what they've got in store for us, then drown our sorrows in caffeine.' She disappeared towards the board, Eli following in her wake.

Midnight slumped. The last thing she needed was to retrain. Her days were already as long as she wanted them to be, and she enjoyed her work.

Across the auditorium, a crowd had formed around the board. Certain departments would remain untouched. Engineering, electronics, medical and coding all had an absolute pass. They were too specialised for change. The only other people presumably free from Necto's meddling were site maintenance and catering. Probably.

Amber was striding towards her, spilling a trail of coffee, mouth hanging open.

'Oh my God . . . I'm still in data analysis, but I've been moved to the social services account as team leader, which means more cash in the bank, or more to spend on glorious me. How cool is that? If Vickson were still here, I'd kiss her.'

'That would take care of your promotion pretty fast,' Midnight said.

'I don't know about that. You managed to burst into her office and keep your job. Damn, I didn't check your name. You've got to be with me, right? We've been together since the start. Come on. We have to find out!'

She grabbed Midnight's hand and dragged her to where the crowd was just starting to disperse. Running her finger down the list of J surnames, Amber turned to Midnight, frowning.

'This can't be right. It says you've been moved to client account management.'

Midnight stared at the board. 'Perfect end to a perfect week,' she said. 'What the hell do those guys even do?'

'Midnight, you have to tell them you're not moving department! You're a data analyst, and you're good at it. '

'Amber, it's fine.' Midnight was all out of fight. She'd been concerned she might not have a job left at all. If the worst that could happen was answering the phone to disgruntled clients, then she wasn't going to storm into HR and threaten to quit.

'It's not fine. They can't separate us. They've bloody well promoted me, and you're much better at the job than I am.'

Behind them, a girl was crying. On the other side, a group of women were clinking coffee cups in an impromptu toast.

'We'll still get drunk together once a month. Nothing's going to change, right?' Midnight slid an arm around Amber's shoulders.

'Everything's going to change. And where's Eli?'

'Here,' he appeared. 'Apparently I'm going over to client management with you. It's a shame. I was enjoying data analysis, what little I'd done of it.'

'I'm losing both of you?' Amber cried. Eli shook his head and disappeared into the crowd, murmuring something about trying to find someone he'd met in his initiation session.

'You've only known Eli a couple of days. I guess they didn't think you'd be so upset about it!' Midnight teased.

'But he's eye-candy! Our team was perfect. I had you to make me laugh, and him to look at. Plus, he has no home commitments. Lives on his own, always available in the evenings, so I thought I'd have someone to do things with after work when you're not available. Which, you know, you're usually not. Not a moan, just a fact.'

'We can still be lunch buddies,' Midnight said.

Amber grabbed Midnight and hugged her hard. 'Every day. You have to promise.'

'Every day,' Midnight laughed. 'We should get moving. Can't be the last ones to leave. That would be a Necto negative.' They both grinned.

Necto negatives were imaginary black marks on their records they'd thought up together during their training. They'd awarded them to each other almost every day since. Midnight was going to miss Amber. She had made her working life better since day one and, although they were chalk and cheese, their relationship just worked. They'd always been there for each other.

People were starting to shuffle towards the exits.

'Take nothing from your former department to your new desk. Confidentiality applies even between departments. Anything relevant will be copied electronically and sent to you by your department head,' some suit announced.

Midnight felt the sudden rise of nausea. 'Damn. Got to go. I'll call you tonight.' She ran for the doors, ignoring the bank of lifts with the impossibly large group of people waiting, and took the stairs instead.

She tripped twice and forced herself to slow down. 'Shit, shit, shit!' Her cheeks were blazing by the time she made it to the department door. Wiping sweat from her face, she walked in faking a relaxed smile.

Richard was busy talking with other data analysts who had their arms full of personal possessions, giving Midnight the space to slip past unnoticed to her desk. She ripped open the drawer where she'd thrown the pen drive with the Profile K applicant's data. If anyone else found the drive, she'd be on an immediate disciplinary, probably followed by dismissal.

The drawer was filled with a selection of pens and cables, a lip salve and a mascara, other drawer detritus. Her fingers just wouldn't close on the pen drive. She put her face down to look into the back.

'Lost something?' Richard asked.

Midnight whipped her head up, catching her forehead on the sill of the desk.

'Bugger,' she said.

'Not strictly office appropriate language, but as you're leaving us, I'll let that one go. Was there something specific you were looking for?'

He found it, Midnight thought. It's in his pocket and he's going to draw this out to torture me. I'm not off to client accounts, I'm on my way to the job centre.

Eli barged between them unawares.

'Just wanted to pick up my lucky pen,' he said. 'And to say I'm sorry I won't be part of this department. I enjoyed yesterday.'

He stuck his hand out to shake Richard's.

'Er, yes, well, good luck. Sorry it was a short stay. Do look after Miss Jones, won't you? She's actually a very good worker. In spite of everything.'

Midnight's fingers closed on the pen drive. She stood.

'That may be the nicest thing you've ever said to me,' she told Richard quietly. 'Thank you. You've been very . . . consistent.'

He blushed slightly, gave a small nod, and wandered off.

However disconcerting it was to be moving departments with no notice, she certainly wouldn't miss Richard Baxter's lectures on taking responsibility and being a team player, never mind his views on how women were more sensitive than men. Hopefully her new boss would have their head firmly in the twenty-first century. Midnight knelt to do her laces and shoved the pen drive into the side of her right boot.

'Ready?' she asked Eli. 'Don't want to be late on our first day, whatever that's going to look like.'

They took the lift, Midnight carrying her few personal possessions and trying not to bite her nails. She'd never been to the floor that housed client accounts before. The signs beyond the lifts pointed to the complaints office and human resources in one direction, accounting and Midnight's destination in the other. She offered up a quick silent prayer to the corporate gods, to keep her away from the complaints end of the corridor, and headed for her new office.

'Does Necto shake things up regularly?' Eli asked.

'Not like this. Random training sessions, security spot checks, and they've moved department heads around before pretty brutally. This is a new one, though.'

'Excuse me, pocket check, please,' a uniformed female announced before they could enter their new department. 'Everything into the trays.'

Midnight tensed. If they told her to take off her shoes she was screwed.

'Am I going to get in trouble? I took some gunpowder tea sachets from the kitchen in data analysis,' Eli whispered.

'Just put them in the tray. They're checking for electronics, nothing else,' she told him, as she began turning out her pockets.

Sara Vickson appeared in the doorway, waving at security. 'Hurry, please. I need to be elsewhere.'

Midnight did a double-take. Sara Vickson had been little more than a name a few days ago, now the director was popping up everywhere. She didn't know whether to be flattered or scared. The officer briefly scanned their possessions and motioned for them to go in.

'I wanted to welcome you personally,' Sara Vickson said. 'This is a new role, one we think will really change how our clients feel we engage with them. We're expecting great things. Now I should be off. I have some changes of my own—'

'Actually, Ms Vickson, can I ask how this happened? I mean, after walking into your office . . .' Midnight's voice trailed off.

Vickson gave what Midnight figured was supposed to be a conspiratorial wink, but which came off more crocodilian than anything else.

'You won my respect,' she said. 'You didn't take no for an answer and you decided to take matters into your own hands. We reward the go-getters, and those who stay loyal to the company. Enjoy the salary bump. And don't forget, this is an expanding empire. We do that by getting our clients whatever they need. Happy clients mean big bonuses. Just give Necto what it wants, and you'll never look back.'

She stalked out, leaving Midnight to look around confused until she spotted Eli beckoning her into a private section of the office, separated from the main area by a huge sheet of glass.

Inside were two desks. One large, one small. Eli sat at the smaller desk, logging into a computer.

'I think I'm your deputy or something. I didn't get a pay rise though,' he added ruefully.

'To be fair, you did only start working here yesterday,' Midnight noted, checking the room for surveillance and wishing she was sharing an office with someone she knew better. 'Listen, sorry to do this and I promise it'll be the first and last time I ever make any requests of this nature, but could you see where the department kitchen is and bring us both some water? It's hot in here.'

'Sure. You don't want tea instead?' he asked.

'No, but thank you. That's not your job. In fact, I need to figure out what your job is.'

Eli headed out of the door to get water. Midnight logged in, went into computer settings and disabled the camera and audio equipment, before digging around in her boot for the pen drive that was already starting to blister her instep.

She had two options: either wipe the pen drive or find a way to get it out of the office. The deletion option was by far the safest. The thing with Necto was that security when you left at the end of the day was actually stricter than when they let you in. The loss of corporate secrets was what they really feared. A pen drive would set off the metal detectors as she went through, and pleading forgetfulness just wouldn't wash.

But deleting it? Letting that information go after all that had happened? She just couldn't. If she was wrong about the Profile K, then Necto weren't at risk anyway. Even if they'd chosen to ignore information they held, they still weren't responsible for what had happened to Chloe Martin. The issue was how to get it out of the building, because leaving it in her desk was asking for trouble.

Eli reappeared and put a glass of water on her desk.

'Thanks,' she said. 'But you were right about that tea. I'll make you one, too. Could you start by compiling a list of all the client accounts we'll be consulting on, then we'll speak to the team heads and figure out what's needed.'

She slipped into the kitchenette and opened every drawer until she found a knife sharp enough to cut into her jeans, opening up the hem of one leg and pushing the tiny pen drive inside. She folded the material back down over her boots, praying that she could convince security that the boot's zip was the problem. Midnight poked her head out of the kitchenette door to find that Eli already had a line of people waiting to speak with her.

There was a lot to unpack about her day. Why her, was the first question. Was Vickson just keeping her sweet to ensure compliance? The fact that they'd sent Eli with her, with no experience at all, was a clear red flag. But the pay rise would make a huge difference and the additional holiday? That alone made the new position worthwhile.

All she had to do was cruise through the day, and not get caught removing company data from the premises. After that, it would be Friday night, and the only plans she had involved hot water, carbohydrates and fermented grapes.

By the time the end of the day finally came around, Midnight started finding things to do that delayed her departure, terrified at the thought of attempting to exit with contraband. It was only when the office became notably quieter that she realised she'd be better off going through security while they were still relatively busy with the end-of-day mass exodus, rather than waiting until she was the only person for them to concentrate on.

'Damn,' she muttered, 'I'm such an idiot.' She ran for the lift, pressing the button uselessly over and over again, as if that would speed it up. 'Calm down,' she told herself. 'Normal day. Nothing to see here.'

Taking a deep breath, she exited the lift, and almost sashayed to the escalator that took her down to the lockers. In the distance, she could see the row of security guards checking people out of the building for the night. Sadly, no miraculous power cut had put the metal detectors out of use. She just had to act like nothing was wrong and say the same things she did every single night when she left. All of which would have been easy had her mouth not been as dry as desert sand while sweat was soaking her back.

It took her three goes to get her key into her locker.

Someone asked her a question. Midnight turned, confused. 'Sorry, what?'

A woman from the communications team was grinning at her. 'I asked if you got the email I forwarded you. It's so lovely when old friends get in touch. I only noticed it because she had such a fabulous name.'

'I didn't read it. It's been a bit of a day with the restructuring. Who was it from?' Midnight had half an eye on security, expecting some omniscient alarm to go off at any second.

'Gemini? A friend of yours from college. You two must have raised some eyebrows with those names!'

'Doesn't ring a bell. Must be a mistake,' Midnight said.

The woman disappeared and Midnight forced herself to pause and breathe slowly for half a minute while she turned on her mobile and calmed down.

'You've got this,' she told herself. 'Just stop acting guilty.'

She chose the lane with the security guard she knew best and put a smile on her face.

'Evening,' she called as she placed her bag into a plastic tray. Her voice was a little croaky and her face felt hot, but in ten seconds she would be out of the door and on her way home.

And if not?

Then she'd be in a secure office with someone from senior management accessing the pen drive, and she wouldn't have to worry about getting up on time for work the next day.

'Is that everything?' the security guard asked, ready to push the tray into the x-ray machine.

'Um, sure, yeah,' she mumbled. Talk about something, she thought. Anything. Just talk. 'At least it's not raining.' Thank God she wasn't working for MI5.

'Supposed to bucket down tomorrow morning though,' he replied.

Midnight stepped towards the metal detector arch, light-headed and suddenly aware that she still had her mobile in her hand, which was an absolute bloody nightmare, because now the alarm was going to sound for sure, and they would do a double-check, and—

The alarm began to blare. Red lights flashed above the archway she was walking through. Midnight wasn't acting at all when she jumped out of her skin but, caught in a valley between terror and desperation, she had a momentary flash of inspiration and sent her mobile phone flying through the air towards the doors.

She dashed through behind it, crying out in horror, then shouting over her shoulder, 'Oh my God, I'm so sorry, I had my phone in my hand. Please let it not be broken. I can't be without a phone.'

The security guard followed her through the archway. 'Is it okay?' he asked. 'How's the screen?'

Midnight held the phone to her chest. 'Dented but not actually smashed,' she said. 'I just hope it turns on again.' She hoped he wouldn't ask to take a look at it before it switched off. She pressed the operating button hard. 'I don't know what's wrong with me today. I think I've got a migraine coming on. They always make me a bit forgetful. I'm normally so careful going through screening.'

She rubbed her head with one hand and looked pained, which wasn't difficult.

'You want me to take a look at the phone for you, Miss Jones?' the guard asked her.

'I think I just need to get home before this headache really gets a hold. I'm not feeling great. Sorry to have caused a ruckus.'

'No problem at all.' He walked back to the security area and retrieved her bag, then delivered it to her. 'You need any help getting home?'

'No, but I appreciate that. I think a walk in the fresh air might be just what I need. See you on Monday.'

Midnight walked out slowly enough, wondered why she felt faint twenty yards outside the building, then remembered to breathe. She was clear of the office, she still had a job, and the USB stick was still in the hem of her jeans. Only her phone and her blood pressure were the worse for wear, and in the grand scheme of things, that seemed like a small enough price to pay. She had no idea what she was going to do with the data on the pen drive, only that preventing its total erasure felt like the right thing to do. Midnight thanked God it was the weekend, and wished she was already home.

Chapter 17

The Applicant

Mae glared at him from the only piece of furniture in the lounge as he tried to catch his breath. He was winded from the kick she'd landed in his solar plexus, and still sore from previous injuries. It had been a rough week, physically speaking.

But now that all the fighting was over, he could take his time. Some idiot on the floor above was playing punk rock so loud you'd be forgiven for thinking it was the seventies, and another couple a few flats along were arguing with their window open. All in all, that was enough noise to distract from the sounds he and Mae had been making, just so long as the row along the corridor didn't turn into a full-on domestic resulting in the police being called.

'Stop staring,' he said, pulling the scarf from around his neck. The matching hat was lying in the hallway where Mae had ripped it off along with a handful of his hair, while boxing his ears. His ski gloves, never worn for any actual snow-based sport, had been stuffed into Mae's mouth and secured with duct tape. He'd even remembered to buy the tape from a pound shop rather than a hardware store. If police found traces of it around her mouth later on – hopefully several days after he'd finished with her – the first place they'd look for him would be on hardware store CCTV footage. There were other things he had with him that the police would be interested in, but the most important one he'd stolen from the back of his parents' pantry earlier that day. Given how long it had been since they'd used it, they were never going to realise it was missing.

Time had dragged. He'd arrived at his parents' at 10 a.m., peeled vegetables, laid the table then eaten Sunday lunch, played cribbage, after which he was finally allowed to depart. That had left him with little time to prepare mentally for what he was about to do, but enough to grab his stuff and follow Mae from the supermarket to her home. The darkness meant she hadn't noticed him, and the cold allowed him to wrap up so well there was no way anyone was going to describe him in any detail to the police, even if they did see him walking behind her.

From then on, it was just a matter of doing as he'd practised. He'd wanted to wait, had cautioned himself against moving too fast, but finally lost the fight against his inner demons. The desire he felt was an unstoppable force.

He followed a long way behind, to ensure Mae was going straight home. When certain, he'd taken a different route through a housing estate, coming out just ahead of her as she was approaching her block. He'd arrived at the doorway to the flats thirty seconds or so before Mae got there, patting down his pockets as if looking for keys, then rooting through his backpack, asking himself softly, 'Where are they?' Mae had walked up behind him, tired, cold and desperate to get inside, and slid her key into the lock, letting him enter after her, because who suspected the man in front of them?

From there, it was just a few steps down the hallway to her apartment and his timing had to be impeccable for that – close enough to shove her inside before she could scream, but a second too soon and she'd be yelling in the corridor.

He'd pretended to be walking past as she'd started unlocking her door, but then it became clear that she knew the people in the flat along the hallway.

'Can I help you? Mrs Favro doesn't take visitors after dark, so you shouldn't knock—' Still sliding that key home, still turning it and pushing forward.

He barged her forward just like he'd planned, but Mae – sweet little Mae who looked like she would weigh nothing and be as easy to break as a twig – reacted faster than he could possibly have anticipated. She spread her arms and legs like a cat being forced into a carrier, tensing all her muscles and pushing back against him. It stopped him in his tracks for a moment, but left him free to cover her mouth with one hand and to punch her in the left kidney with his free arm.

The air whooshed from her lungs and into the palm of his hand like a gift. Her arms and legs folded into her body. He allowed himself a self-congratulatory smile. For a moment there he'd been worried that she was going to be trouble.

She dropped to the floor like a tiny human anchor, all her weight pulling downwards. It was unimaginable that someone so slight could become lead in his arms. The only firm hold he still had was over her mouth, but suddenly she was whipping her head left and right. Bending his body over the top of hers, he fought to stop her from wriggling out beneath him, circling his arm around her neck to stay in control, squeezing to stop her from screaming. Then she flopped in his arms, eyes shut. Just like that. No more thrashing. No more fight.

He checked that she wasn't feigning unconsciousness, then dragged her into her flat and onto a tatty armchair in the lounge, stripping off his gloves to shove them into her mouth and pulling the tape from his backpack.

When he was done, he started preparing the rest of her flat. He made sure all the windows were both shut and locked, closed the curtains, found her mobile phone and turned that off too. Then he switched her ancient television on – a little background noise would be helpful – and chased that up with the radio in her bedroom.

When he was ready, he went back to her. Mae's head was flopped to the left, and she was breathing heavily. He was going to rouse her soon, not that he needed her awake, strictly speaking. It was simply that in his experience with Chloe, he'd found that having her watching what he was doing had heightened his experience considerably. There was something thrilling about having a witness.

Standing in front of her, he began lightly tapping the right side of her face.

'Mae,' he said. 'I need you to wake up.' He slapped her a little harder now. She really was out for the count. 'For fuck's sake. Mae!' he yelled.

She didn't even open her eyes when she pulled her knees up into her chest then smashed her feet, full force, into his core.

He flew backwards, crashing into the wall, watching as she tried to stand but found the armchair she was strapped into far too heavy to move with her. Thirty seconds of thrashing later, she stopped and simply glared at him. There was enough hate in her eyes to start a war.

'Why aren't you crying?' he asked, brushing himself off as he stood. Not that she could answer him – not that he actually wanted her to – but he was curious. 'That was a pretty hard kick. Aren't you scared that I'm going to be angry?'

Nothing. Not a shake of her head, or a raised eyebrow.

Mae was awesome. He looked longingly at her. How cool was a woman who didn't crack, even under that much pressure? He still didn't want to do the sorts of things with her that he dreamed about doing with Jessica. But kudos, anyway. Chloe had been hysterical at a much earlier stage. Her gaze slid to his left and he turned to see what had her attention. Next to him, on the wall, was a clock.

'You're right. It's getting late. We'll be done soon, and then I'll leave.' He wanted to be reassuring. It would be easier to move her into the bedroom if she thought she'd survive. 'Your bedroom's tidy. It shows you have discipline.'

From his backpack, he took a rope with a noose. Her face when she saw it betrayed the first signs of panic, eyes wide as she tried to shrink away, but it was over her head in a heartbeat. He pulled the noose just tight enough to control her.

'I know what you're thinking, but I'm not going to hang you. This is just to make sure you do as you're told. I watched a video of how to tie the knot on YouTube, and it still took me hours to get it perfect.' Mae was breathing so heavily, she sounded like a bull about to stampede.

He felt alive. Gone was the frustration of wanting someone he couldn't have.

'Stand up. I'm going to point a knife in your back,' he murmured. 'I'm not going to use it on you, as long as you keep walking with the rope tight around your neck. Do that until you get to the bed, then lie down. Don't fight me. I don't want to use the blade, but I will. Let's go.'

Mae's legs wobbled but didn't give way. She went slowly, sweating, but the rope stayed taut and he didn't have to repeat his instructions. The flat was just three rooms, with the kitchen at the end of the lounge which doubled as a dining room, a bathroom opposite the front door, and a bedroom opposite the lounge. Even so, it felt like the journey took an age. His skin had started to itch by the time Mae reached her bed. It had to begin now.

'Lie on your stomach,' he told her. That was met by a furious growl but the knife tip in her shoulder blade was persuasive enough.

He tied the loose end of the noose rope around one leg of the bed, threw the pillows across the room to make sure nothing got in his way, then began cutting off her clothing. Mae didn't move, wriggle or kick. She just lay there, so still that at one point he checked to make sure she hadn't passed out again, but when he pulled back her hair from her face, her eyes were open. It scared him a little. Not enough for him to stop. Enough to put her hair back across her face so he didn't have to see that expression.

Then someone knocked on the door. Three times, not too loudly. Friendly, familiar.

Mae's body tensed, and in spite of the gloves and the tape and being face down, she put every bit of life force she had into producing a growl-scream-shriek that might – just might – have been audible from the corridor.

He crept out of the bedroom, quietly pulled the door until it was almost shut, then moved along the hallway to stand with his ear pressed against Mae's front door. Whoever was there knocked again.

Fuck it! They hadn't gone.

'Mae?' a man called. Then words he couldn't understand, too foreign and too fast, but the voice was scratchy and shaky. Unmistakably that of someone elderly.

The applicant rubbed his hands over his face.

Stay calm, he'll go. Stay calm, he'll go. Stay calm, he'll go.

Then the sound of keys jangling.

'No,' he muttered. 'This isn't what happens.'

More calling to Mae from the corridor. He should have known, because the buzzer didn't go to be let in from outside, so the man must have had keys all along.

Instinctively, he reached out and pushed his hands against the door to prevent entry, but that was wrong too, because the man would know straight away that something was wrong.

Deep breath, step away. Hide in the bathroom, behind the door.

Now he could hear Mae again as the key grated in the lock – it needed some WD-40, he thought – but perhaps it was a good thing that she was making a noise because the man, whoever he was, would go to her.

There were footsteps inside the flat, the first two slow and hesitant, then a desperate shuffling no more than four feet from where he was hiding, and the sound of the bedroom door being pushed fully open.

The applicant stepped out and, unheard, covered the ground to where an older man was tripping over his own feet to get to Mae and free her from the ropes. Mae's bulging eyes fixed on the blade diving gracefully through the air towards the man's neck. It sliced so cleanly that he couldn't have felt a thing until he was already collapsing.

The applicant raced back to shut the front door, kicking aside a bag that must have been dropped on the way in.

Don't slam it! he ordered himself. No more noise. Or should he leave, now, while he still could? What if someone was expecting the old man home? What if other people were about to arrive? He thought about that for a moment, then returned to the bag and looked through it. In it was food that barely constituted enough for a meal for two. They weren't expecting anyone else. It had been a care visit, not the start of a party.

Still, the applicant cursed his shoddy preparation. He hadn't watched her for long enough. Due diligence was a real thing.

What he'd had planned for Mae wasn't going to be fulfilling now, anyway. He'd thought he'd have the whole night.

'Just fucking calm down,' he said. 'You have time.'

He hauled the man into the bathroom and pushed his body into the shower, allowing himself only a minute to admire the picture. On any other day, that wouldn't have been enough for him, but now he was out of time.

Rolling Mae over, keeping three fingers inside the noose so it didn't tighten and hurt her, he looked for that furious stare, now the ruse was up. She would know she wasn't getting out alive.

Her eyes were closed. Not squeezed tightly shut, just resting lightly, eyelashes shimmering on her cheeks. He looked more closely. Tears hung from the ends of her lashes. She had loved the man whose life he'd taken, and now Mae was hiding in the comforting dark of unconsciousness until it was over. Not so brave any more.

He retrieved the duct tape, layering it over her mouth to stop the screams that would come. It wouldn't be like his time with Chloe. There would be no artistry or slow burn. He took supplies from his backpack – workman's goggles, his parents' kitchen gadget, and a stack of brand new tea-towels for wiping the blade – and turned up the radio.

There would be some noise, not nice noise. In a couple of hours, the smell would have permeated the corridor. By the next afternoon, it might have been reported to building maintenance. Come the evening, someone would have attempted entry. That was okay. He was going to work fast, then exit through Mae's bedroom window into the night. But he had to see it through, no matter the risk. Stopping was simply not an option.

Chapter 18

It was Tuesday lunchtime, and Midnight found herself standing at police crime scene tape that was both inconsequential and a chasm between her and the flat where another young woman had died.

She'd heard it from Amber, who had visited her that morning from data analysis, entering Midnight's office with the words, 'It's not your guy. I know what you must be thinking but I'm here to tell you it's not.'

Eli had stopped typing and was looking from Amber to Midnight and back.

'Amber, I don't know what you're talking about. Do you want to start at the beginning, but this time in private?'

Eli busied himself. 'Tea?' he asked brightly. 'Anyone? No? Okay then.' He bustled out.

'If you're referring to what I think you're referring to, please don't talk about that in front of Eli. We've known him less than a week, so I don't know if I can trust him yet. More importantly, who's not my guy?'

'I assumed you'd heard,' Amber said. 'Listen, I'm pushed for time. I had no idea how busy it was heading up a team—'

'Amber. What's happened?'

'Where have you been for the last day?' Amber snapped. Midnight took a deep breath, assessing her best friend. Amber never snapped. If she was stressed, she made a joke. This was new. 'Sorry. I know you have a lot going on.' She sat down in Eli's chair. 'Two people were found dead. I didn't want you overreacting, especially now everything's going so well for us.'

Going well was an understatement. Midnight's pay had increased by a full third from her data analysis position, and that had been remunerated far beyond comparable positions in other companies.

'Where?' Midnight asked.

Amber twisted one hand in the other and looked like she wanted to bolt. 'Clapham. That estate they've been talking about bulldozing and redeveloping.'

'Do the police think it's the same attacker?'

'That's my point. It can't be. This is two victims, different sexes, so nothing like last time. I just figured your imagination would be working overtime,' she said. 'I should go, but let's get coffee after work. I'm worried about you.'

'Coffee? I think that's the first time you've suggested we go anywhere other than to a bar. You really must be worried.'

'That's kind of mean,' Amber muttered, frowning.

It was unlike her not to be able to take something Midnight said as a joke, but then they'd been separated for the first time. It was a big change for them both, and all Midnight had been thinking about was herself. Amber had been there for the fun times, but more importantly, she got her through the tough days and the boring days, always with a smile. She made

Midnight look forward to going into the office. Now all that had changed, and there was a hole in Midnight's working world.

'I'm sorry. Coffee would be good,' Midnight said. 'I appreciate you looking out for me.'

Thirty minutes later, she put on her coat, left the office without a word to anyone, and hopped on a bus. Amber's protestations that it wasn't the same killer felt hollow, and Midnight's gut was far more persuasive. Something was wrong. People didn't just randomly start dying like that in one small area of a city.

It had taken Midnight just a few minutes to get the details. The woman's name was Mae. She was in her twenties, had both lived and worked in Clapham, and had died in her own home. The dead man was a relative of Mae's but it wasn't clear if he'd lived there too. It was amazing what people put on social media. Nothing was taboo any more. Some neighbour had revealed the road, block and apartment number of Mae's flat.

Midnight wasn't even sure why she was going there. Guilt, she answered her own question. You're going because you think that maybe you could have stopped it, and now you need to face up to what you've done.

She glanced at the people either side of her along the crime scene tape barrier. Could the murderer be there? His DNA could be on her now, rogue skin cells on her coat. She turned around, staring into the crowd and searching for a face that might fit the image she'd developed of the killer in her imagination. Possibly, terrifyingly, Midnight realised that perhaps he could even see her in the crowd. Was he looking for her as she looked for him?

'Miss Jones?' When she turned back, DI Ruskin was standing in front of her. 'Were you looking for me?'

'No. Maybe. I'm not sure,' she blustered.

Ruskin frowned, then lifted the crime scene tape and ushered her in.

'Come on,' he said. 'I have a flask of coffee in my car.'

The seen-better-days Toyota could have used a valet, but it shut out the wind and offered a little privacy. The passenger sun visor was down, and Midnight could see in the mirror that her mascara had run. She'd been crying. No wonder Ruskin had decided to be kind to her.

'You okay?' he asked.

Midnight nodded. 'How do you do this job? There's so much sadness.'

He took a deep breath in. 'I suppose I'm trying to limit other people's future sadness. All those potential victims who need protecting.' He blew warm air onto his hands.

Midnight liked him. He was fatherly in a way she'd forgotten, and masculine without the bullshit. It was a good combination.

'So is it?' she whispered.

'Chloe's killer?' he asked. Midnight nodded. 'Maybe. We don't have the forensic results from this scene to compare yet, but we do have a DNA source from Chloe's flat. If there's a match, we'll call that positive for a triple murder. Watch this space.'

'Who was the man that died?'

'The second victim's father. His son just released a statement to the press. It was bad timing. In an American thriller, they'd call it collateral damage, but here it's just another old-fashioned murder.'

'So what was the link between Chloe and this woman . . . Mae?'

144

'Can I ask you a question first? What are you doing here? Last time you were passing by, but I know you work so don't you have somewhere else to be?'

'Is it suspicious, me coming here?' she asked. 'Because now I feel like I should have stayed away.'

'Full disclosure, we checked you out after you were spotted near the last crime scene, so no, you're not on my list of people I think might be involved. I'm just curious.'

Midnight gazed out of the window. She wanted to tell him everything, but she had a new contract, and she'd studied it carefully over the weekend. Not only would she get fired if she breached confidentiality, she could end up losing everything if she got sued, and without a reference there was no way she'd find another position in the industry.

'I just felt I had a connection to it. And like I said before, it's all so close. Too close. To where I live, I mean.'

He stared at her for a few seconds, then pulled a flask from the back seat and poured two plastic cups full of steaming coffee.

'Hope you like it strong.'

It burned Midnight's tongue a little, but the coffee was good.

'Do you have a picture of Mae?' she asked.

'I can show you the one we've just released to the press. You sure you want to see?' She nodded and he pulled out his mobile.

Mae was breathtaking. She was Asian, with hair that fell perfectly onto her shoulders, small, cupid's bow lips and eyes the darkest shade of brown, set broadly across her face. The resemblance to Chloe's eyes was notable.

'Did he kill her the same way he killed Chloe?' Midnight asked, handing the mobile back.

'I can't talk about that. Some details have to remain out of the public domain. Listen, Miss Jones—'

'Midnight,' she said. 'As I'm in your car, drinking your coffee.'

'Midnight. I get the feeling there's something you want to tell me. Am I right?'

She shifted her eyes from his and lifted one shoulder noncommittally up and down.

'You'd be amazed what people tell me. Sometimes it's a hunch. Sometimes they suspect a loved one but have no idea how to get past the guilt of reporting them. The point is, if you know something, or suspect something, you can trust me with it.'

Midnight could hear Amber's voice in her head, telling her not to freak out.

'I think I just remembered what you said about killers coming back to the scene. I figured he might be here, and I thought . . . I thought I'd recognise him somehow. It was stupid.'

She finished her coffee and handed him the cup.

'Okay,' he said. 'I should be getting back inside, but promise me something: if you need to talk, call me. The Met police have been having a hard time with public trust lately, but most of us, nearly all of us, are here to do the best we can. Instincts are there for a reason, Midnight. What I've learned from a lifetime of policing, is that people are most likely to die when they ignore their gut.'

'Sure,' she said. 'Thanks for the coffee. I feel better now. I'm sorry for what you have to see and do. I think you're brave. And I believe that you're the good guy.' She left, knowing he was watching her, wishing he would come after her and force a confession from her.

But he didn't.

146

Chapter 19

Ruskin watched Midnight Jones plod back towards the crime scene tape. She resembled a shadow more than a whole person, as if the substance of her had dropped out. He was always wary of spending too much time with witnesses. Sometimes they were just freaks who got off on the drama. For others, a crime offered a way to make a connection. Miss Jones, though, was an anomaly. She made Ruskin want to shake her to see what fell out. There was something she was holding back, but if he pushed her too hard, she'd retreat.

His mobile interrupted his musings, with a message to attend the mortuary for a debriefing. Picking up some chicken soup and dumplings from Donatella's on the way, he drove across town to the place he liked least in the whole of London. This was where every sad story ended. All the good work done there was necessitated by the tears of loved ones. Ruskin was going to move back to Scotland some time soon. He'd wanted so much more for his family than living in a two-up-two-down on a crowded street. At least in Scotland, their money would go further, even if that meant leaving their friends behind. London had given him a great career, endless entertainment and some memorable times, but he'd dreamed of ending his days travelling the world, and if that couldn't happen on a police pension then the next best thing was watching golden sunsets over the lochs and hiking the Highlands. More than anything, he didn't want the last place his body lay before cremation to be that damned mortuary. Deep breath, do your job, be grateful it's not you – his mantra before buzzing to be let in.

The pathologist met him with an outstretched hand to take the traditional offering. They sat together in the staffroom to eat, and Ruskin was grateful for the salty chicken soup softening the chemical air. While they ate, there was no mention of cases or bodies or death, by unspoken agreement. Family was a safe topic, as was sport. Books, at a push, because neither of them found much time for reading. Television was another taboo subject. Ruskin failed to understand why so many people wanted to watch programmes about true crime or fictional crime, unsolved murders, or just misery. If he had his way, all media would be required to be positive. There was enough horror in his world without sitting down to relax with more.

'How's your wife, Jock?' the pathologist asked.

'Fed up with me making promises I don't keep. I'll be home at ten p.m. I'm not working this weekend so I'll have the time to fix that tap. I'd love to go to the cinema on Friday. I'll definitely have Christmas off this year. We can afford that cruise she's always fancied. That sort of thing. I'm carrying both too much weight around my middle and too much guilt on my shoulders in equal measure.'

'I'm sure she understands.' The pathologist smiled softly.

'Aye, she does. But her understanding the demands of this job, and me wishing I had the time and money to treat her better, are two different things. And as for my kids . . . you think the hard bit's when they're wee things, falling over themselves and afraid of the dark. No one tells you it's the pain they'll experience as adults that really breaks you.'

The pathologist waited a beat.

'Problems?'

'Nothing a large amount of cash couldn't fix.' Ruskin issued an uncharacteristically bitter laugh. 'My son and his wife can't have kids. It's driving her into depression and he's become a shadow of the fun-loving boy he used to be. The NHS won't fund any more attempts at IVF so it's the private route only.'

'I'm sorry. That really does cost a lot of money.'

'Aye. Around fifteen thousand for every three rounds of IVF, and that's without factoring in time off work and incidentals. We might have been able to help with a portion of it if my daughter hadn't got herself mired into credit card debt throughout university and the years that followed, then lied to us about it until it was too late to bail her out. She owes money to a lot of people, not just the banks.'

'Jock, I'm sorry. It never rains but it pours.'

'Never a truer word spoken,' Ruskin said. He looked into his empty soup cup, knowing it was time. 'Looks like I've run out of excuses to sit around blethering.'

'Shall we then?' the pathologist asked.

They walked together through the labyrinth of corridors and rooms, brightly lit, largely windowless, white-painted. Coveralls, gloves, masks and hats followed. There could be no suggestion that the evidence had been tainted.

'We'll look at the visitor first. The bodies have been formally identified by Mae's brother. He confirmed that the male was their father. He often popped round to see Mae in the evenings, even if it was late after her work shift. He worried that she wasn't eating properly, and it gave him something to do after his wife passed.'

'I'm meeting Mae's brother later today to update him. So what do we know?'

The pathologist rolled down the covering. The front of the neck had been severed with a hundred-and-eighty-degree cut so deep that almost everything save for the spine had been destroyed. Ruskin had seen the body at the flat first, but it was still shocking second time around.

'It's a single cut,' the pathologist said. 'No snagging or secondary openings. So two things follow. The blade was substantial, by my estimate no less than eight inches long and two inches wide at its base.'

'There was nothing matching that description at the scene. Do you have any idea what sort of blade we're looking for?'

'I'd say a butcher's knife or chef's knife, but high-end or recently sharpened. The blade's pathway was flawless. Death was fast, and while not entirely painless, the best I can say is that by the time this gentleman's brain registered what had happened to him, he would already have lost consciousness.'

'Given the trail of blood from the bedroom to the bathroom, it seems obvious he died first. Did you find any other injuries? Was he restrained or beaten before the murder?' Ruskin asked.

'No. There wasn't a mark on him. Neither defensive, nor any sign that he'd actively fought the perpetrator off.'

'So he was approached from behind? Taken by surprise?'

'I'd say so,' the pathologist said. He pointed to the left side of the victim's neck, just where the severance had stopped. 'This point here is where the blade was pulled out sharply. You can see by the way some of the internal tissues were pulled forward rather than sideways. That's the exit point of the blade. It means the cut from behind was made from right to left.'

'So we're looking for someone left-handed?' Ruskin asked.

'Or ambidextrous, but even then, most people who use both hands favour one or the other slightly, even if it's subconscious. At a moment where both force and precision were required under great stress, they would normally automatically choose their most used hand.'

Ruskin wished he hadn't eaten the soup. 'Poor man. The last thing he saw in this world was his daughter tied to a bed with a noose around her neck. It's hardly peaceful.'

'And yet it was still vastly better than his daughter's,' the pathologist murmured, pulling the cover back over the deceased and pushing the trolley to one side as he manoeuvred another to the centre of the room.

To Ruskin's horror, the pathologist pulled down the large surgical light in preparation for some close-up work. His stomach rebelled a fraction more. It wasn't squeamishness. Ruskin had attended helicopter crashes, vehicle pile-ups and murder–suicides. He thought he'd seen all that the depths of humanity had to offer him.

But this, so soon after Chloe Martin?

'Ready?' the pathologist asked.

'No,' Ruskin answered, entirely truthfully.

'Good. You're still human then.'

Ruskin's fellow officers, privately and quietly, operated something they called a gore score. It wasn't sophisticated and it wasn't nice, but it was a realistic way to warn officers what they were walking into, and it was a means of compartmentalising different crime scenes in your head. Deaths with no external sign of violent attack – hangings, drownings – were a 1. By

151

the time you were attending arsons, shootings, high falls and stabbings you were around the 5 mark. The cut to the old man's throat was bad, probably a 7. He'd thought Chloe was the worst thing he might see for the remainder of his career, and in his head, that was already a 10. Now he had no choice, much as he hated the gore score living rent-free in his brain, to downgrade Chloe's injuries to a 9.

'This is the 10,' he muttered.

'I beg your pardon?'

'Thinking aloud,' Ruskin said. He wanted to ask if they could work from the photos instead, but how could he? How dare he opt not to look, after all Mae had suffered?

'She's not here, Jock,' the pathologist noted astutely. 'The girl you're thinking about is gone. This is a collection of the cells that housed her for a while. I'm going to do this as quickly as I can.'

Ruskin nodded but didn't try to speak. The gore score got his colleagues through walking into nightmare after nightmare. His personal scoring system worked differently. It had no catchy rhyming nomenclature or clever imagery, but in his head, the crime scenes he'd attended – the most memorable ones at least – were filed in terror order, marking how much fear and pain the victim had endured before death. Mae scored a 10 in that table too. He tensed his muscles and held his breath.

Mae's corpse best resembled a Victorian dissection gone horribly wrong.

'If you don't start breathing again, I'm going to ask you to step outside until I'm certain you can proceed without putting your health at risk,' the pathologist said.

The air whooshed out of Ruskin's lungs. He forced his shoulders to drop, peeling his fingers from the edge of the metal table he hadn't even registered he'd been gripping.

'I'm all right,' he said quickly. 'I need a timeline, a weapon, likely noise, and anything you know about what happened to her before all this.' He motioned vaguely in the air above Mae's body. 'Most importantly, what we know about him.'

'Time of death was shortly after we know she returned home. As accurately as I can assess it, within thirty minutes of her father's death. By the time the bodies were discovered the following evening, both had been dead in the region of twenty-one hours. No sign of sexual assault. The weapon took some research, but we have a variety of blades and implements in a vault. One of my assistants managed to find a similar mechanism to the one used, and we've been testing it on a section of pig carcass.'

Ruskin thought of the Cairngorms. Of walking through the valleys as clouds rolled down the mountainsides, purple-blushed at dawn.

'First, I need you to take a look at one of the incisions, so you know what you're looking for. And the type of person you're dealing with.' The pathologist pulled a magnifier over a cut approximately halfway up Mae's right thigh and stepped to one side to allow Ruskin a closer view.

'Focus on the skin at the edge of the cut. It looks rough, with tendrils of skin appearing to have been pulled upwards. The cut itself, seen microscopically, looks jagged, almost zigzagged.'

It was a mess, was what Ruskin could see. From the big picture down to the brushstrokes, everything was chaotic and clumsy.

'How is this the same killer?' Ruskin mused. 'Apart from the timing and the geography, it's almost the polar opposite of Chloe's murder. In the most inappropriate terms, the difference between the injuries is like comparing Van Gogh to a three-year-old drawing with their first set of crayons.'

'Under any other set of circumstances, I'd agree with you,' the pathologist said. 'But we'll get to that. I've chosen this particular injury for a reason. Allow me to just put in an outward clamp.' He opened a metal drawer and took out something that resembled a reverse bulldog clip, inserting it into the leg wound to push back the tissues. 'What you're looking at now is the bone. You can see the line of damage, with the tell-tale raw edges.'

'Yup,' Ruskin managed.

'So the first conclusion is that the killer came with multiple weapons: the sharp knife, used on Mae's father, and a weapon with a serrated blade, but with bigger teeth.'

'More like a saw?' Ruskin looked harder at the bone damage.

'Exactly like a saw,' the pathologist told him. 'But with two blades, I believe. I'm going to give you greater magnification.' He moved a dial.

When Ruskin looked again, he saw two cuts to the bone. Each had gone no more than a few millimetres down, but there were two distinct parallel lines, both leaving tiny bony splinters.

'What did this?'

'The clue was on the skin. Look back here.' He pointed with the end of his pen at the skin first on one side of the incision, then the other. 'Look at the rough skin tagging the knife left. On the upper part of the leg the tags are pulled to the left. On the lower part, they're pulled to the right.'

'Two blades?' Ruskin frowned.

'Two blades working together. That can't happen with a manual weapon. The human hand and brain don't work that well, especially on a surface like soft human flesh.'

'Fuck,' Ruskin sighed. 'Power tool.'

'Quite so. Now some power saws work by moving a single blade very fast backwards and forwards. That's not the pattern here. It took a while to find a match but . . .' He walked across to a cupboard and opened the door. Ruskin wasn't sure he wanted to see what was inside.

'Here you go. It's not exactly the right model. These blades produce an effect that leaves a half-millimetre wider gap between the two incision marks, but it might be as close as you're going to get.'

He handed Ruskin the weapon, only no one else would ever think of it as that.

'An electric carving knife. You've got to be kidding me. He . . . he literally—'

'I wouldn't even try to put it into words,' the pathologist said. 'What you need right now are simple facts. Let me show you our companion sample.'

He pointed Ruskin in the direction of a metal tray with a transparent sheet of plastic over it, then moved the magnifier again to assist.

'We used this electric carver on the pig skin. Now you have to allow for different skin thickness, different fatty deposits, et cetera, but what you're looking at is the same basic pattern.'

Ruskin could see it. 'The skin strands at the edge of the wound are larger here.'

'Yes, I believe that's because the semi-circular arcs on the teeth of the blade are wider than on your assailant's weapon. The smaller the teeth, the shorter the little tufts of skin off the wound. We tried it on a bone sample too. Same parallel lines. When one blade is going one way the other blade goes the other. That's what creates the lines, and the different direction of skin tagging. The fact that it's a power tool accounts for how deep the knife went in.'

Ruskin stepped away from the sample to look back at the rag doll remains of Mae's body.

155

'How long was she conscious?'

'Not long. The pain would have been unbearable. I'm afraid he chose areas where he didn't hit any arteries or she'd have bled out very fast. There were one or two false starts, as if he were practising.'

'He was getting a feel for the weapon,' Ruskin said. 'What about the noose?'

'Used only to restrain and control, I'd say. The bones in her neck were undamaged although there were grazing injuries suggesting it had been tightened while she was still alive. It would have restricted her airways but not fatally, so her breathing would have been laboured but I doubt she'd have been rendered unconscious. Likewise, I found no damage to her trachea, so no, if you were hoping she might have died earlier from the noose, that wasn't the case.'

'We know she couldn't have screamed because of the gag, but what about the noise from the electric carver. Could the neighbours have heard that?'

'Easy enough to cover with other sounds. I gather both the television and the radio were on when officers attended the scene?'

'They were,' Ruskin confirmed.

'Given that all these injuries would have been inflicted in a short period of time, there might have been additional background noise for fifteen or twenty minutes, but not necessarily enough to make the neighbours complain.'

Ruskin stepped away from the body and sat down in the pathologist's chair. 'How many injuries, total?'

'Fourteen.'

'So exponentially less than on Chloe Martin, and that's before we start comparing the methodology. But you still believe it's the same man?'

The pathologist covered Mae's remains, stripped off his gloves and joined Ruskin at the desk.

'We got some results in an hour ago,' he said. 'There was plenty of DNA left at Mae's. Some on the floor, probably from sweat, and a drop of blood that had flown across to a mirror. My hypothesis is that when he first started up the electric carver, he nicked his hand. I asked for all other work to stop at our DNA centre, and they pushed it through. But the incontrovertible evidence is that the same DNA from saliva has now been found on Chloe's left breast and Mae's thigh.'

'So it really was Chloe's killer, no question.' Ruskin let that sink in for a moment. They were dealing with a murderer who had changed his kill method, gone from surgical to butchering, and who had no criminal record they knew of, in spite of how extraordinarily dangerous he was. 'And he was either very excited and drooling, or angry and spitting?' Ruskin asked.

'Take your pick. Both options have the same result. His DNA was also on some skin cells that lodged on a shard of one of Chloe's broken teeth, presumably when he hit her. So the only good news is that you have one psychopath, not two, loose on the streets of London.'

'That's something. But you and I both know he'll kill again, assuming we don't stop him first, and God only knows what he's going to do to his next victim.'

Chapter 20

Jessica stared at the woman at her door, who was holding out a huge bouquet of flowers.

'Do I have to?' she asked quietly.

'Have to what?' the florist asked.

'Accept them. I mean, can I not? Would you tell whoever sent them?'

'If the sender asks, we'll explain that you refused delivery. I have to take a note, in case we get accused of breaching our contract. So, are you taking them? I have other deliveries.'

'I just don't want to give the impression that I wanted the flowers, but I also don't want to make him cross because he knows where I live and—'

The florist put them at Jessica's feet. 'I'll leave them here. That way I can say we delivered them, but you don't have to take them inside. Happens more often than you'd think.'

The florist disappeared and Jessica plucked the card from the plastic holder.

'*A thank you for making me feel so welcome, and a reminder about our date this afternoon. See you at 4. Don't be late! Wx*', she read.

'It's not a bloody date,' she hissed, ripping the note in two and kicking the flowers across the hallway, a trail of water and petals in its wake.

Against her thigh, her mobile began to vibrate.

She sighed. It was him again. Since the accident, he'd found so many excuses to text her that she was considering blocking him. Only then an insurance claim was inevitable, maybe police involvement too. Jessica opened the message.

Hope you like the flowers. Would you send me a photo of them, just so I know they got my order right?

She stared at the ruined blooms. 'Shit.'

Gathering up bits and pieces of flora, she hunted for a vase. It took a while to find intact stems and whole blooms, but eventually she was able to piece together what might pass for a bouquet, taking a close-up shot.

Thanks, she texted. There was no need. 4 p.m. meeting confirmed. Was that clear enough? She wasn't worried about being too obvious. He hadn't taken any of her previous hints. If anything, the more aloof she'd been, the more enthusiastic he'd become, and Jessica had insisted on a mid-afternoon meeting so there could be no misunderstanding. It was not a date.

He replied immediately. Wonderful, although the photo isn't clear. Could you take another? I've booked a table so we don't feel pressured to leave. And don't drive – they have a great wine selection. Jessica rolled her eyes.

Just left my flat so can't take another photo, she replied. No wine for me. Too much work on.

She turned off her mobile, and crushed the flowers into her bin, making up her mind that if matters weren't resolved that afternoon, she was going to contact her insurance company anyway. There was only so much she could take. It had been just over a week since the accident, and he was getting creepier by the day.

The W stood for Willem, surname Foster, but he remained the Cream Bun Creep in her head. He'd stayed for four hours after coming off his motorbike. Four long, painful hours. In that time, he'd made one phone call to have his bike picked up by a recovery truck, and another supposedly to let a friend know he was all right, although to Jessica's ears that conversation had sounded contrived. She wasn't even sure there'd been anyone on the end of the line. He'd lain on her sofa, drinking his way through the whole bottle of wine, intermittently complaining of back pain, neck pain, and aching shoulders. When she'd asked if he wouldn't be better off in his own home, he'd claimed he probably shouldn't be alone until it was clear he didn't have a serious head injury. Finally, she'd told him bluntly that she had an early morning to prepare for and wanted to go to bed.

He'd asked to see her in person today so they could go through repair estimates, see her insurance documents, and discuss general liability issues – his phrasing. Jessica had done her best to persuade him that a phone call would work just as well, but he'd insisted, claiming he had copies of documents to give to her. She'd caved in just to get it all over with in a single meeting rather than prolong the endless texting. Strange that save for her hurried and automatic apology when he'd first fallen from his bike, Jessica had no memory of accepting liability. But today she had a plan, and she was going to see it through.

She washed off every trace of make-up. Instead of the cute low-rise jeans and cut-off top she'd put on that morning, Jessica donned her baggiest jumper and shapeless camo trousers – no perfume, no lipstick, no jewellery. After giving her hair the briefest brush so she could pass as sane on the street, she drove to their rendezvous point. Parking just one street away so she could make a quick escape, she waited until it was 4.10 on the dot before making her way to the Cuban restaurant Willem had selected. She wasn't prepared to be there on time. God forbid he should think she was keen.

'Booking in the name of Foster,' she told the waitress, and was led to a table with a single yellow rose in a jar and a lit candle. Jessica made a point of blowing it out before she sat down. The Creep was nowhere to be seen among the few random diners there between lunch and dinner service.

She squashed her irritation. Was his lateness yet another game or was he planning on making some ridiculous entrance? Still, it gave her a chance to make sure everything was in working order. From her bag, she took out the file she'd prepared. In it, she'd drawn a to-scale(ish) map of the road, marking the position of his bike, and how far out she thought her van had swung while she'd been reverse parking. She'd also obtained estimates for the repairs to her van with which she intended to negotiate. She too, she was going to say, had suffered a stiff neck after the accident. In spite of her stoicism and quick thinking at the event, she'd been left shaken up and distressed after he'd left her flat. So weren't they both in the same boat? Neither had obtained any witness details, after all. He had been, she thought, driving too close to her van, and surely going too fast if he hadn't been able to avoid her vehicle when she'd clearly been parking. Nonetheless, she was prepared to forgo any claim against him if he agreed to do the same. Each to bear their own costs, matter closed, upon which, she intended to block him once and for all.

For her pièce de résistance, she was going to mention that she'd met someone she liked. A girlfriend. Leave him in no doubt that she was not in the marketplace.

She took out her mobile and hid it on the table in plain sight. What he didn't know was that her old phone would be in the handbag she had open on the tabletop, recording their whole conversation. She needed the Creep to agree to let the claim go, and she knew better than to believe he would stick to any arrangement they made. A week later, maybe two, he would have sudden neck pain again, or find something else wrong with his bike. An excuse, no matter how pathetic, to turn up on her doorstep.

'Been there,' she said, pouring herself a glass of water. 'Not doing it again.'

If it didn't work then screw it; insurance company, rising premium, paperwork. She'd just have to sell more cakes to pay for it.

'Excuse me, Miss? Mr Foster just phoned. He apologised, but he's running late. He said there were delays on public transport and . . . something about not having his bike?' The waitress sounded vague. 'He'll be here in thirty minutes. He said you should go ahead and order.' Like hell was she going to order food.

'Just a pot of tea, please,' Jessica said, wondering why the creep hadn't just texted her as usual. Perhaps he'd thought that by letting the restaurant staff know he was on his way, it would be that much more awkward for her to just get up and leave. Manipulative bastard.

It was already 4.20 which meant he wouldn't be with her until 4.50 p.m., dragging their meeting firmly into the early evening.

'Finish it,' she told herself, gritting her teeth. 'Just sit it out and finish it.'

Instead of sitting there fuming, she made plans on her mobile for the following week, listing supplies and new bread recipes.

'Sorry to ask, but is your date coming?' The waitress looked apologetic.

Jessica checked her watch. It was 5.10 p.m. 'Let me call him.' She dialled his number but got voicemail. How long was she supposed to wait? She wanted to go but needed it to be over, and if he arrived to find she'd already left, he'd be hot on her heels with the perfect excuse to go to her flat. She'd give it until 5.30 p.m. If he hadn't arrived by then and she still couldn't get hold of him, she'd leave, keep the lights off at home, and just not answer the door.

At 5.29, the restaurant door opened, bell jangling and shredding her nerves. Jessica wished she'd already left. She stood to greet him but found herself looking at a stranger. That was it. She could go. There was no way the Creep could expect her to wait around any longer. Taking no chances, she grabbed her mobile.

5.30pm. Couldn't get hold of you. Going to a friend's for the night. I'll email tomorrow, she texted. To the point but polite, and it contained an alibi for the rest of the evening. Jessica congratulated herself.

There was a space outside her flat as she drove by but she wasn't stupid enough to park there. Instead, she left her van a couple of roads away – she'd pay for that the next morning when she had to load up – but it was necessary.

The walk to her flat, brief though it was, made her jittery. Jessica had the uncomfortable sense, as she had every day since the accident, that he was watching her. A week earlier, she'd looked out of her bedroom window to see a man across the road staring up at her flat, and immediately panicked. It wasn't the Creep, but it had freaked her out anyway.

She arrived at the door to her building and ran up the stairs to her flat. Her key stuck for a moment, protesting, then gave way and she was in. Jessica reached for the light switch then remembered not to. Her mobile vibrated in her pocket. She left it until she reached her bedroom where her blinds were closed.

Sorry. Plans went awry. Did you make it to your friend's house safely?

'Bollocks,' Jessica whispered.

Also, I took a closer look at that photo. My flowers look damaged. I called the florist for an explanation. They said no damage occurred at their end. Where are the flowers now?

The tea Jessica had drunk rose in her throat. He knew what she'd done.

No. She was allowing her imagination to get the better of her.

Only her key had stuck in the lock, and it had never done that before. Not one time. And now that she stood still and breathed deeply, wasn't there the faintest hint of something in the air that shouldn't have been there? Something spicy and stereotypically male. A cheap aftershave mingling with the normal scents of yeast and cinnamon?

'You didn't,' she said. 'You'd better fucking not have.'

Jessica turned on the lights. It didn't matter now if he knew she was home, but she yanked her curtains across anyway before double-locking her door and putting the safety chain across, then dragging a dining chair over and setting it in front of it, not that she could wedge it beneath the handle properly, but it made her feel better.

In the kitchen, she stared at the bin. The lid, a press-down-to-open type, was up in the air. Had she not closed it after shoving his flowers in there? She racked her brain, but the memory was fuzzy. Nothing else was missing or moved. She checked the kitchen, her bedroom and the bathroom.

She was going out of her mind, that was it. The Creep had got to her so badly that she was sensing him everywhere.

'Bedtime,' she said. 'That's enough for one day.'

It was ridiculously early, but she could get up at dawn and continue to plan the next week's baking. The thought made her feel instantly better.

Throwing off her clothes and cleaning her teeth but deciding against the bath, she climbed into bed and turned off her phone. In the morning, she'd contact her insurance company. Decision made.

She closed her eyes and forced herself to think of better days to come. There was always light at the end of the tunnel if only you looked for it hard enough.

It was as she was in the final throes of falling asleep that Jessica realised she hadn't looked in her pantry to see if anything had been moved. The pantry was the reason she'd rented that flat in the first place. It was seven foot long and seven foot wide, with floor-to-ceiling shelving. She'd had a bespoke chilled cabinet fitted and put hooks across the back of the door for aprons.

She sat up in bed, the beat of her heart too loud in her ears. The pantry was easily big enough for an intruder to hide in, quite comfortably, in fact. Warm enough that they could stay there for quite some time, with bottled water and food to boot. She climbed out of bed and stood with her back to the wall, staring at her bedroom door.

Her pantry no longer felt like the safest space she could imagine. Because what, she thought, if someone had found a way to unlock her flat, identified the ideal place to hide, and just never left?

Chapter 21

After three days of obsessing over every news report, interview, and morsel of information, Midnight had woken, still exhausted, with a fit of shivering and coughing. Feeling only a twinge of guilt, she called in sick then cancelled Dawn's carer and set herself up on the sofa with paracetamol and a blanket. Dawn sat at the dining table, happily colouring. An hour later, there was a knock at the door. Midnight, still in pyjamas and fuzzy-headed, opened up.

'Miss Jones?' A woman held up her Necto identification. The man next to her was holding a box.

Midnight took a deep breath. 'Did I do something wrong? I called in to HR and let them know I was unwell.'

It was the pen drive she thought, panicking. They'd found out and now they were here to collect it and tell her she'd been fired. Every muscle in her body was clenched.

'Actually we're here because you've been allocated a home working laptop. There are certain security measures we need to explain, but senior staff are sometimes allowed external access to our systems. Is there somewhere we can set up?'

Midnight tried to internalise her relief and stepped back to allow them access, wishing her flat were tidier.

'You can use the dining table. We'll go through to the bedroom,' she said. 'Shout if you need me.'

Fifteen minutes later, in jeans and a shirt, Midnight listened as they explained the things she could and couldn't do. She wasn't to touch any of the media settings, every email she sent would be verified for security purposes before it was directed to the recipient, and inbuilt GPS meant the laptop couldn't leave her home without setting off an alarm at Necto HQ, and it was best left on, apparently – something to do with not having to go through security. Midnight nodded at everything they said until they left, when she sat and stared at the screen.

It felt more than a little Big Brother, having something of Necto's in her home. She might have anticipated this response if she'd been calling in sick for a fortnight with a broken ankle, but a single day? Perhaps it meant she could work from home more often – that was definitely an idea worth investigating.

She moved Dawn back to the dining table and settled her with a puzzle, then reluctantly dragged herself to the laptop. The least she could do was check her emails, so there was some record of her making an effort. There was nothing unusual in her inbox that day, so she filled a few minutes with trashing unnecessary mail until she reached a forwarded email about the fellow King's College graduate. Her finger hovered above the delete button, until curiosity got the better of her. There was no Gemini D St John on her course, she was certain of that. So perhaps she was just another master's student the same year she was there. The use of the middle initial in the name felt like a very American touch, which made no sense. All her friends had been British or European. Midnight made a cup of tea and tried to forget about it, but something was annoying her. Rather than let it hang in her brain all day, she called King's College alumni office and explained who she was and gave the name of the person she was looking for.

'There's no one called Gemini St John on our system, I'm afraid, but it's so odd that you've phoned,' the records officer said. 'I took a call just a few days ago asking about you – I've never heard the name Midnight before, and it stuck in my mind.'

Midnight suddenly felt cold.

'What did they want?' she asked.

'Your contact details, but of course I said no, we're very security conscious. Then he asked if we had any graduation photos of your course, and I was looking but then he said not to worry as he'd found one online while I had him on hold.'

'Did he give a name?'

'Not that I recall. He said he was an old friend of yours organising some sort of reunion.'

Midnight thanked her, rang off, and stared at the email from Gemini D St John. What the hell was happening? A fictional person trying to find her at Necto, and now at her old college too?

'What the fuck?' she muttered, grabbing a scrap of paper and writing out the letters of her name, then crossing them off, one by one. 'Gemini D St John is an anagram of Midnight Jones.'

Dawn gave a burst of laughter that Midnight couldn't return. Midnight stood without thinking about it and checked the front door was properly shut, then inspected the locks on all the windows.

Why would someone email Necto asking about her using an anagram of her name?

'Your profile is now being assessed by Midnight J,' she said, trying to control the shake of her hands. 'It's Profile K. That's who wants to find out about me. He thinks I know something about him.'

And why the name Gemini? Did he know she was one of twins?

Another email pinged into her work inbox, and Midnight flinched. She hesitated before looking at it, then told herself to grow a backbone. She wasn't the kind of woman who jumped at shadows.

'Media department automated update,' it read. 'Ref. Chloe Martin murder-related information. Per your request.' Beneath it was an attachment containing a new press release linking Chloe's murder to Mae's. The police had publicly announced that DNA evidence connected the deaths, appealed again for information, and released the details of Mae's case to help jog memories in case anyone suspicious had been seen in the local area.

Midnight's mobile rang as she was reading it.

'Hey, Eli said you were off sick so I thought I'd check on you. You okay?' Amber asked.

'I'm just a bit under the weather. Sorry, I should have called. We were meeting for lunch.'

'No problem. I'm actually going with Eli to choose flowers for his mother.'

'You guys are getting close.'

'Don't get jealous,' Amber laughed. 'He asks loads of questions about you too. Sometimes I think he's more interested in you than in me!'

'Does he? That's . . . nice.'

Amber left to get ready for Eli, and Midnight sank to her knees. Someone out there was trying to get as much information about her as they could. At work, Eli was trying to do the same. There were eyes everywhere, but no one she felt able to trust. Not even Amber, who seemed to be best friends with Eli already. In itself, that wasn't unusual. Amber was one of those people you felt like you'd known forever after just a couple of hours, and she was completely unafraid of leaping into new social situations. It was part of what Midnight loved about her, and she wished with her whole heart she felt able to confide in her the way she used to. The added problem now was that by dragging Amber into her mess, she might just be putting her best friend in danger, too.

There were things she had to do alone, and first up was identifying the person who was looking for her. Before he found her.

Chapter 22

Midnight had lived abiding by the rules. At thirteen, she recognised that she was a better care-giver to Dawn than their parents. She'd never been in trouble, never cheated on a test, never spread gossip. That was why applying to TESU to join their Environmental Public Awareness master's degree course felt huge, despite her good intentions. The £250 she paid to make the application balanced the lie to an extent. The thing that was really freaking her out, was hacking into Necto's system.

Having removed the pen drive with the applicant's data from Necto's office – stolen, Midnight's brain insisted, let's not sugar-coat it – she'd created a giant problem for herself. There was no way she could risk taking it in again to review it, but she needed access to Necto's headset to review the footage.

It had taken her a week from the delivery of her new laptop to figure out a plan that stood any chance of working, and another three days before she could get an appointment slot at TESU for the test. She would have preferred to apply under a different name, but that had proved impractical as applicants were required to upload two forms of identification, including their address and date of birth. So Ms Midnight Jones, biting her nails at 8 a.m. – twenty-one days since Chloe's death, thirteen since she'd found out about Mae – had taken a day of leave on Monday and was in attendance at TESU being given an introductory speech in a large group of applicants.

'Please would you all wait here until your name is called. After that you'll be taken through the paperwork then escorted to a booth. Nothing to worry about, it's pain-free,' the staff member said. It didn't get a laugh. Everyone there was nervous. What Necto did and how they did it was the subject of speculation and conspiracy theory, in spite of the fact that their tests were the gold standard for every human resources department.

Midnight was called to a desk behind which sat a man who held his pen like a cigarette. Her eyes lingered on the yellowing around his nails. She'd smoked for a while in her teenage years, until it had become apparent how much her sister was relying on her. Then she'd stopped, and not just the smoking but everything: eating fast food, night swimming, even squirting fake cream into her mouth from those cans which she'd heard could kill you. No Risk Jones was who she'd become. Until she'd found the Profile K.

They walked away from the noisy reception and into a hallway with multiple doors on each side.

'You're in here,' he said, taking a set of keys from his pocket and opening up. 'Bag, coat and mobile in that locker. Make sure your mobile's switched off. We allow a one-hour time slot per applicant. Once the equipment is on, you shouldn't move out of the chair unless it's an emergency.'

Midnight deposited her belongings in the locker and took a seat.

'I'm going to fit your cuff and glove now.' He slipped the contraption over her arm. 'This measures your heart rate, blood oxygen, temperature, perspiration and hand movements. The technical term is a psychogalvanometer. The headset pinpoints which parts of the footage you look at, pupil dilation, and brain activity. It's actually kind of cool.'

Midnight sat still while he got the fittings right.

'Wasn't that poor woman who got murdered from TESU? It was so awful.'

'Lean back,' he told Midnight. 'Try to relax.' He began threading the wires through clips attached to the chair to stabilise the sensors. 'Chloe used to work in this department. No one here wants to talk about it.'

'Gosh, did you know her? I didn't mean to upset you.'

'I did. Chloe was a good person.'

He took hold of Midnight's head, moving it slightly left then right before adjusting the set to make sure each lens was directly in front of her eyes. 'You have a small skull.' He tightened the strap around the top of her head.

'It's so scary. Do you think it was someone she knew?'

'I think you should concentrate on the course you're applying for. What was it again?'

It took Midnight more seconds than it should have, to remember. 'Environmental Public Awareness, master's. I get confused because I was thinking about taking a different course, but I switched at the last moment.'

'Oh really, what was the other choice?'

'Ouch,' Midnight said, grabbing the back of her head. It was the best she could do for a diversion as she didn't have an answer. 'There's some hair caught.'

He undid it, smoothed her hair then reconnected the headset. 'Looks fine to me. Good to go?'

173

'Sure. Do you lock the door?'

'No. That would be a fire risk. If there's an emergency, the system will shut down, an alarm will sound and a red light will flash simultaneously. There'll be a staff member in the corridor to escort you to a safe place. Press the button under your left thumb and the program will start.' He left, closing the door firmly behind him.

Deep breath. It was time for the technical bit. Midnight had no idea if she could pull it off, but she had to try.

She unclipped the headset, freed her hand from the glove, and moved to the locker to take a keyboard with an inset mouse, the pen drive, and a screwdriver from her bag. Midnight was pretty certain a central system notified TESU supervisors when applicants began their tests, so a long delay before starting would raise questions. She was going to have to move at lightning speed.

First, she unscrewed the panel that covered the front of the computer drives then attached the keyboard through an internal USB port, hoping interfacing with the system wouldn't throw up an error code, then reconfigured the headset to play rather than record data, and plugged in the pen drive. There wasn't time to get back into the chair, so Midnight squatted on the floor, put the headset on, then used the keyboard to fast forward through the preliminary sections.

Viewing the footage second time around was no easier, but she was able to steel herself. Running the applicant's data at eight times normal speed helped, stopping at the point where she'd found it impossible to watch.

With her nails pressed painfully into her palm, Midnight watched. One man was hitting another with a mallet. A woman used explosives on some poor creature, and Midnight was grateful she couldn't tell exactly what it had been. When a masked adult used a lighter to do terrible things, Midnight began to gag.

'Make it stop, make it stop, make it—'

Then there was nothing but white noise in her head. A man, masked and gloved, was standing over a woman tied to a bed, scalpel in hand. She was awake and struggling, mouth gagged. He began making tiny, delicate marks, one by one along her left thigh. Trickles of blood began to flow, blossoming furiously as each droplet hit the white sheet.

Midnight's mouth fell open. She couldn't have made a sound if she'd wanted to. It went on and on, slice by slice, until Midnight couldn't bear it any more.

'How the fuck did they get that footage?' she asked the empty room. 'There's no way that's part of any normal test.'

The young woman wasn't Chloe, but it might as well have been. Midnight wanted to bolt from the room and call DI Ruskin then and there, but she had to finish what she'd started.

The next piece of footage was back to animals, the one after that was water-based. Then came the sound of a chainsaw as a man ran through a forest. Midnight hit fast forward, paused it, and rewound. Because what if that had been the inspiration for Mae's death? Surely no one could break into a flat with a chainsaw and not get noticed – the sound alone would have had everyone dialling 999. She watched, dry-mouthed, as the inevitable happened.

'This is a fucking nightmare,' she whispered.

The clip stopped abruptly and a man approached a woman who was tied to a chair, a wire stretched tight between his hands. Midnight shut her eyes. She got the gist. Midnight switched it off. The ten minutes she'd been watching might have been ten hours. She had no idea if that footage sequence would have been available to anyone had they shown no boundaries or reactions to the preceding clips, or if for some reason the Profile K applicant had been singled out to view it. There was no doubt that Necto had the ability to change the footage shown during a test. The real question was why they would want to.

Unless – Midnight held her breath – unless the killer wasn't the person who'd viewed the footage, but the person who'd selected it, playing some sick game. But that would make the killer someone inside Necto.

'That's not possible,' Midnight said. 'I really am losing the fucking plot.'

There were three rapid knocks on the door. Midnight leapt towards the computer.

'Miss Jones? Is everything all right?'

'One minute, I'm not fully dressed!' she shouted, ripping out the pen drive and keyboard before shoving the computer panel roughly back on, then racing to the locker to shut everything away. 'I . . . got too hot.' She pulled her shirt out from her waistband and undid a couple of buttons before putting the glove back on.

The door opened.

'You okay? Gosh, yes, you do look flustered,' a woman said. 'We didn't get the signal that you'd started, so I thought I should check on you.'

Midnight giggled nervously. 'I was having a bit of a panic attack. Stupid really. I've just invested a lot in getting this far.'

'There's nothing to be worried about. You can't fail this test, it's just about maximising course suitability. You want to press the green button while I'm still here? Then I'll slip out once I know you're okay.'

'Sure,' Midnight said. 'Thanks.' She wriggled the glove back into the right position, and pressed go.

176

Chapter 23

Back at home, Midnight got Dawn into some warm clothes to avoid her catching a chill, and prepared to push her to the supermarket where Mae had worked. What she was doing was unconscionable. She'd never in her life used Dawn as any sort of accompaniment before – prop, her brain insisted, bitch that you are, you're using her as a prop because you're scared to lose your job. Yet here she was, pushing Dawn in the wheelchair they used on long days out when Dawn would get too tired to walk, nearing the entrance to the supermarket on Aristotle Road.

'I'm sorry, sweetie,' she told Dawn. 'I'll buy chocolate cake as a treat. Are you warm enough?'

Dawn nodded. There were odd moments when she seemed to be able to listen and respond, but they were few and far between. Still, they gave Midnight hope that her sister got something from their conversations, more than just the reassurance of hearing her voice. If nothing else, Midnight's day off to make her TESU application had given them an extra half day together, and that was always the best possible way to spend her time.

'We won't be long. I just need to find a shop assistant to talk to.'

Dawn gave a broad smile and reached up to hold Midnight's hand as they entered. Her heart swelled, as it always did when her sister managed a fluent, purposeful movement that had emotional intent behind it.

Inside, the supermarket was only moderately busy. The staff looked subdued. Midnight had to pick her moment carefully. They would have been flooded with attention in the days since the police had released Mae's details.

Midnight picked up a basket, then they made their way past fruit and veg, talking about dinner and breakfast, and what to put in the freezer. She was the very picture of a carer, the unmistakable loving twin sister, and she knew it.

Pausing next to the bread section where a young man was stacking shelves, she gave him a bright smile.

'Hi, is this gluten-free? My sister reacts badly otherwise.'

'Not sure,' he mumbled. 'I only started this week. I can call someone for you.'

'No need,' she said. He wouldn't be able to help her. 'I've just spotted the loaf we normally get. Thanks anyway.'

Midnight picked up Dawn's favourite chocolate cake before moving round to tinned goods, and busying herself choosing items while looking for staff members. An elderly woman, no more than five foot two and wearing a cerise dress with white polka dots, tried to reach a packet of pasta but knocked it to the floor.

'I'll get it,' Midnight said.

'Thank you, dear,' she said. 'Look at you two. Aren't you both just beautiful?'

178

'That's very kind,' Midnight said. 'Do you need any more help? We're not in a hurry.'

'That's all right. I like to take my time. It's the only bit of my day when I get out, really. I never buy too much. I just like the walk here, then I get a cup of tea at the cafe next door.'

'What a good idea,' Midnight said. 'Have you lived around here long?'

'Sixty-five years give or take, since I was a girl. It's changed so much I barely recognise it sometimes.'

Midnight gave up on the shopping and followed her down the aisle to kitchen rolls.

'Talking of change, awful about the poor girl who worked here. Makes me feel scared to live nearby.' She picked up a roll of bin liners and put them in her basket.

'Just terrible. I didn't know her well, mind. Maureen on the tills told me she mainly did evenings, and I don't go out after dark.'

Midnight's heart sank. There were only so many people she could talk to in one visit without arousing suspicion.

'Very sensible. Well, we'd better be going. You made me fancy a cup of tea. Lovely to meet you.'

At the end of the shop, there was only one person on a till. Midnight and Dawn got in line.

'Cake?' Dawn asked, grinning and pointing into the basket.

'Of course, cake. Your favourite. We'll go home now, don't worry.'

They moved slowly while people took their time packing bags and Midnight remembered why she always had her shopping delivered. The elderly woman joined the queue behind her.

'All right, Doris? Got everything you wanted?' a voice said from behind the greetings card display. 'Come on over. I'll open up another till for you.'

179

Midnight stared at her name tag. Maureen was at work.

She followed Doris to the new till, in spite of nearing the front of the queue, and engaged her again.

'Sorry, you mentioned a cafe nearby? Where is that?' Midnight asked her.

'It's Thimbles, this side of the road, past the little toy shop,' Doris said. 'How you doing, Maureen? Things any better?'

'Not really,' Maureen said quietly. 'We've had a string of people in asking about Mae. Bloody ghoulish, is what it is. People should know better.'

Midnight emptied her basket onto the conveyor belt.

'We were just saying as much, weren't we, lovely?' Doris directed at Midnight.

Midnight put Dawn's cake down carefully, leaned towards the women and kept her voice low. 'Absolutely. I get people coming up to me all the time and asking what's wrong with my sister, like they feel like they have the right to our personal information.' She hated herself. 'Who does that? I know it's nothing like what you're going through with Mae. I'm so sorry. You must be devastated.'

Maureen nodded. 'We are. Feels like everyone wants a piece of it. What is it about tragedy that gets people so excited? It was a media frenzy outside when the news first got out,' she said, ringing up Doris's total.

Midnight could have kissed Doris for paying in cash and slowly counting out coins. She let her voice rise back up to normal volume to see what other interested parties might join in.

'It's not okay that women have to be scared walking home around here. This area used to feel safe, even in the evenings. These days I have to think twice about walking my sister to the shops, and it's heartbreaking. Not just Mae, but that poor woman from TESU as well.' Murmurs and nods all round, and now people in the next till line were listening too. 'I heard the police are looking for a link between the two of them. You end up praying it's nothing that could make you a target too,' Midnight said.

'Could be this social medium stuff,' Doris offered. No one was rude enough to correct her.

'I reckon it's just someone who lives local,' the man queueing behind them added. 'Opportunistic, like.'

'They were checking TESU, too,' Midnight said. 'Mae wasn't thinking about applying there, was she?'

Let it be the link. Please, let it be the link.

'No, love. Our Mae had other plans,' Maureen said, running Midnight's shopping under the barcode reader. Midnight couldn't keep the disappointment off her face.

'She could take care of herself too,' the man on the next till put in. 'Kept herself fit, knew some of that martial arts stuff. Whoever did that to her must have got a shock. No way she went down without a fight, bless her.'

'I'm off for that cup of tea,' Doris said. 'I can't stand to think about it any more. Do you and your sister want to join me?'

It would have been impolite not to, and Dawn was enjoying being out of the house. Maureen finished bagging the shopping and Midnight paid.

'We'd love to,' Midnight told Doris.

'What's even worse,' the man on the till next to them was explaining to his customer, 'is that she was about to leave. Mae was so excited. I never saw her as happy as when she got her confirmation letter through.'

Midnight stopped what she was doing. 'Confirmation letter for what?'

181

'For the army, darlin'. Mae wanted to serve her country. Two months from now she was due to start her training. Bloody tragedy. She'd have been amazin'.'

'Come on then, dears,' Doris said from the doorway. 'I'm buying.'

Chapter 24

The Applicant

He and Jessica had lived at opposite ends of the same village. It was reasonably large as villages went. His father had been on the local council and had lectured him often and at length about the responsibilities that came with overseeing the budget for four thousand inhabitants. Catchment areas and bus routes being what they were, he and Jessica had gone to separate secondary schools which also meant they had different friends (well, she had friends).

He was twelve when he saw her first. She was lying in the long grass at the edge of the village green, near the children's play area. The sun had baked the grass brown, and not a leaf was moving on the tree branches in which he had been sitting. Not hiding, exactly. Just sitting, enjoying the day, watching the ice-cream van make its rounds. He had no money for it. His parents said those people were using the vans to avoid paying taxes.

Jessica was sweeter than any ice-cream. He watched as she rolled down a hill with a friend, secreting himself more completely in the foliage and hardly breathing as they came to a stop on their backs, giggling their heads off. Jessica reached out and held her friend's hand for a moment, and the girls had lain there looking up into the endless blue sky until a woman shouted. The friend shot up, racing away and waving. 'Bye Jessica! See you tomorrow!'

Jessica stayed as she was, hand outstretched as if still holding the other one, looking so at peace with the world that he had stopped breathing. He hadn't experienced that bliss again until Chloe, then again with Mae.

He didn't know how long Jessica stayed on the village green, because a bird decided to empty its bowels all over his back, and the thought of her looking up and seeing him like that was too awful. He'd crept down and run home. A few boys had seen him, boys who already shouted names and spat at him when they could get away with it.

'Hey, Birdshit!' they called after him.

He was called Birdshit at school and around the village from then until his parents sent him away at sixteen. Officially, he was being sent away to get a better education. The actual purpose was for him to get what they referred to as a 're-education'.

For four blissful years, he'd worshipped the ground Jessica walked on from afar. He waited for her school bus then followed her home to see where she lived. He spent his weekends wandering the village, hoping desperately to catch a glimpse of her. Those odd moments when she appeared were magical. She wasn't one of those girls who hung out at the bus stop smoking cigarettes with the boys, nor did she wear skirts that appeared to grow shorter with each passing month. Jessica was a jeans and hoodie kind of girl. His mother would have said that she kept herself nice.

He never spoke to her. Not once. By chance one day, he'd been exiting the village shop as she'd been entering and they'd brushed elbows. He'd whirled round to apologise, to look more closely into her beautiful eyes and hear her voice, but Jessica hadn't even noticed him. That was all right, because he had some stuff to work on. Lots of stuff, apparently.

The first time his parents had reacted strangely to his behaviour was when his mother cut herself with the garden shears, causing a deep gash to the palm of her hand. He was eight, maybe nine. His father had rushed her into the house to clean the wound, and he remembered walking into the kitchen. She wasn't crying, but she had her eyes closed against the pain and was biting down hard with her top teeth on her bottom lip.

'Apply pressure to your mother's hand,' his father had instructed. 'I'm going to call the doctor. Push down firmly. It's just blood. It won't hurt you.'

His father hadn't needed to worry. He'd wandered over calmly and pressed the gauze pad down on his mother's hand until a trickle of blood had run out and along her little finger.

It was mesmerising, the beauty of blood. The depth and complexity of it. The way it moved, almost alive, as if it had been trying to escape all along and had finally found its route. He'd peeled the gauze back to see where it had come from, and the gash was breathtaking. Inside was a river, a red tide pulsing upwards and washing her palm. He leaned down to look, and God, then he could smell it and the copper stung his tongue before he even knew what he was doing—

The slap came from behind him to the back of his head, his father stepping back to stare at him.

'He licked it!' his father screamed at his mother. 'He took the gauze off your hand and he . . . he tasted it.'

185

'You're mistaken,' his mother had shouted back. 'Why would he?'

There'd been a scramble to find a clean gauze pad (he'd dropped the first one on the floor) then his parents went to get medical assistance, leaving him alone with orders to mop the blood from the floor then go to his room and not move. There were some threats issued with the orders, the details of which escaped him now, but the next hour had been his and his alone.

He'd seen blood before – his own – from minor grazes and cuts, never spilling more than a drop or two, but this was something completely different. He dabbled his fingertips in the droplets, swirling and painting, smelling and tasting, until it dried out. Then he took his mother's pastry brush from her drawer and used it to transfer the little crimson flakes onto a scrap of foil which he folded carefully and stuck under his bed with a ball of Blu-Tack. Thrilled, but not stupid, he climbed into the shower to wash off the blood.

His father would be having words with him later that night, and he had no idea what to say. That he hadn't planned it? That he hadn't even thought about it? That one minute he'd been holding his mother's hand and trying to help, and the next he'd been unable to stop himself dipping his head to taste it? That didn't seem like something his father would want to hear.

As it turned out, his father simply avoided him for the next week. His mother had cancelled a sleepover to which he'd invited a classmate, stopped having her friends round for tea, and withdrew her hand every time he reached for her. The lesson was unambiguous. What he'd done was strange and dirty, and they were never going to look at him the same way again.

Time passed. The gulf between them lessened, and it was as forgotten as things can be when you've shocked your parents so badly. Everything settled for a year or more until the day a deer tried to hop over the back gate into their garden and became entangled in wire. His parents had both been out at work and he was home alone during a school staff training day. The poor creature had screamed. He'd never heard an animal scream before and it had him running from the house to see what was wrong. The gardener wasn't around, and his parents had instructed him to call them only if it was a matter of life or death, by which he assumed they meant his own rather than some non-domesticated mammal's.

By the time he was close enough to the creature to help, it was too late for either of them. The deer wasn't going to survive, even if he managed to free it, and he had neither the willpower nor the ability to walk back to the house and phone for help.

The deer's legs were awash with red, as was the wire, the fence posts, the bushes, the grass and soil. It was like a dream. Walking slowly forward, holding out his hand, he knew he had to touch it. Even if the deer kicked and bit him, it would be worth it to smell that living mineral scent and wash his hands in its flow.

By the time his parents got home, the deer had breathed its last. They found him sitting on the ground in front of the carcass, naked and red from his hair to his toes. His mother had vomited, run back to the house, taken a full bottle of sherry from the cupboard, and disappeared to the guest room for the night. His father had growled at him to stay where he was, then brought the garden hose and washed him down. Even when the water ran clear, he kept going. By the time his father finally relented, leaving his skin sore, his body temperature approaching something that felt like flaming ice, he realised that his father had been crying as he'd hosed him. It was the first time he'd understood that there might be something truly wrong with him.

There was a psychologist, then a psychiatrist, a therapist, then a hypnotherapist. He told them all the truth until it was clear that none of them wanted the truth. They wanted the lie they were being paid to extract from him. That he'd been going through a phase. That he was better. That he was considering signing up to do a sponsored walk raising money for children starving in some distant country. Good boy. Well done. Much improved. All children did strange things from time to time. It was probably because he was an only child, possibly because he'd been born by emergency caesarian section.

His parents had buried themselves in work. They were often out in the evenings and away at weekends. His time alone allowed him to indulge his fascination unseen and without judgement. Some of the memories were better than others. He'd got carried away with some raw beef and ended up with food poisoning. Then there was his attempt to see how it would feel to watch the blood flow from his own body, making a cut to his thigh that had been deeper than he'd expected, and left him passed out on the bathroom floor. There were other events over the years but worst of all – the last straw, as his mother would tell him almost daily in the five months between it happening and him being sent away to a specialist rehabilitative sixth form boarding school – was what happened with Benjamin Hoffman.

At his new college, he learned to hide his anti-social interest. His parents received nothing but positive reports from college. The cold baths, a Victorian treatment for almost any form of so-called hysteria or strange behaviour, were working. The art therapy sessions were extremely beneficial (they didn't let him use red paint for fear of 'setting him off'). The strict vegetarian diet had quelled his unnatural interest in meat. The early bedtimes and daily exercise routines took care of any other perfectly normal desires he might have. Onanism was dealt with by means of an ice bucket, decades before anyone thought that might be a fun challenge. The therapist insisted on full disclosure of almost any thought he'd ever had, every single memory of Jessica and all of her personal details, a thorough history of his relationship with his mother and father, and every single incident involving blood was jotted down carefully in her notebooks.

In spite of the Benjamin Hoffman event, and the damage done to his parents' reputation, he'd come out of college with an impressive set of A-levels, an offer from the sort of university that would have made any other parents proud, and with an understanding of how to control his behaviour, or so he'd thought.

Now, there were really only a few things he wanted. One of them was probably going to get him arrested and imprisoned for life. The other was Jessica. And given that he had no intention of going near her any day soon, instead he chose women who reminded him of her. Like Chloe. Like Mae. Then there was Midnight Jones. He had the photo of her by his bed, taken at some charity fundraiser for brain-damaged kids, and he looked at it more often than he should. Did she know everything about him, or nothing at all? Could he risk going near her, given that she might already have reported whatever his profile had shown her? Could he risk letting her live? There was so much going on in his head. Too much. And it made it so very hard to sleep. But he felt more alive than he ever had before, in his whole damned life.

Chapter 25

During a lengthy cup of tea with Doris, while Midnight tried to hide the sound of her tapping heel and the fact that she was looking at the clock every two minutes, Dawn had a wonderful time. Doris didn't ask what was 'wrong' with her, didn't condescend, and wasn't the least bit worried about the mess Dawn made eating her cake. On any other day, Midnight would have loved it. Doris lit up the room. She reminded Midnight of her father's mum – the much-loved Granny Apples, named for her tiny orchard that had been Midnight and Dawn's favourite place in the world when they were toddlers. Granny Apples had died shortly after their fourteenth birthdays, and left a hole in their world, or perhaps she'd always filled the hole that their parents failed to plug after her death.

Midnight liked Doris's laugh, as loud and vibrant as her clothes. She saw the way everyone who came and went in the cafe smiled at her, whether they knew her or not. More than anything, she liked the way Doris chatted non-stop to Dawn, patting her hand and making her sister giggle. Dawn, in her own unique world most of the time, had come alive in the older woman's presence, as if she'd always been waiting for her. By the time they were ready to leave, they'd exchanged phone numbers and addresses, and promised to meet up for another cuppa soon. Dawn demanded multiple hugs from Doris before she could bear to let her go, so Doris slipped out, very quietly as Midnight was paying, to avoid upsetting her.

As they were exiting, Dawn began waving and pulling Midnight back towards their table.

'No, honey, we're leaving now. We have to get home,' Midnight said. 'I promise I'll bring you back next week. It's a nice place, isn't it?'

She tried to manoeuvre Dawn towards the door but her sister was having none of it, pulling even harder for their table. Midnight caught a glimpse of something bright pink under the table.

'Doris's scarf!' Midnight said. 'That's what you were going back for. Hold on, I'll get it.' She leaned down to pick up the length of patterned cloth from beneath the chair.

'Dos!' Dawn said, pointing at the scarf. Midnight's heart leapt. Dawn spoke so rarely, and she almost never learned names, certainly not those of people she was unfamiliar with. She looked at her watch. Doris only lived around the corner, and whatever else she wanted to get on with, if her sister was so captivated and happy, then that moment had to be treasured and prolonged. They could walk there, though she was grateful for the wheelchair which would make the journey faster. 'Come on. We'll take it back to her now.'

They made their way down a few side streets until they reached Hedgerow House. Never had a building been so inappropriately named. Doris had explained that it was made up of flats with a warden who could be called on in an

191

emergency, but just the thought of such a vibrant soul living in such a depressingly grey structure made Midnight's heart sink.

She checked along the row of paint-peeling doors and found 16c. Putting a smile on her face, she knocked. Doris opened up almost immediately.

'You left your scarf,' Midnight said. 'We're not stalking you!'

'Dos!' Dawn shouted, holding out her hands.

'Dawn!' Doris shouted back, bending down to give her a kiss on the cheek as if they were old friends parted for months. 'Thank you for bringing that back to me. Come on in, you two. Sorry about the state of the place. I keep asking the landlord to do it up, but there's always some excuse or other.'

'We can't stay, I'm afraid. I have a list of things I need to get on with at home.'

'Just for a minute then,' Doris said. 'I have something for this lovely girl.'

They left the wheelchair outside and went in. It was cold. Much colder than it should have been, Midnight thought, looking crossly at the inadequate windows and ill-fitting door. The walls needed painting, there were patches of damp high in the corners, and the carpet was threadbare, but every inch of every surface had been spruced up with cheerful pictures, patterned blankets and pretty plants.

'I love how you've decorated it,' Midnight called to Doris who was opening and closing drawers by the sound of it in what she assumed was a bedroom.

'Oh, it's mostly tat, but I do like a bit of colour. They can dress me in grey when I'm heading for the grave. Until then, I want my world to be full of colour. Ah, here it is!'

She came back into the lounge and handed Dawn a long soft woollen scarf of every conceivable shade. Dawn's eyes lit up.

'For you, my dear. I thought you'd like it!' Dawn clapped as Doris wound it gently around her neck, draping the ends down her shoulders. 'Made it myself.'

'We can't take it,' Midnight said. 'That looks like it was a lot of work.'

'It was, and I can give it to whoever I like. Now, do you have time for another cuppa?'

'We don't, but you're welcome to our house any time, and we'll make trips to the cafe a regular thing, shall we? I know Dawn would like that.' Doris smiled. 'And I would too. I can't promise much in the way of great hospitality. I'm not a great cook but I have a constant supply of tea and coffee.'

'I'll take you up on that,' Doris said. 'Now get this precious one home before you both get tired out. And you'll call me, won't you, if you need anything? I do like to feel needed, and to get out. This place is all right, but the telly-box isn't what I'd call company.'

Her smile faltered for the first time, and Midnight's heart missed a beat. Lovely Doris, in spite of her natural upbeat personality and her irrepressible warmth, was lonely. She was grateful that Granny Apples never had to live in a place like that. No one should have to spend their final years in such a tiny, dismal box of a home.

'We'll call very soon,' Midnight said. 'And the same goes for you. If you ever need us, just pick up the phone.'

Many more kisses and hugs later, with an ecstatic Dawn stroking her new scarf, Midnight walked home desperate to get the connections right in her head. What was the link between Chloe and Mae?

They arrived home to a stack of post that Midnight knew she should deal with, even though the only thing she could think about was calling DI Ruskin just as soon as she found his card. It was way past time for her to share everything she knew with him. She checked the kitchen and her bedroom, then under the pile of letters, finding one from Dawn's Care at Home Agency marked urgent. Cursing, she ripped open the envelope as she continued to wander around looking for Ruskin's number, stopping as she got a few lines down the letter.

Dear Miss Jones,
We regret that the current economic crisis has made it necessary for us to increase our charges. Our prices will be rising from next week onwards as follows:
Hourly rate between 6 a.m. – 6 p.m. £30 per hour.
Anti-social hours fees between 6 p.m. – 6 a.m. £50 per hour . . .

Midnight's heart was thumping. Other details followed, including a request for an electric wheelchair, and increased notice for late stays, but all Midnight could focus on was the money. She helped Dawn move from her wheelchair to the sofa and got her settled before doing the maths. Fifty hours a week at £30 per hour was £1,500 per week. That was without a late night or time off at a weekend. It was without holiday respite care. That came to more than £6,000 per month, which was pretty much the same as it would cost for Dawn to go into a high-quality residential home, and Midnight had sworn on her own life that she would never, ever do that to her twin. Not a chance. She and Dawn were never going to be separated.

Midnight took a deep breath and tried to calm down. With her exponential pay rise and additional holiday when she could dispense with carers temporarily, and if she stopped booking extra cover for evenings out, they could just about exist. Just about. No margin for error. No margin for the odd bottle of wine or facial either.

She looked at her sister. It was worth it. But she couldn't lose her job. More than ever, they needed financial security. If she hadn't had the promotion, she would never have been able to cope with the rising care prices.

Midnight checked her watch. Amber would be out of work now. If she couldn't call Ruskin and tell him everything she knew thanks to her suddenly precarious financial position, she'd have to find another way forward. It would take more of her time and energy, but she had a skillset and it was time to start using it, although she was going to need some help at the outset. What she needed was someone who could help her understand the nature of the threat. Perhaps then she could help the police without having to give up Necto's corporate secrets. There was only one person she'd ever come into contact with who had the skills and experience in psychological profiling required. That woman had helped Necto develop their profiling software. Midnight had seen her speak, and even been on a training course with her, she just couldn't remember her name. It had been something unusual, and it was on the tip of her tongue.

Hey Amber, having a home day with Dawn. Sorry I missed lunch again – hope you found someone to eat with. Back tomorrow, I promise. You alone? she texted.

Just me and an enormous iced cherry almond bun I bought from the new woman they've got coming in to sell us dopamine through baked goods. You have to try her stuff. It's (almost) better than sex with hot barmen, was Amber's reply..

My iron willpower remains unbroken. She had some nice bread yesterday tho. Hey, wanted to offer a client a bespoke resource. Do you remember the name of the profiler they used to help develop the software? American? She was odd but good, Midnight prompted.

Hold on.

Midnight found DI Ruskin's card in her wallet while she waited for Amber.

Found it. Dr Woolwine. She was weird, Amber wrote.

That's it. Thanks Amb.

Want me to come over? I can bring a bottle.

That was quite the offer, coming from Amber. She always declared that quiet nights in were strictly for the over-forties. Midnight reminded herself how lucky she was to have a friend who was willing to change their own patterns to suit hers, but much as she would have loved to share a bottle of red and pour her heart out, she needed to be alone.

Thanks, but not tonight. Dawn's restless so need to keep flat quiet. Love you. Thanks for info x.

How many times in one day could she use her beloved sister as an excuse? The answer, sadly, was as many as it took.

Midnight googled Dr Woolwine and found a website with the details of the psychological profiling consultancy she ran.

American forensic psychologist, Dr Woolwine, first name Connie, was the sort of person Midnight had always wanted to be. She spoke her mind, not in a way that was crass or cruel, just whatever she thought, almost unfiltered.

Two problems were lodged between Midnight and the person she needed to speak with. The first was an absolutely gigantic lie about the information she needed and why she needed it. The second was funding. How did you approach one of the world's most renowned profilers, ask for her help, and have no money to pay her? If she pretended it was a Necto job, there would be no reason to have a problem paying, so that wasn't going to work.

As she thought about it, Midnight made Dawn a few little triangle sandwiches and filled up a beaker with orange squash.

'No,' Dawn said. 'Moo-moo cup.'

'I think it's in the dishwasher,' Midnight said. 'Can we use this one for tonight?'

'Moo-moo cup,' Dawn insisted. 'Moo-moo cup.'

'Okay, babe. I'm getting it.' Midnight wandered into the kitchen to fetch the old black and white cup Dawn had always loved. Apart from the photo, it was one of the few things left from her parents' era. Midnight wanted to throw it into a furnace. How could her mother have done it? Fathers left all the time. And no, that wasn't okay either, but a mother leaving the child who would always need her? Heartless cow. She threw the moo-moo cup into the bin, burst into tears, then got it out again and washed it.

Shit, she was worn out. She decided to make contact with Connie Woolwine by email, then go to bed.

'Dear Dr Woolwine,' she typed into the query box of the contacts page. 'I work at Necto, London, and I have a query I think perhaps only you can help with. It's not official, so I won't blame you if you say no, but I don't know who else to ask. I heard your talk when the new profiling system was introduced. I was a data analyst then but now I'm in client liaison. Sorry and thank you. Midnight Jones.' She put her contact details in the required boxes, then got Dawn ready for bed.

She accepted the truth while she was putting pyjamas on Dawn and manoeuvring her into bed, that her sister was getting harder to move around. Central London was no place for her. They needed to be in a little cottage in the country where Dawn could spend her days watching ducks and squirrels. Maybe they could even have a cat or a dog. Dawn's existence was just day after day of getting through the hours, when it could and should be so much more.

Five years, she thought. Stick it out at Necto. Get promoted again. Move to a three-bedroom place where she could advertise for a live-in carer who would get paid, in part, with free room and board. Start to save some money. Move to the country. Become a remote profiling consultant. Work online. Spend every day with her sister, learning to make . . .

'Fuck it. Jam or pickles or something,' she said.

Her mobile rang and she assumed it was Amber, swiped the video call icon and said, 'Give me a minute. Dawn needs her teddy. I can't even start to tell you how utterly crap my day has been.'

'Not what I expected, but okay. That sounds as good a place to begin as any.'

Midnight stared into the screen. 'Oh, fuck.'

'You'd think it would be the case that I never get greeted like that, but it happens more often than you'd believe. Midnight Jones, I presume?'

'Dr Woolwine. I'm so bloody sorry, I wasn't expecting . . .'

'That's fine. I interrupted you putting your daughter to bed. I'll call back in a while.'

'Please don't go. I really do need to talk to you.' Dawn began waving and blowing kisses. 'My twin sister,' Midnight explained. 'Dawn, I've got to speak to the lady. I'm putting your star lights on. Watch them for a while and I'll be back to read you a story. Love you.'

There were a few seconds while Connie Woolwine waited and Midnight settled Dawn down, then the bedroom door was shut and Midnight sank onto the sofa.

'Your sister is beautiful. Must be hard, seeing yourself reflected and wondering how you came out the way you did, and how she seemingly got the short straw,' Woolwine said. Midnight didn't even try to answer, it was far too close to her every waking thought. The line crackled suddenly. 'Sorry. I'm in Venezuela consulting on a case. The hotel Wi-Fi is about as reliable as a used car dealership. Anyway, I was intrigued by your note and I had a few minutes to spare, plus I love your name. So how can I help?'

'Yes,' Midnight gave a small cough. 'So, um, I have a situation at work with a profile and I thought it was sort of a software glitch but while I was doing the data analysis, it did seem to me that probably there were some oversights, um, that you might be able to explain—'

'Let me stop you there,' Connie Woolwine said. 'You're lying to me. I don't know why or about what. We can talk about it, and I suspect you have a good reason for contacting me because your baseline emotions are genuine, but everything about you is off right now. So I'm going to hang up, and you're going to decide what you want to say to me. There's no rush. I'm not putting a timer on it or any of that bullshit. You look like someone in need, and I checked you out already, so I know you actually do work for Necto. Take a beat, figure it out, then call me back.'

The line went dead.

Chapter 26

It took no more than five minutes to pull herself together. Someone else was going to die. Another Chloe, another Mae. Then there was the thought Midnight had been trying to cram to the very back of her brain, unsuccessfully. Someone had been trying to get information about her too. It might have been a coincidence, and it might have been a joke, but she was jumping at shadows and lying awake half the night. Midnight knew enough about the psychology of serious crime to understand that violent murders of young women by a stranger were both impulsive and compulsive, meaning the murderer had an itch they needed to scratch, and they weren't simply going to stop. Not now they'd got a taste for it. The only person in a position to help her was Connie Woolwine, and not lying to her didn't require telling the whole truth.

'Good, you're back,' Woolwine said, without any other greeting. She was wearing a black T-shirt that looked the worse for wear, and was sipping from a bottle of beer, her hair pushed back by sunglasses as she leaned into the camera. Midnight got the impression Connie Woolwine could see through her mobile, halfway around the world and into her soul. 'Let's talk.'

'I can't tell you why I'm asking,' Midnight said. 'And I can't pay you. You'll have questions I won't be able to answer. So if you don't want to do this—'

'Why did you lie to me before?' Woolwine asked, her voice light, curious rather than annoyed.

'I can't afford to lose my job. It'll be my sister who suffers if I do. I don't want her to have to go into residential care.'

'High stakes.' Woolwine whistled.

'Can I ask how you knew I lied?' Midnight wished she'd taken her own bottle of beer from the fridge before making the call.

'Lack of clarity. Fidgeting. Looking away from the screen. Vague language. A light sheen of sweat beneath your eyes. Tense neck. You're a terrible liar. It wasn't a party trick.'

'I'll remember that. Thanks for taking my call.'

'I was intrigued. So what's this about? I ask that with the caveat that my time is limited, I'm half a world away, and I can't get heavily involved. I'm yours for as long as this phone call lasts, and that's all.'

'I understand. It's about two murders in London. Well, three actually,' Midnight began.

'Uh-huh. I know a little about them. My work partner, Brodie Baarda, was a former Met police detective inspector. He's been keeping a close eye on the murders as they're on his old stomping ground. He's spoken to some former colleagues about the details. Part of our job is to stay up to date with current crime events. The third death was collateral, so technically not part of the series, I think.'

'That's right. I guess I need to know if watching a video could make someone do something that terrible. Or maybe *how* it makes them do something like that. I mean, what *sort* of person would watch a video then do that?'

Woolwine stayed silent and stared at her. Midnight wanted to look away but didn't dare in case the psychologist ended the call again.

'That's three questions,' Woolwine said. 'But I have one for you first. Why is this your problem?'

'I can't answer that,' Midnight said. 'I wish I could, but the ramifications would be too serious. And because I *think* that maybe I know something, but I don't *know* that I know anything. I just can't shake this link I've made in my head and I need . . .' the tears started again. She knew they might. The last couple of weeks had been bizarre and devastating, and at the same time none of it seemed real.

'Here's what we're going to do,' Woolwine said. 'You're going to take a few real deep breaths with me. Focus only on me. You need to let the stress go to get some clarity. At the moment you're bombarding your brain with too many different signals. No one's mind works efficiently like that. I'm going to answer your questions, with the limited knowledge I have about these crimes and how they may link to the videos. I'm going to say this before I start, and I need you to remember it: whatever you're imagining may not be true. Whatever is happening, you're not responsible for. Got it?'

'Got it,' Midnight said.

Connie Woolwine was the single most confident person she'd ever been in contact with. Quiet, internal confidence. It was almost impossible to look away from her.

'So these videos, are we talking about a movie or a game, some sort of porn or what?'

'I can't tell you much, except that I think maybe the videos were curated because of their extreme violent content. It's not mainstream viewing.'

'All right. We'll start by assuming the man who committed these murders did actually see these videos.' She was writing as she spoke, looking straight into the camera, as if her brain and hand were completely unconnected. Midnight tried to look into her eyes instead of staring at the pen. 'I understand they have the perpetrator's DNA. Given the fact that they haven't identified him, he's obviously not in their database which means, firstly, that he's never been convicted of an offence, and second, it's the first time his DNA has gone on record or the police would be linking other crimes to him as well.'

'How can this be the first time he's hurt anyone?' Midnight whispered.

'Oh, it's not. He's done other things. Smaller things that he managed to keep hidden. So did his self-control bubble just pop or was it something more triggering? You think those particular videos gave him the inspiration he needed to kill.'

'I do,' Midnight said. 'That's exactly it.'

'But there's plenty of material out there. There's the dark net or the backroom stuff they pretend not to have at the worst kind of adult stores. He could have seen similar videos easily if he'd looked hard enough.'

Woolwine was drawing a diagram on the page as she stared into Midnight's eyes. Not at her, Midnight thought. More like through her. It was as if she didn't even know she was still writing.

'Was he so entranced by what he saw that he replicated a video in the first murder?' Midnight was opening her mouth to speak when Woolwine continued. 'Nope. Why would that have been the catalyst? Why not any other video at any other time? Or a book, a TV show, even just a daydream. If this is what does it for him, why not just follow his own instincts and do the things he's been longing to do?' She stopped writing abruptly and chewed the end of her pen. 'Minute of silence please.'

Midnight watched. Connie Woolwine looked left, up, left again. Her mouth was forming the tiny rapid shapes of internal dialogue. She shook her head and closed her eyes momentarily, then the noiseless speech began again. It was more gripping than any movie Midnight had ever watched, as if Woolwine's skull was transparent and Midnight could see all the cogs whirring and turning.

'Okay,' Woolwine said. 'This guy isn't young, by which I mean not a teenager, I'd say mid-twenties at the youngest. These were no clumsy, disorganised, impulse crimes. Compulsive, yes. Impulsive, no. And they're sexually driven but not sex-centric.'

'I don't understand. If the women weren't raped or sexually assaulted, then how can these crimes be sexual?'

'First, because he's actively choosing women to hurt, so there's almost inevitably a sexual undercurrent. But there's something else happening at the crime scenes that's driving him. Something exciting at a primaeval level that gets this guy off, maybe the screaming or the helplessness. It just doesn't come in the form of a vagina. Perhaps it's the simple idea of a woman, or maybe it's that what he wants to do is such a deeply personal thing, he wouldn't get the sense of intimacy with a man that he craves with a woman.'

'So, he wants to hurt her, but he wants it to feel like an intimate experience. Like a micro-relationship?' Midnight offered.

'Perfect observation,' Woolwine said. 'I once tracked a guy across China who was obsessed with men's elbows. He killed five different men amputating their arms so he could play with their elbow joints. It was still sexual, just in his own unique way.'

'Shit the bed,' Midnight said.

'That is a new phrase to me and one I shall be using later. Baarda is going to hate it, so thank you. We'll consider that full payment. Now, back to it. Yes, definitely sexual. Both deaths involved blades from what I've heard. Hmm. But we were talking about him. Where's he been until now? Why nothing like this before?'

'Maybe abroad?' Midnight offered.

'Possibly, but the DNA profile will be with Interpol by now and there have been no hits on their system either. That still leaves the countries who don't routinely store or share DNA data. Let's assume he's British. Got to recreate. Hold on.' She set her mobile down. Midnight could see a basic hotel room, tidy save for stacks of paper and a side wall covered in photos and maps. 'Ignore all that. I'm mid-case. I need more room to do this.' She grabbed several sheets of blank paper and laid them out in a long rectangle. 'Midnight Jones, this is how I work. If it freaks you out, you can leave me to it, and I'll get back to you.'

'No, I want to see. I . . . I think you're amazing.'

'Save the fan-girling until I've given you useful information.' She grinned broadly. 'Right, let's go.'

She drew the rough outline of a woman on the papers. Scaled down, the figure came out about a quarter of the size of Woolwine herself.

'I've got her tied to the bed. She's gagged. There's been a bit of a fight. I've taken her clothes off. What else have I done? Locked the door, closed the curtains, probably got an apron on, or a change of clothes with me, I know this is going to get messy. I want to take it slow because otherwise it won't go the way I want it to, but I'm jacked up. Really fucking excited. You still there, Midnight?'

Midnight tried to stop her mouth from hanging open. She managed a confirmatory grunt rather than any coherent words. Connie Woolwine was—

'You think I'm weird? Don't worry, I get that a lot. Just stay with me.'

And also apparently a bloody mindreader.

'Midnight, you said you spoke to a police officer about the murders, but how much information have they released to the public about the victims' injuries?'

'Limited.'

'Okay, so I know rather more about it than you. Given the fact that it sounds as if you shouldn't be calling me, can I count on you to keep anything I say confidential?'

'Oh God, yes,' Midnight said.

'Then we can begin. My pen is the scalpel.' She looked down at the paper woman. 'You're naked, panicked, conscious, I'm guessing. If you weren't conscious, it wouldn't be exciting. I want to see how you react when I start cutting. Where do I start? The legs, I think. Lighter cuts, to start with. I'm finding my feet, getting to grips with the blade. Although I've prepared for this well, watched my victim to make sure she lives alone, I know I'm going to take my time, so I've practised on other meat. Of course I have. I want to know how that blade will feel as it goes in. Have I practised on myself? How might that have felt?' She paused the dramatisation. 'Damned right, I have. I want to know what the pain feels like. I want to be able to feel what she'll feel with every little cut.'

'How many . . .' Midnight's voice was gravel. 'How many times did he cut her?'

'I don't have exact numbers. But most of her body was cut. Arms, legs, torso, face, I think. It was a lot. Doing this reconstruction now, I'd say more than a thousand.'

'That's not, um, he's not human. I mean, surely it's obvious to anyone who knows him that he's not normal?'

'I think our boy is good at hiding it, and I think he's spent a lot of time and effort getting good at hiding it. Maybe someone helped him, even if they didn't know it. Just a few more minutes now.'

Midnight didn't want to watch and she didn't want not to. She bit into the knuckles of her fist to keep herself quiet.

'You're so scared, Chloe.' Woolwine ran her fingertips over the outline of the head on the pages. 'The first few cuts wouldn't have hurt that much, then when he kept going, the sting would have turned to a burning, and after that the skin would have started to pull apart. You were just longing to fall unconscious, weren't you? Our man, on the other hand, he was just getting going. Didn't stop. Didn't give up. Didn't get bored. Even after you fell unconscious, and you must have, he just kept on going.' Woolwine made mark after mark on the paper, careful with each, breathing in time with every line.

Eventually she sat back.

'Obsessive compulsive disorder, maybe.' She looked into the mobile's camera. 'And please don't think that's about turning the lights off three times when you leave the house. It's so much deeper than that. But then, why this way of killing? What's he getting out of it? Slow burn. No big impact wounds. She stays alive much longer. Her heart keeps beating. Probably unconscious though. She's gagged, so he's not getting the pleasure of watching her beg. What the fuck is it, Midnight? What's the most important thing about this picture?'

'You mean apart from all the fucking blood?' Midnight asked.

Chapter 27

Something smelled bad. Not just a bit off, like milk left out too long, but really nauseatingly bad. The stink was coming from a box outside Jessica's apartment door, her name scrawled on it in angry capitals.

What made it worse was that Jessica had had a good day. A great day, in fact. The new company she'd begun delivering to had been thrilled by her bread samples and already put in an order for more. If her company kept growing at that rate, she'd need help and a larger kitchen. The box was the universe's way of keeping her feet on the ground.

She dumped the box in her kitchen sink and stared at it. Not opening it was a possibility, a very attractive one, in fact. Living in denial felt like the easier option. But then she wouldn't know quite what level of crazy she was dealing with, and imagining what was in the box might well be worse than the reality. She put on washing-up gloves, grabbed a sharp knife and threw open her window before slitting the tape. Inside was another box, and in that was a taped-up bin bag. Gagging,

Jessica pushed aside her dread in favour of anger. She'd spent hours in terror, imagining the Cream Bun Creep hiding in her pantry, only to find that the sole invader was her own imagination, but still, Jessica was convinced he'd been there. His message about the flowers in her bin was way too specific for any other explanation. Now she was so furious she couldn't even see the end of her tether in the distance behind her.

The gifted rat had been dead a while. The vague sense of movement in its fur was nothing to do with the rat itself but came from a swarm of fleas.

'Piece of shit!' Jessica screeched, shoving the lids down on the boxes hard and fast before taking a bin liner of her own and thrusting everything deep inside then securing the top with multiple knots. She dropped it outside her flat door, knowing she'd have to take it out to the communal bins later, but her priority was scrubbing her hands, knife and kitchen sink to remove any possible trace of contaminants.

Six months earlier there would have been no question about the sender. Her ex, Billy, had pulled equally nasty stunts. She wondered for a moment if it could, in fact, have been Billy who'd delivered the rat, but that didn't make sense. Her ex-boyfriend had finally disappeared from her life, plus anonymity had never been Billy's style. He'd always wanted her to know he'd been there. The rat was from the Cream Bun Creep – there was no doubt about it. What Jessica really couldn't understand was how she'd attracted yet another vicious loser. She was a bloody magnet.

The deep clean took an hour. By the end, she was sufficiently furious that she'd made a decision. She'd lived in fear of Billy for a long time. There was no way she was going to do that again. This time she had evidence. The police could check the box for fingerprints, or just . . . something. She could walk to the Lavender Hill police station in fifteen minutes, and hopefully by then she'd have calmed down enough not to either scream or cry.

Outside her flat, she bent down to pick up the rat package. It wasn't to the right of her door where she'd dropped it. It wasn't anywhere on her floor, in fact. She checked the floor above and the one below. Certain that a helpful neighbour must have picked it up, she even checked the bins for a recently deposited black bin liner. For once, the rubbish having been collected that day, it was almost empty.

Jessica stared back up at her flat. The fucker had been there, hiding somewhere. He'd seen her take the box in, and he'd seen her throw it out again, and now he'd run away like the little weasel he was, taking the evidence with him.

Back in her flat, she let out a screech that would have had her neighbours banging on the walls had they been in. Enough was enough. Since the afternoon she was supposed to meet the Cream Bun Creep for their meeting, she hadn't felt safe. She'd seen him everywhere, behind the curtains, in her pantry, even in her wardrobe. Now this.

Well, sod it. It was her turn to be aggressive and inappropriate. It was her turn to have the last say.

Willem Foster had given her his address as part of their details swap immediately after the accident. He'd also said he was driving down her road because he was considering moving into the area, but he was already living in Stockwell, just up the road.

'It was all bullshit,' she said, stomping out of her flat. 'Every word. He knew where I lived and he was waiting for me.'

She took a bus to Union Road rather than risk losing her parking space and found his basement flat. The planter on the windowsill was filled with old brown stalks, and there was rubbish outside his door that looked as if it was there for the long haul. Jessica rang the bell.

Willem yanked the door open, his mouth dropping.

'You,' he said.

'Well observed,' Jessica snapped back. 'We need to talk.'

'I hope you're not expecting me to invite you in, after that email you sent.'

'Do I want to go into the place where you pack up dead rats in boxes? I do not. What I need to say can be said here. Stay away from me. No more deliveries, and no more creeping around my place.'

'Creeping around your flat? Have you been imagining me going through your underwear drawer, Jessica? Maybe taking a quick shower in your place while you were out?' He ran his hands through his hair as if rinsing out shampoo. Jessica tried to speak but couldn't. 'Or was I on your kitchen counter – that's more your thing, right?'

The creep began to laugh, and Jessica knew the only thing between her and a prison cell was that she didn't have a knife in her hands.

'Stop!' she said. 'You fucking freak! Just admit you were in my building today.'

'Not me,' he smirked. 'But if I find whoever got you this upset, I'll buy them a fucking beer.'

She got up in his face. 'It *was* you, you sick, gaslighting, bastard.' That was as much as she could be bothered with. There wasn't going to be any moment of satisfaction, no gotcha. Jessica walked away. She'd said her piece and shown him that she wasn't scared.

It was a while before she heard Willem's door slam. He'd obviously been watching as she walked up his street.

The Cream Bun Creep wasn't the only one.

Chapter 28

Midnight had been cut off from Connie Woolwine when a man had suddenly burst into Connie's hotel room shouting that there had been a break in their case. Woolwine hadn't even said goodbye, just ended the call and gone. Midnight assumed the poshly spoken English male had been her partner. How amazing to be able to just up sticks and go to Venezuela for work. When she'd heard Woolwine speak at Necto, she'd talked about working with the FBI, advising on cases in Scotland, and going undercover at some high security prison hospital. Midnight looked around the apartment. It all felt so small. *She* felt small. Connie Woolwine wouldn't have been scared of Sara Vickson or of losing her job.

After reading Dawn a story, she ran herself a bath and lit some candles. The day had taken its toll, and Dr Woolwine's behaviour had been unexpected, to say the least. Midnight wasn't sure if she felt better or worse for having witnessed it.

It was five hours earlier in Venezuela than the UK so, by the time Woolwine had finished whatever she was doing, it would likely be the middle of the night in London. Midnight decided on giving in to tiredness. She kissed Dawn one last time, did her final check of doors and windows, then settled into bed, drifting off just seconds after her head hit the pillow.

When her mobile started jingling, she was convinced it was the morning alarm. Instead, she was greeted by Connie Woolwine's voice.

'You were asleep,' Woolwine said. 'Crap, it's three a.m. for you. International time differences are so frustrating.'

'Sorry, I didn't know you were going to call back.'

'You'll need a pen and paper,' Woolwine continued. 'I have theories. It was better that we had a break anyway because I needed time to process your suggestion.'

'My suggestion?' Midnight asked, turning on a lamp. 'I didn't know I'd—'

'All the most helpful suggestions are made when you don't know anything about it. I'm going to give you a caveat first and it's the size of a soccer stadium, so take me seriously. At this stage, with only two series-specific deaths, there is absolutely not enough data to profile this killer. I mean that a hundred per cent. It's not just something on cop shows. One can be an anomaly, two can involve coincidences. We see patterns at three. What I'm doing now is spitballing, and so help me God, I have no idea why I'm doing it, other than that it feels to me like you need someone. Say it back to me.'

Midnight wasn't sure which bit. 'You're just spitballing?'

'Good. With that at the forefront of our minds, I want to talk through your idea with you.'

'My idea about . . .'

'The blood. All that blood. I've been trying to imagine how Chloe's bedroom must have looked after she'd bled slowly into those sheets, because her heart wouldn't have stopped for a

213

really long time, and that doesn't feel incidental,' Woolwine said.

'But surely whenever someone's murdered with a knife, there's a lot of blood. It's kind of an unavoidable by-product.'

'Not like this,' Woolwine said quietly. 'Chloe's death was designed to keep her alive for a long time. That could be for one of two reasons. The first is torture, but Chloe would have been unconscious for the latter part as she grew increasingly weaker and went into shock. The second reason is that killing may not have been his primary motivation. Think about it. Why go to all that trouble, take so many hours to kill, then not use your hands? I'd expect strangulation, something more personal. With Mae, he got interrupted, but he still wanted the blood flow before death. The intent is the same, albeit more desperate.'

'So what was his motivation, if not to kill?'

'I'm hypothesising, Miss Jones, that one possible explanation for the mechanics of these two murders is that your killer has Renfield syndrome.'

Midnight frowned and rubbed her temples.

'I'm sorry, I have no idea what you're talking about. I apologise for sounding stupid but . . . Renfield, like *Dracula*? Is this a joke?'

'Definitely not. It's otherwise, although no more helpfully, called clinical vampirism.'

'Clinical fucking what now?' Midnight spluttered.

'Bear with me. It's going to sound ridiculous but the syndrome is no laughing matter, and historically such cases have been linked to other extremely violent crimes.'

'But Renfield was a fictional character,' Midnight said. Her head was aching and she had the strangest feeling that she might be falling down some Carrollian rabbit-hole.

'Ignore the whole undead, living in a coffin, bullshit. Renfield syndrome doesn't have to be entirely about consuming blood, it's also a fascination with it, the desire to touch it, to see it. It's vastly more common in men than in women,' Woolwine explained. 'And I gather there was saliva found on both bodies, in odd places. Given what a mess the bodies were in, there had to be a large enough amount of saliva for it not to just get lost in the chaos.'

'You think he . . .?'

'I think it's a possibility, yes,' Woolwine said.

'I don't understand how anyone gets to a point where they're obsessed with blood. How does that even happen?'

'Like many things in psychology, the seed seems to be planted in childhood or puberty. There will usually be a formative event, maybe an injury to the child or someone important to them, when the sudden appearance of blood is both traumatising but also exciting. Blood-letting in particular gives a sense of power and control. It's part of the reason teenagers self-harm, if that makes sense. Cutting yourself and drinking your own blood is called auto-vampirism. At the most extreme end of the syndrome, the need to have contact with blood is devastating and overwhelming. John Haigh, the man they called the acid bath murderer, is thought to have suffered from Renfield syndrome. This is not something to trifle with.'

Midnight blew out a long, tired breath. 'That's awful.'

'It's not exactly news that this guy is dangerous. To be honest, if blood is his primary motivation, it's good to know, but it doesn't take us a hell of a lot further. Interesting though, cos it's super rare, but there are documented cases. I'd love to get in a room with him.'

Midnight wrinkled her nose at the thought of even being in the same building as a man that sick. 'How are the police going to catch him?'

215

'No idea. Even if we're right about the Renfield's, there won't be any record of him suffering with it. This sort of thing only ever comes out after an arrest. But you think he's seen videos somewhere that reflect both Chloe and Mae's murders, so that's a starting point.'

'I just can't be sure,' Midnight murmured. 'Chloe's yes, I don't know about Mae's.'

'Can you be any more specific about the link between viewing these videos and the person who killed these women?'

Midnight sighed. She desperately wanted to tell Connie Woolwine everything, but with extra money now needed for Dawn's care, she had to be even more careful not to breach Necto's confidentiality terms.

'There are connections in terms of geography, a coincidence of timing, a tenuous digital trail, and my gut feeling.'

'Well, regardless of whatever reason you have for maintaining confidentiality, if the police source material in breach of privacy rights and without a warrant, it's likely to be excluded in court.'

'It feels like I've been wasting your time,' Midnight said. 'I think I should just leave the police to do their job.'

'We're not done here. We only answered the question, *why* does he kill the way he kills? Which still leaves why is he killing *now*? That's possibly the more helpful of the two, because timing often gives us information about milestones in a killer's life.'

'Okay, but let me just go to the kitchen. I need coffee for this.' She plodded to the kitchen, moving around as quietly as possible.

Even Dr Woolwine started whispering. 'So according to your theory, he saw these videos then used the seen methodology to sate his love of blood. The killings are so blade-specific that he couldn't have done anything at this level before, so why was this a trigger now?'

'Like you said before, he could have got this stuff from anywhere. Why replicate these videos?' Midnight asked.

'Has to be because he hasn't got this stuff from anywhere else. Maybe his lifestyle is very restrictive, so he could be in a religious order, or a politician with a wife and kids – no, that definitely wouldn't have stopped him – or . . . maybe he's been actively trying to avoid it.'

'Like, fighting his urges?' Midnight asked, giving in to temptation and pouring a measure of whisky into her coffee.

'Exactly like that,' Woolwine said, walking out onto her balcony. Midnight could see stars all around her. 'I'm at a point where I can't help more without additional information. You need to consider what you're going to do with this information.'

Midnight slumped onto her sofa. 'Maybe it would help the police to hear some of what you've hypothesised tonight. Your partner, he's ex-Met, so perhaps without mentioning me, you could . . .'

'Just drop them a line with my thoughts? I could. And yes, Baarda will pass it all along. I'm not going to ask you what your interest is, Midnight – I know a brick wall when I hit one – but isn't there someone inside Necto who can advise you? When I was consulting, they seemed keen to be the sort of employer you could talk to.'

'Yeah,' Midnight said slowly. 'They do give that impression. Internally, they have other, more pressing considerations. Client confidentiality, for one.'

'I don't buy that,' Woolwine said. 'Client confidentiality ceases to have any legal effect when there's an overriding need to release information in a criminal investigation. In fact, withholding relevant information could get them in serious trouble.'

'I'm starting to wonder if that's the issue, that they might be concerned about their legal exposure for showing the footage that caused this,' Midnight said.

'You're not saying this footage appeared on one of Necto's profiling sequences?' Dr Woolwine's voice was loud in the quiet of the Venezuelan night.

'Shit,' Midnight said. Confidentiality blown, and too late to backtrack.

'That can't be right. I worked with them to set ethical boundaries. There was never a program that went this far. That footage has to pass rigorous standards.'

'I had a Profile K,' Midnight murmured. She leaned her head back and breathed fully. It felt like the first time she'd done so since walking out of Sara Vickson's office. It was out now. She'd told someone.

'You had a what now?'

'A Profile K. For killer.'

'I have literally no idea what you're talking about. That would be completely irresponsible. We didn't develop that set of results. It's a joke, surely, representing some anomaly.'

'Profile K assessments are on the system, we just never found one before. The footage similar to Chloe's murder was part of that profile test. I watched it all. It was pretty fucking disturbing.'

'Then that footage must have been placed within the test specifically, and it must have had a purpose. Are you the only person who knows about this?' Woolwine asked.

'I reported the Profile K to one of the company directors. That was before the first murder though. She reminded me that we're bound by certain rules and, listen, I can get fired. If this comes out they'll know it was me. If I lose my job . . .'

'Who did this, Midnight? Someone inside Necto selected those videos for a reason, maybe for that specific applicant. What were they trying to do? It's so twisted that you can't even be sure the killer isn't inside Necto.'

'That had occurred to me too,' Midnight said quietly. 'I've just been hoping it was too ridiculous to be true.'

A message beeped at Woolwine's end, and she tapped a finger on the screen. 'Crap. The pathologist here has asked to see me and Baarda. We'll be travelling tomorrow, but I'll be in touch real soon, okay? Assume nothing. Do nothing. I don't like this, but we have no idea what it all means yet. As soon as you reported it, Necto would have wiped their files clean and ditched all trace of that profile. There'll be nothing left to find.'

'I have it on a pen drive,' Midnight said softly. 'I smuggled it out.'

'That was risky. Just keep it safe. Damn it, where's my charger?'

Dr Woolwine was clattering around her apartment and throwing things in a rucksack. From the bedroom, Dawn began humming. Midnight checked her watch. It was 4.30 a.m. and there was virtually no chance she'd get Dawn back to sleep now. She cursed herself for waking her sister up two hours earlier than normal.

'Listen, Midnight, before I go I want to make sure you understand exactly what this man will be prepared to do to enable himself to keep on killing,' Woolwine was saying as she hauled on what looked like ancient hiking boots. 'He has an addiction within a psychosis, which means he's about as dangerous as—

The screen went black.

Midnight was staring at it, waiting desperately to hear what she needed to do. Did Dr Woolwine even know she'd been cut off? Midnight tried to reconnect but the line was dead.

Woolwine would call back. She'd said she would. It was bizarre. Connie Woolwine couldn't be more than a couple of years older than her, yet they were worlds apart.

Dawn called to her.

219

'Coming sweetheart!' Midnight put some extra pep into her voice to make up for the dread she was feeling.

Connie Woolwine was a lot. It was all so overwhelming. Part of Midnight wished she hadn't contacted her, only that wasn't fair, and it was cowardly to boot. She'd given up her time, put her faith in Midnight and taken her seriously. Only now Dr Woolwine was gone, if anything, Midnight felt even more alone than she did before.

Jumping up, she went straight to her kitchen and opened the cupboard where they kept rarely used items. Midnight put her fingers into the furthest eggcup and pulled out the pen drive. It would be better in her bedroom, where no one but her ever went. In her wardrobe, she chose a dress with pockets and tucked the pen drive deep inside. She felt safer with it there.

A crash outside her bedroom window made her shriek, causing Dawn to scream. She ran to calm Dawn down, then realised she was being an idiot, and dashed for the window instead. There was no one to be seen. At 4.30 a.m., even in Clapham, the residential streets were deserted. Had it been a dog or stray cat? Midnight reconstructed the noise in her mind. It had been heavy, loud and metallic. Then a scuffling. Maybe a drunk staggering around looking for somewhere to lay his head.

Or maybe not.

Dawn called for her again. Midnight got her sister from her bed and tucked her up in her own. Then she went to the kitchen and took a knife from the block, sliding it under the bed as she climbed in to cuddle Dawn back to sleep.

The woman at King's College had said a mystery caller had found a photo of her. There were no photos of Midnight on the internet, as far as she knew, except one. In it, she'd been raising a glass of champagne and toasting one of those large cardboard fake cheques representing money raised by a charity that had helped Dawn in the past. Midnight had been wearing a long silver dress with her hair up. Nothing like she looked day to day. Nothing like she looked at home. But recognisable enough, she thought, for anyone sufficiently invested in finding her, and who knew where she worked.

'Fuck you,' she whispered into the night, as Dawn snored gently beside her. 'Come anywhere near us and I'll kill you.'

Chapter 29

Amber had a staff appraisal on Tuesday lunchtime, so it was Wednesday before Midnight could get her alone. She was cramming a slice of chiffon cake into her mouth as Midnight threw back a double espresso. In one corner, a group of girls was talking earnestly. Midnight had heard both Chloe and Mae's names mentioned. It felt good to know she wasn't the only person who couldn't think about anything else.

'Seriously, this new girl's cakes are so good, you have to try one. How can you sit there looking at that cart and not want anything?' Amber said.

'Eli mentioned there was new food on offer. I'm not hungry.' But she did want another espresso. 'Amber, there's something I need to talk to you about but it's really, really got to stay between us. It'll sound stupid but I need you to promise.'

Amber giggled. 'Come on . . . really?'

Midnight dug her nails into the palms of her hands. 'Yes.'

'Okay but it'll cost you one of those garlic and cream cheese loaves.' Midnight sighed. 'Come on, be nice,' Amber countered.

'I've hardly seen you and when I do, you look so stressed it freaks me out. We used to have lunch every day and do nothing but gossip and laugh. You know I'm there for you – always have been, always will be – but it would be nice to be able to talk to you with a bit less drama. Also I need a cup of tea now because I ate the cake too fast.'

Taking a deep breath, Midnight stood and did her best to look more normal. 'Tea and bread coming up.'

It took her only a minute to order the tea and an espresso for herself, but several more standing in the queue for the woman at Bake Me A Cake to wrap up Amber's bread.

'Can I tempt you with anything else?' she asked.

Midnight did her best impression of a smile. 'That's all thanks.' She tapped her card to pay.

'I hope you don't mind my saying, but I've seen you before with your sister. My name's Jessica. We must live close to each other. She's beautiful. I mean, you're both beautiful. I always dreamed of having a twin sister. I was an only child and that was pretty boring.'

She handed over the bread wrapped in crisp white paper with a tiny sticker on it to keep it together. Her logo was a pretzel with the company name written in a curve around it. Midnight's social skills finally kicked into gear.

'This is lovely,' she waved the loaf vaguely. 'You've only recently started selling here, right?'

'Yes. I tour lots of local businesses with the cart, but I was thrilled when Necto contacted me. They employ so many people here!'

'They certainly do. Well, thanks for this. And thanks for what you said about my sister. Say hi if you see me again.'

'I will,' Jessica said, as a female security officer stepped forward to ask her something about calories.

Midnight went back to Amber.

'Okay, what's the drama?'

'That psychological profiler whose name you gave me . . .'

'She was pretty hard to forget.' Amber took a sip of tea and settled in. 'So blunt!'

'I spoke to her on Monday night, and she raised some interesting questions about what Necto's up to.' Midnight kept her voice low, grateful for the corner table away from anyone who might overhear. She recapped everything from using TESU's facilities to her conversation with Dr Woolwine, sticking to the headlines.

'So our local serial killer is a vampire? You don't think that perhaps Dr Woolwine has spent too long licking frogs in South America?'

'Amber, this is serious! For God's sake, two women are dead, and there'll be more, because killers like this, who slaughter for their own perverse pleasure, don't stop until they're caught. That's about as well documented as it gets.'

'Great criminal psychology lecture, Midnight, but you need to leave it to the professionals. For fuck's sake, don't you have enough on your plate? You just got a major promotion. Do you know how much more you're getting paid than most people our age? It's, like, five times as much.'

'I can do the maths,' Midnight said. 'Look, I just need to know if you're aware of any developments here.'

Amber stirred her tea thoughtfully. Midnight looked back at Jessica. That security guard just wasn't leaving her alone. 'What is it you think they've been developing?'

'I guess it would have to be military or espionage. Maybe personal defence or private army at a push. Possibly for a foreign government,' Midnight said. 'There are any number of private armies operating across the world. Some are recruiting from African countries or from prisons, or offering an income and a gun to people living in poverty, only those recruits aren't natural fighters. They don't have the stomach for a lot of what they have to see and do. Imagine if you could target people who already have an in-built propensity for violence. I'm guessing this is just early-stage research, getting a feeling for what's possible. But using psychological triggers to create human killing machines is something plenty of dictators and desperados would pay good money for.'

'That would be extremely unethical, probably even illegal,' Amber whispered.

'But not impossible. Not for Necto. And they already have plenty of clients on their books who might be interested in something like that, even if they don't publicise it.'

'Listen, as far as I know, there's nothing new in development. We usually hear whispers about big projects even if the details are hidden.'

Midnight shook her head. 'I'm going to set up a meeting with the development team to see if I can get them talking about what they're working on. Now that I'm in client liaison, I have an excuse.'

'That's not a good idea, Midnight. Vickson warned you about pushing this. If she figures out what you're doing, best-case scenario, you'll be demoted.'

'Then she can't find out. Didn't you date someone in the military team for a while? I just need a name and a mobile number then I can get in touch with him outside work.'

Amber crossed her arms and sat back in her seat. 'You're stirring up unnecessary shit, Midnight. Say I give you a number to call, what are you going to say? "I think the company we all work for, who pay us incredibly generously with some nice perks, is bending the rules a little, so I'm planning on taking them down?" What the fuck?'

'Would you keep your voice down?' Midnight hissed at her.

'Would you get a grip? No one is losing their job for you, and it's not fair to put anyone in that position. You shouldn't even be talking to me about it. It's making me uncomfortable.'

'His name was Sonny something. You met him on the office behaviour course, which was an interesting take-away. I just need his surname, Amber, then I'll leave you alone.'

Jessica walked past, pushing an empty trolley, and gave them a wave.

'That's me sold out. It was nice to meet you. See you around, I hope.' Jessica beamed at them.

'Yeah, take care,' Midnight said. As soon as the words were out of her mouth, she got the horrible feeling that she'd forgotten something, or was late for something. The security guard Jessica had been chatting to sat down at a table not far from Midnight's, and she instinctively pulled her chair a little closer to Amber's

'Sorry, Midnight, but I have to go,' Amber said. 'No hard feelings, this just got complicated. You're not the only one with responsibilities.'

'Oh come on, you have no one to look after but yourself. You party, like, four nights a week. Your main problem is how to fit in all your beauty appointments, and—'

Amber stood, leaning across the table to speak quietly but emphatically. 'You know what, you can just fuck off. That was incredibly patronising.'

Midnight stood slowly, shaking her head with regret. 'Yes, it was. It totally was, and you have every right to be pissed off with me. Amber, I'm sorry. I was completely out of line. It's no excuse but I didn't sleep, I'm scared. Also I feel responsible . . .'

'Well this time, you're not. I think you're a bit addicted to it, being responsible for everyone. You have to take care of Dawn, I get it. But remember when I was an hour late for work and you decided with no basis at all that I'd been murdered? Now you have to be responsible for the choices a global corporation is making. When's it going to stop?' She picked up her loaf. 'You see this necklace I'm wearing? You gave it to me when I broke up with Steve and thought I'd never stop crying. That scar on your ankle is from when you tried to leapfrog a concrete bollard in Trafalgar Square and didn't make it. I picked you up, got you in a cab, took you home and patched you up. And that ring on your finger is the birthday gift I bought you last year. We're good friends, Midnight, so please, for the love of God, listen to me. Drop this. Get on with your life. You'll be fine. Dawn will be fine. That's all that matters. Thank you for the bread and the tea. I don't want to argue with you any more, so I'm going.'

'Fine,' Midnight said quietly. 'Just do me a favour and don't tell Eli about any of this.'

'Why would I tell Eli?' Amber asked.

'Just because I figured . . . the two of you were . . .'

'Is that you trying to protect me again or are you spying on me? And why are you judging him? He's working hard and doing everything you ask.'

'Sure,' Midnight said.

'Then stop being so paranoid. You know, people are a lot less interested in your personal life than you seem to think. I'm going now, before I say something I regret. I need some space.'

Midnight sat back down and stared into the cold espresso. She picked up the cup and tossed it back anyway. It wasn't that Amber didn't have a point, it was just that she didn't have time to deal with it. Later, she would apologise properly, but if Amber couldn't help her, she had no choice but to help herself.

Back at her desk, she found the number for the military applications team and called it.

'Hi, this is client liaison. I was looking for someone in your team, I met him on a training course but I can't remember his name. It's Sonny . . .' She let it hang.

'Aziz? There's no other Sonny here.'

'Yes!' Midnight said. 'Honestly, my memory is shocking.'

'Tell me about it,' the woman on the end of the line said. 'Did you want me to put you through to his extension?'

'That would be great,' Midnight said.

The internal line rang only once before it was snatched up.

'Sonny Aziz, what do you need?'

'Hi, I'm from client liaison and I have a couple of queries. I was told you were someone I could talk to. In fact, I think we met on a training course before,' she said.

'We don't deal with the client liaison team. Military is dealt with from inside this team so you shouldn't have any client care overlap with us,' he said. She could hear him typing rapidly as he spoke, not so much as a pause for the call.

'I know, but I have a request from another client where I think military applications might be helpful so I wanted more information. Would you have time this afternoon? Room 720 is available at four p.m.'

He sighed without bothering to disguise it. Midnight imagined him rolling his eyes.

'I can give you fifteen minutes,' he said. 'Come with a list of prepared questions, so we can get straight to specifics.' Sonny hung up.

Midnight's plan was vague but formed of two halves. First, she'd drop Amber's name into the conversation, build a little trust, find some common ground. Then she would talk about possible uses of military profiling for the police. After that, she'd see how far she could push Sonny with regard to new applications. Vickson had even laughed about how a Profile K applicant would be perfect for military recruitment. Perhaps that hadn't been a joke at all.

At 3.50 p.m. she searched for Eli to give him a task that would keep him busy for the remainder of the afternoon, but he was nowhere to be found. She settled for leaving a note on his desk to say she was taking a conference call in a quiet room, and that she was not to be disturbed.

She took a lift to the conference room floor, laptop tucked officiously under her arm, grabbed a cup of water along the way, and made herself slow down. Better not to seem too keen. She should let Sonny get there first then walk in a couple of minutes late, looking as if it was just one of many things on her schedule that afternoon.

The door to room 720 stuck a little as she was pushing it open, and some of the water dripped down her shirt.

'Damn it,' she said. 'Every time.'

When Midnight looked up, there were seven pairs of eyes on her belonging to Sonny Aziz, Sara Vickson, Eli, Richard Baxter, a security officer and two others she didn't recognise. She took a shallow breath and set the water down on the table.

'Thank you, Mr Aziz, you may go now,' Vickson said.

He slid out of the room without giving Midnight a second look. Her heart was beating too hard, and there were fuzzy lines at the periphery of her vision. It seemed sensible not to try to speak.

'Before we get started, we're going to need your laptop,' Vickson said. 'Hand it to Eli.'

He stepped forward, fingers outstretched.

Fucking Eli. He had to have been keeping an eye on her all along, or at least reporting to Vickson when Midnight wasn't at her desk. Amber had always been too trusting, and now it was clear to Midnight that her suspicions about her friend having a fling with Eli were right on the money. Clearly Amber hadn't even been able to get to the end of the day without spilling everything to him. Between them, they'd screwed her. The only remaining question was how much Sara Vickson knew. Midnight handed Eli the laptop.

'Security, you can wait outside until we've concluded this conversation. Eli, you can go back to work. Somebody should be doing their job,' Vickson said. The uniformed guard exited, only his outline visible through the opaque glass. Eli disappeared without saying a word. Richard Baxter was avoiding making eye contact by fiddling with his tie. Coward, Midnight thought. He wasn't even her boss any more and he was still there digging the knife in. 'Miss Jones, these two people are from human resources and our in-house legal team. They'll need to interview you then run through some procedures. Do you consent?'

'So what's Baxter doing here?' she asked.

'Apparently we're obliged to have someone with you who is on your side, so to speak. Mr Baxter kindly offered,' Vickson explained.

Midnight couldn't contain her laughter. 'The man who threatened to report me to human resources is here to hold my hand? I'm sorry but surely you can see how hilarious that is.'

'I retracted that report,' Richard mumbled. 'And I take no pleasure in what's happening today. You were always—'

'Spare me it,' Midnight interrupted. 'Instead, perhaps someone would like to tell me what, exactly, I'm supposed to have done wrong?' she asked. If Vickson wanted to play hardball, she had some ammunition of her own.

'You exceeded your authority. You contacted a department that should only be contacted at director level. You are using time that should be dedicated to your actual duties to pursue your own pet projects without department head agreement, which means your other responsibilities are not being properly met. I'm disappointed. You're still in the probationary part of your promotion, and, less than two weeks in, you've let both me and your whole team down. I'm asking for an investigation. You'll be suspended for two weeks while we arrange a formal hearing to decide how to deal with this.'

No mention of the Profile K applicant, or their previous meeting. No mention of why Midnight had tried to meet with Sonny Aziz. No mention of the file Sara Vickson had asked her to destroy. Midnight shrugged.

'So I'm being disciplined for being enthusiastic, for exploring new potential client avenues, and for forgetting to obtain a single authority, even when all I was doing amounted to research? This seems disproportionate.'

'Does it?' Vickson snapped. 'Then maybe you've failed to appreciate the sensitive nature of our work. We have rules and regulations for a reason. Many of our clients need guarantees in place regarding confidentiality. When it comes to our military department, we handle information so sensitive that it's a matter of international importance how we conduct ourselves. You know that, Miss Jones, having come from the data analysis department where you are given refresher courses every single year in confidentiality procedures. Were you trying to cause an international incident or did you just think it was fun to potentially get us sued?'

'We should probably stick with the procedure for dealing with this,' the human resources man said shakily. 'There has to be a full interview before any sort of recrimination or disciplining takes place. We can't rush to conclusions.'

'I concur,' the lawyer added quietly.

'And of course, you do have rights,' Richard added stiffly. 'You may want to formalise your own representation.'

Sara Vickson raised her eyebrows. 'You're not being fired, Miss Jones. Not yet. I'm still hoping you might use this disciplinary hearing as a learning exercise. Take some time out. You'll be on full pay while we go through the motions, so consider matters carefully before making any rash decisions,' she paused to let that sink in. Rash, like talking to the police? Rash, like sharing the Profile K data? Midnight wasn't sure which. 'You might like to consider the fact that you won't get a reference from us if we have to terminate your employment, and reputations in this industry are fragile things. You might see that you have behaved unwisely. I'm sure there are some retraining options that we could find. Just to reaffirm your commitment to Necto.'

'Some additional training would definitely be a possibility,' the HR man interrupted, 'but no findings have been made yet. Again, I need to emphasise that you will be given the opportunity—'

'I've got the point,' Midnight said. 'I'm sure Necto won't be in a rush to terminate me. I've always been a good employee. And nothing I've done has compromised Necto. So far.'

'I should hope not,' Vickson said. 'Use the time to think, Miss Jones. We're better off working as a team. I'm sure we both have too much to lose by ending our professional relationship.'

Midnight waited until Vickson had gone before collapsing onto a chair. It took an hour to give the human resources representative her version of what she'd been doing meeting Sonny Aziz, and answering the other allegations.

Richard Baxter opened the door for her to exit and followed her out.

'I am sorry,' he said. 'I can't imagine how it must have felt to be taken by surprise like that.'

'Then why not warn me?' she snapped. Richard's sudden empathy was either fake or triggered by guilt. Midnight was too enraged to care either way. He looked like she'd slapped him.

'Company procedure,' he muttered. 'It would have made things worse.'

'You're hiding behind company procedure? You know how this started, and you know why they're laying the groundwork to get rid of me. Don't pretend to be on my side if you won't tell the truth.'

He breathed heavily through his nose as she turned to go. 'I have a daughter, Miss Jones. About your age, in fact. I worry about her walking home, going out in the dark.'

Midnight turned to face him.

'You never said.'

'I like to keep things professional in the office,' he replied. 'My point is that I understand what you were trying to do. Much as I believe you should have gone about it differently . . . this outcome has been unfortunate.'

Midnight walked back so she was close enough to him to whisper.

'The only unfortunate thing here is Necto's unwillingness to be honest and help the police.' The lawyer exited the conference room into the corridor and gave an unhappy harrumph at Midnight's continued presence.

'Don't worry, I'm leaving,' she said. 'That's more than enough hypocrisy for me.'

She left Richard and the lawyer in the corridor and made her way to security, where she handed in her pass and cleaned out her locker in a way that didn't feel temporary at all. In spite of the fact that the working day was long since over, she found Amber waiting for her outside the office building, looking crestfallen.

'I told you,' Midnight said, walking straight past her. 'You should never have trusted Eli. The timing was all wrong, him turning up out of the blue like that.' Amber was following her like a shadow. 'Why did you feel the need to tell him everything? He went straight to fucking Vickson. I'm on paid leave pending a disciplinary hearing, so if you're waiting for me to apologise for earlier then you can shove it.'

'Midnight, it wasn't Eli.'

'Of course it was. He was right there waiting with them. I had to hand him my laptop and watch him go back to my office to take over my job. I bet he loved every second of it.'

'It wasn't Eli who told Vickson, Midnight. I know it wasn't him,' she stopped walking and let Midnight go ahead. 'Because it was me.'

Midnight managed three more steps before her feet stopped walking. She didn't want to believe it. She needed Amber to be lying to protect Eli. Anything was better than being betrayed by her friend. But Amber's face was full of truth, from the tears in her eyes to the shake of her bottom lip.

'Why?' Midnight whispered.

'They gave me this whole speech about loyalty to Necto and the legal implications of giving away company information. From the moment you went to Vickson about the Profile K, they were keeping tabs on you. Necto is powerful. They made it sound like just knowing what you were doing made me culpable too. Vickson told me she was worried about you, and that she wanted to protect you. Listen, I'm not proud of what I did, but I can't lose my job, Midnight. I love my life.'

'You love your life? That's the phrase you want to pin your betrayal on? Fucking hell, that's not much to show for stabbing me in the back. So you're saying Eli wasn't in on this?'

234

Amber shrugged. 'We discussed some of it, sure, but it was me who told Vickson. When you started talking about arranging a meeting with Sonny, it was a step too far. Midnight, you have to understand, it didn't feel like a choice.'

'So the word "no" has magically escaped your vocabulary then?'

'Midnight, please . . .' Amber was sobbing.

'You know what, Amber, fuck you. Fuck you for taking the piss out of Necto while you can't actually get enough of it, and your tough talk about what bastards management are when you crumble the second you have to look them in the eyes. Fuck your claims of friendship and asking about Dawn, and pretending to be the good guy. We're done.'

'Midnight, I am your friend, I promise. Please don't go. We need to talk!'

'No, we don't,' Midnight said. 'You just need to listen. Our friendship's not over, Amber. For a friendship to end, it had to have been real to start with. Ours never was. Have a nice life with Necto and Eli. They're exactly what you deserve.'

Chapter 30

Dawn's carer was on the pavement as Midnight turned the last corner to the flat; next to her was a police officer taking notes. Midnight broke into a jog that became a sprint when she couldn't see Dawn anywhere.

'Where is she? What happened?' she screeched. 'Is she hurt?'

The carer took a step back. 'Dawn's fine. She's inside with another police officer. You're late again. I've been trying to call you.'

Midnight could have cried. 'I had a tough afternoon, and I forgot to switch my mobile on when I got it from my locker.'

'This is the owner,' the carer told the officer.

'Miss Jones?' She nodded. 'I'm afraid your place was burgled this afternoon. They left a bit of a mess. Do you have any video security? A concealed nanny cam maybe?'

The carer gave her a hard look.

'No,' Midnight said. 'Tell me Dawn wasn't in there.'

'We were at the day centre. We left here at one o'clock. By the time we got back at five, the place was wrecked. I called the police straight away. I've got to go. My kids'll be screaming for their tea.'

Midnight ran inside to Dawn who was still in her wheelchair, while a female officer did her best to chat with her in a reassuring way. Their apartment had been taken apart. Chairs had been turned over, everything was pulled out of cupboards and drawers, even jars of coffee had been emptied into the sink.

Midnight gave Dawn a hug. This was her sister's safe space, carefully designed to make everything familiar and easy for her. The environment remained the same every day. Whether she was showing it or not, the break-in was going to affect Dawn very badly indeed.

'Will a crew be coming to take fingerprints and photos?' Midnight asked.

The officers looked at one another. 'Is anything missing?' one of them asked.

'All our priceless works of art seem to be here, but I'll have to check the safe for the diamond tiaras,' Midnight said. 'Does it matter if anything's missing or not? Someone broke into our home and trashed it. I want them caught.'

'I'm afraid we have limited resources for burglaries, and at the moment a lot of manpower is being used to investigate the local murders.'

'You mean the murders that happened within walking distance of here? I'm familiar with them, thank you,' Midnight snapped.

'Do you have any idea who might have done this? Is there an ex with a grudge?' the constable asked.

Midnight huffed. 'There's no vindictive ex. I don't owe anyone money, and I don't keep anything here that anyone could possibly want.'

'We've taken some photos. You should contact your insurance company. I've left the crime report number by your kettle. It would help if you got an alarm.'

Midnight glared at the officer. 'How did they get in?'

'The carer said the front door to the flats had been propped open, probably for the pile of deliveries just inside the front door. Your lock seems to have been forced. You'll need to call out a locksmith tonight, and you might want to think about staying at a friend's until you can get cleared up. This sort of burglary is usually opportunistic, most likely to fund a drug habit.'

'Is there someone you can call?' the woman constable asked.

'There's no one.'

The officers left. Midnight called an extortionately priced twenty-four-hour locksmith who promised to be there within thirty minutes, picked up a hairbrush and began brushing Dawn's hair. As bizarre an activity as it was with debris all around them, Dawn had to be her priority, and brushing her hair had always calmed her. It was the one thing their mother had consistently done for Dawn, morning and evening.

'This stuff comes in threes, Dawnie. I've been suspended from my job, my best friend betrayed me, and now our flat's been trashed. Feels like we're due some good luck. Let me fetch some hairbands, sweetie. I'll put it in plaits.'

In Dawn's room, Midnight stared at the mattress. The side of it had been slit open, yet Dawn's jar of loose change remained untouched on the floor by her bed – weekly pocket money that Midnight made a point of giving her, from which every now and then they took a few pounds to choose Dawn something new from the toy shop. Either the burglars were stupid enough to have missed it, or the police claim that the break-in was opportunistic was utter rubbish.

'Oh, hell!' Midnight shouted. 'The pen drive!'

She raced through to her own bedroom where the damage was even worse. Her wardrobe was empty, clothes had been thrown all around the place, and she couldn't find the dress she'd hidden the pen drive in. She flopped onto the floor, head in her arms, trying to fight through the shock of what was happening to them.

Dawn's quiet crying was the only thing that gave Midnight the strength to get up again. Her sister had begun rocking. She only ever did that to self-soothe. Midnight wrapped a soft blanket around Dawn's shoulders, settled her with a teddy as a comforter, then began tidying the lounge as best she could. Half an hour later, her fury got the better of her and she phoned Amber.

'I didn't think you'd ever talk to me again,' Amber said. 'Can I just say how sorry I am? I'd never have chosen to betray you, Midnight. I wanted to tell you.'

'They broke into my flat this afternoon,' Midnight said. Her voice was granite. 'They waited until Dawn was out, small mercy, then they trashed the place looking for my copy of the data.'

'Midnight, that's not something Necto would do. I'm sorry for what you're going through but do you really think they're that obsessed with this?'

'Did you tell them about the pen drive? That's all I need to know, Amber. Did you tell them about my trip to TESU and how I hacked the system to view the footage again?'

There was a painful silence at the end of the line. 'I don't think I did. They asked a lot of questions, and I was upset. I can't remember clearly.'

'Well, my place is trashed. They did a good job. I couldn't tell the police anything was missing so they think it's just mindless vandals. They don't even have the resources to send a crime scene investigation team over.'

'Shit.'

'No, no, it's all good. You can call Sara Vickson and tell her they got away with it. Whoever Necto sent were really good at their job. It was too much of a mess for the police to even bother taking fingerprints.'

'There has to be some other explanation, Midnight. It feels like you're taking it all very personally . . .'

'You think it's all in my head? Are you kidding me? They asked you to fucking spy on me, Amber! They identified you as my closest friend, and made you scared enough to think you might lose your job if you didn't tell them that I was still pursuing my—'

'Your what? Your investigation? That's what you were thinking. For the record, they said they were concerned about you.'

In spite of the awfulness of it all, Midnight couldn't stop herself from laughing.

'Oh come on, did you really fall for that bullshit, Amber?'

'It's not bullshit. Sara Vickson was worried that you might put yourself in danger. She said they'd never used any of the footage you described. No one else has ever seen it.'

'Are you seriously suggesting that I made this up in some sort of hysterical fit?' Midnight shouted.

'Not me. Vickson implied that maybe you were having a hard time coping at home and balancing the pressure at work. To be fair, you have been a bit, um, strange recently. You've said some mean things. That's not like you.'

'I'm going now,' Midnight said. 'You were right to think we wouldn't be speaking again.'

She ended the call, gave Dawn a huge smile and made a decision.

*

Doris arrived at the same time as the locksmith. Midnight gave the latter instructions to fit a new lock, the best quality he had, followed by a chain. Meanwhile, Doris sat with Dawn on the sofa, put something musical on the television, and held Dawn's hand as they watched together.

'Cup of tea?' Midnight asked her quietly.

'I'll make tea for us all. Don't need to ask where everything is. It's pretty much all been laid out for me. Helpful burglars, they were.' She gave Dawn's hand a pat then put the kettle on.

'I'm sorry to call you out of the blue. I just need Dawn distracted while I clean. She obviously likes you.'

'Oh, she's an absolute love,' Doris said. 'Little bastards really made a mess. Still, we'll have it spick-and-span in no time.'

'I don't want you helping with this. That's not why I called.'

It was Midnight's turn to have her hand held, and the human contact made her want to crumble.

'Clapham may seem like just an outcrop of that metropolis they call the city, but in my childhood it was more like its own little town. People looked you in the eye as they passed you on the street. We helped our neighbours out. And anyway, I haven't felt like anyone needed me for . . . I can't actually remember the last time. Your phone call took ten years off me. And your sister is doing fine. Together, we're going to get this place all cleaned up. We'll keep the music up loud, sing along, and pretend it's a game. When we're done, there's a lovely Ethiopian restaurant nearby, who deliver. Best food for miles. My treat.'

Midnight didn't fight it. She needed someone to tell her she was okay. Being fed was the icing on the cake, not that she'd let Doris pay.

An hour later, they'd cleared up the worst of it. At one point, Midnight disappeared into her bedroom to try to get hold of

241

Connie Woolwine – if ever she'd needed help and guidance it was then – but the mobile rang a few times then cut off. Midnight almost slid into self-pity but pulled herself up short. What would Dr Woolwine do, she wondered. If she couldn't get hold of her, then the next best thing was to imagine *being* her. Woolwine sure as hell wouldn't sit around and cry. There was enough to do without throwing herself a pity party.

Back in the chaos, Midnight and Doris managed to safety pin the sides of the mattresses together and fit clean sheets, which would have to do until new mattresses were delivered.

'Is this something you need or shall I throw it away?' Doris asked, holding up a small angular piece of red plastic.

Midnight stared at it in the palm of her hand.

'Something important?' Doris asked.

'It's the lid of a pen drive,' Midnight said. 'Where did you find it?'

'It was on the dining table under your shopping bag.'

Midnight examined every inch of the table. The pen drive itself was missing, and if the cap was off, they must have found it. They probably took a moment to make sure they had what they were looking for, then left. Her stomach was a lump of rock, and she'd begun sweating from parts of her body she had no idea could sweat. They had the bloody pen drive – the only hard evidence she had that could potentially force Necto to help figure out the killer's identity. How could she have been so stupid that she didn't realise Necto were on to her from the start? They had some of the best technology in the world at their disposal. Of course they'd been watching her every move.

Doris lowered herself onto a chair, moving noticeably more stiffly than when she'd arrived. Midnight snapped herself out of her sinking mood, and put her energy into caring for the people around her.

'How about that food now?' Midnight asked. 'You've been amazing.'

'Good idea,' Doris said. 'Then you can tell me about all the things that are bothering you. I know upset when I see it. And it's not that this isn't cause enough, it just looks like you've got the weight of the world on your shoulders.'

'My best friend betrayed me today,' Midnight said. In spite of the missing pen drive, that was the thing hurting her the most. It was painful to say the words out loud.

Doris reached out and hugged her. 'Oh, love. Then she was never actually your best friend, was she?'

Chapter 31

The Applicant

Benjamin Hoffman wasn't just having a good day, he was having his best day ever. It was his thirteenth birthday, and that morning his parents had surprised him with a box that he'd opened blindfolded. When the black Labrador puppy had launched himself tongue first at Benjamin's face, he'd started crying and laughing simultaneously. He'd named the little fur bundle Casper, and played with him until he'd fallen fast asleep on the sofa, tucked under a blanket, squeaky toy under his chin.

Benjamin had thought that was that. How much better could it possibly get? Only then, his parents had brought in another box. That one they'd let him open without the blindfold but very carefully. Inside was an older female cat from an animal shelter who'd come from a home with lots of dogs where the owner had died. Smartie took one look around and decided she was home. After a few cuddles and snacks, Benjamin set her down on the sofa next to Casper and she curled up next to him as if she'd been to a job interview and had understood the brief immediately. For an hour, Benjamin sat and watched them, taking a stream of photos and reaching out gentle fingers to stroke them every now and then.

In the afternoon, he'd gone on a bike ride to his grandma's house who lived two miles outside their village. She'd baked cupcakes, bought him the hoodie his mum had told her Benjamin liked, and had spent the previous three months making a photo album of their family going back decades, ending with all the photos of him. The gift had been wrapped in silver paper with a green bow on it. They'd sat together for ages looking at the photos and remembering his grandfather. After that, Benjamin had insisted on mowing the lawn. He did it once a month, and he wasn't going to miss it just because it was his birthday. His grandma deserved better than that. She made him orange squash to go with the cupcakes, and he got cracking. Half an hour later, the lawn was finished and Benjamin set off for home, desperate to get back to Casper and Smartie.

Five minutes into his journey, he saw another boy slowly crossing the road, something cupped in his hands. He recognised the boy from his village but didn't know his name.

'Got something good?' he shouted brightly.

'A frog. I'm taking it to the stream before it gets run over,' he replied.

It was the most natural thing, to hop off his bike and walk with him to the tiny footpath that ran down to the stream.

'Can I see?' Benjamin asked.

The boy opened his hands a crack to allow him to peek in. The frog was sitting there, perfectly calm, waiting to be released. They didn't discuss it, didn't feel the need to introduce themselves, just walked, frog held out in front, through a copse of trees to the nearby trickle of water.

'Could I hold him, before you put him in? I've never picked up a frog,' Benjamin said.

When he was asked about it later, Benjamin would say that he hadn't noticed anything odd about the boy. He seemed normal. A couple of years older than him, fairly quiet, but not scary or unpleasant. Hard as he tried over the next months, even years, he would relive that conversation and try to identify the warning signs he'd failed to spot, but the truth was that there were none. That was because, until the blood started to flow, the boy's behaviour really had been entirely unremarkable.

The boy reached his hands out to meet Benjamin's, setting the frog delicately in his palm.

'Wow, I thought it would feel slimy but it's dry and warm,' Benjamin said. 'It's not even trying to escape.' If anything the frog felt a little too still, as if it were giving up on life. 'How long ago did you find it?'

'A while,' the boy said. 'Do you want to be the person who puts it back in the water?'

'Can I? I mean, it was your find, so I understand if you want to.'

'Nah, it's okay. You can do it. There's a patch along here where it's muddy without too many stones. I reckon he'd like that. I read in a book that frogs like mud.'

'Great,' Benjamin said. 'It's my birthday. My mum and dad got me a puppy and a cat as a surprise. You can come to my house and see them if you like animals.'

'Uh-huh, sure. The mud patch is just here,' the boy said. Benjamin knelt down, careful not to get his jeans wet. He didn't want to make extra washing for his mum. 'I think you'll need to reach out a bit further. We don't want the frog hopping back this way. He might end up on the road again.'

Benjamin wasn't convinced the frog would notice the additional few inches, but the boy had been kind, so he wasn't going to argue about it.

He leaned over, slightly off-balance as he tried to keep his sleeves out of the water, feeling the frog starting to move as it sensed the stream nearby. The boy was watching over his shoulder. There was a near perfect moment when the sun was sparkling across the water in diamond flashes, the stream splashing over tree roots and rocks, and they were both holding their breath as Benjamin lifted his upper hand.

Then the boy stumbled, falling forward to land heavily across Benjamin's shoulders. Benjamin went onto his knees, but the boy didn't manage to right himself so Benjamin kept going forwards into the mud patch, both forearms down in the water, squelching heavily beneath the water. Finally the boy got his balance, and lifted himself off Benjamin's back, landing on the bank next to him. The boy began laughing, and Benjamin forced himself to laugh along. His parents wouldn't be cross. They'd probably think it was all quite funny. Benjamin wished he didn't have to get cleaned up when he got home because he wanted to go straight in to see his new pets, and now he'd need a shower and a change of clothes.

The next thing he felt was warmth, which was odd given that the water was so cold. He looked down at his lower arms. The stream was swirling raspberry ripple.

'Don't worry,' the boy said. 'I can look after you. I know what to do. Let me see.'

Benjamin was trying not to cry, but he could feel the sting of the cuts in his arms and the amount of blood was making him panic. Below him, where he'd fallen, there was ice in the water, only that couldn't be right because it was summer.

'Glass, under . . . the mud . . . hurts . . . need my mum.'

The boy was peeling Benjamin's sleeves back, and the air on the wounds was a sudden agony, and now the blood wasn't seeping through his clothes any more, it was a river in its own right.

'Don't feel well,' Benjamin stuttered. His head was swimming.

'Lie back,' the boy said. 'Here, I'll help.' He put one arm around Benjamin's shoulders and laid him on the ground. The world was going fuzzy.

'Have to . . . stop bleeding.'

'Yeah, I'll sort it out,' the boy said.

He had each of his hands over Benjamin's forearms, and now the blood was all over him too, and the sheer redness was nauseating. The boy was sitting on Benjamin's chest and it was getting harder to breathe and impossible to speak. He wanted to ask the boy what he was doing, tell him to get a grown-up, but then the boy's face was pressed against one of his arms, and something was moving, snake-like, against the cut.

'I'll get help,' the boy said, sitting up abruptly. 'Holding your arms up in the air will slow the bleeding.'

He stood, wiping his mouth with the back of one sleeve, as he walked away. Benjamin both wanted him to go and was terrified of being alone. Freezing cold, weak as the almost dead frog who had not hopped in the end, but practically fallen from his hands into the river, he let the world slip away.

The next thing he heard was his mother crying. By the time he'd opened his eyes, his father was standing over her, cradling her. Benjamin wanted to tell them that he was all right, but his mouth wouldn't form the words. He slept again.

The next time he awoke, they were ready for him. He tried to raise his arms to hug his mother, but they were bandaged and packed so tightly he couldn't lift the weight of them.

'Oh, thank God,' she cried. 'You're awake.'

'Don't upset him,' his father said softly. 'He'll be okay now. How are you feeling, Ben? The doctor's on his way.'

'M'okay,' he slurred. 'Thirsty.'

'You'll be dehydrated,' his father said. 'They gave you a lot of painkillers and they had to do an operation on your arms, but everything will be all right.'

He slept again, and dreamed of trying to do a painting for his mother to put on the fridge door the way she used to when he was little, but every new colour he put on his paint brush came out red.

Recovery was slow. The doctors explained that he'd lost a lot of blood and needed vast numbers of stitches and a transfusion. His parents told him that the boy he was with had flagged down a passing car and saved his life. For the first few days, Benjamin had wondered if he'd made it all up in his head. Had there even been a frog?

His parents told him the police had checked out the river and found deeply embedded shards of glass hidden in the muddy patch where he'd been releasing the frog.

'Such awful luck,' his father said. 'If you'd been just a little further up or down the bank, you'd have been fine. They didn't find glass anywhere else.'

Benjamin began to cry.

'Oh, baby,' his mother cooed. 'Don't get upset. The scarring looks bad now, but it'll fade, and the important thing is that you didn't lose the use of your arms. I know the skin feels tight and painful but—'

'He did something to me,' Benjamin said. 'That boy. I think that maybe he pushed me into the river deliberately.'

'What do you mean?' his father asked.

'When I was bleeding, he . . . I don't know.'

'You're still in shock,' his mother said, smoothing his hair.

'He licked my cuts, like he was enjoying it.' Benjamin began crying again. He hated that he felt like crying so often.

'Ben, I'm sure it just felt like that. The boy said he was trying to get the bleeding to stop.'

'He didn't,' Ben shouted. His parents both sat back. 'He sat on my chest and he, I don't know, it was like he was getting as much of my blood on him as he could. I couldn't move and I couldn't get up.' He choked on the tears and the saliva in the back of his throat until his mother held him and he could breathe normally again.

Other parents would have decided it was all in their child's head. Another father would have whispered to their wife that their son was probably hallucinating, and his wife might have whispered back that their boy would seem more like himself in a week or two. But Benjamin was the sort of boy who could be depended on to tell the truth, even when he'd experienced the worst the world had offered him.

A week later, when Benjamin was safely reinstalled back home and being helped to heal by a very energetic puppy and an even more patient cat, his father reappeared from a sudden trip out, as white in the face as Benjamin imagined he'd been when the ambulance had rescued him from the riverbank.

His parents disappeared off into the kitchen, leaving Benjamin watching TV. He turned down the volume, feeling a wave of guilt at listening in, but stayed very still as his father talked in low tones.

'I felt I had to. After what Ben went through, it seemed only right. I expected them to be angry that I'd even suggested it. I thought they might throw me out on my ear or threaten to call the police. But they just sat there and listened, no reaction at all.

No anger or disgust. How can that be? I told them every single thing Ben told us, and they didn't look shocked in the slightest.'

'You don't think . . .' His mother didn't finish the sentence and his father didn't reply. There was a lengthy silence.

'Perhaps we should put the house on the market. Make a fresh start. Get Ben away from here,' his father said. 'Your mother can come and live with us, wherever we go. Benjamin loves her and he's going to be off school anyway while he recovers. I'll let the police handle it from here. I don't want any member of our family to have anything to do with those people, ever again.'

He could hear his mother murmuring agreement.

Ben closed his eyes and breathed out. Moving was good. Never seeing that boy again was good. Benjamin didn't go on social media very much. He didn't have a mobile phone, and his parents rarely used theirs, but he knew about sexual assault. He'd been taught sex ed at school and knew all about consent. What was strange about everything that had happened to him, was that the cuts, the blood loss, the scars and the pain weren't what kept him awake at night. It was the sense that his body had been invaded. The feeling that he'd been . . . violated. That was the word he learned later.

Something had been done to him and taken from him. His nightmare was the lack of power and sense of helplessness, and the feeling that the boy had been just waiting for him to come along that day. And the sure knowledge that the glass, that bad-luck-just-happened-to-be-right-there glass, hadn't been an accident at all.

Chapter 32

Midnight clutched her mobile. It was time to call DI Ruskin. Necto putting her on two weeks' suspension pending a disciplinary hearing was a one-way street, so how much more did she have to lose? Her employer was done playing nice, so she was done too. She'd considered her options since getting suspended and come up with nothing except that it was time for the truth. On Thursday afternoon, she dialled Ruskin's mobile.

'DI Ruskin,' he said.

'Hi, this is Midnight Jones,' she said. 'There are a few things I need to tell you. Things I wanted to tell you from the start, but I wasn't allowed to then, and now I think I'm about to lose my job, so their loss might as well be your gain.'

'Okay,' he said. 'You sound a little . . . strained. Before you tell me anything, are you all right?'

Midnight had no idea, that was the truth. From the second she'd found the Profile K applicant her world had been turned upside down. She hadn't wanted it, hadn't asked for it, in fact she'd done everything in her power not to burn her world down. Now everything was up in flames whether she liked it or not.

'Okay is subjective,' she said.

'I get it,' he said. 'So tell me what's been happening.'

'Necto's profiling system picked up an anomaly called a Profile K. That describes someone with not just sociopathic responses and boundaries, but beyond that into psychopathy. The applicant took his test at TESU. Then Chloe died, and she worked at TESU. That coincidence alone was enough to make me sure that these things are connected. Everything happened in the Clapham area. Then Mae died, so I took a look at the footage the applicant watched, and it had one scene very closely resembling the method used in Chloe's death, and another that could roughly relate to Mae's. Necto says it doesn't have the applicant's details, and that a Profile K isn't real, just a poorly chosen name for a set of data beyond anticipated profiling levels. But there are too many coincidences. Also I kept the data – fair warning, I actually stole it – then yesterday my flat got burgled and it's gone. I think Necto took it to ensure they didn't get caught up in the investigation.'

Midnight heard Ruskin take a deep breath and hold it for a few seconds.

'It's disappointing that the only solid evidence no longer exists,' he said. 'Without it, I'm not sure what the evidential link is between the Necto test and the murders, if there even is a link. Is this why you were at Mae's house after her body was found, because you felt responsible?'

'Yes! God, yes, I felt terrible. And now I've waited too long and Necto have made sure I can't help you. I'm so bloody sorry. I was such a coward.'

'Well, hang on a minute,' he said. 'First of all, you've told me now, which a lot of people wouldn't have done. Also, there are a few things here you can't be certain about, like who burgled your place, and, more importantly, whether or not this applicant actually is the killer. So let's take it one step at a time.'

'Sure,' she said. 'Whatever you need from me.'

'Right now, I need you to sit tight and look after yourself and your sister. It sounds like you're going through a lot. Who should I contact at Necto to talk through all of this?'

'Sara Vickson. That's who I reported it to at the start. She looked at the applicant's file and told me to delete it from my system.' She could hear Ruskin's pen as he made notes. 'I can't believe you're actually going to speak with Necto. Now that I've told you everything, I feel like such an idiot for not having said something before.'

'That's not a problem,' he said. 'I'm guessing a company like Necto has a whole minefield of confidentiality clauses in its contracts.'

'You have no idea,' Midnight muttered. 'There's another thing. It'll sound stupid but someone sent me an email at work under an anagram of my name – like they were trying to get my attention. Then someone else called my university alumni office to get my personal details.'

'And you think?'

'I think it could be the Profile K. He would have been sent my first name and the initial of my surname when I was working on his file. I guess the idea that I might have some insight into his nature might have sent him over the edge. I really think he could be the killer, so . . .'

'So you feel like you're being stalked by Chloe's killer too?' Midnight couldn't even respond. She knew how it sounded.

'Listen, I can hear in your voice how stressful this has been. I'm going to call right now and make an appointment to see Ms Vickson today, and I won't be taking no for an answer. You just hang on in there. If I have anything to report back, I'll call you.'

Midnight didn't want him to hear that she was crying.

'Thank you,' she managed.

The tears she cried once she ended the call were ninety per cent relief, nine per cent guilt and one per cent self-loathing. It shouldn't have taken her that long to do the right thing, but it was done. Whatever the consequences for her, she still had Dawn. As long as they were together and safe, she could cope with anything.

Doris had saved them, the night before. They'd cleaned up the mess from the burglary together, eaten together, and she'd even read Dawn a bedtime story before Midnight had seen her safely into a local taxi. Dawn, in spite of the trauma of the burglary and Midnight's frantic mood swings, had been blissful in Doris's presence. Midnight had watched the two of them at the table, the most unlikely of friendships, and realised what her sister was missing – a sense of extended family. Now sweet, lovely Doris had appeared and it felt like there was a chance that the hole in their lives could finally be filled.

Midnight pushed Dawn's wheelchair a little faster along the street to the cafe where they'd first had tea together. She didn't have anything better to do. It was true that there were job applications to be filed and budgets to be drawn up, but she didn't have to pay the carers again until she found a new job, once Necto had finally bitten the legal bullet and sacked her. Until then, she was on full pay, not using up any of her holiday, and determined to spend time with her sister. The teashop was full. Doris was in a corner, in a bright yellow jumper paired with a purple skirt, holding the two last available chairs with a strategically placed handbag and coat. Midnight parked the wheelchair outside and helped Dawn inside. They chatted as they looked at the menu.

'I used to bake,' Doris said. 'Don't bother these days. Seems such a waste just for me.'

'I met a girl at work yesterday who lives near here. She has a baking business. Goes round local companies with a trolley.'

'I might know her, then. What's her name?' Doris asked, waving at a waitress.

'Jessica at Bake Me A Cake. Her cakes looked lovely. Tea for three, please,' Midnight told the waitress. 'Also a Bakewell tart, apple turnover and a slice of the ginger traybake.'

'I once won a Women's Institute award for my Bakewell tart . . . Midnight, you all right, dear?'

Midnight's face had paled. Talking about Bake Me A Cake had closed a circuit in her mind, and now she knew exactly why Jessica had made her feel uneasy. She had to talk to her, and there was no time to lose.

'Doris, I have to make a call. Will you be okay with Dawn for a minute?'

'We'll be right as rain, won't we?' She gave Dawn's arm a squeeze as Midnight dodged between tables to get outside.

Her mobile offered up a number for Bake Me A Cake instantly. Midnight dialled.

'Hello, you've reached Jessica at Bake Me A Cake. I'll get back to you as soon I can. Leave your name and number.' Her voice was as bright and friendly as it had been the previous day when Midnight had been focused on Amber.

Midnight left a voice message, doing her best to sound casual rather than terrifying, reminding Jessica that they'd met at Necto but making it clear that she really, really wanted to speak with her and that she didn't want to wait.

Four hours later, Doris having insisted she would look after Dawn, Jessica entered the bar wearing a pink top with a sweetheart neckline and a black miniskirt with sheer tights. Midnight waved to catch her attention from the booth she'd been holding and wondered how best to explain why she'd asked for a meeting.

'Hi,' Jessica said. 'Hope you haven't been waiting long. I was trying out a new bread recipe and it took longer than I'd anticipated.'

She actually smelled of freshly baked bread, Midnight realised. Men had to flock to her. There was something so pure about Jessica. The thought didn't make what she was about to say any easier. They passed the first few minutes with small talk.

'I've got to be completely honest with you,' Jessica said quietly. 'I've only ever dated men so this is a leap. I hope you can bear with me if I'm a bit of an idiot. Just contemplating going on a date feels like such a monumental thing, but I'm so glad you called and . . .'

Midnight's mouth fell open and she started shaking her head.

'Jessica, I'm so sorry. I just realised how my call must have sounded.'

'Ugh. I'm so embarrassed.' Jessica dropped her face into her hands.

'Don't, please, this was my mistake. If someone called me out of the blue and asked to meet me I'd have thought the same thing. I would have been clearer, only I wanted to say this in person.'

When Jessica picked her head up again, her eyes were red. Midnight reached across the table and took her hand.

'Please don't be upset. I'm unbelievably flattered. If I were a bloke, I'd be sitting here thinking how lucky I was!'

Jessica burst out laughing and wiped a stray tear away with the back of her hand. 'I'm sorry. I've just been in the wars a bit emotionally, and when you called I was so excited that I didn't even stop to think about it. I've been trying to figure out a way to meet someone. Also, I seem to have stopped sleeping lately, so my judgement is clearly a little off!'

'Perfect storm. I know that feeling.' A waiter delivered wine. 'You joining me?'

'Maybe I should just go,' Jessica said.

'Actually I still need to tell you something, so could you give me a couple of minutes? The wine is optional, but I sure as hell need it.' She poured two glasses and raised hers in a mock toast. 'To me, suspended from work, recently burgled, probably soon to be bankrupt with little or no hope of ever having what might pass as a normal relationship. That make you feel any better?' She grinned.

Jessica picked up her glass and knocked it against the rim of Midnight's.

'Holy shit. That really does deserve a glass of wine. What happened with Necto? You were only there yesterday.'

'That's part of what I need to talk to you about, and it comes with a slightly personal comment. I'll give you the potted history.'

Jessica sat and listened as Midnight explained everything. By the time she was up to date, there was only an inch of wine left in the bottle.

'Jeez,' Jessica said. 'That's terrifying, not to mention appalling. I'm just . . . not sure what it has to do with me.'

'Yeah, that's the thing. Have you seen photos of Chloe and Mae?' Midnight pulled out her phone and brought up images of the two women side by side.

Jessica stared. 'My eyes,' she said softly. 'You think. . .'

Midnight didn't need to look, she'd noticed it the first time she'd seen Jessica. Her eyes were so wide apart it was hard not to stare. It made her striking rather than ruining her looks, but it also undoubtedly attracted attention. 'That's why I'm here? You think that because of my orbital hypertelorism, I might be a target.'

'Sorry, I didn't catch the medical term.'

'It's a genetic thing. I have a mild case, but it can require operations and bone restructuring. I'd say these two women just have very wide-set eyes, but it stops short of what I have.'

'It's your mouth too,' Midnight said. 'Forgive me for being so personal. You have this tiny, sweetheart mouth, like both the victims. The combination of the wide eyes and small, round lips makes your face really heart-shaped and, I mean, beautiful. You must attract a lot of attention. After what you said, I realised you live locally, like Chloe and Mae. So I wanted to warn you. I'd have felt awful if something happened and I hadn't.'

'Oh shit,' Jessica muttered. 'The Cream Bun Creep.'

'What?'

'There's this guy. He used to work for a company I deliver to, and he was always a bit slimy. Hanging around too long, asking personal questions. Suddenly he wasn't there any more, and I was really relieved, but then he turned up in my road and there was a crash between his motorbike and my van. I was reversing and felt responsible – he *made* me feel responsible – and he pretended not to recognise me. Anyway, things got nasty

259

and I was convinced for a while that he'd broken into my flat.' Jessica shivered and pulled her jacket over her shoulders.

'Did you call the police?'

'There was nothing to report. I didn't tell anyone until you.'

'What's his name?' Midnight asked.

'Willem Foster, at least that's what he told me, but as soon as I suggested we report it to our insurance companies, he backed off, so now I don't know if anything he told me was true. Please tell me this isn't the guy who killed those other women. He was in my flat, Midnight. He has my personal details. I think he even delivered me a dead rat a few days ago.'

'I'm in touch with a detective on the case. He's a good guy. I'm sure if I pass him the details, he'll check Willem out.'

'That's good,' she nodded. 'Do you think we could call your detective tonight? I have the details from Willem's driving licence, and his insurance too. We could call your detective from my place while I pack a bag. I can't stay there until I know it's safe. I've been through one abusive relationship. It took all the strength I had to get on my feet again.'

They slipped out of the bar together, Jessica indicating the route.

'We should move fast,' Midnight said softly. 'It's not safe to be out.'

Chapter 33

They hurried along side by side, Jessica recounting the weirdness of her interactions with Willem. The streets were busy enough to slow them down, and crossing Clapham's roads took time. Twenty minutes later, Jessica opened the door to the apartment block and let Midnight in. The lights flicked on as they took the stairs to the first floor.

'You don't have a photo of his driving licence, do you?' Midnight asked. 'I feel sure I must have seen him somewhere, probably just because he's all I've thought about recently, but—'

'That's so annoying,' Jessica said. She jiggled her key in the lock. 'This has been getting worse lately. My key doesn't want to work again.'

Midnight's blood felt like it dropped several degrees in temperature. She reached up a hand to pull Jessica away as the key finally engaged the lock, freeing the door. They fell forward together into the flat, landing heavily on their knees. And there he was, waiting for them.

Willem Foster, also known as the Cream Bun Creep, was lying on his side, eyes wide open. Something organic-looking was shoved deep into his mouth and most of his blood appeared to be on the carpet. A dining chair was on its side, and streaks of speckled blood climbed the walls like tracks of old ivy. The air was thick with the worst of bodily scents.

'Ah, ah, ah, ah,' Jessica was saying.

Midnight began pulling her backwards out of the flat and into the corridor.

They helped each other to their feet and fled down the stairs, crashing against the outside door before ripping it open and running onto the street.

'Was he . . . was he dead?' Jessica asked.

'God, yes. Do you know him?'

'That's him. Willem. What do we do now?'

Midnight was already dialling 999. Jessica pointed towards a battered van while Midnight was asking for help. They climbed in, locked the doors behind them, and waited for the lights and sirens.

'Who the fuck did that to him?' Midnight asked.

'I don't know, but I don't want the police to think it was me. He was in my flat! How did he get in there?'

'And how did whoever killed him get in there?' Midnight asked. They stared, open-mouthed and shaking, at the brightly lit upstairs windows in Jessica's flat.

A minute later, the road was being closed off, every window filled with faces peering out at the drama, as the machinery of the law took over.

They were escorted to a police van. Blankets were draped around their shoulders. Takeaway coffee appeared with unnatural speed, laced with sugar. After the police came two larger vans from which people emerged in the process of pulling on white suits. A variety of Jessica's neighbours were escorted out, carrying overnight bags. Presumably they'd all been asked to find somewhere else to stay while the corridor was processed. A man appeared carrying a bag of equipment, and everyone stood back to let him through.

'Pathologist's here,' one of the police officers said to another. 'We'll get some answers soon.'

They waited and watched.

Midnight studied Jessica as she sipped the steaming coffee, aware of how little she really knew about her. She'd accepted everything Jessica had told her about Willem Foster without question, except that now a man was dead on Jessica's floor, and she was Jessica's alibi for the time she'd been out of her flat. Not that she thought Jessica was capable of such a thing. Willem Foster had been stabbed, over and over again, by the looks of it. You had to be really crazy to do something like that to another person. Or very, very angry.

'It wasn't me,' Jessica whispered.

'That's not what I was thinking.'

'It's what I'd have been thinking. I turn up to meet you, tell you all about this guy, then take you back to my place and there he is, dead on the floor. Of course you're wondering if it was me.'

Midnight took a deep breath. 'Yeah,' she admitted. 'It had crossed my mind. I'm sorry. That's not a reflection of you. I'm not sure which way is up at the moment.'

A forensics officer put his head into the van. 'Sorry to have to ask this, but because you entered the scene, we'd like your outer clothes to be taken for examination. We can swab your shoes here and return them to you immediately. You might have picked up some trace evidence that will help, and we need to exclude you from the investigation.'

'You need to exclude me as a suspect?' Jessica asked.

The man gave as reassuring smile as he could while nodding. 'Of course,' Jessica said. 'Are you able to bring me a change of clothes from my flat?'

'Not until the scene's been fully processed, and that won't be tonight. We'll provide you with crime scene suits for you to travel in. Do you have relatives or friends nearby?'

'No,' Jessica said. 'I moved here to get away from my ex-boyfriend. I haven't got a social circle yet.'

'You can stay with me,' Midnight said.

'No, you'll be feeling wary. I can book into a hotel. I don't want to impose.'

'No way. A man was just killed in your flat. You shouldn't be alone tonight.' She took hold of Jessica's hand. It felt like ice in spite of the burning hot coffee cup she'd just been holding. A woman who introduced herself as a detective constable climbed into the van.

She made notes of their names, dates of birth, addresses.

'So, Jessica, you know the man upstairs as Willem Foster. Is there a reason he was in your flat tonight?' the constable asked.

'I didn't know he was there. I suspected before that he'd broken in. I let him in to recover after a traffic accident three weeks ago, while we exchanged details. He stayed for hours, much longer than I wanted. I did wonder if he'd found a way to copy my keys while I was making him a drink or in the loo. Another time I thought he'd left a dead rat outside my door. I went round to his house to ask him about it.'

'A dead rat? Are you sure?'

'Yes. I got home and found it outside my door in a box, it was gross. That was just after I'd told him to deal with the accident claim through my insurance company a few days ago. He'd been kind of stalking me.'

'Did you happen to see what was in his mouth when you entered your flat tonight?' the detective constable asked.

Jessica shook her head.

'It was a rat. Dead and decomposing, but definitely a rat,' the officer explained.

Hands across her mouth, Jessica doubled over, and did her very best not to be sick.

Chapter 34

'Well, a rodent in a corpse's mouth is something I never thought I'd come across, which will teach me not to assume I've seen everything there is to see yet,' the pathologist said to the other crime scene operatives in the room. 'The rat's not fresh. From the decomposition, I'd estimate it's been dead a few days and I'd say it's infested with fleas, so we should warn the homeowner. She'll need to treat this carpet.'

'Given the amount of blood here, I'd say the fleas are the least of her problems,' DI Ruskin said, walking in and surveying the damage.

'Jock, I wasn't expecting to see you on this one. Are you not busy enough with your serial killer?'

'I've handed that over to someone more senior, and I'm only filling in here until they allocate another DI to it. This is a mess and a half. The rat has some relevance, I'm told. What are people like?' Ruskin put his hands on his hips and shook his head. 'The detective constable spoke to the person renting this place who found the body. She has an alibi going back a little over two hours, during which time she walked to and from a local bar, and was at the bar with witnesses for an hour. How does that fit with time of death?'

The pathologist shook his head and raised his eyebrows. 'This is a very recent death, but you know I can't be quite that precise. More than an hour, less than three, but that's all I can give you. He hasn't lost that much internal body heat, but then he's indoors, the central heating is on, he's fully dressed and lying on a carpet. Blood loss was extremely rapid, and death would have taken just a few minutes. Grab a step to kneel on. If there's trace evidence on the floor anywhere, it'll be right in front of his mouth because this took some doing. Also, put on a mask. You're not going to want to breathe this in.'

Ruskin did as the pathologist suggested and was immediately grateful for the advice.

The rat's two back legs were hanging down below Willem Foster's bottom lip, its tail limp and dangling onto his chin.

'Christ almighty, it looks as if he was in the middle of eating it,' Ruskin said, narrowly avoiding gagging as he spoke. Speaking involved breathing in, and the stench was incomprehensibly awful.

'This is a large, adult male rat. Its head, I believe, has been pushed deep into the victim's throat,' the pathologist said. 'I want to wait to remove it during the postmortem so I can assess how much force was used.'

'Do you have any idea of the sequence of events?'

'His hands aren't tied, no restraints were used at all, in fact, so I'd say the killer surprised the victim, stabbed him multiple times, he fell to the floor, and the rat was probably pushed into the mouth while he lay bleeding out. He must have been too weak to pull the rat from his mouth, or it wouldn't still be in situ. One of the stab wounds,' he pulled the shirt apart and pointed to a deep wound in the upper chest, 'most likely hit his heart. The blade was long and sharp. We're assuming it's the one on the floor just behind the body.'

'How many wounds?' Ruskin asked.

'Eight that I can see right now, plus some additional defensive wounds on his hands. The stab wounds on the torso were purposeful. The intent was to kill, I can say that with some certainty. You can't push a knife into a body this far and think anyone could survive it.'

'Could a woman have done this?'

'Strength-wise? Absolutely. That knife was sharp enough, as long as the victim didn't have much prior notice of the attack, that any adult could have inflicted those wounds. They're all either forwards or ever so slightly downwards in angle so the perpetrator couldn't have been much shorter than the victim, more likely the same height. He's approximately five foot ten.'

'Maybe they were up on their toes, or wearing heels,' Ruskin offered.

'Possibly. The attack was frenzied, one stab after the other, because you can see that all the wounds bled at the same time. The heart was still beating while each wound was made.'

'So the whole attack from start to finish might only have taken a minute?'

'Exactly. There's a lot of blood involved, though. There would have been a substantial flow from the earlier wounds when the knife was withdrawn each time, and some spray which you can see on the walls. Finally, when they were inserting the rat into the mouth, they would likely have been kneeling in blood.'

'So if the woman who lives here did this then went out, she must have a magic formula for getting cleaned up,' Ruskin said.

'There are some partial footprints, right foot only, leading towards the door, still slightly wet. At first glance, they look large, suggesting a man's feet. They're not full prints, so I'd say whoever did this made a real effort not to get too messy – they knew what they were doing. It's possible they left in a hurry and didn't have time to get fully cleaned up.'

Ruskin thought about that for a moment. 'With that much blood everywhere, it would have been all over their clothes, unless they'd really prepared and were wearing something like the suits we're wearing now, shoe-covers and all. Let's say they got disturbed, took the coveralls off, bundled them into a bag, maybe made a mistake in the last second and trod in a patch of blood. Possibly didn't even realise. They got out into the hallway and onto the street with no visible sign of what they'd done. It means it wasn't an impulsive crime. Nothing spur of the moment. Pretty much meticulous.'

'I agree, and there's further evidence to back up your theory. Here's what we found in his pocket . . .' the pathologist reached out a hand to an assistant who passed over a small plastic evidence bag.

Ruskin took it and held it up to the light. 'A key. Is it a match for this apartment?'

'Looks likely. It needs processing for DNA and prints before we start doing anything else with it, but I'd say so. Do you see the little cardboard tag attached?' Ruskin nodded. 'It has a single capital J handwritten on it. Does that relate to the woman who lives here?'

'I believe so,' Ruskin confirmed.

'The deceased also had a pair of ladies' underwear in his pocket that we've bagged and tagged. We need to check the whole place for his prints to see what else he was up to, and take her prints to see what interaction if any she had with this body, then we can figure out if anyone else was involved.'

'That's one scary love triangle,' Ruskin said. 'The woman

who lives here – Jessica – apparently knows this guy. There's some suggestion that he'd been stalking her.'

'Well, if she didn't do it, then someone else in her life is very dangerous indeed,' the pathologist said, standing.

'Any chance it was someone known to him? Maybe the deceased wanted to intimidate Jessica, brought someone with him as an accomplice, but then the two of them got into a fight?' Ruskin suggested.

'Anything's possible, but the rat thing is weird. Say you're right and the two of them came here together. Maybe the accomplice wanted to steal something or got sloppy, and there's unanticipated conflict . . . why spend the extra time posing the body with the rat?' the pathologist asked.

'That may well prove to be the million-dollar question,' Ruskin said. 'I'll get back to the station, put in a preliminary report, and identify a team. Someone'll be in touch tomorrow to talk through your postmortem findings.'

'Sir,' the detective constable appeared. 'Did you want to come out and speak to the witnesses yourself?'

'No. There's no point me getting involved. Take thorough statements, and make sure they're both available to come into the station in the next few days. It's not my case.'

'You got somewhere better to be, Jock?' The pathologist gave him a smile.

'I actually do,' Ruskin said, patting the pathologist on the shoulder and walking out.

Chapter 35

The detective constable reappeared in the police van. 'The detective inspector wants to know if you have a key with a cardboard tag, and a J on it?' she asked Jessica.

'No,' Jessica said. 'I wouldn't need to put my own initial on my keys.'

'Good point,' the detective constable said. 'Have you ever given a copy of your key to anyone else? A cleaner, maybe?'

'No one has a key except me.'

Jessica sounded exhausted, sad and scared.

'Is there anyone in your life you think might be capable of this? Someone who maybe kept an eye on you, without you even knowing it?'

Jessica leaned forward, pressing her hands over her stomach.

'Your ex?' Midnight suggested.

'Billy? This can't be him,' she said.

'Was he abusive?' the constable asked.

'Yes.' Jessica's voice was faint. 'But he's gone quiet lately. He kept calling for ages after we split up. I changed my number, more than once, and cut ties with all our old friends. I even moved. I figured he'd got bored of me. I've only had one nasty text recently, but I can't be sure it was from him. It wasn't from a number I recognised, so I deleted it and blocked the sender.'

'Was Billy ever physically violent?'

'No broken bones, just bruises and scratches. The psychological part was worse. There was a lot of bullying and controlling behaviour,' Jessica said. 'No sign of this, though. I never thought he was capable of killing anyone.'

'Did you find a weapon?' Midnight asked the police officer. 'Because that would have fingerprints on.'

'The weapon appears to be a kitchen knife, but we haven't been able to establish yet if it's from this kitchen, or a blade that was brought in from the outside,' the constable said. 'In any event, we'll need to take your fingerprints, to exclude you. Did either of you touch the body?'

They shook their heads.

'All right. We'll take statements from you both, then drop you wherever you need to go. Please make sure we can speak with you in the coming week, and don't leave the area.'

It took another two hours to jump through all the hoops. By the time the police car dropped them off at Midnight's, they were too exhausted to talk. Doris took one look at their faces and the crime scene suits, obviously decided against asking any questions at that moment in time, gave Midnight a hug so tight it took her breath away and told her to call the next day, then hopped in a cab home. Dawn was peacefully asleep in bed, so Midnight converted the sofa bed and found pillows and blankets, while Jessica changed into borrowed pyjamas and scrubbed her hands and face.

'I honestly thought it was Willem, when you were talking about the man who killed Chloe and Mae. I wanted it to be him, so he could be arrested and stopped, and I could just hate him. Now I feel like I'm responsible for his death, and I don't know what to do with that. And . . . oh shit . . . I'm going to let all my clients down tomorrow. I was supposed to do the trolley at three different companies. How long are the police going to be at my place? I have to get into my kitchen—'

'Jessica!' Midnight said, taking hold of her by the arms. 'Your kitchen is closed for the next twenty-four hours, days probably. You can't cook in that place until it's been deep cleaned. It may take police a lot longer to process everything.'

Jessica let out a shuddering sigh.

'I'm sorry. It's all been such a shock. I don't think I'll ever feel safe in that flat again. I'll have to give notice to leave. All I'll ever see in my lounge is that body.'

'I get it, but that's tomorrow's problem. For now, we should be grateful you're safe. We went looking for a serial killer and instead we found a dead body. I'm betting that we wake up in the morning to the news that your ex has been arrested. Once that happens, you'll have both the Cream Bun Creep and your former boyfriend out of your life forever. Fresh start. You can start getting out there. We'll find you someone who won't hurt you or take advantage of you. You deserve a good woman.'

'I do.' Jessica gave a small laugh. 'What about you?'

'I deserve some work–life balance, less financial pressure, and real friends who are there when I need them.' Midnight's phone pinged. The screen notified her that an email had come into her private account, but the sender's address was just a jumble of random numbers and letters. 'Apologies, I need to check this.'

She considered deleting it – there were viruses and scams everywhere – but it couldn't hurt her as long as she didn't open any attachments, and there was always the possibility that it might be to do with her parents. Midnight opened it, skim-read it, then did another take.

'*Sorry I didn't do more*,' it read. '*I wanted you to know that you were right. Don't share these. They'll know.*' At the bottom, a series of documents were attached.

'What the fuck?' she murmured. 'This has to be from Necto.'

'About your disciplinary hearing?' Jessica asked.

'Sneakier than that. I can only open these files on my laptop. If this is what I think it is, the virus will infect my laptop and wipe my drives. It's Necto's way of making sure I haven't got any other evidence against them that they didn't find when they sent their toy soldiers here. If I can isolate it, though, and save it, I might just be able to turn the tables on them. My coding skills are pretty rudimentary, but not non-existent. I need to negotiate a leaving package, and this might be a stick to beat them with.'

'I'll make more coffee,' Jessica said. 'That's way over my head.'

'Think, think, think,' Midnight muttered. 'Okay. Let's try this.' She disappeared into Dawn's bedroom, using only the light from her mobile screen to guide her, then reappeared a few minutes later clutching a laptop with dented corners and a scratched-off logo.

'Not the latest technology then,' Jessica smiled.

'A few years ago, I let Dawn have this laptop so she could watch her favourite shows while we were out. I bought her an iPad after that, and just never got around to throwing this out. I need a charger though.'

She disappeared again, and Jessica started rifling through the kitchen cupboards looking for ingredients.

'You don't mind?' she asked, gesturing at the assortment of ingredients on the kitchen counter when Midnight reentered.

'Go for it,' Midnight said, plugging the old laptop in and drumming on the coffee table as she waited for enough charge to switch it on and run it off the mains.

'I stress bake,' Jessica explained. 'Have done as long as I can remember.'

'Who taught you?' Midnight asked.

'My mum, but she's gone now. What about you, where are your parents?'

'Touring the world, probably camping on a beach in South America right now. The only thing they taught me was how to let people down. Baking would have been better. Here we go, lucky it still works after the number of times it got dropped. Bloody updates. This'll be a while.'

'I know it's a stupid question, but you said you have a work laptop. Why don't you just log into this email on that? If it corrupts everything, that's Necto's problem.'

'Not stupid at all, but I don't trust it. They just appeared with it one day when I was sick, told me not to tamper with any of the settings or turn it off. It's a wonder they didn't accompany me home to take it away . . .' Her voice trailed off, and she moved her head slowly to stare at the laptop that was sitting on a bookshelf across the room.

'Midnight, you okay?' Jessica asked, sifting flour into a bowl.

'Holy crap,' she whispered. 'That's how they found out about the pen drive. It wasn't Amber. I told Connie Woolwine about it.'

'I don't understand. And why are we whispering?'

Midnight put a finger up to her lips and walked across the room to the laptop, opened it up and began typing furiously. A couple of minutes later, she leaned into the laptop.

'Fuck you,' she said, then pressed and held a button, before storming over to a chest of drawers and shutting the laptop away.

'Oh my God, were they . . . listening to you all this time?'

'Yes. There's software that allows them to input keywords, so if I talked about anything they were interested in, it would have alerted them.'

'Wow, what sort of company does that?' Jessica asked, wide-eyed.

'I thought Necto was changing the world. Turns out they were, just not the way I want the world to change.' She looked longingly at the mixture Jessica was stirring up. 'This has been such a shit day. I don't suppose there's any chance those cakes will be ready soon?'

'I'm making microwave cupcakes, so yes, give me five minutes.' She gave Midnight a brilliant smile. 'Cake makes everything better.'

'I wish that were so,' Midnight said, dashing tears away before they could fall. 'Now I just need to deal with that email.' She logged in and opened the email, clicking on a series of attachments, skim-reading as she went, and issuing a stream of softly spoken expletives.

Jessica put the cakes in the microwave and went to sit next to Midnight.

'All those documents say confidential at the top. Did someone send you them to get you in trouble?' Jessica asked.

'I don't think so. There's a briefing paper, a client letter, some medical notes, and this,' Midnight tapped the screen, 'a report on a Necto test subject. What the actual fuck?' They settled in silence to read it.

Subject [redacted] attended [redacted] College, from age 16 to 18, on a full boarding basis. Contact with parents was limited. Parental referral related to repeated criminal behaviour although the subject had never been charged with, or convicted of an offence. Subject is a 32-year-old heterosexual male, unmarried, currently single and living alone. His address is [redacted]. He graduated from [redacted] University, since which time he has worked in white-collar positions, for no more than 12 months per post. To date, he has still not come to the attention of the authorities.

Student files obtained from [redacted] College note that the student was unsettled for the first year but that reformative therapies appeared successful in his second year. Available documentation includes therapist notes, medical records, academic notes and parental letters. The subject was originally referred for developing psychological problems that involved increasing violence with forward planning and targeting vulnerable subjects, obsessive behaviour, anti-social behaviour and unhealthy appetites. It was considered that, but for the intervention, the subject would have continued to offend in increasingly serious ways. Records showed that subject had a substantial obsession with one particular female, [redacted], from his childhood village, about whom he repeatedly spoke in counselling sessions. The female's personal details are contained within the counsellor's notes and it is possible that even now she remains a focus of the subject's attention. We recommend ongoing surveillance of this female as the subject appears to have moved within a short distance of her home address in London.

[Redacted] College managed his psychological development with a range of therapeutic and punitive techniques that prevented further offending and reset the subject's proclivities and tendencies, allowing him to function relatively normally within the community. He is considered a good test subject

for an attempted psychological reset to study reactions to targeted stimuli on inactive psychosis.

'What do they mean by a psychological reset?' Jessica asked.

'I'm not sure, but I have a bad feeling about it. After all, if this student was functioning better, coping normally in society, then a reset could only mean undoing all that good work, right?'

'So they're trying to . . . bring back the monster?' Jessica whispered.

Midnight nodded slowly. 'I think that's exactly what they were trying to do.' She reached out and took hold of Jessica's hand without realising she'd done it.

Subject was invited for free testing using a specially drafted letter directed towards his particular interests and strengths. At this time, he has confirmed a testing slot but not yet attended for testing. At testing, subject will be shown footage tailored for him specifically.

The aims are to use subliminal messaging within the test to pinpoint specific psychological weaknesses. Necto will put surveillance in place to assess behavioural, sociological and psychological changes in the subject. The results for this subject will be compared with other test subjects in the same study to determine the effectiveness of the technology. Reports will be made to the client [redacted] on the effectiveness of the technology for (i) psychological weaponisation, and (ii) enemy unit psychological warfare. At the present time, the study is progressing on time and to target.

'Are they . . .' Jessica took a deep breath. 'Are they seeing if they can mess someone's brain up so badly that they start hurting people?'

'They are.' Midnight dropped Jessica's hand, closed the file and shut the laptop. 'No wonder Vickson tried so hard to shut me up. What the fuck have they done?'

Chapter 36

'Whoever did this for me took one hell of a risk. This isn't just whistle-blowing. Sending out research like this is corporate theft.'

'Do you have any idea who sent it?'

'A good friend. Someone I judged too quickly and too harshly. First, I owe them an apology, then I need to decide what I'm going to do with the information.'

'I'll give you some privacy,' Jessica said softly, before disappearing in the direction of the bathroom.

Midnight tried to imagine what Amber must have done to access the documents. Lying, at the very least, maybe getting access to another department and someone else's computer. Possibly even password theft. However she'd done it, it had involved serious threat to not just her job but also her liberty. Probably, having dug a bit deeper, Amber had realised that Necto were prepared to do some very bad things to protect their secrets, and betraying Midnight to Vickson had been the perfect cover for it. It must have been terrifying. Midnight made the decision to call her in spite of the hour. What she had to say couldn't wait.

Her mobile went unanswered for a few rings until a sleepy-sounding Amber picked up.

'Do you know what time it is?' she asked.

'I'm sorry,' Midnight said. 'And not just about the time. I should have had more faith in you. Please don't say anything, because this is all on me. I know we have to be careful. Necto has been listening to me at home. But thank you, and I want you to know that I love you.'

'I appreciate the apology but honestly it could have waited until morning.'

'By then I'll have made my mind up about next steps,' she kept it vague. It was a long shot that Necto were listening to Amber's calls, but far from impossible. 'What you've done for me is far more than I deserved.'

'Are you being sarcastic, or are you drunk?'

Midnight heard the flick of a light switch followed by a male groaning and mumbling.

'Oh bugger, I'm sorry, you're with someone. I didn't mean to disturb you.'

'We were sleeping.' Amber sounded irritated. 'Listen, I've said I'm sorry, but I think you need to take some responsibility for what happened too. You didn't have to take it this far, not with Dawn depending on you.'

Midnight pinched the bridge of her nose and tried to follow the conversation.

'I get that,' she said, 'and I know you went out on a limb for me, so . . .'

'Midnight, it's really fucking late and you're not making any sense. Did I miss something?' Amber's tone evolved from irritated to really pissed off.

Midnight let that sink in, panic rising slowly from her stomach to her head.

'No. No, you didn't miss anything. Busted, though, I had a few drinks and lost track of time. You told me several times not to get involved, and I wouldn't let it go. I should never have blamed you for the suspension. That was all on me. So thank you for . . .' The words stuck in her throat like a giant lump of undercooked pastry. 'Thank you for trying, even if I was too stubborn to listen.'

'Well, that's okay, and yeah, you should have listened. I hope you come to your senses and give them the reassurance they're looking for. It's not too late to keep your job.'

'Uh-huh,' Midnight murmured. 'I guess it took this to make me realise just how good I had it.'

'Turn the bloody light off,' the man in the background muttered.

'I have to go,' Amber whispered. 'We should get lunch next week. I'll put in a good word for you with Vickson, let her know you want to put things right.'

'That'd be great. Thanks Amber,' Midnight said. 'Sleep well.'

Jessica reappeared and took the cupcakes out of the microwave.

'Thank God I woke her up,' Midnight said. 'If she'd been awake, I'd never have got away with that.'

'With what?' Jessica asked.

'It wasn't Amber who sent me those documents,' she said softly. 'She's never been that good a liar. If it had been her, she'd have let me know it.'

She'd wanted it to be Amber, Midnight realised. Perhaps that's why she'd leapt to the conclusion that Amber had been the one to help her rather than consider whether or not there was any evidence to link Amber to the disclosure. If Amber had done it, she thought, she'd have found a way to reach out – even if the message had to be coded somehow – to let her know. The excitement Midnight had felt at repairing the friendship shrivelled into disappointment.

'Who did send it then?' Jessica began cleaning the kitchen.

'I guess it must have been the one person I was certain I couldn't trust. Eli. I was so worried about the timing of his arrival on my team that I never shared anything with him. I suspect Amber did though, so Eli would have known all about it.'

'Can you call him?'

'No, and I've got a horrible feeling he might have been in bed with Amber. Someone was there, and she and Eli were starting to get very friendly. If I call him now, Amber will suspect that whatever I was just talking about to her actually applies to him. She's not stupid, and I can't be sure she won't report back to Necto like she did before. I don't want to get Eli into trouble.'

'So what can you do with those documents anyway?' Jessica asked.

'Allude to the contents without being specific when I negotiate a leaving package, and I can tell DI Ruskin that everything I suspected was right. I'll have to stop short of handing over the stolen documents as I don't want to get anyone in trouble. Ruskin was supposed to be talking to Sara Vickson, so I'm hoping there's been progress. I'll call him in the morning. It's too late now.'

'Yeah. Earlier, I thought I might never sleep again, but now I can hardly keep my eyes open.'

Midnight checked her watch. 'Dawn will be awake at seven o'clock on the dot. Let's regroup tomorrow.' She stood, stretched, and padded towards her bedroom.

'Midnight?' Jessica said. 'Thank you, again. It took a leap of faith for you to invite me here. I don't know what I'd have done without you today.'

'No biggie,' Midnight said, gently switching off the light.

In her bedroom, she tried once more to get hold of Connie Woolwine, but didn't even get a ring tone. She gave up for the night and fell asleep – by some miracle – in less than a minute.

Outside in the light-polluted dark, two men watched. Both wanted to speak with the women inside. One sat in his car, lights off, huddled down in the seat. The other sat on cold stone steps, hidden by a doorway, a scarf around his face. The same rain obscured their views. The same vehicles passed them both. One was a hero, the other was a killer, and each had broken the law. Neither one knew the other was watching.

Chapter 37

The Applicant

He had to kill again. If in the past he'd been able to pretend that it was something less than murder, and that death was only a side-product of fulfilling his needs, he couldn't any more.

Midnight Jones was no longer a distant possibility of a threat. She'd found Jessica. His Jessica. Pieces were falling into the puzzle of his identity faster than he could possibly have anticipated, and he wasn't coping well.

Finding Midnight had been easy, although it had taken some patience waiting outside Necto's office, identifying her from the photo he'd found, then following her home. The first time, she'd hopped on a bus and he'd been too far behind her to do the same. The second time, she'd walked home and that had worked out fine. Since then, he'd spent some time watching her flat – ground floor, thankfully – although she kept the curtains closed most of the time. To his amazement and delight, he'd discovered that she had a twin. And no one else lived with them.

This time, learning from the problems at Mae's flat, he'd done his research properly. No more being impetuous, because that was going to get him caught. Midnight's flat looked out onto a quiet street with a small strip of grass between the lounge window and the road. If he broke in through there, he'd be spotted whatever time of day it was. The bedroom windows, though, were at the side of the building, and with garages between the windows and the road. Midnight's bedroom protruded further than her sister's, which gave him even more cover to break into the sister's room. If he was quiet enough, no one would be any the wiser.

He would tie them both up – Midnight would be compliant if her sister's life was under threat – then take his time. He'd have all night if he did things right. He even had a new weapon with him, and he was excited about trying it out. More than just excited. He couldn't wait.

That was why he was sitting outside the flat on a cold stone step, in the dark, getting rained on. It should have happened hours ago, only then his world had shifted on its axis, and Jessica Finch had appeared with Midnight, both of them dressed in white coveralls. He'd slapped his face to wake himself up, convinced he was hallucinating. But no, both Midnight and Jessica had reappeared, showing an old woman out into a taxi.

It had been a busy day. He'd taken some time in the afternoon to check on Jessica, only to find that as she'd been leaving her building, the scumbag who'd been stalking her had entered. The scumbag had been dispatched quickly and appropriately enough, but so fast that he hadn't taken any real pleasure from it. That idiot had been planning on leaving yet another dead rat in Jessica's place – not a mistake he'd ever make again.

Fortunately, good planning meant that he had spare clothes with him in preparation for that night, so he'd been able to change out of the bloody garments before making his way to Midnight's. It had all been going so well. Then without warning, the two most important women in his life at that time had climbed out of a police car right in front of him.

That was hours ago, and he hadn't been able to leave since then. He could see their outlines as they walked around the lounge-diner behind the curtains.

Jessica's appearance meant that he was right to be concerned about what Midnight knew. She must have been looking for him. Did she have his name? His address? Surely not, or the police would have come a-calling, which meant he had no time to lose before killing her. Perhaps it was best done then and there. His backpack had everything he needed to get in through the window, to tie them up and to dispatch them.

But then there was Jessica. His inspiration. The woman he'd always believed he loved.

Only now . . . did he? Had it been a simple teenage crush taken to new heights by his desperate loneliness? It was so hard to tell what was real any more. Suddenly Jessica was a risk too. If she was hanging around with the woman who'd profiled him, she was a loose end he could no longer leave hanging.

Three women in one flat. So much blood. Even if half the night had gone, there was still time.

A light went off inside, and he stood to get a better view. There were still other lights on, but the women were moving around now. He needed to hang back, but the excitement, the possibility, the thought of how it would feel and smell and taste, was making him twitch. Another light went off, and now the flat was fully dark.

He needed to get closer, to listen and look. One of them might still be awake and scrolling or texting. The streets were quiet, and that was good. He could spend some time waiting for them all to be fast asleep before breaking in.

He began crossing the road, moving diagonally to get behind the garages where he wouldn't be seen, then—

A car slammed its brakes to stop just inches from his legs, suddenly putting on its lights. He threw up an arm into his face, but too late. The driver had seen him and was shouting something he couldn't hear.

He stared longingly at Midnight's flat, just metres in front of him, but stepped backwards instead, breathing hard, grateful to be in one piece. The car pulled away.

He had to go home. He had no choice now. The driver had seen his face so clearly. Anything that happened that night would lead straight to a Photofit, and he'd worked with enough people that one of them was bound to identify him.

It wasn't fair. He was ready. He needed it. Now he'd have to retreat like some miserable dog with its tail between its legs.

Bide your time, his inner voice cautioned. Maybe not tomorrow, but perhaps the next day. Let the dust settle. They'll be worth the wait.

Chapter 38

Dawn loved the enormous, fluffy, multicoloured jumper that Doris was wearing so much, the two of them were just cuddled up on the sofa, pointing out all the different colours.

'Doris?' had been Dawn's first word that morning. Midnight had promised to phone Doris that evening to arrange another get-together, but was pre-empted when the phone rang half an hour later, only for Doris to ask if they were in the mood for a visit. She'd arrived shortly after with a bag of food to make them all shepherd's pie for lunch, several bottles of bubble mixture, and three new children's puzzles which were exactly right for Dawn. Midnight had hugged Doris tight, overwhelmed by gratitude.

'That's all right, my lovely,' Doris had muttered. 'I'm here as much for myself as I am for you. Now you get on with whatever you need to be doing. I'll put the kettle on.'

Midnight had introduced Doris properly to Jessica, then Dawn spotted the bubble mixture and puzzles, and any hope of chatting longer was gone.

'Doris is lovely. You're so lucky to have met her,' Jessica said. They were lying on Midnight's bed with the door shut, so that nothing they discussed upset either Dawn or Doris.

'I know. It's like she woke something in Dawn. The agency carers are fine, but very matter-of-fact, like they don't want to get too attached because it's just work. When we met Doris, though, she filled a need in Dawn straight away. If I believed in anything as unscientific as fate, I'd say we were supposed to have met her. Does that sound stupid?'

'It sounds wonderful. I hope there's someone out there that I'm supposed to meet. I could do with the universe taking care of me a bit.' Jessica gave a weak smile. 'When I woke up this morning, for a few seconds, I'd forgotten about it. Then when I remembered, I wasn't even shocked. It was like, yeah, that happened. What's wrong with me? A man got stabbed to death in my flat and it's as if I couldn't care less.'

'Willem Foster scared you. It doesn't make you a bad person if you don't care what happened to him, it makes you sensible. It's just one more threat eradicated from your life.'

'Yup. Not the only one, though, apparently.' She turned onto her side to face Midnight. 'I like your place. It feels safe and homely. You're amazing to have looked after Dawn all by yourself for so long. Do you miss your parents?'

Midnight thought about it. 'No. They've been gone for years, and I have Dawn so that's their loss. My parents weren't always terrible people. When Dawn was little they were good with her. They never missed an appointment, and our house was adapted to make it easy for Dawn to play safely. It's like they ran out of steam. When they saw me get into my twenties, I think they realised what they'd missed and wanted a chance to be young and carefree again.'

'Hard on you, though.'

'It was. It is, if I'm honest. But this whole nightmare has been a reality check, weirdly. I don't want Dawn to be with carers all day, and I don't want my sister to be stuck in some tiny flat in the middle of a city. We need more space than this, and better quality of life. When Necto sacks me, and after I've used the contents of those leaked documents to command a fair pay-out, I'm going to start looking for a new place. I'd like to watch the sunset without the distortion of smog. What about you? I guess you'll be looking for a new place to live, too.'

Jessica shrugged her shoulders. 'In my dreams, I live in a townhouse on four levels. One entire floor is this gorgeous kitchen, with huge ovens and pantries, and doors that open onto a garden so it never gets too hot and I can feel fresh air on my face. As it is, there's enough blood on my carpet right now for me to open it up as some sort of house of horror. I hate blood. Always have. The way it drips. The way it dries. It even smells disgusting.'

'Chloe and Mae's killer doesn't hate it,' Midnight said. 'I spoke to a psychological profiler about the crime scenes. Dr Woolwine's amazing. We talked for ages. I was hoping she'd contact me again, but she's on a case abroad and now she's not answering her phone.'

'Well, I wish your Dr Woolwine was here now,' Jessica said. 'She might have some idea who killed the creep in my flat.'

'I bet she would,' Midnight said. 'She had this theory about the serial killer, to do with the saliva on the victims' bodies. Said it might be something called Renfield syndrome. People are so fucking weird, it's hard to believe we're all the same species.'

Jessica stood up and stretched. 'Do I even want to know what Renfield syndrome is?'

'It's a sort of nod to Bram Stoker's *Dracula*. It's also called clinical vampirism, only without the undead. Some people get

291

obsessed with blood, tasting it, drinking it. The whole thing freaks me out.'

'Here's to that. When I was a kid, there was a rumour about some boy in our village doing something like that. There was this other boy who lived near us . . . I forget the details. Something happened, like an accident or something, this kid got hurt, and he swore the teenager drank his blood. It was all anyone could talk about for weeks. The boy who got hurt left school. His parents put their house on the market and everything. No one ever saw the family again.'

'What happened to the kid who did it?'

'People said he went to a new school. I wouldn't have recognised him anyway. I'm not sure I ever met him.'

Midnight stared at her. Jessica was beautiful. Stunning, but unique. Unmissable, really.

'Do you believe in coincidences?' Midnight asked.

'Not really,' Jessica replied. 'Except for meeting you in the middle of all this. That was pretty lucky.'

'I'm not convinced it was luck,' Midnight said slowly. 'I think it was a combination of geography and corruption.' She made a decision, got up off the bed and walked into the lounge. 'Doris, we have to go out and we might be gone for a few hours. I'm going to call a carer, but you're welcome to stay as long—'

'You most certainly will not pay anyone to look after your sister when I'm here already and having a lovely time. There'll be hot food ready when you get back. Don't insult me by suggesting any other arrangement.'

'I don't know what we did to deserve you.'

'My mother believed that people appear in your life when you most need them, and she was a very wise woman,' Doris said.

Midnight leaned down, wrapped a tight arm around Doris's shoulders, and kissed her on the cheek. 'Like mother, like daughter.'

She stood again and beckoned to Jessica. 'Let's go. I'm driving, you're navigating. No time to lose.'

Chapter 39

They negotiated a bumper-to-bumper M25, then made their way south towards Guildford, conscious of every minute that ticked by.

'DI Ruskin's mobile number is in my wallet,' Midnight said. 'It's on a white card.'

'Found it,' Jessica said. 'Get off this road at the next exit. My old village is just a few miles away.'

'How old were you when you moved away?' Midnight asked her.

'My parents divorced when I was sixteen. They sold the house, and I never went back to the village again. Hold on, his phone's ringing.'

'Put it on speaker,' Midnight told her.

'Ruskin,' he answered.

'Thank God. This is Midnight Jones. I wanted to talk to you about a theory I have. I'm on my way to—'

'Miss Jones, I can't speak to you. I'm about to go into a meeting,' Ruskin said.

'But it's about Chloe and Mae's murderer.'

'I'm not actually on that investigation any more,' he said. 'In fact, I'm not with the Met Police at all, as of the end of my shift last night. I was made an offer, so I took retirement using up my annual leave to exit immediately – it was long since overdue. You should contact whoever's taken over from me. The incident room will be able to put you in touch with the senior investigating officer.'

'But I told you everything. You were supposed to speak with Sara Vickson. And since then I've received new information about Necto's involvement.'

'Miss Jones, I'm sorry to be blunt, but my enquiries at Necto proved fruitless. However, they did explain that they have serious concerns about your mental health, and that you're currently suspended pending a disciplinary panel. My advice would be to set aside your obsession with the murders and focus on preparing for your hearing.'

'He has my name!' she shouted. 'He was told about "Midnight J", that I work at Necto, and he knows I'm the one person who understands exactly what he is! I think the killer might have Renfield syndrome which is—'

'Mr Ruskin, we're ready for you now,' a woman cut in, albeit muffled in the background. 'Ms Vickson will join us shortly to go through the terms of your contract offer.'

Midnight's mouth went dry. 'You're at Necto.'

'I have to go,' Ruskin said. 'I felt obliged to pass on my concerns about your mental health to the investigating team at the Met before I left. Necto were adamant that you might be disruptive to their investigation.'

'How much did she offer you?' Midnight asked softly. 'It's great pay, right? Four, maybe five times your police salary? Great perks, too. Let me guess, you're going to be their inside man liaising with police forces across the UK.'

'The role was open . . .'

'Funny how that happens,' Midnight said. 'Nice holiday package, private health care. And you still get your police pension. Boy, did you fall on your feet.'

'I have a family to think about. Ten years at Necto and I can give my wife a more comfortable retirement than we ever dreamed of. Do you have any idea how much she missed out on because of my career? Parents' evenings together, school plays, birthday celebrations. Medical appointments where she was given bad news and had to handle it alone, for fuck's sake. My wages were never enough to give her the lifestyle she deserved. I just want to give her, and our kids, a brighter future. I earned that. I sweated blood and cried tears for it. I had to see things the general public have no idea about. And my kids . . . there are things they both need. Things I should have been able to help them with long before now. This job at Necto is the payoff for years of slog in the police force, and you can't tell me I don't deserve it. Plus, there's a chance to do some real good here. The technology being developed has so many uses—'

Midnight ended the call. No arguing, no drama. Just a dead line and silence.

'Fucking Necto!' Midnight screeched, thumping the steering wheel.

'Do you want to, maybe, pull over?' Jessica asked. 'Just until you've calmed down.'

'No,' Midnight growled. 'I do not. And don't worry, I'm fine. The only idiot here is me. I should have seen that one coming. Necto are good at recruitment. They took a police officer who appeared to be the most caring, experienced, principled man imaginable, and they bought him. But not until they'd made him discredit me.'

'So whoever we call about this is going to . . .'

'Think I'm imagining things? Yup. Exactly that,' Midnight finished for her.

'And I'm the girl with the dead body in her apartment, part-victim, part-suspect. Which makes this part-shitshow, part-nightmare, doesn't it?' Jessica said. 'You know what? I bet they have one of those crime line phone numbers.' She jabbed madly at her phone screen.

'We need a name first,' Midnight reminded her. 'This boy from your village with the blood fetish might have left the country. He might even be dead. Let's see what we can find out, then we'll figure out a way to tell the police about it.'

Jessica gave directions. The centre of the village had retained its countryside character, with old houses nestled around a duckpond, the obligatory thatched pub and a church, beyond which was a sprawling housing estate.

'Do you think you'll recognise the house?'

'This estate's new, but the rest is familiar. After the rumours started about the blood-sucking incident, a group of us went to the house for a dare. Stupid kids' stuff,' she said. 'The building was imposing. I remember a cockerel weathervane.'

They drove into a warren of country lanes, windows down as they looked around.

'Stop!' Jessica shouted. 'I think that's it, through those trees. You can just make out the side of the house.'

Midnight found a long gravel driveway and left her car at the end. They smartened themselves up, snapped photos as subtly as they could, and went to see who was in. The garden was large but had been left to go wild, save for a small mowed area of front lawn. Thick hedges hid the front elevation from the road, and there was woodland to the back. The windows were clean but the paintwork was peeling. A sign on the front door declared that no sales talk would be entertained, while an ageing Volvo sat in front of a garage further down the drive.

'Here goes nothing,' Midnight said. 'Remember the story and keep it simple.' She rang the bell, half-expecting to hear a Dickensian chime.

Eventually, a man appeared, opening the door a couple of inches. Midnight put him in his late sixties or early seventies.

'Hello,' Jessica said brightly. 'Sorry to call unannounced. My name's Jessica and I used to live in the village. I lost my parents recently, and I'm putting together a scrapbook of my childhood for my own kids.' The man stared. 'I was friends for a while with the boy who lived here, and—'

The man issued a burst of laughter. Jessica stopped talking.

'Teddy didn't have any friends,' he said. 'Not that we were aware of.'

'You're his father?' Jessica asked. 'I assumed the house had changed hands over the years. I was going to ask if you remembered the owners. So how is . . . Teddy?'

The man folded his arms and a woman appeared at his back. They were equally tall and skinny. His hair was grey, hers was entirely white.

'What do these two want?' the woman asked.

'This one claims to have been friends with Teddy,' he said, pointing at Jessica.

The woman echoed his earlier derisive snort.

'My name's Jessica,' she said. 'It's so lovely that you're still here. I wish I'd had that much consistency in my life. Teddy's very lucky.'

'Jessica,' the woman took small step forward, looking her up and down curiously. 'I remember Teddy mentioning you. He didn't talk much about other children as a rule. Did you go to school with him?'

'No, our house was the other side of the village so I fell into a different catchment area,' Jessica managed, her voice getting smaller with every passing word. 'Then my parents divorced, so they had to sell our house. Where did Teddy go?'

'Moorview, then Manchester University,' Teddy's father said. His wife tutted.

'And what's he up to now?' Jessica asked.

The man took a slight step forward. 'He's working in London, whereas you seem to be as free as a bird to knock on strangers' doors on a weekday during office hours.'

Midnight let Jessica bluster through that one as she peered inside. The interior was much like the outside, neat but disintegrating.

'Sorry,' Midnight said. 'But we've been travelling a while and I'm desperate for the loo. Would you mind?'

'Actually we would,' the woman said. 'I'm not sure who you are.'

'A friend of Jessica's. I drove her here. It's not always safe for women to knock on doors alone, so I guess I'm a bodyguard of sorts.' She offered a meek smile and a gentle laugh. They returned neither.

'There's a petrol station outside the village. They have facilities,' the man said. 'You should go.'

'Of course,' Jessica said. 'We don't want to keep you. I'm glad Teddy's doing well. I work in London too, actually. Is there any chance you could give me his mobile number so I can get in touch with him?'

The woman actually huffed. Midnight tried to keep a neutral expression.

'I can take your mobile number and give it to him next time he calls, in case he would like to be in contact with you,' the man offered.

'That'd be great,' Jessica said, reaching for her handbag. Midnight caught her hand.

'Great idea,' Midnight said. 'Do you have a paper and pen?'

She took a bold step forward to get her head inside the front door. Both the man and woman stepped back away from her.

'The back of that envelope will do,' Midnight said, pushing further forward and grabbing a letter from a stack that had been left on a table next to the door. 'We can use this.'

'You will not,' the woman snapped, snatching the envelope back. 'I'll fetch my notepad.' She took a few steps along the hallway to a table with a landline telephone on it.

'Wow,' Midnight said. 'It's lovely that you've kept your house so . . . original.'

'The number,' the woman called.

Midnight trod gently on Jessica's toes. She gave a number and followed it with, 'Please do ask him to call. I'd like to see who else he remembers from here and try to find them online. Does Teddy use any social media? That might be the easiest way for us to get in touch.'

The man screwed up his face. 'I sincerely hope not,' he said. 'It kills the brain cells.'

'You're right there,' Midnight said. 'And you can't trust it. You never know who's got your information these days.'

'Yes, well, we agree on that,' he said.

'Always nice to meet a fellow sceptic,' she stuck out her hand until her fingertips were just touching his. He unfurled his fingers slowly and took her hand, as if he didn't want to, but his digits had a mind of their own. 'Mr . . .?'

'Hawthorne,' he said.

'Sally . . . Bowles,' Midnight replied, kicking herself for the clumsy musical theatre name theft. 'We should go, Jess. That petrol station has my name on it.'

Mr and Mrs Hawthorne watched them walk up the drive and off their property before shutting the door.

'Talk about sinister,' Midnight said. 'It was like a Shirley Jackson novel.'

'I think they're just old and a bit mistrustful,' Jessica said. 'She didn't like you, though. What was that thing with the envelope?'

'I was trying to get a surname,' Midnight said. 'Turns out, you just have to apply standard English handshake pressure. Tell me that wasn't your actual mobile number.'

'Of course it wasn't. Even if Teddy Hawthorne isn't who you think he is, the rumours about that kid went on and on. I don't want him in my life.'

'Him, or his parents.' She shivered. 'Right, I'll get us home, you get on your mobile and see what you can dig up about Teddy, Ted, Edward, Theodore or Eddie Hawthorne. He might not be using social media, but he has to live somewhere. We have an approximate age, he works in London, and we know about his education. That should be enough for the internet to work its intrusive and highly dubious magic.'

Chapter 40

The Applicant

From the outside, it was like any other sixth form college. Located at the edge of Exmoor, too far from bus stops and train stations for public transport to be of use, trips home during term times were discouraged, and additional fees could be paid for students to remain in dorms during the holiday periods too. Teddy was starting an A-level course, in the normal way a sixteen-year-old would, studying maths, geography and chemistry. He'd wanted to do biology, but given it included some dissection and mention of subjects Teddy had been banned from discussing, everyone agreed that chemistry would be the less triggering option. That was where any similarity to a normal sixth form reached an abrupt full stop.

His parents told him remarkably little about his new home before dropping him off. An intimidating stone entrance hall with grand pillars loomed at the top of a curving driveway. Members of staff were standing waiting as they pulled up. His mother had packed more clothes than he thought was necessary for just the six weeks until half-term, but they'd agreed a generous tuck shop allowance and said he didn't have to write all that often.

As they pulled up, he saw there were girls arriving too. Teddy's heart soared. Girls were so much better company than boys. They were softer, easier to pal around with and much nicer to look at. As he'd had to leave his precious Jessica behind, at least he could look at the girls there and find the one who looked the most like her. Strange that his parents hadn't mentioned it was a co-educational school. It would have been a selling point for him. The decision to send him there had been made under a cloud, of course. The Benjamin Hoffman debacle had seen him pretty much trapped in his bedroom for the whole of the summer, and the boarding school option was only announced to him in mid-August, but he hadn't fought it. The village, his mother had explained, had been consumed with gossip since Benjamin . . . she never had found a way to finish a sentence with Benjamin's name in it.

The police had talked to him. He'd denied any knowledge of how the glass got into the river. Bumping into Benjamin on the road had been nothing more than a coincidence (which was true; any child would have served the same purpose). Benjamin had made rather a strange allegation, the officers said. Something about Teddy (long pause) licking the wounds? Maybe even sucking them? (Another long pause.) His parents, to give them their due, had kept poker faces the whole time.

'Poppycock,' his father had said. The Hoffman boy was clearly hysterical, likely in shock. Teddy was simply helping. Were the Hoffmans trying to get money out of them? How ridiculous. The police had gone on their way shortly thereafter. If an offence had been committed, it was hard to tell and even harder to prove. Benjamin Hoffman was going to be all right, mostly. Perhaps, one officer had suggested, just keep a low profile in the village for a while. His parents had managed to maintain their composure until the police were driving away.

Teddy had wanted all hell to break loose. That would have been preferable to what actually happened.

'Go to your room, son,' his father had said. 'It's bedtime.'

'But it's only five—'

'Bedtime,' his mother had repeated. 'We'll talk in the morning.'

The next morning, his mother had opened his bedroom door to slide in a breakfast tray, then closed it again. His father had fitted a lock to the outside of the door. Teddy had an ensuite, and food was provided three times a day, so his basic needs were met. He was able to open his window and stare into the garden but the drop made illicit excursions impossible. They delivered him books and puzzles, and weren't cruel or abusive, they just stopped all meaningful interaction. The next long conversation they had was to show him the brochures for a private school called Moorview College. A week later they'd packed up the car, his parents had said a stilted farewell, and Teddy had been shown to his dorm.

The girls, it turned out, were housed in a different building. They wouldn't eat together, socialise, or even have assemblies in the same hall. They did share classes but the girls sat on one side of the room and the boys on the other. Speaking, passing notes, or giving each other what teachers called 'the eye' resulted in caning, not that caning was legal, but who was going to complain? Parents sent their children to Moorview with the expectation that their child would return to the world a better human being, by any means necessary. The cane, Teddy found out, had a split end that would cause twice the damage, twice the pain, and that gave it more flexibility for a better whipping motion.

Moorview taught Teddy to study hard and get good results. It made him grateful for the little pleasures in life. And it made him compliant. That was what Moorview was very good at indeed.

For those who could afford it, Moorview's mission was to ensure their graduates would fit into mainstream society. Did you have a child showing a tendency towards homosexuality? Drug abuse? General teenage sloth, rudeness, bad habits? Sign on the dotted line. And there were special programmes for those teenagers displaying really deviant behaviour. Had your child attacked someone? Did you get the sense that there was something deeply wrong with your child, so that even the best therapist couldn't help? Moorview was the answer.

Teddy had only memory snapshots of his time there. Sometimes, not even memories, just fears that rose up to overpower him temporarily, before he got himself back on the straight and narrow. Candle wax was one memory. Food withdrawal was another. And the terror of wet bed sheets.

He'd graduated from Moorview a straight A student and gone to university with all those former appetites and deviancies locked into a psychological strongbox and tucked away – or so he'd believed – forever. He watched no television, no films, read no books other than textbooks, saw no plays and listened to no music other than classical. At university, he knew better than to let himself slip back into his old ways. He kept eyes front in lectures and handed in his work on time, and if he never used his mind to push boundaries or experiment, then he always turned in properly referenced work with accurate conclusions.

Since university he'd stuck to safe jobs where only factual work was required of him. He'd been a good employee, always on time, never disruptive. He'd looked at women occasionally but never wolf-whistled, never accidentally brushed them on the tube. Most importantly, he hadn't slipped. Whatever he'd thought about in the small hours, when other men crept from their wives' sides to watch porn on their phone in the bathroom, or when women considered the mechanics of pressing a pillow over their snoring husbands' faces, he'd never acted on his desires. He'd witnessed an accident once between a bus and three pedestrians, choosing to run from the blood rather than letting himself be consumed by it again. He even purchased processed food rather than risk the excitement of entering a butcher's shop. Moorview College had worked its monstrous magic on him. And if they hadn't cured him entirely, then at least they'd made him bury his true nature so deep down that it should never have seen the light of day again. Life had become much easier since he'd learned to suppress the savage – the redder, as he thought of it – side of his nature. He'd tried so very hard to be normal. Teddy had wanted to remain the man his parents had sent him to Moorview to become.

He'd located Jessica in Clapham when she'd started her own business and put a headshot on her website. The first time he'd seen her again in person had been the closest thing to a religious experience he could imagine. Her face and body, all grown up now, had been exactly as he'd fantasised, night after night, through all the lonely years. Even if she did attract the very worst sort of men.

After finding her, he'd kept his distance as he had back at home. It had been enough for a while to know she was nearby, to see her living her life, not all of it good, but he'd been taught not to intervene. He lived by rules, and those rules had saved him.

Until the letter from Necto. Until the test. Until he'd seen all the things he'd tried so hard not to see for so long.

If he'd stayed in touch with anyone from Moorview, he'd have known that he wasn't the only one who got the letter. If he'd thought about it, he'd have wondered how Necto got his name and why they thought he might be a good candidate for their new profiling test. If Moorview had destroyed their records when they'd changed hands and become an international language school, things might have been different. But the files had sat in the basement, in neat plastic folders; every detail of every disturbed child recorded. Until someone finally found a use for them, and a way to make money from them. Necto was such a force for good, investing in the community.

Chapter 41

'Tell me I'm not the link.' Jessica stared out of the window as they drove home.

'I can't,' Midnight said kindly. 'But that doesn't make you responsible.'

'I don't get it. I never spoke to him, didn't know I'd ever crossed paths with him, and yet he mentioned me to his parents? Maybe it was another Jessica.'

'Did you know another one about your age in the village?' Midnight asked.

Jessica didn't answer, but slumped down further in her seat. 'I'm going to call it in,' she said. 'The police will deal with it.'

Midnight didn't bother arguing. It was only right to let the police know, even though what they had was no more substantial than a red piece of wool linking photos, maps and psychological syndromes around boards in their minds. She had the email from the Necto whistleblower, too, for whatever that was worth.

Jessica dialled. 'Yes, hello,' she burst out, 'I need to . . .' Silence. A long wait. She put her hand over the mouthpiece of her mobile. 'Voicemail, loads of beeping, there must be a lot of messages on here,' she whispered. 'Oh, hello, my name is Jessica Finch.' She gave her mobile number. 'The man I believe you should be looking for in relation to the murders is Teddy Hawthorne. He works in . . . somewhere in London. We don't have his address, but he has an obsession with blood. I knew him when I was a teenager. Please, call me back.' She ended the call. 'Why does none of it sound as compelling when I try to explain it on the phone?'

'Because we need Dr Woolwine to explain her theory to them. I've got an idea. Go online to a site called Personal Insights. You'll get a warning about it not being secure, and it's not, so sorry about that. Log out of everything first, social media, email, any apps with your financial information on them.'

It took Jessica a few minutes. 'What now?'

'These apps find people's details with very little preliminary information. They're a bit dodgy, illegal in a few countries, but as soon as one shuts down, another opens up.'

'Will I get in trouble?' Jessica asked. Midnight took her eyes off the road to stare at her. 'Yeah, point taken, everything's relative,' she said. 'Right, Teddy—'

'Edward,' Midnight corrected her. 'There's no way his parents registered his name as anything as human and fluffy as Teddy.'

'Edward Hawthorne. It's asking for an age. He was in the school year above me, so I'm guessing thirty-two. Now it wants a city: London. Sex, male.' She hit submit and waited.

'His parents said he went to Moorview. Do you know it?' Midnight asked.

'Never heard of it. Definitely wasn't a local sixth form. Here you go. It's found five Edward Hawthornes in the London area. That's amazing. Have you ever checked yourself out?'

'Yup,' Midnight said. 'It's terrifying. Read me the list.'

There were only two options in the area of the murders. 'Check out social media,' Midnight said. 'If we're right, one of those guys will be avoiding having a public profile like the plague. The other one might be a bit less shy.'

'Got one. Eddie "the Ed-Ster" Hawthorne is on Facebook, Insta and TikTok. Shaved head and a face tattoo. Not going to blend in.' She tapped a few more keys. 'The other guy is missing in action in terms of information. And his address is . . .'

Midnight was quiet for a few seconds. 'Write it down and let's go.'

'Midnight, no. That's crazy. You don't know what you're getting us into. We can't just knock on his door and ask if he's killed anyone lately.'

'We don't need to do that. Come on, we're back in Clapham already. You heard what his father said, Teddy's most likely at work. Let's just drive past his place and see what it looks like.'

'You can't be serious.'

'Jessica, Necto has seen to it that the police think I'm losing my marbles. Even if we just find his front door, we can maybe get his DNA. I know there was DNA at the scene of both Chloe and Mae's murders. If we got a match from here too, it would be case closed. No more having to talk through theories or profiles,' Midnight said.

'We're not going in, right?'

'I'll keep you safe. You can stay in the car if you'd prefer.'

'I would actually,' Jessica said.

They parked on a road that looked as normal as every other street in Clapham. 'This can't be it,' Jessica said.

'I know what you mean. Like, you should get a sense that something's going on here. Damn, I can't see any building numbers. It must be on that side of the road, though.'

They got out of the car.

'It's all commercial property,' Jessica said. 'So it has to be one of the flats above those industrial units there.'

'The entrance must be to the rear. There's a passageway. You wait here.'

'I can't see who's coming and going from here,' Jessica said. 'I'll stand in front of the fish and chip shop. Is your phone charged?'

Midnight checked. 'Yes, and I'll keep it in my hand. Phone me. No need to say anything. If it rings, I'll come straight back out.'

'Fine. No risks. Give me your word.' Jessica folded her arms and waited.

'Too bloody right,' Midnight said. 'Just don't freak me out unnecessarily. If my phone rings, I'm going to come racing out, probably having a heart attack. Give me a second. I've got some wipes in the boot I can use for collecting samples.' She popped her boot, fiddled around, and slammed it shut.

Jessica took up her post outside the chip shop window, grateful beyond belief that there were plenty of people coming and going, and that it was still daylight. She peered into the passageway between the buildings, which was just wide enough for a small car to drive into a parking area with communal bins and industrial unit drop-off points, then stood back and waited.

The area at the back of the buildings wasn't the least bit intimidating. There were bins, a few stray bags of rubbish, a motorbike half-concealed behind a signpost, some smashed pallets, and an old stack of chairs. At the back of each industrial unit, a staircase rose up over a basement area to the flats above. Midnight double-checked Teddy's address then walked along looking at the buzzers.

'Thirty-five A and B,' she muttered. 'Here we go.' Teddy's place was 35B.

Midnight took the steps at a jaunty semi-jog, as if she were no more than a delivery person with a lot to do that day. Deep breath, try the buzzer first.

It gave a metallic grating sound. Midnight looked up. The noise issued through both the doorbell unit and a partially open window on the top floor. She kept an eye on the curtains above, but there wasn't the slightest twitch. Mr Hawthorne had been right; Teddy was at work. She pressed the button for flat 35A. There was no response from that flat either, but looking up at the closed windows, no curtains, filthy glass, she wondered if anyone was living there. She took a wipe from the pack, carefully cleaned the door handle, then folded up whatever DNA she'd captured and pushed the wipe deep into her pocket. It still wasn't good enough. That handle could have anyone's DNA on it, from landlords to delivery drivers, even would-be burglars. The only handle she could guarantee would have clear traces of Teddy's DNA was the one on the door of his individual flat.

Midnight checked the area once more. There was music playing, a backdoor into an opposite unit standing open, the sounds of plates clattering deep within. Traffic was heavy on the road where they'd parked. It was mid-afternoon. What could happen?

Below the steps, she'd already spotted the basement. It had to be a storage or utility area for the units above, which meant there was a good chance it would access the staircase to Teddy's apartment door.

She made sure she hadn't missed any calls, looked for CCTV cameras, then jumped down the three feet into the basement cavity, wiping dust from the window with her sleeve before peering through it. It definitely wasn't a residential room. There was an ancient clothes airer gathering cobwebs, parts of a bicycle, and a dried-up mop and bucket.

'Two minutes,' she said. 'Up the stairs, wipe the handle, down the stairs, get out.'

From the rear waistband of her jeans, secreted beneath her jacket, she pulled the large flathead screwdriver she'd taken from the basic toolkit she kept in her boot in the absence of a shed. Jessica hadn't needed to know. Even from across the road, it had been obvious that the building was in a sufficiently bad state of repair that getting in wouldn't be impossible, so long as she could do it without being spotted. The window frames were wooden and rotting, with only single glazing. Midnight kept low and slid the screwdriver up the vertical window frame, putting forward pressure on when it hit the catch, pushing the head of the tool under the lever and trying to pop it up. Nothing.

'Shit,' she muttered. The wood had split slightly but the catch was holding. Midnight tried again. More movement, but still no success. 'Works in the bloody movies,' she said. She took another look over the top of the basement wall. There was still no one around. One last go. She shoved the screwdriver deep into the bottom corner of the window where the paint was at its flakiest, pushing hard enough to make the wood groan. Keeping the pressure on, she forced the tool upwards, snagging the bottom of the internal catch. It moved.

'Oh fuck,' she muttered. 'I actually did it!'

There were a few wasted seconds as she stalled. She didn't care that she was committing a crime. She had no intention of breaking into any private spaces, or stealing anything. All she needed was for Jessica to stay alert if anyone was approaching. If Midnight encountered anyone inside, her plan

313

was to pretend to be on her mobile, having a conversation about building safety. Taking a risk wasn't the same as going in with no Plan B.

She climbed inside, slid over a countertop, hopped down, then pushed the window closed again. The handle felt loose and floppy but it wasn't obviously vandalised. For all anyone knew, it could have broken when someone tried to open it from the inside, she told herself. Midnight stopped and listened. There was no noise. She was alone in the building, and it was time to move.

A sliding door accessed a staircase up to the ground floor. It squeaked enough to reassure her that it was rarely used, but not enough to make it difficult to get through. Even inside the building, she still had a mobile signal, and there was enough light that she didn't need to put her torch on.

'So far so good,' she muttered.

The industrial unit was in front of her facing out onto the road, so presumably the stairs she was taking skirted around the side of that. The fact that she'd entered at basement level meant there had to be one additional flight of stairs to get her into the accommodation area of the building. Midnight turned a corner towards the detached edge of the building, so somewhere there had to be a double-back to a hallway between the two flats. In front of her was another sliding door. She put on a cheery face, mobile in hand, ready to act like a building inspector, and stepped through.

It was a lounge. Basic and tidy, if sparse, nothing out of place, but definitely a sitting room rather than a corridor.

'Bollocks,' Midnight said. 'This isn't a hallway! Which flat am I in?'

A door with a peephole was the exit into the main hallway, double-locked, needing a key to open it.

'Curtains,' she said. 'There were curtains in thirty-five B.' She raced through another doorway and found an ensuite. A further door out of the bathroom took her into a bedroom.

There was the open window through which she'd heard the first buzzer she'd pressed, and the curtains she'd seen.

'I'm in his flat,' she said. 'Shit it, I'm in his frigging flat.'

The bed was made, and the flat looked normal enough, but at the far edge of the bedroom a roof ladder was down below an open hatch, two suitcases on the floor at its base. Midnight stopped in her tracks. Could Teddy be up there? Was that why he hadn't heard the door buzzer? She tried to quieten her breathing, grateful that she hadn't banged any doors and that her phone hadn't rung. Her heart was beating out of her chest. She grabbed her mobile and set it to silent. Leave or look, she asked herself. There was no movement above her head, no creaking. The flat was as still as it could be. Fighting her own persistence, wishing she could just let it go, she crept to the bottom of the ladder. There was no sound at all, not even the movement of air from above her. He's at work, she told herself. He's paying rent and living alone, so he has a job. Stop driving yourself crazy.

She took a step back and her heel caught one of the suitcases. It toppled over with a bang and Midnight cried out. She fled to the bedroom doorway then forced herself to turn and look back. Nothing. No Teddy, no bogeyman chasing her. Absolutely nothing except a fairly tidy room and those cases.

'Teddy's running away!' Midnight said. 'He must know he's going to get caught soon.'

She raced back into the bathroom, pulling open the cabinet above the sink. There, exactly as she been hoping for, was a comb. She couldn't take the whole thing – he'd know straight away that someone had been in – so she pulled out a couple of stray hairs, careful to put it back where she'd found it, and closed the cabinet.

Midnight checked her mobile again. There were no missed calls. She was going to be fine. All she had to do was get out, same route she'd gone in, and make sure she left the doors as she'd found them.

'Calm down,' she told herself. 'Just don't pass out. Sixty seconds and it'll all be over.'

Chapter 42

Jessica was starting to freak out. She knew it had only been a few minutes. In terms of distance, Midnight was just around the back of the block. There weren't any other street entrances in or out. No one had driven or walked into the alleyway. It was fine. The staff in the fish and chip shop were laughing as if they hadn't a care in the world. A police car had even gone past, an officer raising her hand at a teenager. The kid had smiled and waved back. Community policing at its best.

'Excuse me, love,' a man stuck his head out of a passing van. 'Do you know where the nearest petrol station is?'

'No idea, sorry,' Jessica told him.

She looked into the alleyway, terrified that someone might have sneaked through in the five seconds she was distracted, but she was panicking unnecessarily. Even so, Midnight was taking too long. Jessica pulled out her mobile to check how many minutes had passed, as a man wandered out of the chip shop, barging straight into her. The mobile went flying, hit the metal bin next to her then skittered into the road, landing just under a parked car.

'Sorry, I didn't see you! Here, hold this.' He dumped a warm paper bundle in her arms and rushed over to retrieve her mobile, getting down onto his hands and knees to reach under the car.

'I'll get it,' she said. 'It was my fault. I should have been standing further away from the shop door.'

'I think I've found it,' he said. Jessica heard scraping as he pulled it back out. 'Not good news, I'm afraid. Have you got insurance? I know a great repair shop but there's a lot of damage.'

He stood up sheepishly and gave her the handset. The screen was completely smashed. Tiny shards of glass prevented her from tapping it, and the screen was full of pixelated lines.

'Oh God, not now,' she said.

'Can I help? Use my phone if you need to make a call. Do you need a cab or something?'

'No, but thanks, I can sort it out.' She kept half an eye on the alleyway, feeling herself start to sweat.

'Okay then,' he said. 'Well, sorry again.'

Jessica brushed the worst of the glass away and waited for him to disappear. She had no choice now but to go after Midnight and hope no one followed her to the back of the building. The man who'd obliterated her phone crossed the alleyway, stopped for a few seconds to eat a handful of chips, then took out his own mobile before turning ninety degrees and heading towards the back of the buildings.

Jessica's jaw dropped.

'Holy fuck, not right now,' she said. If Midnight was doing anything stupid, which given the delay seemed entirely possible, the last thing they needed was a witness. She raced after him. 'Excuse me!' she called. He was walking ahead of her, turning the corner to the back of the flats. 'Actually, I could use some help. Hello?'

He heard her, finally stopping at the base of a set of steps. There was no sign of Midnight anywhere. Jessica wasn't sure if that was good or bad.

'You all right?' he asked. 'Do you need the details of that repair shop?'

'Yes, please,' she replied loudly, hoping the sound would echo around the quadrant to wherever Midnight was. 'That would be . . .' Some metres away, only half-concealed, was a motorbike. Jessica didn't know much about bikes generally, but she knew that one, with its customised paint job. That was Billy's bike. She'd been on it enough times to know she wasn't mistaken. The man, still munching chips, followed her eye-line to the bike.

'Everything okay?' he asked.

'Not really,' she said slowly, taking a few steps past him towards the bike. 'I recognise that—'

The tip of the blade pressed through her hoodie hard enough to sink into her skin right onto a vertebra. She felt the trickle of blood before she'd even registered the pain.

'Walk up the steps,' he said. 'I know you think you can scream for help, but I'll kill you. Or worse, I'll leave you alive but so badly injured, you'll spend every minute of the rest of your life wishing you were dead. I don't care if I get caught, that's what you need to remember, Jessica. At least I'd have the memory of covering myself in your blood. There's no way for anyone to reach you before I sever your spinal cord.'

'Please don't hurt me,' she said.

'I'm not intending to,' he whispered. 'We're long overdue a conversation. You have so much to thank me for. I'm going to hand you my keys to open the door. Not a word, not a sound.'

She did as she was told, too scared to run or fight. Too scared, even, to cry. Inside the building, he locked the door behind them, knife still pressed into her back. The blade was a fire in her flesh.

'You really didn't recognise me?' Jessica didn't answer. 'That's disappointing. Up the stairs, and go careful. I don't want to hurt you any more than I have already.'

'You could just let me go,' she said. 'If you really don't want to hurt me, let me leave.'

'And miss my chance to tell you how I feel? After all these years of loving you from a distance? No, that wouldn't be right. I'd like you to know me, Jessica. It's time.'

She took the stairs slowly. What hurt more than the knife in her back was how easily she'd been fooled by a bag of chips. She didn't know what she'd expected Teddy to be, but an open, apologetic man wasn't it. Worse, it now occurred to her that he'd recognised her and simply waited until she got her phone out, orchestrating the collision to make sure she couldn't call anyone. She and Midnight would have been better off swapping roles, which raised another question: where exactly was her partner in crime?

At the top of the stairs there was a door on either side. She had no idea if there was anyone else in the building, and much as she didn't want the knife to slip any further inside her body, she had to make some sort of noise.

She stumbled, dropping the mobile she was still clutching back down the concrete steps as she went to her knees. Teddy reached forward to grab her, forced to move the knife from her back to the side of her neck. Jessica gave a loud cry, terrified, no acting required.

'No one's living in the other apartment,' Teddy explained patiently. 'And it's only me in my flat. The unit downstairs has

320

been empty for a while. But I fully appreciate that you felt you had to try that. If we could move past it now, that would be best. All I want is some time with you. I've waited a really long time to tell you how I feel – longer than you could possibly know – but what I'm really curious about, is why you happened to be standing near the entrance to my building today.' He handed her his keys one more time. 'Open up, then go and sit on the dining chair. No heroics. If you know who I am, then you'll know why that would be a bad idea.'

Chapter 43

Everything happened at once. There was a clattering in the hallway beyond the main door out of the flat, then Jessica – her voice unmistakable – cried out. In the stillness that followed, Midnight could hear a man's voice, low and calm, but not make out the individual words. A second later, a key was sliding into the lock and Midnight was running for the bedroom. It was far too risky to hide under the bed or in the wardrobe, so she took the loft ladder, grateful beyond belief that it didn't creak under her weight.

The door slammed, and she could hear the man's voice again. Jessica was crying softly as his voice rose and fell evenly. He was giving instructions, Midnight realised, as she crawled to the rear of the loft on her hands and knees. Most of it wasn't boarded and a wrong movement would be disastrous. She figured the direction she was going would put her over the top of the bathroom. As she crawled, she could hear their conversation more clearly. Behind a pile of old rugs and discarded sections of carpet, she lay out flat, tried to stop herself shaking, and listened while she attempted to formulate a plan.

'Hands behind your back, wrists together. Put one ankle next to each chair leg. Well done.'

'That hurts,' Jessica said. 'It's too tight.'

'Relax. If you fight it, it'll hurt more.'

He was fitting restraints on her, Midnight thought. She had to get a message to someone. A call wasn't going to be possible. If Teddy realised there was someone else in the flat, Jessica would be in even more danger. All she could hope was that his feelings for Jessica would buy them enough time to get assistance.

She took out her mobile and sent a text to DI Ruskin, then forwarded the same message to Amber. Doris only ever used her landline, so there was no way of getting through to her.

S.O.S. she typed. Trapped in loft 35A Jaggard Way. Killer is Edward Hawthorne. He has a hostage, Jessica Finch. 999 HELP.

'I'm curious, how did you find me?' he asked. 'I dreamed of us meeting, but I never wanted it to be like this.'

'I was meeting a friend,' she said. 'That's why I had my phone out. I was about to call him.'

'A boyfriend?' Teddy asked.

Midnight could hear furniture being moved around.

'Just a friend,' Jessica replied. Her voice was a tight little knot at the back of her throat. Midnight realised Jessica had no idea at all that she was in there. She thought she was entirely alone. Hearing Jessica's terror was somehow worse than experiencing her own.

'Good. You've had enough bad experiences with men, but you have me to thank for saving you. Did you like what I did with that rat? I took the first one from your door so you didn't have deal with it, then when I saw him go back again . . . well, he got what he deserved.'

323

'That was you?' Jessica's voice was trembling. 'Thank you.'
Silence followed, then Jessica cried out again.

In Midnight's imagination, Teddy was stroking her face and God only knew what else. She needed a weapon, something bigger and heavier than the screwdriver she was still clutching.

Midnight ran her hands around in the semi-dark, feeling for anything in the loft that might help, preferably a baseball or cricket bat, maybe a wrench or a hammer. She let her fingers work their way beneath and inside the roll of carpet next to her, slowly, carefully. If she knocked anything, Teddy would hear it.

The first thing she touched was plastic, a thick pouch with a seam up the side. She ran her fingers a few feet along the seam to the end, found a ziplock-style opener and pulled. The stench hit her at the same moment something flopped out onto her legs. Midnight grabbed it to push it away and found herself holding fingers.

She dropped them and slapped a hand over her mouth, pushing her nails into her cheek. The smell would have been warning enough, if only her brain had enough time to decode the message. The plastic had been holding the gases in, but now the stink of decomposition was in the air and it was unmistakable, irrespective of whether or not it was her first time in proximity to a dead body. It smelled the way she imagined the corpse would look in daylight – rotten and oozing and undone.

When she could breathe without screaming, Midnight let go of her mouth. She didn't want to touch the body again, but there was no stopping herself. Who was it that Teddy had murdered, and why was their body hidden up here when he'd left his other victims where he'd killed them? She forced her hand back under the carpet, into the plastic sack, and took hold of the fingers again. It was time to establish priorities. The dead body was horrific, but not a threat. If she wanted to live, she was going to have to get brave fast.

'For fuck's sake, just do it! This is a victim. The monster's downstairs,' she muttered beneath her breath.

The hand belonged, unmistakably, to a man. It was large and swollen, the fingers fat and immoveable. Fighting back panicked tears and trying not to breathe through her nose, she reached further in to find he was wearing a jacket. She slid her fingers into the pocket nearest her. It was empty. Taking a deep breath she leaned across and tried the other side, finding the leather square of a wallet.

Pulling a section of carpet over her head, she risked a few seconds of light from her mobile to look at the driving licence she'd found. Just like that, the mystery of Billy's sudden disappearance from Jessica's life was solved. Teddy really had been paying attention to Jessica, killing off anyone who was a threat to her. But leaving Billy's body to be found might have led the police to Jessica, and that could have put her on notice that someone was watching her. Teddy was psychotic, but he was definitely not stupid.

A phone jangled in the room below. Midnight realised she'd lost track of what Teddy had been saying to Jessica. Everything stopped as he walked across to answer the call.

'Hello Mum,' Teddy said. 'I wasn't expecting a call. Is everything all right?'

Fuck, Midnight thought. Oh holy fucking fuck.

'Jessica? Yes, I do remember her.'

Midnight listened hard. Jessica wasn't making any noise at all and, given that it was her one opportunity to scream for help, she could only assume he'd put a gag over her mouth.

'She was there earlier today?' Teddy's voice was getting louder now. 'Yes, sure, you can give me her mobile number. I'd like to call her.'

There was a pause.

'Thank you. Yes, I'll see you Sunday. Beef would be great. Mum, I can't talk long, I'm in the middle of cooking.'

Midnight began searching frantically for anything at all that might give her an advantage. They were out of time. Even if it was a risk, she had to dial 999. She might not be able to speak, but if she let the call roll, they might be able to locate her.

As she pressed the numbers, putting her mobile on silent, she heard Teddy say, 'Two girls? What sort of car were they in? No, it's not a problem. I keep telling you, I'm fine now. Listen, something's burning. See you Sunday.'

The game was up.

'Where is she?' Teddy shouted at Jessica. Midnight heard the rip of tape as he released Jessica's gag. 'Is she downstairs in a car, waiting for you?'

'She went home,' Jessica sobbed. 'She was going to fetch some friends to come back with her. That's why I was waiting on the street.'

Clever woman, Midnight thought.

'Did you call the police?' Teddy shouted. 'Did you?'

Jessica paused fractionally too long.

'You didn't,' he said. 'Well done. But why would she leave you here alone? If you went back to our village, it's because someone made a connection between you and me. So what were you doing this close to my flat, just at the entrance to . . .'

Midnight saw something metallic glinting in the distance as she spun her mobile torchlight wildly around the loft. Metal was good. It offered at least the possibility of a weapon. She glanced at her phone, hoping against hope that Ruskin or Amber had passed on her SOS and someone was trying to triangulate her signal and get help there.

Below, she could almost hear the tick of Teddy's brain as he tried to figure out what they'd been up to.

His footsteps echoed out of the lounge and onto the concrete staircase that led down to the basement room. As he went, Midnight shot across the attic, grabbing the end of what turned out to be a heavy chain, and wrapping it around her forearm.

Down below, Jessica was crying and screeching for help. Teddy's footsteps beat a path back up the stairs and into the lounge.

Midnight heard a slap, and the crash of flying furniture. 'Someone was in my house!' he yelled. 'Where the fuck is she?'

Midnight started, and a section of chain fell from her hands, banging down on a wooden rafter and echoing around the loft. Time stood still.

'Well, hello,' Teddy shouted. 'There's a mouse in my house.'

'Please don't hurt her,' Jessica begged. 'She was just looking out for me.'

'*She* was looking out for you? The things I've done for you, Jessica. I saved you from Billy. I could see he was hurting you and I made sure he couldn't come after you again. And Willem. But now someone else is getting all the credit. Are you kidding me?'

'I know you killed Willem and Billy for my sake. I'm so grateful. You were there like a . . . like a guardian angel when I was in danger, and I know you care about me. I think that maybe I could learn to care about you, too.'

'Could you? There was a time when those were the only words I wanted to hear you say. But you don't know me. We lived in the same village for years. You never recognised me then, and you don't recognise me now.'

'I'm so sorry,' she sobbed.

'You're just sorry I'm calling you out for it. We've spoken in the street. I've said good morning to you.'

Jessica didn't respond. Midnight could imagine her face, shocked, dumbfounded, terrified.

'And when you dropped something out of your basket at the supermarket, I was there to pick it up for you. Our fingers actually touched, Jessica.' He was shouting at her now, and Midnight was imagining him picking up a blade and thinking that just maybe it was time for his obsession with the 'girl next door' to be over. 'And when your ex-boyfriend was hanging around at night outside your flat, watching you, I took him and I kept him here for you, and then I killed him for you. And you didn't even fucking well notice!' Teddy was screaming at her now, and Midnight knew with stone-cold certainty that Jessica was breathing her last. 'I loved you! I fucking loved you, Jessica. That's why I never hurt you. I could have done, do you understand that? I could have hurt you whenever I wanted, but I chose other women. I hurt those other women so that I didn't hurt you. And you don't even recognise me? What a fucking idiot I've been all these years. What a fucking joke!'

Midnight heard footsteps now, through the bathroom, plodding, heavy.

All she could think of was Chloe, Mae, Mae's father, Billy, Willem Foster. Could Teddy be reasoned with? Not a chance in hell. But there was Jessica to think of, downstairs, tied up, with no way of defending herself.

She shifted to the loft hatch, but not close enough to be grabbed or stabbed, dragging the chain with her as quietly as she could. Teddy was deranged, but she was an analyst.

A tactician. All she needed was a fraction of a second to take him by surprise at the top of the ladder. The momentum of a fall, the weight of the chains on top of him, might just be enough to give her the advantage.

'What're you doing up there, mouse?' he asked. He was close now, probably just at the bottom of the ladder.

Midnight bit her tongue. Silence was the fastest way to lure him up towards her. The chains were slippery in her hands and it was hard to get enough oxygen into her lungs.

'What could you possibly have been doing in my flat? Let me think.' He grabbed the ladder and rattled it. It was all Midnight could do not to scream. 'You didn't want to meet me. If you did, you'd have waited until I was in. You didn't want photos of me, or you'd have waited until you saw me on my way home.'

He put one foot on the bottom rung and it shifted with the extra weight at its base. Midnight clutched the chains harder, ready to hurl them at him.

'I'm guessing you were evidence gathering. You were with Jessica, weren't you, when she discovered Willem's body?' He let loose a long, ragged sigh. 'Well, you've left me with a big problem, because now I have to get rid of you and the evidence. Even worse, I've got to dispose of Jessica, and I've spent years loving her. A lot of years. It's a shame there's so little time. I could have had much more fun doing this another way.'

A few clicks sounded from below, and the ladder came flying up into the loft in its folded sections. Midnight threw herself away instinctively. The loft hatch slammed upwards. She cried out as the loft went from dusky to fully dark. Her phone screen had turned black from inactivity and was issuing no light at all. She dived for the loft hatch door, but there was already a lock engaging on it.

'Let me out, you bastard!' she yelled, hammering on it. 'Fuck you!'

Teddy was already walking away. She could hear his footsteps disappearing towards the bathroom then into the lounge. Jessica was sobbing, trying to speak, but with the loft hatch closed Midnight couldn't catch the sense of any of it.

She felt along the wooden beams with her hands, reaching out to find her mobile. Her hands found Billy first, then her phone.

'Hello?' she shouted. 'Police! Can anyone hear me? Are you there?' She switched her phone out of silent mode. There was nothing at the end of the line. Putting the brightness up, she checked the home screen. There was just one signal bar, and that was flickering in and out.

More crashing of furniture below. She had to find a way to get help. It was a long shot, but not impossible that Billy still had a mobile on him that might prove more useful than hers. She stripped the last bits of carpet from his body and put her torch on.

'Oh God,' she gasped. 'Oh no, no, no.'

Billy's face had been destroyed. Midnight didn't want to look, but ignoring it wasn't an option. Flaps of skin, lifted off in semi-circles, had turned his face into a messy jigsaw puzzle.

'He's a biter,' Midnight whispered. 'Renfield syndrome on fucking speed.'

Jessica had stopped screaming again. She suspected more tape had been applied as she searched the bloody remains of Billy's body for his phone. There was nothing. Teddy was dangerous but not stupid. He'd probably dumped the mobile on a bus and let it ride until the battery died.

She heard footsteps in the bedroom below. Drawers opening and closing. No more voices. Midnight sat quietly and tried to get a sense for what he was doing. Finally, a door slammed hard. She could hear Jessica whimpering.

'Jessica!' she yelled. 'I'm still alive. I'm going to find a way to get to you.'

Back at the hatch, Midnight smelled it. Faint at first, like being in the kitchen at a birthday party when the candles had just been blown out. So subtle she might have missed it. But then there was the noise, a soft crackling followed by an intake of air, as if the fire was greedy, wanting more.

'No, no, no.' She tried turning the latch to release the ladder back down, but whatever Teddy had done to the lock, it was irreversible from the inside. 'He's burning it down!' That made sense – it was undoubtedly the fastest and cleanest way to get rid of all traces of himself, and the evidence that could link him to Chloe and Mae's murders. That, and the fact that he didn't have the time to kill them slowly which was clearly what he preferred. More to the point, he must have known that smoke inhalation was going to kill Jessica and her, long before the flames reached them, making sure of his safe getaway.

Smoke twisted slyly through the cracks around the hatch, a blue haze in the mobile's torch light, pretty to look at, nasty to taste. The gentle crackling was fiercer now, more insistent. Midnight shuffled away, trying not to cough, pressing 999 on repeat but the call just wasn't going through. She grabbed the carpet offcuts and laid them over the hatch to keep the smoke out, aware as she did it that the temperature was rising.

'Jess!' she yelled. 'If you can hear me, bang something! Let me know you're alive!'

She listened but could hear nothing from the area below, save for the fire that had begun its destructive movement between rooms. The loft space was too hot already, the atmosphere toxic. Midnight got onto her belly and pulled her top up over her mouth and nose.

Scrabbling around, she found piles of useless debris: another ageing suitcase, old paperwork in boxes, a bin bag of clothes, a flowerpot and a stuffed squirrel.

'Fuck's sake,' she muttered. 'There has to be something.' She grabbed the flowerpot and tried smashing it hard onto the floor between the rafters. It didn't even make a dent.

Sitting up, she did her best to stamp with her trainers. She needn't have worried about her foot accidentally going through the ceiling below. Some builder had made damned sure building regulations were complied with.

'Billy,' she muttered, throwing herself to the end of his body and unlacing his huge boots. They were thick biker boots, with dense heels and metal plates down the back. 'Come on, come on,' she said. Billy's feet didn't want to exit. Even through his socks she could feel the bizarrely liquid swelling of his ankles. It took every ounce of her strength as she coughed and choked to yank them off.

The heat was becoming unbearable, and lying on the floor wasn't helping any more. The air was almost gone. Midnight's heart was pounding and she was beginning to gag. Panic was a ghoul with its hand resting on her shoulder.

'Not going to die here,' she muttered as she dragged the boots onto her own feet. 'Not like this.'

The boots were far too large for her, but just the weight of them gave her hope. Midnight settled herself on a beam and held on tight. The air was glowing all the colours of sunset.

She began to kick. The strength it took felt like lifting a bus. Her lungs screamed for more oxygen, the light from her phone no longer cut through the smoke, and her skin was past sweating and dried out, fit to split.

The floor was starting to give, she could feel it flexing with every blow she dealt it, but not fast enough. Surely by now someone would have noticed. The fire brigade had to be on their way. But fast enough to save them? No fucking way.

Midnight raised both feet in the air together and slammed the metal backplates of each heel into the floor at once.

She slid, grabbing desperately for the beam but it was too hot for her to keep hold. There were a couple of seconds of free air where she suddenly, stupidly, realised she had no idea what she was falling into – if the fire had reached all around the flat by then – then she landed hard on her ankles in a cloud of thick, grey smoke. The kitchen area at the far end was on fire – that had to have been where Teddy had started it. Flames were through the ceiling above the hob, and fanning out towards them.

Midnight knew better than to fall prey to the temptation of suddenly breaking a window and inviting in a rush of oxygen to feed the flames. There were seconds left to find Jessica rather than minutes. On her knees, choking, eyes streaming, lungs burning, she covered the floor area getting her bearings. It was Jessica's hair she touched first.

Her hands reached around, assessing the situation. Jessica was still attached to the chair but it was partially broken and on its side. Midnight checked for a pulse and found none, but there wasn't time to be thorough. What she could feel was dryness everywhere. Teddy hadn't cut Jessica, thank God for small mercies. Her fingertips found Jessica's cheek and slapped hard, twice, three times. Jessica jerked beneath her hand.

Midnight tried to speak, to issue orders, but the air was a thick plastic gas in her mouth.

Instead, she grabbed Jessica beneath her arms and began yanking her backwards towards the sliding door and the staircase. Teddy, thank God, had done them that one favour and left it open. Jessica was a dead weight, hands still tied behind her back, one ankle still attached to a chair leg, but at least the other had come off.

Not dying today. Fuck you, Teddy. Fuck you.

Heave, pause, heave, pause.

Then they were on the stone staircase down to the basement area. The cold concrete beneath them was an oasis.

Midnight dropped Jessica to slide the door back across. It went halfway which bought them a fraction more time, but not far enough to keep them safe. Jessica was groaning and moving her head, but was nowhere near conscious enough to move herself.

Aware that it was going to hurt her friend, Midnight had no choice but to drag her down the stairs, cradling her head, and hoping the rest of her body wouldn't be too badly damaged, the smoke pursuing them as they went.

Outside there were still no sirens, though there had to be flames showing in all the windows.

Midnight took hold of Jessica's head again, positioning herself on the stairs below her, then pulled her to the edge of a step and let Jessica's body thump down as she braced against the potential for them both to tumble in one giant ball of broken bones.

They kept going, bumping, almost falling, further from the smoke with every step, until the corner and the second section of stairs. Midnight had to rest a moment. Her arms were burning with lactic acid, and her stomach wanted a chance to vomit. She waited until Jessica had landed next to her then bent away to spit.

Jessica's body spasmed, her free leg flying out to kick the wall, unwittingly pushing the rest of her body forward. She was rolling down the stairs before Midnight could grab her, banging her head as she went, breaking the remnants of the chair.

Midnight tried to scream but couldn't. Instead, she clattered down after her, cradling her head at the foot of the steps before the crashing began above them.

'Collapsing,' she whispered. She looked up at the countertop she'd climbed over to get in. There was no way she was going to be able to lift Jessica up there. Even if her lungs hadn't been pushed to their limit, she would never have the strength to haul a dead weight up onto it.

Dangerous as it was to move her after the fall, Midnight had no choice but to pull Jessica to the far edge of the basement away from the burning lounge at the top of the stairs.

'I'm coming back,' she told Jessica. 'Promise.'

Midnight dragged herself to the counter, opened cupboards for handholds, then pulled herself up, every inch of her body protesting. At least the heat had subsided and the smoke was less, but the building was beginning to moan and screech, and there was no way of knowing how long it would be before it collapsed.

She reached for the window and let in an icy waterfall of blissfully fresh air. Calling for help wasn't happening. Her voice was sand in her throat. Instead, she half-climbed half-fell out, standing in the well of the basement, all but done, the dregs of her strength failing.

'There's a woman there!' someone shouted. 'Help her!'

Midnight could hear feet hitting the pavement, voices coming from all sides, hauling her up into the courtyard, then sirens at last, vehicles turning down the alleyway. Midnight pointed inside, trying to make herself heard, falling into someone's arms. Uniformed women and men rushed in, pushing the crowd backwards, shouting instructions. More sirens, and suddenly Midnight was being loaded into an ambulance, an oxygen mask on her face, seeing everything from above, no more than an onlooker at the scene.

She managed to grab the arm of a paramedic. She pulled the mask from her face. 'My friend?'

'In a different ambulance. They're taking her to the hospital. We'll be leaving in a minute but we need a couple of the fire engines to move.'

The oxygen in her lungs was incredible. She was given a bottle of cold water to sip from when she needed it and watched from the safety of the ambulance as firefighters swarmed the building, extending ladders and unrolling hoses. The road had been closed, members of the public moved back; a perfectly choreographed dance.

'Dawn,' she murmured. 'And Doris. Where's my phone?' She patted her pockets. It was long gone, melting in the attic, most likely.

Sitting up on the stretcher she discarded the mask, finished the remainder of the water, then climbed out of the ambulance, limping towards a police officer who was keeping the public back.

'Listen to me,' Midnight said. 'Very carefully, can you do that?'

'You don't look well,' she said. 'You need to go back to—'

'No, you have to call this in right now. The man who killed Chloe and Mae, the killer that half of London's police are searching for, is called Edward Hawthorne, goes by Teddy.'

'Miss, you need medical help. I'm calling the paramedics over.'

'He lived in that flat, the one that's burning down. Will you call it in?'

The officer looked around.

'I don't have time for you to get a senior officer here. Say the name back to me.'

The officer didn't hesitate. 'Edward Hawthorne. Goes by Teddy. Lived in that flat.'

'He left after setting the building alight. He had suitcases ready, so he's probably trying to leave the country. The bastard wanted to kill my friend and me because we figured out who he is.' The officer had grabbed her notebook. 'The main point is this. He probably thinks we're both dead, but when the ambulance that's leaving now takes my friend to hospital, she needs a police guard. Can you organise that?'

'Yes,' she said. 'I'm going to make sure that happens. But I need you to get medical help too. We'll need a full statement from you. If what you've said is right—'

'It is, but I have a vulnerable sister at home with an elderly carer. I'm going to check on them, then I'm driving straight to the police station to help.'

Midnight didn't wait for a response.

Chapter 44

Midnight dug her car keys from the pocket of her jeans, beyond grateful they were still there.

She drove up to the police barrier, explained that she needed to follow Jessica's ambulance to the hospital, then turned off at the next road to race home. Later that night she was going to have to get medical help herself – her lungs felt like she'd inhaled acid – but she wasn't going to leave Doris alone caring for Dawn, and Dawn needed to see her, if only for a few minutes. It wasn't just for their sakes, she could admit that. To walk into her own home, to hold her sister and to see her smile, was what Midnight needed.

Her constant, forever love.

She parked on the double yellows right outside the flat. Never mind the ticket, they were welcome to tow her damned car if they wanted. What mattered was getting inside. There was a real risk that she was about to vomit – her stomach didn't like the smoke any more than her lungs had, or perhaps it had been the near-death experience making her nauseous.

Either way, she needed a bathroom and some time curled up on the bed with Dawn. It occurred to her that Doris was going to require a much more detailed explanation of what had happened at some point, but the thought of putting any of it into words when she walked through the door was too much for her. In fact, she thought that even the shower might have to wait. She really needed to just collapse. Her head was swimming again as she let herself into their flat and locked the door behind her.

She was welcomed by absolute silence.

'Hello?' she called. 'Doris?'

She looked around the lounge-cum-kitchen-diner. Freshly washed plates and cutlery were on the draining board, the television was off and Dawn's iPad was on charge. Doris's handbag was on the table, her coat hung up next to Dawn's by the door.

Midnight let out a slow, shaky breath.

In spite of the sunburn effect of the flames on her skin, in spite of warm clothes, in spite of the central heating, ice water was dripping down Midnight's spine. Her muscles began to contract, her breathing slowed. What she felt, bubbling over the top of the numbness of escaping from a burning building, was her body preparing for fight or flight. Only Midnight didn't need to decide which of those two options she would take. Even if she did still have the option to exit to safety, to call the police and wait for backup, she could no more have left her sister than she could put her into a care facility. Some things were simply impossible.

There were three closed doors between her and finding out exactly what was going on in her flat. One went to her bedroom, another to the main bathroom, and the other led into Dawn's room.

Not that she believed it would do much good, but Midnight slid the largest knife she could find from the block and held it in front of her as she went.

She approached her own bedroom first, keeping her steps light and slow as she made for the door, turning the handle slowly, trying to remember to breathe, the adrenaline making her jittery and nauseous. There was nothing there. No mess, nothing out of place. No one there who shouldn't have been. The millisecond of relief was swamped by the certain knowledge that worse awaited her.

Her hand was slick with sweat as she tried to turn the knob of the bathroom door. At first she thought it was locked. She wiped her palm on her jeans and tried again, bracing herself.

Inside, face down on the floor, was Doris.

Midnight refused to allow herself the luxury of a reaction. There was blood. A lot of blood. Too much, in fact, for a woman of Doris's age to have lost, all from a wound in her scalp. Midnight looked around but there was no obvious weapon. It seemed much more likely her assailant had slammed Doris's head into the wall. There were fingermarks in the bloodstream, long strokes, as if someone had taken their time running their fingertips through the stickiness.

She needed to help Doris – if she wasn't beyond help – but she couldn't risk being taken by surprise while she was doing so, and she had to find Dawn. There was a sense that she was being physically torn in two as she forced herself out of the bathroom, and away from their new friend. Midnight squashed her fury and terror deep down. She re-engaged her brain, that calculating part of herself she'd always believed could and would get her out of any sort of trouble, that had got her out of Teddy's loft using only a dead man's boots. Boots she was still wearing, like some grotesque gothic clown, even now.

She gripped the handle to Dawn's room. Her palm wasn't sweating any more, and the chills had abated. Her sister needed her. Whatever she had to do to save her life, she would.

The door opened with no trouble at all, and inside was near darkness. Curtains closed, lights off.

'I want you to know that you're not to blame for any of this,' Midnight said. 'You've never been guilty, really, for any of it.'

'Pretty words, mouse,' he said. 'Is Jessica all right? The fire is all over social media. I saw an ambulance leaving. Was she in it?'

Midnight stepped further into the room.

At the far end, Teddy was sitting in the old chair with Dawn on the floor at his feet. Once upon a time, that chair had lived in their parents' lounge. Midnight hadn't saved much from their past, but she'd kept that. It was enormous, and needed refurbishing, but it was comfortable and Dawn loved it. She was busy playing with a light chain that alternated colours as you touched it. It was her favourite thing. Clever of him to have found it.

'Jessica's still alive,' Midnight said. 'Or she was, when I left her. Injured from falling down the stairs, and suffering smoke inhalation, but alive. Hey, Dawnie,' she added softly. 'I'm home, sweetheart. Sorry I was gone so long.' Dawn gave her a brief, bright smile before focusing again on the lights, and Midnight felt a flash of deep gratitude that her sister had no understanding at all of the danger she was in. She left the door open wide, both to maintain an exit and for some visibility, and took one more step inside. 'How did you find me?'

'I waited near my flat with Billy's motorbike. I saw two ambulances, and paramedics running around with stretchers, then they brought you out. I'm impressed that you managed

341

to escape. I figured you'd come back here to your sister if you were still walking and talking, so I got here first. If you lived, I'd have you. If you didn't, I'd have her.' He glanced down at Dawn, and the rage Midnight felt was enough to flatten a city. 'I knew it was you up in my loft, but if I'd have given that away, you might have sent the police here. I didn't want that.'

Midnight's smoke-addled brain wasn't working well enough to make all the connections.

'You knew about Dawn? I don't—' Her brain finally did its job. 'It was you. That Gemini St John stuff. How long have you been watching me?' Just the thought of it was a violation. Teddy at the window, spying on her and Dawn. Teddy waiting for the opportunity to do what? The same things he'd done to Chloe and Mae?

'Most recently, I was here last night. Before that? Several times. I am curious though, what you thought about me. Midnight J, tucked away in her ivory tower of an office, looking into my brain. Were you fascinated or terrified?'

Midnight swallowed hard. She couldn't get into an argument with him. She needed to give him what he wanted, which seemed to be appreciation, or at the very least to let him feel seen.

'I think . . . I was just worried about you. It must be hard to live inside your head. I can't imagine it. Thank you for not hurting Jessica at the flat, by the way. That was a good thing, and not easy. I don't think you ever planned on hurting her. I mean, you got rid of those other people who were hurting her. Willem was bad news.'

'He was more than just bad news,' Teddy said. 'He would have hurt her eventually.'

'Well, he won't be doing that again. You taught him a lesson. Good for you. Do you mind if I come and sit with Dawn? She'll get restless in a moment if I don't hug her.'

'You can,' he said. His voice was soft and easy-going. 'But it's important that she doesn't make any sudden moves. It would be dangerous. Throw the knife out into the lounge first, then come on over.'

Midnight did as he'd instructed. It was impossible not to feel like prey approaching an anglerfish.

'Sit all the way down,' he said. 'I don't want you jumping up.'

As she sat, Midnight saw that he had his hands on Dawn's shoulders. Dawn beamed at her, entranced by the lights, completely unaware – thank God – of the danger she was in, and most importantly, unharmed. Around her neck was a scarf in a rigid semi-circle. Midnight tried and failed to figure out what it was.

'Teddy – can I call you Teddy?'

'You can,' he said.

'Thank you,' she held one of Dawn's hands as she spoke, stroking it with her thumb. Doris had curled her hair. Thinking about that knocked the breath from her lungs. It was such a sweet thing to have done, and now Doris was alone in a heap on their bathroom floor. Midnight had to hide her loathing of the man who'd done that. 'Teddy, I believe you're suffering from an illness called Renfield syndrome. I think it's been with you a long time. I want you to know that, because the things you've done were driven by an urge you weren't equipped to deal with.'

'Stop it,' he said. 'I've had plenty of people talk to me like that – explaining how I should feel, diagnosing me, exploring my psyche.'

Midnight dragged the name from her memory.

'Moorview,' she said. 'What kind of college was that?'

'The kind that puts an electric shock through your balls if you masturbate,' he said. 'The kind that gets you to reveal your innermost thoughts then whips the urges out of you.'

Midnight took a deep breath. 'I'm sorry,' she said. 'You were so young.'

'Don't be sorry. It worked. For a while, anyway. At least I got to protect Jessica. I actually loved her. She didn't seem all that impressed when I told her that. Could you hear us, from the loft?'

'Very little,' she said honestly. 'But I can understand why you'd fall in love with Jessica. She's incredibly sweet, and very pretty.'

Dawn set down the string of lights and began to wriggle.

'Stay still, honey,' Midnight said. 'Just a little longer.'

'No. Want cuddle. Tired,' she said. She was starting to frown. Midnight knew what was coming.

'She looks exhausted,' Midnight said. 'How about I put her to bed? You have me here now. No defences. I'm not trying to trick you or fight you. I just want my sister to be safe.'

'How do you know it's not your sister I want?' He leaned forward in the armchair to watch her reaction.

Midnight kept her face blank. 'So why wait for me? Why not just do whatever you had planned, then leave?'

He grinned. Midnight wondered if Chloe or Mae had had time to notice the well of emptiness she was seeing in his expression.

'Maybe I wanted you to watch,' he said.

Dawn began to struggle. He gave a quick tug on the scarf around her neck, and now Midnight could see that it had ends poking out from the scarf, in the form of long wooden handles. Dawn gave a cry, but some ancient self-preservation reaction kicked in, and she stayed still, staring terrified at Midnight.

'Dawn,' she took hold of both her hands, 'I'm going to put you to bed in a minute. Shall we say our prayers like when we were little? Close your eyes, stay very still and think about

344

Mummy and Daddy.' Midnight looked up at Teddy, ignoring the last thing he'd said. What she needed to do was distract him. 'You did a test recently at TESU. Psychometric testing but more intense, remember?'

'What I remember is meeting Chloe afterwards. There must have been fifty people in the waiting room, but the only face I could see was hers. She was talking to some woman and smiling, at one with the world. I asked her about bus routes, and she was so . . .' his voice drifted into silence.

Midnight's heart sank. Necto had not just shown Teddy footage that had set him off on a killing spree, they'd done so at a venue where, by tragic coincidence, his perfect victim was in attendance.

'Teddy, what you experienced that day has affected you. The people who designed the technology wanted it to have an effect on you, so they could watch what you did. They planted special footage there just for you, so when you logged in to do the test you saw footage that no one else was ever exposed to.'

'The videos?' he asked.

'Yes,' she whispered. 'The videos.'

Teddy looked up and away into the distance.

'I was intrigued. The letter spoke to something in me.'

'It was designed to do that,' Midnight said. 'It may have looked like generic advertising, but they wrote it just for you.'

'You say that like it was a bad thing, but they . . . liberated me,' he said. 'They reminded me of the things I used to want. It was like someone was looking inside me and projecting all my dreams onto a screen.'

'They didn't liberate you, they triggered you. They got hold of Moorview's records. Everything they did was calculated, right down to inviting Jessica to sell her products at Necto, to keep an eye on her too. That's where I first saw her. I'd started putting the pieces together in my head before I could even see the bigger picture, but we were all manipulated, Teddy. Including you. What they've done is monstrous.'

'You think I'm a monster now? Which is it – am I the victim or the perpetrator?'

He moved forward again so that he had a knee either side of Dawn's shoulders, gripping her tight. Dawn began to moan and struggle.

'Please don't hurt her, Teddy. She's completely innocent. What is that around her neck?'

He looked down at his hands, eyebrows raised. 'I wrapped it up. She's not going to get hurt while the scarf's on there.'

Midnight drew her knees up a little to get her feet flat on the floor. 'What's underneath the scarf?'

Teddy pulled back his shoulders. 'You want to see? I could take the scarf off.'

'Not with my sister sitting there,' Midnight said. 'Sometimes she can't control her movements. Please just tell me.'

'If you really want to know.' He pulled the handles out for a clearer look. 'It's a cheesewire. Chef's kitchen quality. I bought it on the internet. It's amazing, the things they let you buy that really have no business in the hands of normal people.'

Midnight's heart stopped beating for a few seconds. That last video was running through her mind now, in glorious technicolour. He was holding a fucking garrotte. She didn't speak again until she knew she could do so without crying or screaming.

'Why did you choose a cheesewire?'

'Because with the right amount of force behind it, it's fast.' His face lit up, his carefully controlled expression dissolved into childish delight. 'So fast that – get this – the heart gets no signal from the brain to explain that things have, you know,

346

come apart. It continues to beat for quite a while, but you can see everything. Where the neck severs you can literally see the blood pumping. Can you imagine that?'

Midnight could, and the effect on her was debilitating.

Dawn lurched to the side, reaching out for a stuffed toy that was under her bed.

'No!' Midnight grabbed her, hugging her tight, keeping her upright. 'Please, Teddy, take it off her neck. Put it on me instead. Please just promise you won't hurt her.'

'I can't promise that,' he said. 'I'd be lying. One of the other things Moorview taught you was to never lie.'

'Didn't Moorview also teach you not to kill?' Midnight asked.

'They tried,' he said. 'They definitely figured out that I was capable of it. I guess, however hard they tried, long-term I was always—'

Midnight grabbed the umbrella that had been on the floor next to her, and leapt forward, shoving it next to the wooden handle of the cheesewire, pushing it down then pulling it forward, as she used her body weight to push Dawn backwards against Teddy, getting some separation between Dawn's neck and the wire. She smashed her forehead into Teddy's hard enough to leave them both reeling.

Dawn was wailing and screeching as Midnight pulled the umbrella against the cheesewire, straining every fibre of her body, teeth gritted, growling with effort. Teddy was reaching forward with his jaw, gnashing his teeth, trying to find the flesh of her face and get a bite, even as he held onto the handles of the wire.

Even with the scarf over it, Midnight could hear Dawn gurgling with the pressure. The umbrella, a child's version, was half plastic and starting to give as Teddy pulled tighter.

Midnight let the umbrella go, thrusting forward into Teddy's body again as she raised a foot to tuck one of Billy's huge boots behind the wire, shoving it away from Dawn's neck.

'I'm gonna fucking kill you. Both of you!' Teddy was shouting, Midnight on top of him, Dawn between his knees, none of them able to move without giving away their physical advantage or getting hurt.

'Let her go!' Midnight screamed. 'You animal! Fucking let my sister go!'

Seconds passed, eye to eye, and nobody moved. Without warning, Teddy released Dawn as he brought up one fist to smash Midnight in the side of the head, and his other to grip her by the throat. Dawn fell to the floor as Midnight fought him. She held onto enough consciousness to know that Dawn was crawling away, sobbing.

'Help!' Midnight screamed. 'Someone help!' She needed to make Teddy panic at the thought that someone might come. It was early evening. People would be home from work and still awake. She kept herself wrapped around Teddy as he tried to get up from the chair, shifting her hands up to his face as the blows kept coming, feeling for his eyes, pushing her thumbs deep into the sockets.

When his teeth found her lower jaw, the agony was every pain she had ever known in her life combined and compounded. It was white and blinding, breath-stopping and spectacular. The world slowed down. Her thumb tips weakened in their search for his eyeballs.

Don't give in, she thought. Not yet.

She couldn't scream any more. The pain had ended any chance of her getting a breath out, and now he was clamping down harder, grinding his jaws left and right over her lower jaw, as if he could make them one. Her neck was wet, and she

348

wanted to give in, to let him kill her fast because that was what was going to happen whatever she did, and the thought of the pain carrying on was killing her anyway.

Fight! Fucking fight!

She took her thumbs from his eyes and shoved them hard, one each side, up his nose, ripping his skin apart.

His jaws flew open and it was Teddy's turn to scream and gasp for breath, but then he had her throat again and the squeezing, the pressure, the nauseating dizziness and the pain in her lungs was the end of the fight.

Don't hurt Dawn, she thought, knowing she couldn't be saying it out loud.

Please don't hurt my sister.

Her hands were flopping, arms falling to her sides, his blood mingling with hers as the battle came to a close.

And then more blood hit her face. More than she'd ever thought could come from a living body, so hot it shocked her. She tried to yell but the blood was in her throat, cloying, disgusting.

Teddy's hands fell away, his body limp, toppling into her, the weight forcing her backward to the floor, thumping loosely over her.

Another body collapsing next to hers, tiny, frail, reaching out a hand.

'You're all right, dear,' a weak voice said. 'We're all right.'

Midnight pushed Teddy's body off hers and wiped blood from her face. There was enough light from the lounge to see Doris lying on the floor at the side of Dawn's bed, clutching her chest with one hand and her head with the other.

Teddy's head was half separated from his neck, gaping open. His body, as he'd predicted, had taken a moment to realise what was happening.

'Dawn?' she called out. 'Baby, it's okay. I've got you.' She crawled to the bed and reached out a hand for her cowering twin sister. 'Stay there. It'll be okay.'

She kept the lights off as she made her way into the lounge to phone for an ambulance on the landline. Dawn didn't need to see the mess that was Teddy's cheesewire-severed body.

When help was on its way, she managed to stand and stagger back through to Doris.

'Try to breathe,' she said. 'Ambulance is coming. You saved us, Doris.'

'He was . . . hoisted by his . . . own petard,' she panted. 'I'm not sorry.'

Midnight took Doris in her arms, one arm extended to grip Dawn's hand under the bed, until the ambulance crew arrived.

Midnight's lungs were giving in by the time they reached her. 'Keep my sister with me,' she whispered as they began preparing to intubate her. 'She has to stay by my side.'

Chapter 45

Some angel had put them on the same ward, not just Midnight and Dawn, but Jessica and Doris too. By the time Midnight regained consciousness, twenty-four hours later, Jessica was out of her bed and sitting next to Midnight's. Dawn's bed had been rolled next to Doris's so they could hold hands as they watched television together while they waited for Midnight to wake up.

Midnight's jaw was agony. She woke up feeling Teddy's teeth clamped around it, as she panicked, trying to scream.

'It's okay,' Jessica stroked her arm. 'You're safe. The nurse said you'd wake up in pain. They left this button thing you can press for more painkillers.'

Midnight tried to speak and couldn't.

'They had to operate,' Jessica explained. 'He did quite a bit of damage to your jaw, broke it, in fact, which the surgeon said he'd never known a human to have the strength to do with their teeth alone.'

Midnight tried to remember the sequence of events. It came back to her all at once.

'See keed 'im,' she murmured through the contraption that was keeping her jaw in position, pointing at Doris to make herself clear.

'I did kill him, lovey. He played a blinder on me, mind. Came to our door, said he was a plainclothes officer, and that you'd been in an accident with your friend Jessica. Said he needed to get some identification from me before he could tell me the details of the accident. I let him in, turned my back, and he grabbed me. Believe me, putting that cheesewire round his neck was no trouble at all. Thank the Lord that you and this precious girl are all right.'

'Ank oo,' Midnight said, her right hand over her heart.

'Don't be silly, my darling, you don't need to thank me. If you hadn't come back when you did, I wouldn't have survived and neither would your sister. If you ask me, we all saved each other.'

'Oo ah 'ight?' Midnight asked her.

'I'm fine. Bump to the head, a few stitches . . .' Doris said.

'Loads of stitches,' Jessica added softly.

'And they gave me some fresh blood! Imagine that, someone else's blood pumping around my veins. Might make me younger and stronger, you never know.'

Sort of what Mr Renfield's motivation was, Midnight thought. Personally, she never wanted to see another drop again.

She turned to look Jessica up and down.

'Don't you worry about me, I'm fine. Broke an ankle on my way down the stairs, some cuts to my wrists from the cable ties, slight concussion, and it turns out that smoke inhalation is absolutely horrific. But I'm alive, thanks to you. The fire brigade said you kicked your way through the ceiling to save me. Is that right?'

Midnight shook her head and pointed at herself.

'Oh, okay, you were just saving yourself?' Jessica laughed. 'That makes much more sense.'

Midnight caught sight of a pad of paper and a pen, and motioned to it. Jessica handed it over.

'Teddy killed Billy. His body was in the loft,' she wrote.

Jessica took a deep breath. 'I thought so. I saw his motorbike at the back of the flats. I don't know how he lured Billy there, but Teddy must have planned it really well. Billy was big, and he was strong.'

Dawn was holding her arms out in Midnight's direction and waving her hands. Jessica got up on her crutches, helped Dawn off her bed, and guided her across the ward. She climbed onto Midnight's bed and snuggled down beside her.

Midnight held her tight, trying not to cry, and failing. Doris smiled from the other side of the room. Jessica went back to her own bed and rested her ankle.

'Oh, you had a visitor before, but you were still out of it from the anesthetic,' Jessica said. 'Someone from Necto . . . a man.'

Midnight frowned. Was it Eli who had helped her with the documents, or perhaps newly civilian DI Ruskin coming to apologise for not listening to her earlier?

'It was Richard someone or other. I didn't catch his surname,' Jessica said.

It had to be Richard Baxter, Midnight thought. Her old boss. That was utterly bizarre. Had he visited out of a sense of duty or guilt, or to give her information about her employment status? She certainly wouldn't be appearing at her disciplinary tribunal any time soon.

Midnight clicked the button for extra pain relief, shifted down in the bed and set the pen and paper aside. Everything else could wait. She had her sister in her arms, friends who she very much hoped might become more like the family she needed, and the chance to rest. That was enough.

Chapter 46

'Thank you for your evidence,' the select committee chair said. 'You're free to go, Miss Jones, but should you wish to watch the remainder of proceedings, you may take a seat in the public area.'

It had taken six months to convene the hearing after Teddy's death, and it took three days for the committee to hear evidence and consider documents on formulating ethical guidelines and legislation for future psychological testing software.

Richard Baxter had given evidence on Necto's 'special projects'. He was offered anonymity and given whistle-blower status, but chose instead to show his face and give his real name. Midnight left the hearing when he did, catching up with him in the corridor.

'Richard,' she said. 'Do you have a minute?'

'Miss Jones, I was told you'd finished your evidence. I'm surprised you wanted to stay a second longer than was necessary.'

'I needed to see it through,' she said. 'I'm also looking forward to seeing Sara Vickson squirm.'

'Quite right too. Are you recovering?'

'I am. You came to see me at the hospital, I gather. Thank you.'

'Not at all,' he said. 'I live quite nearby.'

'Not for the visit,' she said. 'For the documents you sent me about what Necto was doing. I didn't realise it was you at the time, but when I made some enquiries, it became obvious. You risked your job for me. It was brave of you.'

'I should have done more, sooner,' he said. 'Perhaps then you wouldn't have . . .' He gave an uncomfortable shrug. 'I keep thinking, if only I'd supported you at the earliest opportunity. I allowed myself to be a slave to the Necto way of thinking for far too long.'

'Is that why you stepped in to accompany me at the disciplinary hearing?'

'It is,' he said. 'I knew then the gesture was far too little. I went away wondering what my daughter would have made of it all. I couldn't discuss it with her, of course . . .'

'Company policy?' Midnight asked, a half-smile playing on her lips.

'I deserved that,' he shrugged. 'Necto and Sara Vickson were so adamant about getting rid of you, I felt it was my duty to find out why. Hence the documents I discovered. But even then I wasn't brave, far from it. I sat outside your flat, the night I sent the email. I wish I'd knocked on your door and done more to help.'

'I doubt it would have made any difference,' Midnight said, laying a gentle hand on his arm. 'What will you do now?'

'Ah, well, I've rather landed on my feet. Necto offered me a position as head of ethical compliance. The old departmental heads are all out on their ears and there's been a substantial shake-up. I was hoping to talk to you about coming back. We need good people with a sense of right and wrong, to shape the direction the company goes in. Will you consider it?'

'That's very kind,' she said, 'but no. Necto have paid me a substantial sum in compensation. Enough to move out of London and take my sister to a house in the country which she'll love, and someone I respect very much has already been in touch about me working with her in the future.'

'Popular young woman,' he smiled. 'Whoever it is, they're lucky to have you. I nearly forgot, Jock Ruskin handed in his notice. I tried to persuade him to stay, but he said the Highlands were calling. Something about preferring to live with less, than to live with a heavy conscience. He wanted you to know.' Midnight nodded. 'Well, I should be off. Plenty to do, and the boss should always set an example.'

Midnight couldn't help but grin. She watched him go, then slid quietly back into the hearing where a new witness was reading a statement.

'. . . represent the owners of what was previously Moorview College. The college as it was when Edward Hawthorne attended closed down some years ago and stood empty for a period. When it was purchased, the new owners found records in the basement, containing details of the children who had attended, their various diagnoses, treatments, prognoses, as well as lengthy logs with disclosures from the children, their medical notes, psychiatric histories and so on. Approximately eighteen months ago, the new owners were approached by Necto Corporation to sell them those documents. Necto had been identifying institutions that ranged from specialist schools such as Moorview, to foster homes, young offenders' institutions and psychiatric facilities, to identify subjects for their product development work.'

'In breach of confidentiality?' the chair asked.

'The records didn't relate to any pupils of the new owners,' the witness responded. 'Legally speaking they didn't owe any duty of confidentiality.'

'The fee Necto paid was substantial?' he was asked.

'My client has made the decision to withhold the precise figures involved, as is their right. The records were passed to Necto. They had nothing more to do with it.'

'That information was then used to identify and help locate potential targets to conduct experiments on, to see what use could be made of Necto's new technology. We all know how it turned out,' the chair remarked.

'On my client's behalf, I would like to reiterate that they accept no responsibility for—'

'Yes, yes,' the chair said. 'They accept no responsibility for any of what followed. I think we all have the picture. You are dismissed.'

More details were revealed. The letter sent to Teddy Hawthorne had been perfectly pitched to pique his interest. He and a few select others had been chosen as subjects who might show signs of substantial new or regressive behaviour following Necto's testing. The committee accepted that Necto had not intended the murderous consequences, and that they could not have foreseen the extent of the damage Hawthorne would cause, only that they were reckless and unethical in their testing. Necto's stated aim – the extent to which they would admit what their intentions had been – was to see if triggers could be used to change behaviour outside of known therapy or institutions. It was, Necto claimed, the only way to ensure test subjects were completely unaware of what was happening, so they did not change their behaviour knowingly.

Teddy himself had started a new career working from home, directing repair and rescue mechanics to breakdowns across the UK. All he needed was a phone and his laptop, allowing him to work from almost anywhere, and giving him the freedom to watch, stalk and study his victims with few restrictions.

Jessica's Bake Me A Cake company had been invited to work with Necto only once Midnight had highlighted Teddy Hawthorne as a potential problem, so they could keep a closer eye on their subject through the object of his obsession. She had been no more than a pawn to them, albeit one they'd believed to be entirely safe.

Chloe's family attended the hearing, as did Mae's. Billy's stayed away. Mr and Mrs Hawthorne made no appearance either. The committee made wide-reaching recommendations for regulation and change around developing new technology for military use. Much good it would do, Midnight thought privately. Corporations like Necto made their own rules. Internally, laws barely touched them.

Sara Vickson was brought to court with a witness summons, and gave her evidence using one-word sentences wherever possible, a permanent scowl on her face. There were no surprises in what she said. Didn't know – couldn't remember – hadn't anticipated – Necto's thoughts and prayers to the families of the deceased.

Vickson accepted that the school records had been used to identify study targets. Yes, it was also possible that confidential disclosures made by students to school counsellors, psychotherapists and teachers might have been taken into account when identifying how study targets might react, although she couldn't go into specifics. Had Necto been watching Teddy Hawthorne since he had undergone their psychological testing? Yes, Vickson said, but only within the confines of the law. There had been no listening devices or video feeds placed in his flat. Necto would never cross such a line. It had all been so unfortunate. Lessons had been learned, Vickson reassured them.

No, Necto hadn't been listening to Midnight through the work laptop. No, they hadn't burgled her house to steal a pen drive, they claimed. All of that was unhappy coincidence, and the company remained deeply concerned about Midnight's wellbeing. On and on it went. Midnight wondered just how far Necto had gone that they weren't admitting. They might not have anticipated the results of what they'd done to Teddy, but they were sure as hell responsible for them.

When Vickson finished, Midnight slipped out behind her into the corridor.

'Ms Vickson, I want to talk,' Midnight said.

Vickson sighed. 'Something along the lines of "I told you so"? That's incredibly tiresome of you.'

'Actually, no. I just wanted to understand how it happened. Why it happened. Wouldn't it have been easier to just hand all the information to the police at the outset, as soon as you realised how dangerous the situation was?'

Vickson gave a bitter smile. 'You really never understood your employer, did you? Necto doesn't get things wrong. They don't fail. They don't accept responsibility. They're too big for those things. You think I was going to be the person who told them they'd fucked up?'

'But . . . women died.'

'Women die every week, Miss Jones. They die because they burn their husband's dinner when he's had too much to drink. They die because they dishonoured their father. They die because police officers can't be bothered to properly investigate stalking claims. Women are disposable. The same way it was always made clear to me that I was disposable at Necto.'

'It's not the same,' Midnight said.

'It's exactly the same to Necto. They're developing technology that will change the world, weapons that will change the shape of warfare forever. You think a couple of women's lives seemed too high a price for them to pay?'

'But it's unethical. Unthinkable. It's criminal.'

'It's life, Miss Jones. This is what big corporations are. Tobacco companies deny that nicotine is addictive. Chemical companies poison whole communities. Car manufacturers know it's cheaper to pay for the odd death rather than recall a whole make of vehicle when they realise it's dangerous. This happens every day in every country across the globe.' Her face fell. 'I'm sorry, Midnight. I wish the world was a better place, but it's not. So if you can't beat them, joining them is the only sensible option.'

'I guess Necto's the right place for people with that attitude. You controlled Amber like that, and I'm guessing Eli gave up any information he had about me rather than lose his job, too.'

'You say that as if either Eli or Amber owed you loyalty. Necto is a place of work. It's a transaction. Employees do what's asked of them and in return they're given money. They get paid when they're at work, when they're on holiday, when they're sick and in pension provision. So of course your colleagues provided information when required to do so. They understood the nature of the relationship. For what it's worth, your friend Amber did so very hesitantly. As for Eli, he's ambitious and he was offered an opportunity to be especially helpful. Ambitious young men, in my experience, think no more of loyalty than they do of treading in a shallow puddle. It barely makes a splash.'

'And how much did Necto pay for your severance and scapegoat package?' Midnight asked.

Vickson shoved her hands deep into her pockets and raised her eyebrows. 'Three million. If you'd been smarter, earlier, you could have had the same without the pain.'

Midnight shook her head. 'That's the thing,' she said. 'Unlike you, I wasn't for sale.'

The injury to Midnight's jaw had taken months to heal, and the scarring would be life-long, but her face was easier to live with than the nightmares.

She bought a house in the country that allowed them to have both a cat and a dog, both elderly and from rescue centres. Benjamin Hoffman's parents would have approved, had they ever crossed paths. Midnight thought the change for Doris would be hardest of all, a life-long Londoner who loved the busy streets and constant noise, but their replacement grandmother filled their days with laughter, companionship, and outrageously bright outfits that were completely at odds with the surroundings, and which nevertheless seemed to fit right in. They looked after one another, gave each other space, and packed their cottage full of love, colourful quilts and takeaways every Friday evening. Some habits were harder to break than others.

Midnight sat in her home office, looking out into the back garden. Necto had paid for all of it, from the tiny orchard with its apple, pear and plum trees, to the goat pens featuring John-Boy and Mary Ellen, characters from one of Doris's favourite old television shows. Midnight had no idea what it was, but saying goodnight to each goat made Doris laugh, and that was all that mattered. Granny Apples would have loved it. She'd have loved Doris too. All in all, they'd ended up in a better place with a bigger family. If Midnight had to find a silver lining in what they'd been through, then that was it.

The payment had been compensation for all Midnight, Dawn and Doris had been through, preventable as it was, plus a hefty sum for the loss of her job. All in all, it had turned out all right, if you excluded the horrors that lived on in their memories. Amber had made contact only once. It was a voicemail. An apology, and a plea for Midnight to call her back. That one thing, Midnight had been unable to do. She hadn't wanted to punish Amber, she just hadn't felt ready. It seemed possible that there might come a day when she could reach out, but it would need more time. Richard Baxter had told her that Amber was still employed at Necto, another promotion under her belt. After all, Amber had stayed quiet, and at Necto that was currency.

Her laptop beeped. Midnight had been expecting the call. She hit a couple of keys and the screen lit up with a picture of a woman in a white shirt, sleeves rolled up, chewing a pen.

'Hi, this is Midnight.'

'Midnight Jones, looks like you had an adventure,' Connie Woolwine said. 'How you doing?'

'I have a scar on my jaw,' she turned to the side to show it, 'where a man tried to bite through my face. I'll never trust another corporation again. And it turns out that Renfield syndrome is very real indeed. His college did an incredibly good job of conditioning him out of his natural tendencies, then Necto got him to snap again, which was what they were trying to do. They just didn't expect to make quite such a good job of it.'

'I should have seen the biting thing coming. It's a feral animal thing, and in this case I'd say it sprang directly from his blood obsession. Violent offenders almost always ramp up the damage they do each time they kill. To go from tasting blood to drinking it, then on to biting, was a foreseeable path. I'm sorry you had to go through so much, Midnight.'

363

'Well, on the upside, I have a mortgage-free house in the Dorset countryside, with a menagerie of animals.' She gave a rueful smile. 'My sister is happier than I've ever known her, and we've adopted a septuagenarian called Doris, who we love. How about you?'

'We got kidnapped in a Venezuelan jungle, had to be rescued by some very dodgy private hire soldiers, then got arrested during an attempted coup. Now I'm back at my family home in Martha's Vineyard. Sounds like you and I should meet for a coffee when we're on the same continent.'

'You should visit us here,' Midnight said. 'My friend Jessica comes down for weekends. Her baking is the best thing since sliced bread, excuse the pun, and we have fresh eggs. I'd like to talk to you about what happened.'

'Then I'll come,' Connie said. 'Baarda has to head home to see his kids anyway, and I have clients in the UK. How are you sleeping?'

Midnight sighed.

'Yeah, thought so. I can help with that too, if you'll let me. It's a big thing coming face to face with what most people hesitate to call evil. Syndrome or not, psychiatric illness or not, sometimes it helps to acknowledge what you've dealt with and allow yourself to know that the fear you felt was grounded and justified.'

'Uh-huh,' Midnight said. She couldn't trust herself to speak. Tears were already splashing the desk her elbows were leaning on.

'I'll be with you in a week,' Connie said. 'Hang on in there, Midnight. And while I'm visiting, I'd like to talk some more about the job offer I made you. I think it might be exactly what you need.'

Midnight dashed an arm across her eyes.

'I'm so flattered, but I really can't leave my sister. We've just settled here, and after everything that's happened . . .'

'I know. Baarda and I are getting busy. We travel a lot, and I have more work than I can cope with. I need someone running a base for me, remotely, I mean. Someone I can always call, day or night, who can check things out, analyse data, do research for me when I'm in the field and pressed for time. Does that sound like something you could do from where you are?'

'Yes!' She had to stop herself from standing up and yelling it. 'I mean, sure. Absolutely. And I'd love it, really. Thank you, Dr Woolwine.'

'Call me Connie,' she said. 'And you should know from the get-go something that Necto will never understand. You can tick boxes and set flowcharts, have a computer system with symptom recognition that takes physiological measurements, but so much of profiling is about gut instinct. It's also about persistence, often to the point of annoying people, and calling out BS when you come up against it. Everything I've heard about how you took on the Hawthorne case makes me think you'll be the perfect team member with Baarda and me. It's not always easy, though. You sure you haven't had enough of the darker side of human nature already?'

Midnight thought about it.

'I think, awful as it was, that I persisted not just because I was worried about more women getting hurt, but also because it seemed to me that finding Teddy Hawthorne was a solvable problem.'

'More to the point, Midnight, is the fact that faced with the worst the world had to offer, you fought and prevailed. There's no category for those qualities on a standard CV. That's what I'm looking for. Someone who doesn't fit the mould.'

'Then I'm your candidate. Thank you, Connie.'

'No problem. I can't wait to meet you in person.'

Midnight ended the call and stared at the photo of their parents she'd put up on the wall. They'd managed to make a twenty-minute video call the previous evening. It was fine. They asked all the right questions, made sure both she and Dawn were okay, then said how well they were coping and that it didn't seem like there was any point them rushing back to visit. That was okay with Midnight. Dawn had smiled and waved at them, but she didn't get upset or emotional. Her needs were being met in a way that didn't require their parents to be present. Midnight decided it was time to let them go. Not to end contact with them, just to put their relationship into the box it deserved – distant relatives.

She had more important matters to expend her mental energy on. So many people had suffered to get her the home she'd always wanted, and the job opportunity she'd dreamed of. She rubbed the scar on her jaw. The best way she could honour the dead was by making sure fewer victims followed in their wake. Teddy Hawthorne was deceased, but there were others like him who needed to be found and stopped, and a life lived without risk was no life at all. It was time to start a job that really mattered.

Midnight switched off her laptop and wandered out into the garden to join Dawn and Doris. There was just time to enjoy the end of the afternoon sun.

Acknowledgements

Several years ago, my husband and I made a film for a global medical research company about the future of drug production. Our research and client visits were astonishing. It opened up a whole new world unlike any other industry we'd worked in. That experience stayed with me, and what I learned was that most of the products we believe are futuristic are already being investigated somewhere by someone. When I began researching the existing technology for this novel, it became clear that everything I was picturing had already been developed. Just – as far as I know – not misused in the way I've written it. Working with my husband on that and years of other projects gave me a new lease on life, and I'm grateful every day for the inspiration David brought, not to mention the laughter, marketing assistance, and cups of tea.

This book, perhaps more than all the others, was a journey. The people who got me to the end of it are superstars. So thank you, one and all, to Helen Huthwaite my brilliant editor and soother of nerves, Elisha Lundin on desk editing, Sammy Luton on sales, Claire Ward on design, Emily Chan on production, Maddie Dunne-Kirby and Ella Young on marketing, Gabriella Drinkald on publicity (no one works a room like Gaby), Georgina Ugen on digital sales, Molly Robinson on audio, Rhian McKay for the copy edit, Amanda Percival for all things international, Emily Gerbner, Jean Marie Kelly and Sophia Wilhelm who are my 360 team in the USA, and Peter Borcsok who is head of sales for HarperCollins in Canada. This isn't just a list of names. Books only succeed through the team's blood, sweat and tears. Launching a book is more technical than it looks, more precarious than anyone realises and more demanding than these people are given credit for. So if you enjoyed this book, lovely reader, and I hope you did, then spend a minute with me thanking the people who put it out into the world.

I wouldn't be functioning at all without my agent team, from the unstoppable Caroline Hardman to her trusty partner in crime Joanna Swainson, my foreign rights wizard Hana Murrell, and the lovely Aaminah Badat. And, as ever, to Gabe for the TikTok videos, Sollie for the pep talks and Evangeline for the hugs. You are the reason I keep writing.

Looking for your next explosive crime thriller?
Why not try *The Institution*?

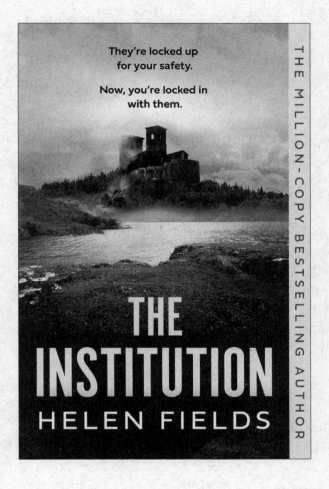

Available from all good bookstores now.

If you loved *The Institution*, then why not try Helen Fields's iconic DI Callanach series?

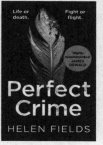

Available from all good bookstores now.

And if you enjoyed the DI Callanach *Perfect* series, we think you'll love these fantastically twisty crime thrillers . . .

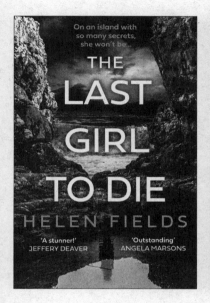

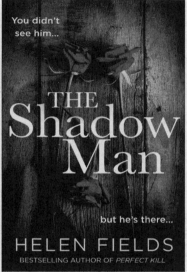

Available from all good bookstores now.